Judith

A NOVEL

Judith

A NOVEL BY

Lawrence Durrell

Edited and introduced by Richard Pine

OPEN ROAD

INTEGRATED MEDIA

NEW YORK

Editor's Introduction

Judith is an adventure story which is both romantic and tragic, embracing twin love affairs, and it is also a political drama of considerable poignancy which contains resonances even for the geopolitics of today.

This Introduction sets the scene in 1940s Palestine, on the eve of British withdrawal from the League of Nations Mandate (under which it administered Palestine from 1922 to 1948), with the impending invasion of the newly created state of Israel by its Arab neighbours. It describes the genesis of the novel, and the many elements in Lawrence Durrell's mind as he was writing it, as well as explaining the discrepancies between the novel and the film of *Judith*, released by Paramount Pictures in 1966.

The Genesis of *Judith*

Following the appearance in 1957 of *Justine*, the first volume of *The Alexandria Quartet*, and the republication of the *Quartet* as a single volume in 1962, Lawrence Durrell rapidly became one of the most celebrated and controversial novelists not only in the English-speaking world but also throughout Europe, thanks to translations of the *Quartet* into French and German.[1] On the strength of this acclaim and notoriety, Durrell was approached in 1960 by Twentieth Century–Fox to write a screenplay for a film about Cleopatra, on which he worked throughout that year and 1961, although he eventually withdrew from that project, and is not named in the film credits.

Then, in September 1962, he was in Israel, researching the background for another film, *Judith*, which would feature Sophia Loren in the title role. Little is known of the circumstances in which the film's producer, Kurt Unger, commissioned the script from Durrell for Paramount Pictures; their correspondence appears to have been lost (it does not exist in either of the major Durrell archives) so that, as in the case of *Cleopatra*, we cannot establish precisely Durrell's reasons for withdrawing from the film project, except to say that he was dissatisfied with the changes in the storyline made by subsequent writers.[2]

Durrell worked on the first draft of *Judith* in late 1962 and early 1963, before meeting Sophia Loren. 'A sweet creature, great dignity and style', he recorded.[3] Although he lost interest in the film studio's revisions to his storyline, he went so far, in August 1964, as to visit Israel again during the shoot, where he and Loren made a short travelogue for CBS Television. 'I acted her off her pretty little feet', Durrell wrote.[4] Given the nature of the political and paramilitary context of *Judith*, it is worth noting that Moshe Dayan, who, as Israel's Minister of Defence, facilitated the CBS feature, had in 1939 been imprisoned by the British for his part in illegal arms importations by the Haganah (see below).

As with so many of Durrell's finished works, *Judith* began as a sketch, the substance and detail of which would be amplified and enhanced as the project developed. After his preliminary reconnaissance in Israel, Durrell wrote to a friend, 'Just finished tracing the

---

1 *Justine* was shortlisted for the Prix du Meilleur Livre Étranger in 1957, and its sequel, *Balthazar*, won the prize in 1959.
2 Cf. Gordon Bowker, *Through the Dark Labyrinth: A Biography of Lawrence Durrell* (London: Sinclair-Stevenson, 1996), pp. 306, 313.
3 Quoted in Ian MacNiven, *Lawrence Durrell: A Biography* (London: Faber & Faber, 1998), p. 533.
4 Quoted in ibid., p. 540.

border without anything to boast about'.[5] As I discuss below, this was typical of his method of constructing a story, prior to elevating it from a basic idea to a higher level of literature.

In the first draft of *Judith*, the central character, Judith Roth, is a distinguished scientist in her own right, who has been 'sprung' from Germany by the Zionists, in order to work on papers by her late father, a Nobel Laureate physicist. Loren objected to the characterisation, telling Durrell 'I am not an intellectual', asking instead if Judith could be portrayed as a simple 'woman of the people, not a doctor type'.[6] As a result, Durrell completely rewrote the story, making Judith into a refugee/survivor of the concentration camps who has been married to a Nazi Colonel, Günther Schiller. Schiller is now aiding the Arab preparation for the impending attack on the new-born state of Israel.

It is significant, from the point of view of this publication of *Judith*, that Durrell approached the storyline and the text in a quite different manner from that of *Cleopatra*. The extant versions by Durrell of *Cleopatra* are written in the conventional screenplay format: 'stage' directions describing atmosphere and movement, followed by dialogue:

> Open slowly on the dark town: palm trees, shadows, a waning moon. The camera enters a room in the palace through curtains stirred by the dawn wind, moves across the strange arabesques of tessellated floors towards a huge bed of fantastic design.[7]

The text of *Judith*, by contrast, is written descriptively, and, while the dialogue is dominant, it is integrated into the narrative in a novelistic style. In the absence of any full treatment for the scenario of *Judith*, we can assume that, while, in the scenario for *Cleopatra*, Durrell was suggesting the way the director might use the camera's eye, in *Judith* he was employing the eye of the reader to achieve his effect.

As a result — it seems — of Loren's intervention, Durrell had, by the end of 1963, written two versions of *Judith*, the second replacing Judith the scientist with Judith the victimised mother in search of her

---

5 Quoted in ibid., p. 532.
6 Ibid., p. 533; and MacNiven, e-mail to the editor, 10 October 2011.
7 L. Durrell, '1st Cleopatra treatment', c. 1960, in Southern Illinois University, Carbondale, Collection 42/13/5.

child by Günther Schiller. A copy of the second version is held in the archives of Paramount Pictures, and it is presumably from this text that the later scripts were derived. The Durrell archive at Southern Illinois University also contains a document labelled 'Judith. Palestine 1947', indicating that Durrell was actively involved in the early stages of the film treatment(s), with perceptive remarks as to the political situation, such as the following:

> Jerusalem: The holy city is like a symbol of the Palestinian political situation. The Arab and Jewish community sharing the town, each believing that it will be liberated in the near future for its own people. The Jews have always considered Jerusalem as their capital but they know that the Jordanian Arabs will try in every way to take this city from them.

Durrell includes a note at the end of this document:

> We must keep in mind from the very beginning of the story the need of creating a sequence to show the threat hanging over the future of the emerging country. The threat, as will be made clear in the end, is the surrounding Arab States which are opposed to the creation of an independent Jewish state.[8]

The film of *Judith*, directed by Daniel Mann, starred Sophia Loren in the title role, with Peter Finch as Aaron Stein and Jack Hawkins as Major Lawton.[9] It is significant that Paramount succeeded in securing the services of both J. P. Miller and John Michael Hayes as screenwriters. Miller, who was principally a playwright, won an Emmy nomination for *Days of Wine and Roses* (1958). He worked on five versions of the script for *Judith* between 1 March and 9 July 1964. Hayes had previously worked with Alfred Hitchcock, one of his most notable scripts being *Rear Window* (1953), for which he received an Oscar nomination, followed by *To Catch a Thief*, *The Trouble with Harry* and *The*

---

8 Southern Illinois University, Carbondale, Collection 42/17.
9 The *Aberdeen Press and Journal* reported on 20 August 1964 that 'The countries of the Arab League will ban all films starring Sophia Loren unless she withdraws from a picture being made in Israel about a Jewish refugee'.

Man Who Knew Too Much. He then went on to earn a second Oscar nomination for his adaptation of *Peyton Place.* Hayes took over the script from Miller on 1 August 1964 and continued with it (another five versions) until 12 March 1965.

A curious anomaly is the fact that the story was serialised (two months after the release of the film) in *Woman's Own* magazine as 'The Epic Story of One Woman's Torment', but differs in several details from the episodes in the film (and the film contains elements that are not included in the story).[10]

As late as 1972 — that is, after the publication of his next major novel sequence, *Tunc* and *Nunquam* — Durrell was still contemplating publication of *Judith*.[11] We do not know at what stage he decided to merge the first two versions of the novella into one story, splitting the Judith character into Judith (still a scientist) and Grete (the wife of Günther Schiller) and introducing the character of David as Grete's lover, to balance the relationship between Judith and Aaron Stein. This development almost certainly came after the release of the film of *Judith* in January 1966. Durrell's title for the expanded novel was 'Double Scenario'. This was presumably a working title, intended to indicate that there were now two storylines: that of Judith (as in the first version) and that of Grete, who replaced the 'Judith' of the second version. It is an unwieldy title, and I have therefore preferred to retain 'Judith' as the title of this expanded novel. The typescript (which was most likely prepared by a professional typist) contains some anomalies, which Durrell clearly did not have the opportunity to correct. Some of these have been silently corrected; others are discussed below.

Durrell's writing styles

Throughout his career as a novelist, Lawrence Durrell wrote on two levels: intense, passionate, intellectual novels such as *The Alexandria Quartet* (1957–1959), and lighter, less serious, more easily written (and more easily read) stories, which he disparagingly referred to as 'pot-boilers'. In fact, the chronology of his published work indicates

---

10 *Woman's Own,* 26 February–2 April 1966.
11 Letter from Juliet O'Hea, Durrell's agent at Curtis Brown, to Durrell, 26 June 1972.

that, in most cases, the 'serious' and the 'lighter' works alternated, as if, having completed a demanding undertaking such as the *Quartet*, he turned to story-telling which allowed him to continue in the obsessional writer's craft without trying to reach for the literary stars.

In 1937, Lawrence Durrell was living in Corfu, and had already published his first novel, *Pied Piper of Lovers*, and, under the pseudonym of 'Charles Norden', his second, *Panic Spring*; and he had written the novel which he later regarded as carrying the first sound of his true voice, *The Black Book*. (The pseudonym was used because *Pied Piper of Lovers* had not met with critical acclaim.) Having attracted the enthusiastic support of Henry Miller for *The Black Book*, Durrell wrote to him:

My double Amicus Nordensis. He is a double I need … You see, I can't write real books all the time … Once every three years or more I shall try to compose for full orchestra. The rest of the time I shall do essays, travel-books, perhaps one more novel under Charles Norden. I shall naturally not try to write badly or things I don't want to: but there are a lot of things I want to write which don't come into the same class as *The Black Book* at all.[12]

To which Miller forcefully replied:

Don't … take the schizophrenic route! … You must stand or fall either as Charles Norden or as Lawrence Durrell. I would choose Lawrence Durrell if I were you … If, as you say, you can't write REAL books all the time, then don't write. Don't write anything, I mean. Lie fallow … Why couldn't you write all the other books you wish as L.D.? Why can't L.D. be the author of travel books, etc.?[13]

As a result of this retort from Miller, Durrell did 'kill off' his dou-

---

12 Ian MacNiven (ed.), *The Durrell–Miller Letters 1935–1980* (London: Faber & Faber, 1988), p. 81.
13 Ibid., pp. 84, 86.

ble, and continued to write the travel books, essays and novels under his own name: his memoir of Corfu, *Prospero's Cell* (1945), was his next major prose work, and if we examine the chronology of his prose publications thereafter, the alternation of 'real' books and lighter stories becomes clear: *Cefalù* (later republished as *The Dark Labyrinth*) in 1946, *Reflections on a Marine Venus* ('a companion to the landscape of Rhodes', 1953), and *Bitter Lemons* (about his years in Cyprus during the *Enosis* crisis, 1957) led up to the appearance between 1957 and 1959 of the work with which his name is most frequently associated, *The Alexandria Quartet.*

Of his works up to this point, *The Dark Labyrinth* is the least demanding: a didactic novel on a programmatic basis, with each character confronting his or her personal destiny within the framework of a Cretan labyrinth. When he was writing it, Durrell told Miller, 'I have deliberately chosen a cheap novel formula ... A rotten book but with some small lucid moments and one or two good lines'.[14] Readers of *Judith* will readily see that not only does this novel have 'some small lucid moments' — some of them of great beauty and, usually, poignancy — but that the Durrell hallmark of memorable phrases and acute insights is, though to a lesser extent than in his 'real' books, present throughout, in his commentary — sometimes cynical, always with a wry humour — on the behaviour of his characters.

Durrell's view of *The Dark Labyrinth* as 'a rotten book' is so self-deprecatory as to be absurd, especially when it has in fact been very highly regarded by the critics. This, and other books in the 'cheap novel formula' were, in fact, the product of what Miller had foreseen as his 'fallow' periods. *Judith* — unpublished until now — was written in the difficult years for Durrell between the completion of the *Quartet* and his struggle with its successor, the twin novels *Tunc* (1968) and *Nunquam* (1970), which were drafted in parallel with *Judith* under the working title 'The Placebo'. In these 'fallow' years, during which he was preoccupied with the ill-health of his wife, Claude, he also produced his translation of the nineteenth-century *Pope Joan* by the Greek author Emmanuel Royidis, and most of his 'Antrobus' sketches of diplomatic life as he had observed it while working at the

---

14 Ibid., p. 186.

British Embassy in Belgrade, then the capital of the Yugoslav Federation.[15] Yugoslavia had also given rise to his 1957 novel of espionage and suspense, *White Eagles over Serbia* — another example of his capacity for a storyline which grips the reader without making exceptional literary demands.

In fact, almost all Durrell's novels combine the dual elements of what Kipling called 'the game' and 'the quest', as exemplified in his *Kim*, which Durrell himself called his 'bedside book'. The 'game' involves a secret which must be discovered in the book's *dénouement*, and the 'quest', which runs parallel to the public 'game', is the individual's pursuit of self-knowledge. The reader's attention and loyalty are sustained by the author's capacity to entwine the two within a single narrative structure.

G. S. Fraser (a wartime contemporary of Durrell in Egypt), who wrote the first major study of Durrell's work, recorded that 'the Wodehousian humour of the Antrobus stories, the Buchanesque thrills of *White Eagles over Serbia*, have helped to keep the pot boiling. Durrell, with typical versatility, was working when I visited him in Corfu on the script and general advice for an American film, a documentary one, about the voyages of Odysseus'. In relation to *Judith*, Fraser remarked, 'this was obviously a hastily novelized filmscript and one wondered even whether Durrell, who had written the script, had himself done the novelizing'.[16]

The level at which the author can pitch his narrative depends on many factors, such as the basic material of the plot — which, as in the case of *Judith*, might be quite deeply researched — and the evolution of the characters as the writing progresses. But it also depends on the author's emotional and material circumstances: financial and other necessities might dictate the composition of a 'pot-boiler' when the writer would prefer to pursue a more intimate and introspective line of enquiry (even though that would still demand a clear storyline). And the reverse might be the case, as it was with Durrell after the

---

15 Miller also advised Durrell not to waste time on the 'Antrobus' stories (quoted in MacNiven, *Lawrence Durrell*, p. 571). Durrell had written to Miller: 'I didn't send you *Esprit de Corps*; thought you mightn't find it funny. I had to pay for the baby's shoes somehow and wrote it in a very short time' (*Durrell–Miller Letters*, p. 306).
16 G. S. Fraser, *Lawrence Durrell: A Study* (London: Faber & Faber, 1968), p. 40.

success of the *Quartet*, when he started to address the twin themes of *Judith* while considering its potential as a filmscript.

Not only might Durrell denigrate the literary value of one of his minor works, but he was also capable of reducing his masterpiece, *The Alexandria Quartet*, to its basic elements, referring to it as no more than 'sex and the secret service'. In the simplest terms, this reduction accurately reflects the twin themes of the 'quest' — the search by several of the characters for the meaning and practice of love — and the 'game', the web of conspiracies, political and religious movements and chicanery which provides the context in which that idea of love is tested and pursued.

When writing *Tunc* and *Nunquam*, Durrell noted that the 'irresistible book themes are Quests, Confessions and Puzzles'[17] and in doing so he expressed the elements which constitute the framework within which his — and any other author's — characters act out their lives. Whether in a Proust or an Agatha Christie, quests, confessions and puzzles provide the author with the momentum of the book and the reader with the reason for continuing to read it. They are the writer's stock-in-trade, and Durrell emphasised this in referring to what he called 'the minor mythologies',[18] the genres of popular literature which have been consigned by critical prejudice to the status of 'lowbrow'. But the creation of an art-literature rests on the foundations of a much more popular genre: the telling of a compelling story, and *Judith* is such a story.

One of the most striking features of Lawrence Durrell's writing, on any level, is his innate absorption of the context and his ability to bring it vividly to life. When writing *Judith* he conducted extensive research, as was his practice with any work which depicted actual events.

Durrell's knowledge of the Levant enabled him to create scenes redolent of specific times and places. Given greater consideration, it is likely that he would have deepened the characterisation of Judith, Aaron, Grete and Lawton, to match the charming and sympathetic caricature of Isaac Jordan with which the novel opens. But the main

---

17 Southern Illinois University, Carbondale, Collection 42/19/8; cf. Lawrence Durrell, *Nunquam* (London: Faber & Faber, 1970), p. 52.
18 Lawrence Durrell, 'The Minor Mythologies', *Deus Loci*, NS7 (1999–2000), pp. 11–20.

players in this adventure represent positions which had become somewhat institutionalised in the course of the Mandate situation: Judith as
a scientist with a Zionist mission; Aaron as the speaker of the *leitmotiv*
'Israel must get itself born'; Grete seeking her child and her warmon-
gering husband; Lawton the reluctant soldier, caught between personal
feeling and military duty. Lawton, in fact, in his hesitant performance
of that duty, and his pathetic wooing of Grete, shows us that, besides
being a political and human fiasco, the playing out of the last years of
the Mandate was a great drama, which Durrell captures in both the
general and the specific.

It is Durrell's ability to create strong images both of concrete
realities — such as the ambience of the kibbutz — and of emotional
states that lifts *Judith* from a reportage to a work of suggestive and
imaginative fiction. (Theodor Herzl, the father of modern Zionism, had said that his manifesto *The Jewish State* was not written
'in the irresponsible guise of a romantic tale',[19] and Durrell was
equally true to his craft in avoiding excess in the portrayal of the
parallel love stories.) His 'political' background made it possible to
include elements in the storyline, such as the unsuccessful blockade with which it opens, Günther Schiller's meeting with Grete
and his subsequent suicide, the encounter between the childhood
friends Aaron and Daud, and the threat of deportation to Cyprus,
all of which are linked thematically and organically to the situation
in Palestine at that time.

It is remarkable that such themes and narrative devices recur in
Durrell's work: in *The Avignon Quintet*, for example, the wife of the
psychiatrist Schwartz (as in the case of Schiller and Grete) is sent to
Buchenwald, and his subsequent sense of guilt leads to his suicide.
Another recurring feature of Durrell's writing is his insistence that the
story never ends, or that it may have multiple endings. In a memo-
randum to Paramount, he suggested that 'my own story ends here,
but there is no reason why one could not continue it along the lines
already discussed'. And the novel ends with an ambiguity: 'Or so it
seemed'. Similarly, *The Alexandria Quartet* had closed with the pen-
ultimate sentence 'Once upon a time', and *The Avignon Quintet* ends

---

19 Theodor Herzl, *The Jewish State* (London: Penguin, 2010), p. 1.

with an 'opening': 'the totally unpredictable began to take place!' Such was Durrell's interest in improbability and relativity that he resisted any definitive conclusion to anything he wrote.

The political context: Palestine, 1920–1948

Specific events such as the United Nations vote in favour of partition (29 November 1947) and the British military and administrative withdrawal from Palestine (14–15 May 1948) provide the pillars on which the personal fortunes of Durrell's characters rest.

Despite two notable exceptions (discussed below) where Durrell seems to have nodded, his scenario for *Judith* is accurate in two very important respects: its portrayal of the political situation towards the end of the British Mandate in Palestine, and its awareness of the tensions between Arabs and Jews which had built up over the previous half century. As a former British diplomat and government functionary, with extensive experience in the Levant (Egypt, Cyprus and the Dodecanese) in addition to his observations of the Cold War while stationed in Yugoslavia, Durrell was in pole position to employ this experience in the service of a novel which would incorporate both a love story (in fact, two) and the elements of a political thriller.

An introduction of this kind is necessary because, as Albert Hyamson noted, writing shortly after the British withdrawal, his own account of Palestine under the Mandate would be for

the guidance, instruction and also warning of those to whom the welfare of Palestine present and future is of account, necessary as an assistance in dissipating the fog of propaganda in which the whole subject is shrouded and has been for the greater part of the past generation.[20]

The fact that little has changed, in the more than sixty years since Hyamson wrote that, underlines the need for readers today to appreciate the unhappy background to *Judith*.

The following pages therefore indicate the political context within

---

20 A. M. Hyamson, *Palestine under the Mandate 1920–1948* (London: Methuen, 1950), p. v.

which *Judith* is set, and the reasons for Durrell's not merely providing political and religious tensions as background (as he had recently done in the *Quartet*) but bringing that context into the novel as a character in its own right. In fact, the points of history, from the inception of modern Zionism in the 1890s to the 'Balfour Declaration' of 1917 and the start of the British Mandate (from the League of Nations) in 1921–22, are matched meticulously by Durrell and woven into the fabric of the story which binds together Judith, Aaron, Grete and David; the Jewish Agency; the Haganah; and the impending vote at the United Nations to authorise the partition of Palestine.

In weaving together the crucial elements in the history of Palestine — the Zionist pursuit of a Jewish homeland, the Arabs' resentment at being displaced from their ancestral lands, and British frustration at the impossibility of implementing the terms of the Mandate — Durrell captured the ironies, injustices and ignominies of that history. The personal quests of Judith, for the fulfilment of her father's scientific work, and of Grete, for her lost child (a feature also of Justine Hosnani in the *Quartet*) are set within the brutal period when the inevitability of British withdrawal from Palestine and the equally inevitable Arab–Israeli conflict not only brought to a head these three strands of history, but predicted and, indeed, precipitated the Middle East crisis which persists to this day. Given that the film of *Judith* (and the serialisation of the supposed excerpts from the filmscript) appeared in 1966, there is an uncanny prescience of the Six Day War that would erupt slightly more than a year later.

The role of Major Lawton in *Judith* and the episode in which Colonel Macdonald makes arms available to the kibbutz ('A Gift for Ras Shamir', pp. 261–263) highlight the ambivalence of both British policy and personal affiliations which runs throughout the period of the Mandate, and they also make clear the fact that the Mandate itself was based on what at best can be described as a misconception, and at worst as a series of deceits and betrayals. The founding document of the conflict was the 'Balfour Declaration' of 1917, a statement by the British Government that it supported 'the establishment in Palestine of a national home for the Jewish people', while also guaranteeing 'that nothing shall be done which may prejudice the civil and religious rights of existing non-Jewish communities in Palestine'. One might therefore assume that Britain wished to see Jews and Arabs living in co-operation, harmony and mutual respect. There were, however, several other factors which not merely complicated the fulfilment of the project and flawed the ground of the Mandate, but actually created a situation impossible of resolution.

Not least of these was another document, secretly agreed upon between the British and French governments and known as the 'Sykes–Picot Agreement', which made similar promises to the Arabs in respect of the same land area. As a Royal Commission of inquiry into the Palestine situation reported in 1937:

> Under the stress of World War the British Government made promises to Arabs and Jews in order to obtain their support. On the strength of those promises both parties formed certain expectations ... An irrepressible conflict has arisen between two national communities within the narrow bounds of one small country.[21]

George Antonius, the principal apologist for the Arab cause prior to the Second World War, referred to the Sykes–Picot Agreement as 'a shocking document':

> It is not only the product of greed at its worst, that is to say, of greed allied to suspicion and so leading to stupidity: it also stands out as a startling piece of double-dealing.[22]

The Commission, whose report would be suspended until after the Second World War, recommended partition of the country, on which Antonius commented:

> Forcible eviction [of settled Arabs] or subjection to a Jewish state ... runs counter to the lessons of history, the require-

---

21 Quoted in A. J. Sherman, *Mandate Days: British Lives In Palestine 1918–1948* (London: Vintage, 1994), p. 13.
22 George Antonius, *The Arab Awakening* (Philadelphia: Lippincott, 1939), p. 248.

ments of geography, the natural play of economic forces, and the ordinary laws of human behaviour.[23]

As I shall discuss below, it was an early example of 'geopolitics', but in this case, taken together with the Balfour Declaration, it meant that the British right hand was unaware of what its left-hand counterpart was trying to exploit.

At the same time, the fact that the Sykes–Picot Agreement and the Balfour Declaration were mutually exclusive points not only to a lack of foresight by the British (during a time of acute anxiety as far as the conduct of the world war was concerned) but also to a level of incompetence, if not of dishonesty. As Jonathan Schneer remarks, 'the Balfour Declaration was the highly contingent product of a tortuous process characterized as much by deceit and chance as by vision and diplomacy'.[24] As a Palestinian commentator has recently written: 'on what basis did the British believe that they were entitled to promise to the Zionists land that belonged to others?'[25]

Even though the Balfour Declaration had avoided saying that Palestine would become the home of the Jews, but stated, rather, that a home would be established *in* Palestine, Balfour himself and Lloyd George (the prime minister at the time of the Declaration) told Winston Churchill (at that time Colonial Secretary) in 1921 that 'by the Declaration they always meant an eventual Jewish State'.[26] In the following year, a British White Paper aiming to clarify the situation stated that

When it is asked what is meant by the development of a Jewish National Home in Palestine, it may be answered that it is not the imposition of a Jewish nationality upon the inhabitants of Palestine as a whole but the further development of

---

23 Ibid., p. 404.
24 Jonathan Schneer, *The Balfour Declaration: The Origins of the Arab–Israeli Conflict* (London: Bloomsbury, 2010), p. 369.
25 Dawoud El-Alami in Dan Cohn-Sherbok and Dawoud El-Alami, *The Palestine–Israeli Conflict* (Oxford: Oneworld, 2001), p. 144.
26 David Fromkin, *A Peace to End All Peace: The Fall of the Ottoman Empire and the Creation of the Modern Middle East* (London: André Deutsch, 1989), p. 520.

the existing Jewish community, with the assistance of Jews in other parts of the world, in order that it may become a centre in which the Jewish people as a whole may take, on grounds of religion and race, an interest and a pride.[27]

Whether or not British policy — or lack of it — for the development of a Jewish homeland in Palestine was based on the strategies of war, on imperialist imperatives, or on a genuine sense of philanthropy, it is incontestable that British support was vital to the Zionist cause, and, as Sir Henry Gurney (the last Chief Secretary of the Palestine Government) put it, 'The undertaking given by Britain to facilitate the establishment of a Jewish National Home in Palestine represented the only attempt made by any nation in history to help the Jews'.[28]

The ambivalence and apparent lack of policy on the part of the British administration was due in part to the fact that many in the army were pro-Arab, despite acknowledging their admiration for Jewish endeavours and the fact that an Arab attack on Jewish settlements would most probably be overwhelming. At the same time, the Jewish Agency, set up in 1922 under the terms of the Mandate (and the organisation responsible for 'springing' 'Judith Roth' from Germany), had become 'an undisguised alias for the Zionist Organization',[29] while 'under the authority of the Jewish Agency, the Jewish community in Palestine had created its own virtual state within the superstructure of British administration'.[30]

This state-within-a-state, tolerated by the British, had an undercurrent of violence in its vigilance against Arab attack, but also in its own occasional attacks on British installations, including the bomb blast at the British headquarters, the King David Hotel in Jerusalem, which killed eighty officials. Under the aegis of the Zionist Organisation (forerunner of the Jewish Agency), a paramilitary defence organisation called the Haganah, was instituted in 1920, 'because Britain failed to defend them [the Jews] effectively during the pogroms of that year'.[31]

27 Quoted in Hyamson, *Palestine under the Mandate*, p. 36.
28 Quoted in Sherman, *Mandate Days*, p. 237.
29 Hyamson, *Palestine under the Mandate*, p. 116.
30 Sherman, *Mandate Days*, p. 29.
31 Schneer, *Balfour Declaration*, p. 376.

In the 1930s, the Haganah ran parallel to two other armed groups, the Etzel (known by the British as 'Irgun'), led by the future prime minister Menachem Begin, and Lechi, better known as the 'Stern Gang', led by Avraham Stern, composer of its anthem, 'Anonymous Soldiers'. Another member of Irgun was yet another future prime minister, Yitzhak Shamir, who was one of those who sanctioned the assassination of Lord Moyne (the British minister of state in Cairo) in 1944.

That the British military turned its back on many instances of arms smuggling is indisputable; members of the armed forces may well have preferred the Arabs to the Jews ('I wish the Arabs would come and wipe the whole lot out' was the view of one soldier),[32] but it was considered necessary for the Jews to be armed in preparation for the Arab onslaught that would follow British withdrawal. 'Arms acquisitions, training and even manoeuvres had been winked at as long as they were reasonably discreet.'[33] In 1937, Churchill was unequivocal: 'To maintain itself, the Jewish State must be armed to the teeth, and must bring in every able-bodied man to strengthen its army.'[34] In *Judith*, Durrell, as already mentioned, even went so far as to show a British officer donating arms, ammunition and other equipment to Ras Shamir on the eve of the Arab attack, a detail which he most likely derived from the well-known fact that 'especially towards the end of the Mandate there were numerous cases in which weapons, ammunition and other material were "lost" from military stores'.[35] The less palatable side of Haganah activity is also to be found in *Judith*, when Aaron declares proudly:

"Another big trouble this afternoon at the Jaffa gate with fifteen killed. *Six* British, my dears, and two Jews. All the rest Arabs. Tonight they are going to have a go at the Haifa factory."

"I don't see why you sound so elated," said the doctor with a little shudder. "It's horrible." He looked suddenly chastened, like a scolded puppy, and nodded in agreement, his face grave

---

32 Quoted in Sherman, *Mandate Days*, p. 87.
33 Sherman, *Mandate Days*, pp. 151–152.
34 Quoted in Robert Fisk, *The Great War for Civilisation: The Conquest of the Middle East* (London: Harper Perennial, 2006), p. 451.
35 Sherman, *Mandate Days*, p. 61.

again. "The horror is not of our making, alas!" he said in a different tone. (p. 30)

The pro-Jewish or pro-Arab feelings of the British must also be seen in the context of the imperative within the Mandate, that nothing should jeopardise the Arab population. It has been said of the first High Commissioner, Herbert Samuel (himself a Jew), that 'as a Jew and a liberal Englishman he would be ashamed ... if it turned out that the establishment of a Jewish state involved injustice towards the Arabs'.[36] At the same time, as the Arab apologist George Antonius put it,

In face of the abominable persecution to which Jews in Central Europe are nowadays subjected, it is not only desirable but also urgent that room be found for the relief of the greatest possible number ... [But] The cure for the eviction of Jews from Germany is not to be sought in the eviction of the Arabs from their homeland; and the relief of Jewish distress may not be accomplished at the cost of inflicting a corresponding distress upon an innocent and peaceful population.[37]

One of the most poignant elements in the story is the apparent indifference of the British military towards the impending, inevitable, Arab–Israeli conflict. 'The army could not avoid taking a position in favor of one side or another, and it was clear enough in Palestine its sympathy was with the Arabs'.[38] When Judith is being escorted by Aaron to the kibbutz after her arrival in Haifa, their truck is searched by an army patrol. Aaron protests that the army is not doing enough to protect Jews from Arab attack. 'You want us to be eaten by the Arabs', he says. 'Personally, I don't care who eats who', the sergeant retorts (p. 33). And when Judith meets Rebecca Peterson at the kibbutz, she asks, 'But don't the British keep the peace?' to which Peterson replies:

When it suits them. I think they would be rather glad if their

---

36 Tom Segev, One Palestine, Complete: Jews and Arabs under the British Mandate, tr. Haim Watzman (London: Little, Brown, 2000), p. 192.
37 Antonius, Arab Awakening, pp. 403, 411.
38 Segev, One Palestine, Complete, p. 193.

Arab friends wiped out the kibbutzim; we are an embarrassment to them. On the Lebanon side we are well protected
because we control the crown of the mountain and the settlements are spread out along it — good defensive positions with
steep cliffs the other side. On this side, alas, it is not so good
because the Syrians are astride the crown and we are down in
the valley. (p. 43)

Not only does Durrell thereby create a sense of insecurity, of a peaceful and beautiful valley surrounded by latent, and soon-to-be-explicit,
hostility, but he represents the reality of kibbutzim, such as both the
real and the fictional Shamir, with an air of pathos that immediately
wins the reader's affection and sympathy. This becomes particularly
effective when Grete is introduced to the children's quarters, and experiences the various psychological weaknesses which are the facts of
life carried within these future builders of Israeli society.

From a reading of *The Alexandria Quartet* we can infer that Durrell himself had far greater sympathy for the Jewish cause than for the
Arabs (his second and third wives were Alexandrian Jews), and the
Quartet, anticipating what Durrell would write in *Judith*, features an
episode of gun-running into Palestine — in this case aided by Coptic
(Christian) Egyptians. Permeating *Judith* is the *leitmotiv* uttered by
Aaron ('Israel *must* get itself born' — p. 88) and David Eveh ('Israel
must become a reality, a sovereign state' — pp. 114–115); and, finally,
with the UN vote in favour of partition, Major Lawton realised that
'Israel had been born' (p. 195). The prophetic dream of Theodor
Herzl had come true: 'The Jewish State is essential to the world; it will
therefore be created ... A State is created by a nation's struggle for
existence.'[39] In *The Alexandria Quartet*, this geopolitical imperative
is recognised by Nessim Hosnani, a (Christian) Copt, who fears the
extinction of non-Muslims in his native Egypt. For him the creation
of a Jewish state in Palestine would represent a counterbalance to the
extension of Islam: 'if only the Jews can win their freedom, we can all
be at ease.'[40]

---

39 Herzl, *Jewish State*, pp. 4, 78.
40 Lawrence Durrell, *The Alexandria Quartet* (London: Faber & Faber, 1962), p. 533.

But this development brought its own nemesis: as Rebecca Peterson says to Grete:

> For so long we have been living in insecurity, dependent on the good will of strangers, on the charity of others... Now, all of a sudden, we exist on paper as a place called Israel. This is a momentous step forward, for we have now become a sort of world commitment. But you know as well as I do that if Israel were to be swallowed up by the Arab states, nobody would lift a finger to save her. At last, my dear, at last we are all alone with our own destiny. It depends on us whether the state can get itself born and fix itself among the other small nations. (p. 213)

The period of the Mandate saw the accelerating process of this conflict, in which 'Two competing national movements consolidated their identity in Palestine and advanced steadily toward confrontation.'[41] David Ben-Gurion, prime minister of Israel 1948–1953 and 1955–1963, simply said, 'Everybody sees the problem in relations between the Jews and the Arabs. But not everybody sees that there's no solution to it. There is no solution!'[42] As one commentator had said as early as 1905, 'The two movements were destined to wage war until one defeated the other, and the fate of the entire world depended on the outcome of this struggle'[43] — a view echoed continuously since then by observers such as Robert Fisk, author of *The Great War for Civilisation: The Conquest of the Middle East*:

> The Arab–Jewish struggle ... is an epic tragedy whose effects have spread around the world and continue to poison the lives not only of the participants but of our entire Western political and military policies towards the Middle East and the Muslim lands.[44]

Despite manifestations of anti-semitism in Britain in the nineteenth and early twentieth centuries, pro-Jewish opinion in England

41 Segev, *One Palestine, Complete*, p. 6.
42 Quoted in ibid., p. 116.
43 Najib Azuri, quoted in ibid., p. 105.
44 Fisk, *Great War*, p. 448.

had in fact been evident since the seventeenth century: Sir Henry Finch published his *World's Great Restauration or Calling of the Jews* in 1621; in 1840 the Foreign Secretary, Lord Palmerston, declared that 'There exists at present among the Jews dispersed over Europe a strong notion that the time is approaching when their nation is to return to Palestine'[45] — an early expression of the view that the 'dispersed' Jews constituted a nation, with the concomitant suggestion that they therefore deserved statehood. The prime minister Benjamin Disraeli (himself a Jew who had converted to Christianity) wrote of the Middle East in his novel *Tancred, or The New Crusade* (1847), while the theme of Jewish re-awakening permeates George Eliot's *Daniel Deronda* (1874–1876), as surely as it becomes the *leitmotiv* of *Judith*.[46]

Also, whether or not the British, in 1917, needed to woo Jewish support worldwide for the continuation of the world war, that war had been preceded in 1914 by the remark of Herbert Samuel that 'Perhaps the opportunity might arise for the fulfillment of the ancient aspiration of the Jewish people and the restoration of a Jewish state'.[47]

Previously, locations other than Palestine had been mooted as a possible 'home land': in 1903, Joseph Chamberlain (the Colonial Secretary) and Lord Lansdowne (Foreign Secretary) had suggested Uganda as a destination;[48] other possibilities under consideration were Mesopotamia, Western Australia, British Honduras and British Guiana (all within the British remit) and Brazil, Mexico and Texas.[49] Balfour himself, as prime minister in 1903, had been involved in the offer of Uganda, a proposal sometimes referred to as the 'first Balfour Declaration'.[50] But Theodor Herzl, having considered the alternatives of Argentina and Palestine, had no choice but to opt for the 'restoration' of the Jewish state in Palestine: 'our ever-memorable historic home'.[51]

---

45 Quoted in Hyamson, *Palestine under the Mandate*, p. 8.
46 Eliot's character Mordecai argues: 'The effect of our separateness will not be completed and have its highest transformation unless our race takes on again the character of a nationality.... There is a store of wisdom among us to found a new Jewish polity' – George Eliot, *Daniel Deronda* (Ware, UK: Wordsworth, 1996), pp. 442–443. Eliot was also prescient in predicting, 'We may live to see a great outburst of force in the Arabs' (ibid., p. 434).
47 Quoted in Schneer, *Balfour Declaration*, p. 125.
48 Cf. ibid., p. 112.
49 Cf. Hyamson, *Palestine under the Mandate*, p. 25.
50 Cf. Segev, *One Palestine, Complete*, p. 40.
51 Herzl, *Jewish State*, pp. 1, 30.

In 1921, the year following the commencement of the British administration in Palestine, Winston Churchill, who had just become Colonial Secretary, declared:

It is manifestly right that the scattered Jews should have a national centre and a national home to be re-united and where else but in Palestine with which for 3,000 years they have been intimately and profoundly associated? We think it will be good for the world, good for the Jews, good for the British Empire, but also good for the Arabs who dwell in Palestine... they shall share in the benefits and progress of Zionism... There really is nothing for the Arabs to be frightened about... No Jew will be brought in beyond the number who can be provided for by the expanding wealth and development of the resources of the country.[52]

There is a telling clue in Herzl's 1896 manifesto, *The Jewish State*, as to the strategic importance of a Jewish homeland in Palestine: 'We should there form a portion of a rampart of Europe against Asia, an outpost of civilization as opposed to barbarism'.[53] Herzl was perhaps recognising what would come within a couple of decades to be called 'geopolitics' — the relations between states based on geographical location — which in our own time has provided us with ways of understanding strategies relating to the balance of power in regions such as the Near and Middle East. As early as 1915, the British prime minister H. H. Asquith had referred to 'the carving up of the Turks' Asiatic dominion',[54] and, as the Ottoman empire crumbled as a side-effect of the First World War, distribution of lands previously under Turkish rule became a priority for the victors.

It has been argued that Britain had no strategic benefit, at the time of the original Mandate, for undertaking it.[55] And in 1945, perhaps in an effort to sustain the argument for British withdrawal, Churchill said he was 'not aware of the slightest advantage that has ever accrued

---

52 Quoted in Fromkin, *Peace to End All Peace*, pp. 520–521.
53 Herzl, *Jewish State*, p. 30.
54 Quoted in Antonius, *Arab Awakening*, p. 264.
55 Cf. Segev, *One Palestine, Complete*, p. 4.

to Great Britain from this painful and thankless task'[56] — a position not inconsistent with his view of the situation over twenty years earlier (quoted above).

Nevertheless, Palestine represented an important — if not vital — land bridge to Arabia and India, and in the same year that saw the 'carving up' of the Ottoman Empire, the military correspondent of the *Manchester Guardian* newspaper opined that 'the whole future of the British Empire as a Sea Empire ... depended upon Palestine becoming a buffer state'.[57] A. J. Sherman's observation, that 'British occupation of Palestine was undertaken in full awareness of geopolitical realities'[58] cannot be easily dismissed: it leads us towards the essential element which is familiar to everyone today: oil. In 1921 a British government minister had foreseen this: 'while, in present circumstances, Palestine was of no real strategic value, it was desirable to keep it. Who knows, maybe one day oil would be discovered there'.[59] With the increasing awareness of oil exploration in Iraq in the 1930s by companies such as the IPC consortium of British Petroleum, Shell and Gulbenkian, geopolitics entered a crucial phase, which Durrell effectively introduced into *Judith*: Judith's father had been working on a turbine which the Jews (soon to become Israelis) might turn to advantage:

"Oil is what we have in mind," said the Professor. "It is also what the Nazis had in mind; they had plans for the Rumanian oil-fields which would have been helped by this idea. By the same token, the British, Americans and Arabs would all be profoundly interested." (p. 60)

And when Judith and Aaron argue about the intensity of the Zionist drive towards statehood and the significance of the United Nations vote on partition, oil again features as a factor in the geopolitical debate:

---

56 Quoted in Sherman, *Mandate Days*, p. 171.
57 Quoted in Fromkin, *Peace to End All Peace*, pp. 270–271.
58 Sherman, *Mandate Days*, p. 15.
59 Quoted in Segev, *One Palestine, Complete*, p. 199.

"And what of the Arabs?" she said harshly. "They will torpedo your vote. You know they will. Who is going to sacrifice good oil to their displeasure?"

"The risk is there — we must take it. It is the only way."

"It will end with a massacre."

"That we can face up to as the worst extremity; but we sabras[60] are not going to stretch out our little white throats to the Arab's knife. But we know that in the longest run we must live with them, cooperate with them. At the moment British oil interests won't let us. That's the point." (p. 134)

The Mandate, officially approved on 22 July 1922 by the League of Nations (the forerunner of the United Nations), came into force on 29 September 1923, although the British had been in occupation of Palestine, militarily and administratively, since July 1920, in the wake of General Allenby's capture of Jerusalem from the Turks in 1917. The Mandate empowered Britain to govern Palestine, with explicit responsibility to support the establishment of a Jewish national home, while (an echo of the Balfour Declaration) safeguarding the rights of the existing population. It also provided for the introduction of self-government, which both Jews and Arabs would reject. It has been argued that these three imperatives were incompatible,[61] and, given the increasing suspicion and hostility between the indigenous population and the newcomers, it seems that the impossibility of carrying out the terms of the Mandate may have contributed substantially to the ambivalence and lack of clear direction on the part of the British. 'One senior official ... estimated that the British had never in fact had a policy for Palestine, "nothing but fluctuations of policy, hesitations ... no policy at all" '.[62] Durrell had given an indication of his own feelings on this point in *The Alexandria Quartet* when his character Pursewarden, based in Egypt, says, in relation to British activity in the Middle East as a whole, that 'it is neither coherent nor even a policy — at any rate a policy capable of withstanding the pressures which are being built up here'.[63]

---

60 See Glossary.
61 Cf. Hyamson, *Palestine under the Mandate*, p. 139.
62 Segev, *One Palestine, Complete*, p. 9.
63 Durrell, *The Alexandria Quartet*, p. 473.

Today, with growing momentum towards long-deferred statehood for the Palestinians, it is perhaps surprising that partition was not on the table as a condition, rather than an option, from the beginning: as David Fromkin observes,

> Since the Balfour Declaration contained no geographical definition, Churchill's advisers concluded that Britain could fully reconcile and fulfil her wartime pledges by establishing a Jewish National Home in Palestine west of the Jordan and a separate Arab entity in Palestine east of the Jordan.[64]

While partition remained unacceptable to both parties, and particularly to the Arabs, it was the only possible means of carrying out the terms of both the Balfour Declaration and the Mandate.

There are two points in *Judith* where Durrell seems to have nodded — to have condensed the historical events of two or three years into a much shorter timescale. For example, there are two references to the Jewish strategy of referring the questions of the Mandate and partition to the United Nations — one by Professor Liebling (p. 61) and one by Aaron (p. 130). However, both these statements were made in early 1945 according to Durrell's chronology, and although the United Nations had been mooted since 1942 and came into existence in October 1945, it did not hold its first assembly until January 1946. No doubt, if Durrell had revised *Judith* for publication, such anachronisms would have been corrected, as, perhaps, would have been the fact that both Liebling and Aaron employ the same expression: 'to bounce' the British out of Palestine and into the United Nations.

But the most glaring example of a 'seacoast of Bohemia' error is in Durrell's depiction of the Syrian, Daud, as a 'prince' and Daud's references to the 'King' of Syria: since 1936, Syria had been a republic, although its independence was only recognised internationally in April 1946. Again, this would no doubt have been noticed if Durrell's typescript had been submitted to his principal publishers, Faber & Faber; I have preferred to let it stand.

However, in the final version of *Judith*, one element just before the

---

64 Fromkin, *Peace to End All Peace*, pp. 504–505.

anticipated Arab attack confuses the reader, since it places one event just before another, which, in strict chronology, it should succeed. I have therefore transposed chapters 26 and 27 in order to maintain the chronological unfolding of events.

Another writer who studied the Palestine crisis in depth was Leon Uris, whose novel *Exodus* (1958) predates the earliest drafts of *Judith* by four years, and which was filmed by MGM in 1960. There is no evidence that Durrell was familiar with either the book or the film; the fact that the same note is struck in both books indicates their authors' familiarity with the commonplaces of the situation: ships landing illegal immigrants, people necessary to the Zionist cause being concealed in crates, gun-running (and the British attempts to prevent such activities) and the importance of oil as an economic necessity. The action of some refugees, on reaching land, to kiss the sacred ground, appears in both novels; the close childhood relationship of Aaron and Daud is also prefigured in a Jewish–Arab friendship in *Exodus*, but with a happier outcome.

Exodus, which is based on an actual incident, also puts the difficulty of the Jewish task firmly before the reader: 'Some people are out to resurrect a nation that has been dead for two thousand years.'[65] Uris reminds us that 'the British were caught in a tangle. They were as far away from a final answer on the Palestine problem as they ever had been.'[66] He was as alert as was Durrell to the geopolitics of the region: as one British official says, 'The only way we are going to hold the Middle East is by building a powerful Jewish Palestine. I don't speak of Jewish interest but I speak of British interest.'[67]

The continuing crisis in Israel-Palestine remains a topic of concern and interest, especially in Britain, where the problem may be said to have started. The screening in 2011 on the UK's Channel 4 of *The Promise*, written and directed by Peter Kosminsky, which commutes between a 'Judith' scenario of 1947–1948 and the present day, harshly emphasises the perennial nature of the conflict.

Naturally, the situation continues to be a central element in the

---

65 Leon Uris, *Exodus* (New York: Bantam, 1959), pp. 19–20.
66 Ibid., p. 95.
67 Ibid., p. 174.

thinking of Jewish writers, not least of whom is Amos Oz, who has described his own experiences of the 1948 conflict in his autobiography, *A Tale of Love and Darkness* (2005), and, more cynically, in novels such as *A Perfect Peace* (1985). Oz favours a 'two-state solution' which involves partition:

> Israel is the only homeland of the Israelis.... At the same time, I regard Palestine as the legitimate and rightful homeland of the Palestinians. As it seems that Israelis and Palestinans cannot share their homeland, it must be divided between them.... The conflict between Israel and Palestine is ... a tragic collision between right and right, between two very convincing claims.[68]

Immigration: the kibbutzim

The situation became acute not only because the Mandate envisaged a form of what today we would call 'power sharing' (similar to that between nationalist/republicans and loyalist/unionists in Northern Ireland) but also because the Arabs realised that the huge increase in the number of Jewish immigrants threatened their own existence in the disputed land.

In 1914, Jews constituted less than one-ninth of the population of Palestine (85,000 out of a total of 690,000), the vast majority of whom were immigrants. By 1920, despite the fact that the Jewish proportion of the population had decreased, some Arabs had begun to attack Jewish property.[69] From 1923 onwards, immigration — technically under a quota system administered by the British — increased significantly, with many Jewish refugees from anti-semitism in Russia and eastern Europe. As Durrell shows us in the case of the 'Ras Shamir' kibbutz, Jews acquired land from Arabs, and formed agricultural settlements, helping to create the impression that they were industrious and enter-

---

68 Amos Oz, *Israel, Palestine and Peace: Essays* (London: Vintage, 1994), pp. xii, 69.
69 Aggression between Palestinian Arabs and Jewish settlers had existed as early as 1891: Cohn-Sherbok and El-Alami, *Palestine–Israeli Conflict*, p. 134.

prising, in contrast to the lazy and indifferent Arabs. At that time, Churchill said that

> Left to themselves, the Arabs of Palestine would not in a thousand years have taken effective steps toward the irrigation and electrification of Palestine. They would have been quite content to dwell — a handful of philosophic people — in the wasted sun-scorched plains.[70]

As the Director of Education in the British administration commented:

> It is difficult not to sympathize with the majority, and the Jews do not tend to make themselves popular; but one feels too that the Arabs are a lazy and unenterprising people, and if they do lose ground they will do so largely owing to their own lack of effort.[71]

This is reflected by Durrell in the painful interview between Aaron and his Arab childhood friend Daud (pp. 166–169), in which Daud, with the backing of the British commanders in the Syrian army, demands the return of the valley of 'Ras Shamir'. First, there is the fact that Aaron's grandfather had bought the valley from the Syrians, as had the founders of so many other Jewish settlements. Secondly, there is the incontrovertible evidence of their success in creating a thriving agricultural community, as Peterson has already explained to Judith:

> It took thirty years and about two hundred lives to drain what was stinking marshland and turn it into the richest valley in Palestine. The Arabs never did anything with it, and were glad to sell it off bit by bit — now, of course, they would like it back. (p. 46)

Although it was hoped that Arabs and Jews might live as neigh-

---

70 Quoted in Fromkin, *Peace to End All Peace*, p. 523.
71 Quoted in Sherman, *Mandate Days*, p. 26.

bours, in harmony and partnership, this proved impossible in the light of Arab apprehension. In 1920 there were only thirty kibbutzim, with a total population of 4,000, constituting only 2.5% of the Jewish population in Palestine. Nevertheless, the kibbutzim

> were guardians of Zionist land, and their patterns of settlement would to a great extent determine the country's borders. The kibbutzim also had a powerful effect on the Zionist self-image.... The agricultural ethos prevailed as a patriotic symbol; the labor movement succeeded in identifying its rural, pioneering worldview with the entire Zionist movement.[72]

During the 1930s many more agricultural settlements were started, including fifty-three kibbutzim.[73] Durrell's portrayal of the determination at 'Ras Shamir' to succeed and to protect the Jewish people, evident in the characters of Aaron Stein, David Eveh and even the non-Jew Rebecca Peterson, is typical of this endeavour.

Durrell locates the kibbutz 'Ras Shamir' in the eye of the storm, in Upper Galilee, at the northernmost point of Palestine (the 'Galilee Panhandle'), bordered on the west by Lebanon and on the east by Syria. In doing so he took liberties with the 'real' Kibbutz Shamir, which is close to the Syrian border (as it was in 1948) and under the Golan Heights, which Israel sequestered from Syria in the 1967 Six Day War and continues, controversially, to occupy. In *Judith* the children of the kibbutz remain within the compound, whereas in 1948 the children of Kibbutz Shamir were evacuated to the Haifa region.

Durrell also played with the orientation of Shamir, locating it, for ideological reasons, on, rather than near, the river Jordan, and below Mount Tabor, rather than Mount Hermon, which is close to the 'real' Shamir. He also embellished Shamir by locating it on the site of a Crusader fortress, of which many survive, especially in Syria, to this day. *Ras* is an Arabic word (*rosh* in Hebrew) meaning 'peak', or 'head', while '*Shamir*' suggests 'rock' or 'flint'. This emphasises the location of 'Ras Shamir', nestling at the head of a valley between the hills that rise up

---

72 Segev, *One Palestine, Complete*, pp. 249, 257.
73 Ibid., p. 379.

on either side of the Jordan, underlining its vulnerability to attack as well as its religious significance on the Jordan.

Shamir was founded in 1944 by mainly Romanian immigrants who were members of the Marxist Zionist youth movement (whereas 'Ras Shamir', according to Aaron Stein, had existed for thirty years). In 1948 its co-ordinator of defence was a woman, Surika Braverman. If Durrell knew this, it may have prompted him to use the figure of Rebecca Peterson in confrontation with Major Towers before the Syrian attack. Although it was always vulnerable (and was the subject of Syrian assaults at a later date: for example, in 1974 three members of the kibbutz were killed during a terrorist raid), Kibbutz Shamir was not, in fact, attacked after British withdrawal in 1948, despite expectation that it would be one of the first kibbutzim to bear the brunt of any assault. Due to these expectations, the kibbutz was well fortified, on lines very similar to those depicted by Durrell in *Judith*.[74] There is no record of Durrell having visited Kibbutz Shamir, although he was clearly aware of its significance.[75]

The Nazi attempt to destroy European Jewry, the Holocaust, created the huge wave of immigrants, both during the 1930s and the world war and its aftermath, which made the crisis so acute. This was, of course, totally unexpected. 'It was never conceived by the British Government that Palestine would of necessity become the country of refuge for hundreds of thousands, potentially millions of desperate Jewish refugees, of all ages and conditions, with no place else to go.'[76] But, as David Ben-Gurion wryly observed,

> Had partition been carried out [before the Second World War], the history of our people would have been different and six million Jews in Europe would not have been killed — most of them would be in Israel.[77]

---

74 Haim Canaani (ed.), *Shamir during the War of Independence* (Kibbutz Shamir, n.d.).
75 Kibbutz Shamir has grown significantly in recent years, from a population of 600 in 2006 to 800 in 2009, of whom a quarter are children. Today it is one of the most advanced kibbutzim, engaged in the manufacture of optical equipment as well as in agricultural production.
76 Sherman, *Mandate Days*, p. 90.
77 Quoted in Segev, *One Palestine, Complete*, p. 414.

The conditions in which these refugees travelled were indicative of both their determination to escape from persecution and their passionate desire to reach the new homeland. Tom Segev quotes the observations of one British officer watching the disembarkation of such a shipload:

> They stepped ashore after long weeks of horrible crowding on the decks of barely serviceable vessels; the conditions were worse than on old-time slave ships.... Amazingly, he saw no misery among the passengers, only exultation. A strange light shone in their eyes. When the immigrants made out the cliffs of Mount Carmel and the blue mountains of Galilee, they would break out in song ... ancient Hebrew melodies.[78]

Durrell captures it well, when Judith assists at a disembarkation where she meets Grete Schiller:

> Now Judith had the chance for the first time of witnessing the different reactions of these arrivals. Some had thrown themselves on the ground, others were laughing and crying, others kissing the wet sand. Most of the refugees were wearing on their backs all the clothes they possessed. (p. 72)

Durrell himself had witnessed scenes similar to what he describes in chapter 9 of *Judith*, 'Operation "Welcome"', in which ships dodged the British blockade of the Palestine coastline in order to set ashore their illegal human cargo. In 1946 he and his second wife, Eve, had travelled on a Greek naval vessel as part of a rescue of refugees from a sunken ship:

> Eight of the refugees had died when the ship had run aground and sunk, but some eight hundred had reached land and were spilled about under the moonlight in a natural amphitheatre. The sight had a weird, ghostly unreality. Larry and Eve spent the next morning ashore, monitoring radio transmissions and talking to the refugees.[79]

---

78 Ibid., p. 230. See also Sherman, *Mandate Days*, p. 130.
79 MacNiven, *Lawrence Durrell*, p. 333.

Introduction

One of the problems for assimilation of Jews into the state of Israel was the fact that they came from so many different backgrounds and cultures. Although Herzl had argued that the Jews were a cohesive entity for which the homeland would be provided ('We are a people — one people'),[80] it had equally been argued that 'There is no Jewish race now as a homogenous whole', and that a Jewish homeland in Palestine would be composed of 'a polyglot, many-colored, heterogeneous collection of people of different civilizations and different ordinances and different traditions'.[81]

The state, Israel, would be a home not to a homogeneous people but to disparate peoples from sixty or seventy countries (the number varies in *Judith*), many of whom had no common language. As Amos Oz has written,

The Jews from ninety-six different countries of origin ... shared a common literary, liturgical and cultural tradition [but] ... One need spend only a couple of minutes on any street here to discover that there is no such thing as a Jewish race. Jews are not an ethnic group and the only unifying force is in their heads.[82]

Durrell, alert to the pathos and the macabre humour of the situation, addresses this in *Judith*, when he has Rebecca Peterson say of a neighbouring settlement:

Tell them from me that they are just a bunch of Glasgow Jews thriving on the sharp practice they picked up from the Scots. Tell them, moreover, that we honest lowland Jews from Poland, Latvia, Russia and Brooklyn hold them in massive contempt. (p. 44)

And the places from which they have come provide the names of their settlements: Brisbane, Brooklyn, Odessa, Calcutta, Warsaw,

80 Herzl, *Jewish State*, p. 8.
81 The Liberal politician Edwin Montagu, in 1915, quoted in Schneer, *Balfour Declaration*, p. 146.
82 Oz, *Israel, Palestine and Peace*, p. 53.

Glasgow.... Durrell may also have borrowed something of the same sense of heterogeneity from *A Chair for the Prophet* (1959) by his third wife, Claude Vincendon:

How in Heaven's name could they expect a national alchemy to fuse and homogenize in an already overflowing melting-pot — Germans and Russians, Spaniards and Englishmen, and the hordes of street-arabs?[83]

In the late 1930s George Antonius pointed out a crucial defect in Arab self-promotion:

The Arabs have little of the skill, polyglottic ubiquity or financial resources which make Jewish propaganda so effective. The result is that, for a score of years or so, the world has been looking at Palestine mainly through Zionist spectacles and has unconsciously acquired the habit of reasoning on Zionist premises.[84]

American support for Israel has, until recently, been unwavering and largely uncritical,[85] and this has created a climate of public opinion in which the world has seen the Israelis as the 'victims' of history and the Arabs as the aggressors. Antonius went on to say that

The fact must be faced that the violence of the Arabs is the inevitable corollary of the moral violence done to them, and that it is not likely to cease, whatever the brutality of the repression, unless the moral violence itself were to cease.[86]

Since it was impossible to persuade Arabs and Jews to sit at the same table for discussions, co-operation was out of the question, as was the long-term goal of a binational state. The manifest sympathy for the Jewish problem, precipitated by the revelation of the Holo-

---

83 Claude, *A Chair for the Prophet* (London: Faber & Faber, 1959), p. 9.
84 Antonius, *Arab Awakening*, p. 387.
85 Cf. Fisk, *Great War*, p. 463.
86 Antonius, *Arab Awakening*, p. 409.

caust, served to occlude the position of the Palestinian Arabs. The 1948 attempt by Syria, Lebanon, Jordan, Egypt and Iraq to stifle the infant state of Israel, followed by those of 1967 and 1973, reinforced the world's view that Israel was a vulnerable state which deserved support. It was only with the recalcitrant move by hardliners in the Israeli invasion of Lebanon in 1978 that public opinion began to accept that there was a Palestinian side to the problem which had been neglected, perhaps because it had not been articulated as effectively as the Israeli side. As Amos Oz has said,

> the wars we led in 1948, 1967 and 1973 were a matter of life and death. Had we lost those wars, Israel would not exist today. By contrast, the Lebanon War was optional ... [it] was not a matter of life and death.[87]

The intensity of mutual fear and repulsion is expressed graphically in two declarations: in 1928 Chaim Shalom Halevi said of the Arabs: 'They hate us and they are right, because we hate them too, hate them with a deadly hatred';[88] while in 1944 the Nazi-oriented Grand Mufti of Jerusalem, Haj Amin al-Husseini, urged: 'Arabs, rise as one man and fight for your sacred rights. Kill the Jews wherever you find them. This pleases God, history and religion'.[89] Such expressions make explicit what is only slightly diminished by diplomatic manoeuvres such as the Camp David Accords engineered by President Jimmy Carter in 1978 between Egypt's President Sadat and Israel's Prime Minister Begin. Anyone who witnessed, during the Six Day War, King Hussein of Jordan saying of the Jews, 'They will be our enemies until the end of time' will appreciate not only the depth of Arab feeling but also the inevitable fact that reciprocal Jewish feeling would be expressed with equal force by Israeli statesmen such as Benjamin Netanyahu.

As General (later Field Marshal) Montgomery said in 1939, 'the Jew murders the Arab and the Arab murders the Jew. This is what is going on in Palestine now. And it will go on for the next 50 years in all

---

87 Oz, *Israel, Palestine and Peace*, pp. 46–47.
88 Quoted in Segev, *One Palestine, Complete*, p. 307.
89 Quoted in Fisk, *Great War*, p. 444.

probability'.[90] He was wrong only in his fifty-year forecast. Again, there are geopolitics at stake, as Robert Fisk has pointed out:

The 1948 war threw up extraordinary portents of other, later, Middle East wars — of events that we regard as causes of present danger but which have clearly been a feature of conflict in the region for longer than we like to imagine.[91]

One need not make any exaggerated claims for *Judith* as a work of great literature: its origins as a film project indicate that it belongs with a collection of Durrell's writings ('a lot of things I want to write which don't come into the same class as…') at a level slightly lower than his major works. But its continuing relevance to the painful situation in the Middle East today makes it a compelling example of Durrell's ability to write a story which also conveys an enduring sense of hope and tragedy.

---

90 Quoted in Segev, *One Palestine, Complete*, p. 442.
91 Fisk, *Great War*, p. 460.

Acknowledgements

The Editor wishes to thank the following for their assistance in the preparation of this publication:

Dr. James Bantin, Curator, Special Collections, Morris Library, Southern Illinois University, Carbondale;
Anthea Morton Saner, formerly Lawrence Durrell's agent at Curtis Brown;
Anna Davis, currently agent for the Lawrence Durrell Estate at Curtis Brown;
Brewster Chamberlin, author of *A Chronology of the Life and Times of Lawrence Durrell*;
Ian MacNiven, author of *Lawrence Durrell: A Biography* and editor of *The Durrell-Miller Letters 1935-1980*;
Dr. Yaacov Lozowick, Director of the Israeli State Archives;
Dr. Hagai Tsoref, Israeli State Archives;
Yehudit Massad and Joan Halfi, archivists, Kibbutz Shamir, Israel;
Jenny Romero, Special Collections Department Co-ordinator, Margaret Herrick Library, Academy of Motion Picture Arts and Sciences, Los Angeles;
Patrick Sammon, a colleague in the Durrell School of Corfu, who gave

considerable assistance and advice during proofreading;
and in particular my colleague Dr. Anthony Hirst, Academic Director of
the Durrell School of Corfu, for professional support, also for assistance in
compiling the Glossary, and for preparing the text for printing.

Glossary

ADC *Aide-de-camp*: usually an assistant or adviser to a senior officer.

ATS Auxiliary Territorial Service: the title of the women volunteers' branch of the British army, 1938–1949.

BEA British European Airways: precursor (with British Overseas Airways Corporation) of British Airways.

C-in-C Commander-in-Chief.

D.P. Displaced Persons.

G.S.O.2 General Staff Officer, 2nd Grade.

H.E. His Excellency: title usually applied to an Ambassador.

H.M.G. His Majesty's Government: at the time in which *Judith* is set, the British monarch was George VI (reigned 1936–1952).

MI Military Intelligence.

MT Military Transport.

N.C.O. Non-Commissioned Officer.

O.C. Officer Commanding / Officer in Command.

UNO United Nations Organization.

WT Wireless transmitter.

Technical terms, proper names, foreign and obscure words

ack emma: from an obsolete military 'phonetic alphabet', these are the words representing the letters A and M. Thus 'four ack emma' means '4 a.m.'

acroflavin: acriflavine hydrochloride: a topical antiseptic.

Camberley: a town about 30 miles southwest of the centre of London, home to a Staff College for training British army officers.

Carley floats: life rafts based on compartmented ovals of copper or steel tubing.

cutty pipe: a pipe whose shape is based on that of traditional clay pipes, but without the long stem.

Druze: the Druze are an Arab people whose religion stems from Islam but has distinct esoteric features; the Druze live mainly in Syria, Lebanon and Israel.

duffle: a duffle coat, made from a coarse woollen fabric, widely used in the British navy from the First World War; typically fastened with two or more wooden or horn toggles through loops of rope or leather.

francs-tireurs: literally "free shooters"; a term often used for irregular forces or partisans, but here appearing to mean simply 'marksmen' or perhaps 'snipers'.

Gauss: Carl Friedrich Gauss (1777–1855), brilliant German mathematician and physicist, whose conjectures are still being followed up today.

German colony: a compound to the southwest of the Old City of Jerusalem, established in the late nineteenth century by a German Messianic Christian sect.

Hafiz: fourteenth-century Persian lyric poet.

Immediate (as in 'an Immediate'): an instruction for immediate action.

I-tanks: infantry tanks designed to accompany (and sometimes to carry on the outside) foot soldiers into battle.

Jewish Brigade: Jewish Infantry Brigade Group. A unit within the British army, formed in 1944, which fought against the Germans in Italy. After the Second World War many members became involved in illegal Jewish immigration into Palestine.

Judas (as in 'a Judas'): a small hinged or sliding panel in a door which allows observation of the person on the other side.

Juliet: a high quality cigar. The full brand name is 'Romeo y Julieta', used by two different companies, one in Cuba and one in the Dominican Republic.

Kalmuk: the Kalmuk people, who live on the western shore of the Caspian Sea, are of Mongol origin.

Lager: German for 'camp'.

Mactaggart forts: military fortresses built throughout Palestine from 1938 (including one in the Hebron) on a model designed by Sir Charles Tegart; Tegart's name is commonly misspelled 'Taggart'. Durrell may have deliberately added 'Mac', or it may be a slip of his memory.

Miko: evidently, from the context, a top-secret intelligence report. It has not been possible to verify the term. Durrell may have invented it, or misremembered some term he had once been familiar with. It could, perhaps, be an acronym for 'Military Intelligence Covert Operations', with the C changed to K.

Mills bombs: a range of hand grenades named after its inventor, Sir William Mills, and first produced in 1915. A new type, the Mills 36M, was produced during the Second World War.

Oxford Shorter: *Shorter Oxford English Dictionary*, first published in 1933, in two large volumes.

sabra: a Hebrew word for a Jew born in Palestine. It first came into use in the 1930s. It refers to the fruit of the prickly pear; equivalent to 'a rough diamond'.

specie: money in the form of coins.

Tellers: Teller mines: German-made anti-tank mines.

Tobruk: as part of the North African campaign, Tobruk was the site of a battle and a siege in 1941.

Verey lights: flares fired from a pistol, to illuminate the sky, named after their American inventor, Edward Wilson Very.

Judith

1

The Secret Rendezvous

The old "Zion" was something of a miracle-ship to the loafers upon the quays and wharves of Haifa; they said that she had no right to be afloat at all. They might perhaps have said the same of old Isaac Jordan, her skipper. As for real sailors who saw the old hulk bustling across the oily harbour water towards the outer sea, they respectfully removed their pipes and spat, gazing after her with a kind of awed sympathy bordering on horror. The Naval Station Commander, catching sight of her from the broad glass windows of the signal station, was apt to utter a pleasantry to his Number Two: "There she goes, with all the grace of a flat-iron!" Yet he noted with a professional eye that her speed was respectable considering her age; only her stability was somewhat questionable. She was about as stable in a head sea, he told himself, as a soap dish. Isaac was a madman to take her to sea. And yet, he had been doing it for years now.

Isaac had bought the "Zion" for a song in the thirties and harnessed her to the trade of smuggling despite her shape, which suggested that her original designer had intended her for use only in shallow estuaries, on lakes, or perhaps as an auxiliary to a dredger. It was with misgivings that he turned her nose to the open sea for the first time, for he was uncomfortably aware of her duckboard lines. Yet she was steel-built, he told himself, and his confidence was rewarded, for, though she fumed and wallowed and stank, she answered the wheel quite well at ten knots, and her pumps worked in an approximate fashion. What more could one ask?

Deeply relieved, Isaac took out a heavy insurance on her and put her to work, aided by his crew of ruffians of all nationalities, clad in rags and tatters, like gypsies. He had spent many happy years in her, now smuggling currency, now gold bars, specie, forged stamps, hash-ish, antiquities… everything one could think of. "Zion" was his accessory after the fact.

As for Isaac Jordan himself, he was a stout grey man in his sixties, heavy of build and absolutely wedded to his cutty pipe. People said he slept with it in his mouth. In summer he wore a soiled yachting-cap of ancient cut and an equally soiled suit of pyjamas with a blue stripe. On the breast pocket of these, however, he sported a number of First World War decorations, both English and French, which earned him a certain measure of sympathy and even latitude from the port naval authorities. In winter, this impressive display was transferred to the breast of his coarse blue sweater of the kind issued to submarine artificers and worn under a sheepskin-lined duffle. Isaac was something of a character in the port and did not allow it to be forgotten that he was an ex-Naval Commander, "Retired R.N.". Moreover, those who might have been forgiven for believing that his medals were from the prop-room, so to speak, soon found to their chagrin that they were real and had been awarded him for services described as "gallant" in the official citations. This, then, was Isaac's own rather eloquent way of enjoying his retirement and his small pension; it may have been a tiring, if lucrative, profession, but he was suited to no other. The only really maddening thing about him from the point of view of the naval authorities was that they could never catch him *in flagrante*; even on the few occasions when "Limpet" had pounced on "Zion" and boarded her, they had found her cargo innocent, indeed, quite unexceptionable. Isaac smiled and spat over the side with a kind of mournful satisfaction. Nor did he spare young Derek Noble of the "Limpet". "Call yourselves a Royal Navy, eh? It's gone down since I left it, that's all I can say." And if Noble did not choose to bandy words with him on the high seas it was because he knew very well that the banter would be continued at leisure over a glass of buttered rum in the Chatham Bar in Haifa the following evening.

Within the last few years, however, Isaac had somewhat changed the nature of his trade. Stirred by the fate of his fellow-Jews in Germany, he had volunteered to smuggle weapons into Palestine for the Jewish Agency. The journeys were longer and more dangerous, the profit nominal. Nevertheless, the old "Zion" plugged up and down the eastern Mediterranean full of crates demurely labelled "Agricultural Machinery". His landfalls were many and curious, and seldom the same twice running. He brought all his skill and experience to bear now in blockade breaking, for the British blockade was tight. So far he had been successful — indeed, so successful as to cause a great deal of bad language and impotent signalling between the corvettes and destroyers which maintained the patrol of the northern reaches of the country. Isaac was always either inside or outside some statutory sea-limit, to the intense fury of "Limpet", "Termagant", "Havoc" and several others of the iron bloodhounds of the Fleet. They made books on him, they laid bets on him, they dreamed of catching him, but so far he had always managed to slip through the mesh. Derek Noble became so infuriated that he spoke darkly of putting a torpedo through "Zion" in the harbour "just to show that damned old rogue Jordan". Other commanders developed their own theories about Isaac's facility for disappearing at sea; these varied between notions of black magic and ideas of dematerialization. Isaac himself suggested mildly that the "Zion" was really a submarine. Once clear of harbour, he had only to submerge... No wonder "Limpet" always made a fool of herself.

On the spring dawn in question, they had been playing this elaborate game of cat and mouse along the shores of Turkey in a light but highly convenient sea-mist — convenient for Isaac, that is. The chase had been full of promise for young Noble, for it was clear that "Zion" was making a secret landfall somewhere along these forbidden headlands; the only question was whether he could intercept her on the homeward leg. In his mind's eye he saw himself gazing down through her hatches at rows of neatly stacked rifles or grenades while Isaac puffed his pipe, for once completely at a loss for an explanation. That would be a moment to boast about. In fact, he had excited himself so much by the prospect of this encounter that he had stayed up on the bridge to brood upon it, as he stared into the vague darkness ahead with its packets of shifting mist. Somewhere out there the "Zion" plodded along, unconscious of the warship dogging her. On the other hand, they were getting uncomfortably near the forbidden sea-limits, Turkish territorial waters. He must be careful.

At about four-thirty, when the horizon had just begun to etch itself on the darkness, "Zion" slid off the radar screen and evaporated. Noble groaned slightly at the information and put down his night-glasses with a gesture of weariness. He drank some coffee and heard a waggish Signals Officer remark: "Gone to ground — we'll have to start digging." Noble turned "Limpet" through a slow arc of ten degrees and sighed. The dark coast ahead, he knew from his charts, was deeply indented and fretted with creeks and harbours; some of them had more than one entrance or exit. With her shallow draught, "Zion" could penetrate anywhere. Moreover, Isaac was not called upon to be law-abiding as "Limpet" was. "Too bad, Sir," said a sympathetic voice. Noble shrugged off the sympathy with hauteur. "You wait, we'll catch her on the home leg," he said, though his voice lacked conviction. He felt suddenly sleepy — the dawn was coming up. "Limpet's" engine drummed softly and her screw gnawed rhythmically in the still sea. He shook his fist across the intervening sea-miles of mist and darkness. "Ah, you wait!" he said. Well, once more they would have to cruise up and down in desolate fashion, like a cat before a mousehole, waiting for "Zion" to re-emerge on her homeward run. Peevishly, the young commander decided that it was time to turn in.

Surely this time everything would be different and they would catch old Jordan on the hop? One never knew in this game.

2

A Landfall in Turkey

But by this time Isaac and his crew were fast asleep, disposed about the deck in inelegant positions, shrouded in sacks and tarpaulins. The young Yemeni boy, alarm pistol in hand, stood on watch, listening to the rhythmic throaty snorting which vibrated on the early morning air. Such arms as they carried were laid within easy reach of the sleepers. Isaac had not forgotten, before turning in, to haul down the tattered Red Ensign his ship bore and to substitute for it a Turkish merchant marine flag, carefully selected from a huge bundle of assorted flags — a veritable library — which he kept stowed in a locker. He had debated for a moment or two whether or not to back it up with a plague signal as well, but had finally discarded the idea — it might savour of over-acting. So they slept peacefully like a litter of cats, while the sun soared out of the sea and threw its cool shadows of cliff and headland upon the still waters in which "Zion" lay.

It was mid-morning before the direct sunlight woke them, glaring down on their unshaven faces and creased eyes. The Yemeni boy brewed tea with a studious air and added condensed milk to it as he handed round the tin mugs. Yawning and stretching, they looked about them with satisfaction. They were quite alone in a harbour of natural rock, distinguished only by the fact that there was an abandoned jetty with a small rusty crane, together with the anomalous remains of a light railway which, at some time in the distant past, had connected with a stone tip jutting from an abandoned quarry on the hillside. But the workings had long since been abandoned, the miners had gone. It was a desolate corner, overgrown with shrubs and arbutus. Tortoises crunched about, hunting for warm stones on which to doze; lizards flickered among the rocks, bent on the same errand. High up in the blue a golden eagle sat motionless, staring down at them. The cliff-tops were deserted; so was the narrow rutted road which climbed up into nowhere. Isaac rubbed his hands with pleasure and sipped the nauseating ship's brew with unction. They were hours too early for the rendezvous, and this too was very pleasant: Isaac was a methodical man and liked to take his time. The crew smoked and lounged, while from the galley came the pleasant odour of a beef stew with olives.

Nadeb, the engineer, went so far as to climb the nearest cliff and sweep the horizon with the glasses, but the few smudges he picked up were too distant to identify. It pleased him, however, to imagine that they were "Limpet" and "Havoc" sniffing down a false trail. He made a signal to the ship and cried, "We've lost them!"

"For how long, I wonder," said Isaac thoughtfully, thinking of the return journey ahead of them. Nadeb had turned the glasses onto the Turkish coast now, sweeping the cliffs slowly and methodically. He picked out the distant smoke of a little town or hamlet, but no trace of guard posts or sentries. He came slowly down to sea-level once more and sat upon the jetty, dangling his long legs. "It's absolutely deserted," he said, in a tone touched with regret — he enjoyed excitement and was a choice shot with a pistol or a rifle. "Not a soul about."

Isaac grunted happily as he filled his pipe.

"With any luck we'll have the same mist tonight," added Nadeb. "It will be an easy run, smooth as milk."

"Touch wood."

"Touch wood."

Both did so and smiled. Isaac rose and stretched, emitting a fragrant cloud of smoke from mouth and nostrils. "I should say they will be here by five or six — then a quick load and turn-around, and... our troubles will begin." He was not really as pessimistic as he sounded. They fell briefly to business now, standing the "Zion" in close alongside the ramshackle pierhead under the crane, and making her fast to the still-sturdy bollards. Then, as the crew fell to darning socks or playing cards, Isaac spent an hour with his pocket Bible, pencil and pad. He had contracted a schoolboy passion for playing county-cricket in this fashion, letting each letter stand for a number of runs scored. The life of each batsman was determined by the emergence of the letters "O" (out), "B" (bowled), "C" (caught), and so on. He had in fact managed in this singular fashion to play his way twice through the Bible without actually reading a word of it. He was in the middle of Judges now. It looked as though Surrey was going to beat Kent.

So the day passed in fitful lounging, punctuated by intervals for food and wine; some of the crew went ashore and skidded pebbles along the flat surface of the water. The sun was warm too, too warm. The Yemeni slept. The atmosphere was that of a leisurely picnic in some London park. They had almost forgotten their assignment, it would seem. Nadeb played patience earnestly, swearing softly from time to time.

A cry brought them to their feet: on the top of the headland stood the small and stocky figure of a young man. He wore a dirty mackintosh, cloth cap and long jackboots. He signalled with a kind of tentative urgency, the purport of his gestures being to enquire whether everything was normal. Isaac nodded and gave the pre-arranged reply by shaking hands with himself like a Chinaman. The young man nodded and pointed away across the cliffs; he disappeared at a lurching run.

"Here they come," said Nadeb. Isaac, carefully consulting his watch and then the now westering sun, only grunted agreement. In a little while the noises of motors gradually grew upon the silence and increased in volume, until at last the two lorries appeared against the sky with their loaded crates jogging. They changed into bottom gear and, slowly as snails, dipped down upon the rough cart track, grinding and screeching. Beside them walked a little group of officials wearing a uniform which vaguely suggested a Customs Service; rather ahead, and accompanying the young man, walked a tall man in plain clothes who had the indefinable air of a plainclothes policeman. They advanced with grave courtesy, and Isaac and his crew stepped forward to meet them.

The young man in the jackboots had a strong and purposeful air which suggested that this was his responsibility, his operation. His handclasp was rough like his voice. He said "Karageorge" and gave a stiff, sawing bow, full of grave awkwardness. Isaac responded with a bob, and, taking his pipe from his mouth, announced himself as "Jordan".

"Everything is in order."

"Excellent."

After a grave ritual of handshakes, they turned their united attention to the loading operation: the lorries were run carefully onto the slip and the squeaky crane was brought into play to shift the crates aboard. The young man now touched Isaac's arm; he had begun to look nervous and his lips trembled. "You'll have to hurry," he said in a low voice. Isaac turned from the chaffering crew and the officials to look at him. "Hurry?" he said. "Why?"

The young man turned aside and beckoned to him with a short choppy gesture: he wanted to tell him something which must not be overheard by the rest of the group — or so it seemed. Not that there was any apparent danger, for everyone was talking amiably, the officials in low voices. Money was being exchanged and papers which looked like Bills of Lading. Isaac walked over to the young man who uttered a few words — words so apparently surprising that the old man let the pipe drop from his mouth and only just retrieved it before it fell to the ground. His face had gone blank. He gazed uncomprehendingly at the crates. "Which ones?" he asked hoarsely. The young man licked his lips and answered, "Number Two and Three. They are marked." Isaac turned upon him with sudden incoherent expostulation. "But, my God," he burst out, "surely you could have...?" A gesture from the young man silenced him. "There were great difficulties. The Agency had trouble. There was nothing else to be done."

"Goddammit," said Isaac, striking his knee. He turned to the "Zion" — the crates had been loaded swiftly and expertly, the formalities seemed to be all but completed. He took one startled look at the young man's face and began to hurry down the slip towards his boat. At the pierhead he said a hurried farewell to the officials, yelling "Engine-room!" over his shoulder in a voice which earned him a startled look from his engineer. He clambered aboard awkwardly and added: "No time to be lost. Cast off." This sudden burst of urgency puzzled his crew but they obeyed. The engines throbbed and the "Zion" turned her black snout in a slow arc towards the harbour entrance, her wake beginning to fan out under the screws. Isaac waved incoherently to the group on shore and added croakily: "Full ahead there." Nadeb remonstrated in a shocked tone. "Full ahead? You'll spring her plates." But a glance from Isaac quelled him, and the "Zion" began to throb in every rivet. Isaac whistled and beckoned to three men. He hissed: "Axes and crowbars. And look quick about it." They looked at him in a dazed fashion but he made a savage, throat-slitting gesture which electrified them into action. Isaac himself unbuckled the heavy fire-axe which was strapped to the thwart beside him. "Nadeb," he said, "round the first headland we heave-to, see?" Nadeb did not see. "What are we going to do? Break up the bloody ship?"

Isaac beckoned him close and lowered his voice, aware how far sound carries on water. "There are people in two of the crates."

Nadeb expelled a puff of air with relief — so the skipper had not gone mad after all. Then he too began to look concerned. "People — in *there*?" He felt a sudden surge of indignation. It was as if a trick in bad taste had been played on them. Why had they not been warned? The little party on the rocky road stared at the "Zion" as she fumed along. "Wave, you fool," said Isaac, as with his free hand he waved a hallucinated farewell.

The first headland was on them, and now the ship turned sharply east and headed for land again, running in the shelter of the tall cliffs; a convenient cliff lay ahead. Nadeb leaped forward like a cat and muttered to the somewhat listless bearers of axes and crowbars. The news galvanized them. They moved in a cluster to examine the crates in question, carefully noting their perforated sides and the slant of the battens which held them together. They waited in sickened apprehension until the "Zion" switched off and wallowed in the still waters of the little creek and Isaac waved them urgently into action. Then they fell to work like maniacs with the backs of their axes, tackling the yellow crates. Isaac himself ran forward to lend a hand.

Had there been a watcher on the cliffs, he would certainly have concluded that the little group of men had gone mad. They banged and crashed at the wooden crates, tearing and pulling away at them with hammers, crowbars, even their hands, as if their very lives depended on it.

In the brilliant light of the westering sun, the smooth sea gleamed and glittered like a jewel, dark when it was shadowed by the shouldering cliffs. The scene itself was certainly an incongruous one: these men flailing away at the crates, tearing off long strips with their hands and tossing them overboard. The wood floated silently beside the boat in the water, with an air of astonishment, its stencilled markings clear for all to see. They ate into the first crate like gourmets into a cheese, forcing the battens apart, squeezing and pushing. It disgorged a mountain of filthy straw such as might line a stable floor, stinking with excrement, but not a word, not a noise of a human being. They called hoarsely, but no answering voice greeted them. They had virtually dismembered the box now. They threw down their implements and plunged into the muddle to recuperate the human beings they had been told existed beneath all this elaborate packing. At long last they managed to extract the first two occupants, whose bodies lay coiled in that nest of dirty straw like maggots in a cheese. Quickly, tenderly, they were laid upon deck in the brilliant soft sunshine and Isaac clawed at their tattered rags in order to lay his shaggy ear upon their hearts. Behind him he could hear the booming and crashing as the second crate was attacked. "They are both dead," he said at last, sadly, still crouched on one knee, his wily old face wrinkled a thousand ways.

The older man had a beard of patriarchal cut and snowy whiteness and immensely long, dirty fingernails. The youth could not have been more than fifteen. The smashed and buckled fibre suitcase had a few dirty clothes lolling from it. Both bodies wore small metal identification discs on the forearm, though whether of Nazi provenance or not he could not tell. Isaac puffed grimly at his pipe as he consulted them. "Father and son," he said under his breath, sitting back on his haunches and looking at them. "Father and son." Behind him surged the racket of the axes busy upon the second crate. They had been lying as if asleep, entangled in a travesty of sleep, their arms round one another; now, in the relaxation of death, their attitude suggested a helpless and yet somehow triumphant surrender. Sincerely moved, Isaac got up, shaking himself like a dog, and waddled aft for a drink of water. Then he took up an axe and joined his crew in their assault on the second crate which they had already half demolished.

Judith heard them coming, but as if from a very long way off. The crate itself echoed like a gigantic sounding-board to the boom of their implements, so that she imagined something like the distant stampede of a horde of elephants whose foot-falls shook the world. Each axe-blow seemed to land in the centre of her brain, deafening, beheading her. Her mouth she kept pressed to a perforation in the wood which enabled her to drink in air with long, laboured inspirations. Somewhere in the straw beneath her she could hear the voice of the religious fanatic muttering away — like the sound of a bumble-bee trapped in a spider's web, now faint and distant, now gathering strength again. Outside the confines of this blind world the racket was infernal. But now, gradually, extraordinary strips of blinding sunlight and blue sky appeared, tearing at her eyeballs. It was as if she were an entombed queen hearing the picks and shovels of the archaeologists approaching her. Voices called and she tried to answer, but her lips and throat had swollen — or so it seemed. The hot and rank odour of straw scorched her lungs. A groping hand touched her shoulder and she shrank away with pain, for her body was a mass of bruises. The daylight was pain, the pain blindness; she shrank from her rescuers.

Then with a splintering bang the walls of this stuffy universe gave way and drew back; sweet air rushed in. The blue sky pierced her like a spear. She shut her eyes fast against it and felt herself scooped up and carried, to be laid down somewhere on a hard deck among voices, the lapping of water, and the smell of hot machinery. No, it was beyond belief, she must be dead! But a rough calloused hand raised her head, a hairy face brushed her body and a voice said soberly: "Well, this one's alive all right." Alive! The voice itself sounded so incongruous that she wanted to laugh, but in her weakness all she could manage was a tree-frog's croak and a few thin tears squeezed from under long lashes. The air, the light, were enticing, but still she could not bear to open her eyes.

"Well I'll be damned."

"They had no right..."

"We're not a hospital-ship." Nadeb's voice rose to a plaintive squeak.

13

But they were busy about some other frantic business, tearing at straw and pulling at strips of crackling wood. She was left for a moment in the oasis of her own thoughts, wheeling and scattering like notes of dust in sunlight. Then she gave a gasp, for someone had emptied a bucket of salt water over her head. The shock seemed to start up her fever again; she began to tremble once more, her teeth to chatter in her head. Isaac mopped her face with a clean handkerchief, swearing softly under his breath. She heard him give an order: "Something warm to drink from the galley." They stayed like this for a long moment, like a tableau of exhaustion — the old man was breathing as hard as she was. "Hurry up, there!" he cried.

Meanwhile her fellow-stowaway had been disinterred from the crate which smelled like a carnivore's cage, and disposed upon the grubby deck. He too was alive, but he presented a strange picture to their startled sight. His long bony body was topped by a fierce hawk's head dressed in a tangle of greasy ringlets falling to his shoulders. His pale blue eyes had the glare of delirium in them and his lips moved incessantly. He still had his voice, though it had been worn down in long patches to a mere whisper. It was not easy to say whether they had a case of extreme fatigue to deal with, or one of insanity. His eyes roved madly here and there, as if searching for something. From an occasional passage of croaks and whispers, they gathered that the subject-matter of his impassioned monologue was religious; he was reciting holy texts. He drank thirstily, slobbering water all over himself, and then suddenly took fright, drawing himself away from his rescuers, sliding along the deck on his long yellow palms like a seal. He found a thwart and pressed his back against it in terror, shouting "Keep away," and extending a long bony finger at them. They watched him with an exhausted and mutinous curiosity. He stayed thus for a long moment with yellow teeth bared. Then, as suddenly, he joined his hands upon his soiled and tattered waistcoat and in a small, plaintive voice, like a sick child, added: "I am Melchior." And at once fell into a deep sleep.

At the sound of his voice the girl opened her eyes on the trembling sky; a chain of images floated incoherently across her mind, evoked by the voice and the terror in it. They scorched her mind. She saw, but very indistinctly, Isaac leaning over her with a cup of tea — only he was wearing a Nazi uniform and his eyes were glaring as fiercely as her own. She raised an imploring hand and turned her head away. The shadows of men fell on the deck, she counted them. They were men in uniform and their footsteps on the hollow decks of the "Zion" sounded like the tramp of feet in jackboots.

"Ah!" she said in a desolate ringing voice full of resignation, "So you are taking me back."

"Yes." Isaac's homely voice sounded like the rasping of a professional storm-trooper. "Back."

They had already rigged up a bunk in the evil-smelling forecastle and she allowed herself to be carried down to it, speechless with fatigue. The hot drink was delicious and she would gladly have drunk more of it, but she fell asleep on the second mouthful. As for her companion, they did not move him, but put some blankets over his sleeping form with a pillow for his head. This done, the crew sat down in exhausted attitudes all over the ship and swore with surprise at being saddled with such unusual passengers; without a word of warning, too! They scratched their heads, gazing at Isaac.

He, for his part, was thinking in terms of extra rations and the hundred and one hazards they still had to face. The possessions of the refugees lay about the deck and he started to gather them: a smashed fibre suitcase, again with its entrails extruding like a squashed bug, a small haversack with the end of a cracked mirror sticking out of the side. That must belong to the girl. He carried it down to her and watched her sleeping for a moment in the uncomfortable bunk. From time to time she was shaken by a sudden gust of short breathing, like a child after crying itself to sleep. Her features were well formed; her forehead was high and white and her closed eyes framed by broad serene lashes. But she was filthy. Her hair had been cut off in a clumsy series of rats' tails and all down one side of her neck ran the livid line of some skin infection. She smelt of the concentration camp.

Isaac shook his head and went on deck again, calling out "Engine room!" in his hardest tones, recalling everyone to their senses again. There would be time, he told himself, to smash up the other crates and dispose their contents in the hold once they were on their way. But he must not ignore the exacting timetable which alone might give them an even chance of breaking the night blockade.

"Zion" snorted and shook and lifted her bows towards the outer sea, which was already taking on the gold and peacock tones of evening. "About five hours," said Isaac, looking at his watch. Their landfall that night would be another deserted harbour off the long spit of Famagusta in Cyprus. Somewhere out there on the opalescent horizon, the ships of the blockade cruised, restless as greyhounds. A faint evening sea-breeze, damp with the promise of mist, was slowly rising from the east. He took it on his cheek with satisfaction as he consulted a compass bearing. It was beautiful, it was calm — as deceptively calm, perhaps, as the two figures which lay side by side on the prow: the dead man and his son. Isaac went forward and sat by them for a while with Nadeb, gazing at their stillness and pallor as he loaded another pipe. They looked, he thought, as if they were listening for something. He was possessed by a great calm, a great resignation as he felt the slow swell of the sea under "Zion's" keel. The sun was sinking into a deserted horizon. A couple of gulls hovered over them with curiosity, crying shrilly. He turned to Nadeb. "What do you know about burial at sea?"

"Nothing. I'm not religious."

"Nor am I. We'll have to do something, read something."

"Well, you have a Bible."

"What about weights?"

"There's some pig-iron in the ballast. The boy shouldn't need so much. But there's no spare tarpaulin."

"We'll use some flags from our collection. Not likely to see a use for the Latin Americans, are we?"

The two men sat smoking and deliberating as the "Zion" plunged on towards the outer sea. Nadeb finally leaned forward and, with a sharp movement of the wrist, snapped off the small identity discs. He sat holding them in his hand.

"Identity," he said reflectively.

"Yes," said Isaac shortly and surprised himself (for he was not, as far as he knew, of a philosophic turn of mind) by adding "It doesn't seem to matter, to make much difference when you are dead, being a Jew or not. It's while you're alive, my boy."

Nadeb grunted and busied himself in disposing the limbs of the corpses, lashing their ankles together and passing a cord round their breasts to pinion their arms securely. "About time," he said sombrely. "The rigor is beginning to set in. Here, knot this one."

They stood for a moment gazing down at their handiwork. The shaggy prophet from his nest of blankets amidships gave a sudden quavering cry and moaned: "And the Lord shall recognize his own." They looked at one another and smiled grimly.

"We must move him below," said Isaac slowly. "We can't have him screaming once we are off the coast. Nadeb, there's some morphia in the medical kit — it would give him some sleep. I'd like to radio the Agency about them, but I don't see how we dare. We might give our position away."

He padded back to the locker and busied himself with sorting flags. Nadeb called for a sail, needle and twine. "Well," said Isaac at last, having made his selection. "One can be Brazilian and the other Chilean. It will puzzle their Creator. What else to do?"

They waited until darkness before performing their perfunctory and awkward ceremony and consigning the bodies to the sea. Then they carried the gaunt figure of the prophet below. Lastly, all hands fell to breaking up the remaining crates and shipping their contents — automatic weapons in glistening water-proof covers. That, at least, was a job with which they were familiar.

Night had fallen.

3

Arrival in Darkness

For two days and nights she lay in a pleasurable doze of exhaustion, lulled by the swing of the sea to healing sleep, or woken by the sudden shutting off of the engines and a silence punctuated by the thud of feet on the decks and the hoarse voices of the crew about their business. She had begun to recover not only her reason, but her self-possession: Isaac no longer wore a Nazi uniform when he came down to give her food by the dim light of a pocket torch. At first he had had to feed her, but now she could even sit up in the evil-smelling bunk, although she ached in every limb. The old man asked her no questions, though from time to time he placed a rough hand on her brow to reassure himself that she was no longer feverish. The touch of his calloused palm was delicious and reassuring. For her part, she only showed concern for the fate of her haversack, and a deep relief when Isaac turned the torch on it. "Give it to me," she said in a hoarse but melodious voice, and placed it behind her head like a pillow. Isaac tended her silently and with concentration, like a gardener, and his pains were rewarded sooner than he had expected, for by the end of the second day she was able to reach out a hand and say: "I want to try and stand. Will you help?" To his delight she could not only do so, but could also walk.

"Nothing broken?" he asked anxiously.

"No. Just bruises. I must be blue all over."

"They'll go."

"I know. When do we… arrive?"

Isaac gave the small ghost of a chuckle.

"Tonight. Very late."

"Tonight?" She opened her dark eyes very wide and gazed at him. Isaac nodded.

"We are through the sea-blockade and on the coast now. Unless we are picked up by a patrol-boat we should…" But he was too superstitious to complete the sentence, and simply contented himself with touching wood.

"What luck!" she said.

"Indeed."

The news itself was intoxicating. She stretched her arms and yawned; then she tried out her newly formed legs once more.

"You see?" she said, "I can walk okay."

"But now you are going to sleep. No noise please. I'll wake you when the time comes. By the way, the man who calls himself Melchior. Is he a relation or a friend?"

"Never saw him before. I don't know who he is. I hardly know… who I am any more. We were taken from the cellar of a house by a man. It is all very confusing. How they got me out of Germany I don't know."

Isaac nodded sympathetically, for the story was a familiar one. The girl sat down, reflectively, and considered the matter with her head on one side. "If you asked me, I couldn't tell you. I've seen nothing but the inside of cattle-trucks, cellars and lorries for weeks." Her lip trembled, but she recovered herself and smiled at him wanly.

"Good girl. Now drink this and sleep," said Isaac in a voice of command. "Everything will be all right."

She closed her eyes again, smiling. The phrase was both reassuring and richly ironic. Isaac padded back on deck with the empty cup and plate. "She's all right," he told Nadeb with satisfaction. "But the other chap…" The prophet posed a problem, for he was still feverish and noisy despite the morphia. They decided that he would have to be strapped to a stretcher to be taken ashore.

19

Meanwhile "Zion", at a reduced speed, was scouting the confines of the dark coast. Here and there shone small starlets of light from the distant villages. But the sea was deserted and calm. Once more Isaac had managed to sidle between the waiting ships and strike land; but he was now in an even more dangerous area, with the risk of mines and patrol-boats to think about. Yet something told him that the journey would be successful. If only the rendezvous worked out... He consulted the phosphorescent hands of his watch and turned the "Zion" a few points east, until they were running parallel to the long beaches, and close enough to hear the waves breaking on them. At four they discerned the faint etching of a fortress and a deserted sea-mole. Skirting it, the "Zion" switched off and lay wallowing in the shadow of the tall ruined structure, waiting for contact. In the silence they could hear the faint exclamations of the prophet below decks and the sound of their own anxious breathing. All was still.

Then a light blinked and the "Zion" answered with a pocket torch. A long silence and then came the sound of cars, and a boat pulled in alongside with a dark figure in it. Isaac whispered something and chuckled. "You are on time, at least," said a gruff voice approvingly. Reassured, the crew began to talk in normal tones again.

"First a stretcher-case," said Isaac, and the boatman grunted. "Less bloody noise!" he said angrily, and their voices dropped once more. "The 'Roach' has been patrolling all evening; and she may be back soon. So cut out the talk and act."

While two of the crew fetched up the feverish prophet and lowered him into the boat, others threw open the hatches and began lowering their freight overboard into the dark water. The "agricultural machinery" in its glistening slip cases of water-proof plastic slid easily and elegantly into two fathoms of water. Floats were set to mark the spot.

The boatman had vanished into the darkness with his stretcher load, promising to come back for the girl. All was purposeful disorder and confusion as the holds were emptied of their contents. In fact, things were going so well that Isaac allowed himself to chuckle and rub his hands; he went below to find the girl already awake and sitting on her bunk with her haversack slung.

"Everything is going like clockwork," he said, and even as he uttered the ill-omened words he heard a warning whistle from the shore and the scudding of feet about the decks. He climbed back on deck, motioning her to follow. Nadeb had already cried "Look!" and was pointing eastward to the two long pencils of searchlight which moved towards them on the dark coast, gracefully swinging this way and that like the antennae of an insect as they explored the coves and reaches of the indented land. Isaac permitted himself a couple of dreadful swear-words. "It's the 'Roach'," he said, almost biting through his pipe-stem with vexation.

"The stuff's all overboard, Skipper," said Nadeb, jumping about like a cat on hot bricks. "We can't be caught here now!" Isaac knew this only too well. He roared "Engine-room!" and, turning to the girl, said: "I'm sorry — you'll have to go overboard. There's no time to lose. Nadeb will take you."

"Zion" began to throb and stagger. It all happened so fast that there was no time to exchange a word or a thought. As the two pencils of searchlight strayed slowly, purposefully, towards them, she felt herself lifted and lowered over the side by Isaac's strong arms. Nadeb climbed down beside her. The sea came up in a smooth cold sheath under her armpits, making her shudder. "It's only fifty yards," said Nadeb in a whisper. "Put a hand on my shoulder. Mind — not a ripple, not a splash!" She did as she was told and, as the "Zion" drew away, the boom of her screw threw up foam onto her face, blinding her. With eyes shut she lay and felt the strong shoulders of Nadeb beginning to work, dragging her. "Zion" had been swallowed in the darkness. After what seemed an eternity, she felt sand under her feet and then pebbles. They lay in the shallows for a while, getting their breath; then Nadeb stood up and dragged her unceremoniously to her feet. They reached the shadow of a lemon grove before the searchlights arrived to light up the deserted fort.

The girl shook herself like a wet dog. They stood thus in the shadows of the trees and watched the chalky light of the patrol-boat's searchlights throw everything into relief — the medieval fort, the mole and the wooded shores of the cove. Every leaf on the trees stood out with sudden incandescence as the beam swept over them and away again. The engines of the boat made hardly any noise as they carried her towards them. She felt the light on her and was tempted to turn back into the thickets around, but Nadeb said: "Stand quite still." They stood thus intently; she could hear the water dripping from her. After a slow and methodical exploration of the beach, and of the three or four deserted fishing-boats anchored in the cove, the "Roach" turned north again and increased speed. Nadeb grunted with pleasure. "They've missed the float," he said. Adding with a chuckle, "They will catch 'Zion' up in half an hour and search her. Good!" In his mind's eye he could doubtless see Isaac's expression of innocent outrage as the boarding-party tackled him.

A figure had detached itself from the shadows and approached while they stood watching: the girl jumped as she felt a hand on her arm. The voice of a woman, low and composed, said, "Are you Judith Roth? I think you must be?"

"Yes."

"Take my hand. It is not far." The girl felt a warm strong hand in hers, and allowed herself to be led away into the dense shadow of the grove among the trees. She was tempted at first to feel alarmed, but finally resignation overcame her: for so long now she had been handed like this from person to anonymous person, like a parcel. But at least for the first time she appeared to be expected. They knew her name, she told herself, smiling. It was like being recognized by long-lost friends. They waited in a ditch while a long convoy of lorries rushed past, their headlights lighting up the tall trees beside the road and throwing up a plume of acrid dust. And here Nadeb took his departure. "Goodbye," he said, shaking her hand, and added as a surprising afterthought: "Welcome to Palestine!" Before she could thank him he had dematerialized and been swallowed up by the darkness.

The woman still held her hand with cool composure. In the half-light the girl looked at her with curiosity: she was of slender build and appeared to be dressed in some sort of apron. She was watching the diminishing light of the convoy on the long straight road. "Now let's cross," she said, and still held onto the wet hand of her charge. They crossed a number of fields in darkness. At last they turned into another lemon grove and paused before the door of what looked like a large deserted barn. The woman pushed open a door and gently led her into what must once have been a granary. Yet a big fire blazed in the hearth and clouds of steam rose from cauldrons of hot water. Two old women, clad like Bessarabian gypsies, were busy with sponges upon the body of what seemed to be a dead man. Judith Roth looked around her with surprise. The dark-haired woman pressed her hand and smiled at her, as if anxious that she should not be alarmed by the unfamiliarity of their surroundings. "This is a temporary transit hut," she said, "for our refugees. Some of them are in bad shape, you know."

The corpse on the long trestle-table opened its mouth and crooned gently. Though apparently still asleep, he had begun a long rambling recitative in which the name of the Jordan river kept creeping in as a leitmotif. The Jordan would wash his sins away if only he could reach it — such was the burden of the song. Judith's companion chuckled briefly. "The old boy's going to be in luck when he realizes we've got the Jordan outside the front door." The two women hummed under their breath as they filled the sponges and crushed the warm water over his emaciated body. They were humming some strange old melody, full of quarter-tones and odd syncopations of rhythms — it was uncanny — as if they were washing a corpse before laying it out. The woman followed the direction of the girl's gaze and said: "He will feel much better for a wash and a change of clothing. Afterwards, I'll sedate him for the night. I'm a doctor, by the way. Naomi Hourzan. Come by the fire now and strip."

Still dazed by the rapid succession of events, Judith Roth complied like some dumb animal. Her fingers wrestled numbly with her tattered clothing. The doctor helped her deftly and tactfully, talking quietly to her. The old women crooned softly as they dried the body of the recumbent prophet, combing his beard and hair, and dusting his body with talc. Naomi Hourzan dragged a long low table across to the fire-light and motioned her charge to lie down while she busied herself with a small suitcase from which she extracted a stethoscope. "You've been expected for some time," she said. "Now lie still, I want to look you over."

"Expected?" said Judith Roth numbly. It all seemed part of the weary phantasmagoria of the whole journey with its mad air of desperate improvisation, its changes of scene. The firelight made her feel

23

drowsy. She felt the cold node of the stethoscope on her back. Once or twice she winced as the cool deft hands touched her, and the doctor returned to the tender spot to reassure herself that nothing more serious than a bruise was the cause of the pain. "Well," she said at last, "so far, so good."

Judith Roth lifted her head and said slowly: "There's nothing broken, Doctor. But I haven't had my period for months now, and I have got some skin infection — probably syphilis, or something as disagreeable."

She turned on her back and pointed at her throat.

The doctor lowered her dark head for a moment to examine the red rash at close quarters. She smiled. "Nothing of the kind. You simply have the traditional scabies of the camps. It will wash away in a fortnight. I have something for that, you'll see."

She was called away by the two old witch-like women, for the prophet had now been washed and dressed anew in a baggy suit of clothes. He had begun to snore. Deftly, the doctor gave him an injection. Smoothly, they decanted him onto the stretcher and bore it away through the door. Judith sat watching them with a dull and uncomprehending eye.

The door opened again and the doctor returned with the two old women. "Now for your bath," she said. "Lie back and enjoy it." Obediently, Judith Roth lay back and closed her eyes. It was a luxury to feel the warm steam rise around her. The loaded sponges crushed the warmth into her body, the water drained onto the earth floor of the barn. The women took up their slow meditative crooning again. How rich and sweet was the smell of the warm soap-lather! She felt their hands sliding over her, sliding over her breasts and flanks. While they worked, the doctor sat down and took up pen and paper. "Well, I shall be able to report your safe arrival at any rate," she said, "but I must fill in the data for them. It's a bore, I know. Age?"

"Twenty-nine."

"Last address?" At this Judith gave a harsh laugh. It would have sounded vainglorious to have given the name of the camp where she had spent the last months. Her laughter ended with a sob.

"I mean home address," said the doctor quietly; "you never know when it will be of use, for example, if you have other family."

"I haven't," said Judith. "Our house is now a Headquarters for the Hitler Youth. My whole family is dead. Luckily my father died before all this… started. He used to say he was proud to be a German. He could still afford to be in those days."

"Gently," said the doctor. "I did not want to upset you."

"Then why don't you leave me alone? Have I come all this way to fill in forms?" Her eyes glared from the mask of soap. The old women made soothing noises.

The doctor took a turn up and down the room with her hands behind her back. She drew a breath and said mildly: "You see, I know nothing about you except your name. I was asked to report on what physical shape you were in. This I propose to do. But as for the rest of the questions, we can leave them — though I can see their point in asking them. Occupation, for example. I see they have put you down for Ras Shamir in the north. I happen to be the doctor of Ras Shamir myself, so we shall meet again. But it would be a help to know if you had any special skills which might be of use to the kibbutz. It's a farming community, living a hard life."

"As far as occupation is concerned," said Judith Roth incoherently, "I have spent six months digging up corpses with a spade and breaking them up into smaller and more convenient pieces. Frozen corpses." But then she suddenly groaned and turned her head from side to side. "I am so sorry, doctor," she said. "It was stupid of me. Please forgive me!" and she extended a soapy hand to touch the doctor's.

"There's nothing to be sorry about."

"But there is. I am being unpardonable. Forgive me."

The two old women had turned her now onto her front and she was able to raise her head and smile at the doctor, her eyes full of tears. "I used to be a mathematician before the university sacked me. You see, doctor, I was sent to a camp first of all by mistake, I think. Then I was released because they hoped I would lead them to some information they wanted. Some papers of my father's. Well… the Agency kidnapped me. Otherwise I imagine I should be back by now in… I won't mention the name, and now I'm here in a strange place where I don't know a soul. It's confusing. Doesn't make sense."

"Well, Rebecca Peterson appears to know you, or something about you."

"I have never heard the name before."

"She's our camp secretary. It was she who asked for you at Ras Shamir. I saw her signature."

"She asked for me?"

"By name."

"Rebecca Peterson," said Judith Roth, and, after deeply considering, shook her head with certainty. "It means nothing to me."

"Well, as I said, I saw her signature."

But she was dry now and able to consult the fragment of mirror tacked to the wall of the barn with a grimace of disgust. She dismissed the name from her consciousness — sent it to join the hundred other mysteries of this long journey into the unknown. All she knew now was that she was hideously ugly with her hair cropped in this fashion; she borrowed a comb from the doctor and swept it back furiously. "Can you lend me a scarf?" was all she said, and the doctor smilingly handed her one, reflecting that when a woman can still think about her looks she is definitely off the danger list.

"You are going to hate the clothes I brought," said the doctor, "but they were all I could find. Mostly they all wear blue shorts and white tops, the land-workers. But it is at least a dress."

"What is more important," said Judith Roth soberly, "is that it is clean."

The women had been clearing up the trestles and stacking them. The doctor took Judith to a small whitewashed cubicle with a truckle-bed in it. "Now, my dear," she said, "you are going to sleep. I can't do anything about you until tomorrow evening when I am driving back to Ras Shamir. We need some papers prepared for you. Manya has orders to feed you, but you must lie low. This place is near the road, and if the British suspected we were using it they would certainly make a police raid. If that should happen while I'm away, hide in the orange grove until they leave. As for the old man, he's going to another place and arrangements have been made to fetch him, so don't bother your head about him, understand?"

"I understand."

The doctor yawned suddenly, exposing small white teeth. "I am going to sleep for a couple of hours before I leave. I shall come for you at five tomorrow... no *this* evening. Good-night, Judith."

"Good-night."

She lay for a long time with open eyes, watching the white light of dawn increase in strength as it shone through the skylight. Then she dozed, and the whole kaleidoscope of her memory began to throw up its bewildering and fragmented patterns. The children were dancing about, pelting her with snowballs, crying "Jew, Jew, Judith, Jew..." Somewhere very far away, and belonging to a world so distant that it seemed to glow with the memory of a paradise now lost, she heard her father's voice talking to her, rapidly and confidently, about the glories of being German.

Her sleep was a shallow and troubled one, hampered, curiously enough, by her new sense of cleanliness. The hot water had alleviated her fatigue quite sensibly. She muttered her way in and out of remembered laboratories and classrooms, in and out of the calculus and the bewildering tangle of magnetic fields where once she had been quite at home.

At midday she woke, sighing, and heard voices. Rising, she peeped through the door and saw that the door of the little room opposite was open. Three Orthodox Jews, in their long black coats and spade-shaped hats, were talking to the prophet earnestly and with elation. Their voices rose and fell. Moreover, the prophet himself, Melchior, was already up and dressed in new clothes of a rabbinical cut. He appeared to have regained his sanity at a single bound. His eyes shone, he embraced his visitors, answering them fluently in Hebrew, and making eloquent gestures with his hands. They had tears in their eyes and were obviously under the stress of emotions based in reverence and relief. He must, she thought, be some great Talmudic scholar or rabbi. Presently the little party made ready to leave; Melchior's smashed suitcase was picked up reverently by one of them as they crossed the main room to the outer door. Once outside, they latched it carefully behind them and their voices faded softly, exultantly, into silence. She was alone now, and she examined her quarters with a desultory curiosity, walking about the gaunt room to look out of the barred windows which gave onto the dense shade of a lemon grove. Some fat crows lobbed about in the rank grass.

After a while one of the old women appeared with a stew-pot and a tin plate and spoon and set them down before her with smiles. Judith ate ravenously while the woman watched happily. She spoke a little imperfect Yiddish and, struck by her gypsy-like appearance, Judith questioned her, only to find that she was a Jewess from Bessarabia who had been in the country a number of years. "Then you speak Hebrew?" said Judith in Hebrew, which she spoke slowly but with tolerable correctness. The old woman chuckled and made an indefinite sign with her hand: "I am still learning. It is hard."

She gathered up the eating utensils and took herself off again, closing the door softly behind her and leaving Judith once more alone. Time hung heavy that afternoon, and the girl was thoroughly bored with her own company by the time the doctor reappeared in the doorway; she was dusty but exultant as she threw her satchel on the table. "I've had a stroke of luck. I got the papers we need. Usually they take time to obtain. I was afraid you might be stuck here for a week. How are you feeling?"

"I'm quite fit."

"Good. Then we can start right away. But first of all here is your identity card." She rummaged in her satchel and produced a suitably creased and thumbed document. Judith saw with surprise that it actually had a photograph of herself stapled to it. "How did they get that?" The doctor smiled. "The Agency boys think up everything. You should have no trouble anyway. Especially once you are up at Ras Shamir with us." She consulted her wrist-watch briefly and reflected. "I think we should move off," she said, "as I still have three more people to pick up."

A dilapidated lorry was parked off the road under the trees with a fat morose-looking girl at the wheel. Its interior was loaded with light wooden crates such as are used for fruit-packing. As they climbed in, the doctor introduced Judith to the girl, whose name was Anna, and in response to her greeting Judith received an ill-tempered nod. They set off along the dusty road with a roar, travelling northward, Anna driving with sullen concentration. The road ran for the most part along the sea-line and Judith looked curiously about her at the new landscape with its exotic vegetation. The jogging of the ancient vehicle was pleasant and conducive to drowsiness — indeed already the doctor nodded beside her. Twice they turned off the main road and ran into an olive-grove to halt somewhere near a cluster of tattered and abandoned-looking sheds, out of which emerged other passengers; two weary-looking girls of Judith's own age, approximately, and a stout rosy woman in her late forties. They were each given an identity card before being shoved aboard over the tail of the lorry, to make themselves as comfortable as possible among the crates. Anna greeted them all with the same brusque contempt. "Come on," she said sharply. "We're late as it is."

They ran northwards now, into the eye of the westering sun along the peaceful olive-groves powdered silver with dust. There was a good deal of military traffic on the road but it all seemed to be moving in the opposite direction. "Must be something up in Jerusalem," commented the doctor, "I expect we'll hear about it this evening." Anna shook her head and muttered. The rest of them did not speak. The girls looked dazed and tired, while the ruddy-faced woman had wrapped her head in a scarf and fallen into a doze. They were all perhaps as recent arrivals as herself, thought Judith, dazed by haphazard travel and the dangers they had traversed. The lorry jogged on steadily with the sea to their left and the rough red outcrops of sandstone and granite on their right, cradling little valleys of green vegetation. A smudge of smoke appeared on the further edge of the coastline and the doctor pointed to it and said, "Haifa."

The road began to curve and twist now, and on one of these curves they suddenly saw a figure detach itself from the shadow of an olive-tree and come racing down to the road waving its arms. It cleared the ditch at a bound and stood on the crown of the road with its arms outspread. A ripple of anxiety ran through them at the sight, and Anna for a moment increased speed as if she intended to run down the signalling figure, but all of a sudden she grunted and slammed on her brakes. "It's Aaron," she said, and her ugly face split into a smile. "So it is," said the doctor. "What is he doing here?"

The figure facing them was that of a robust and broad-shouldered man in his late thirties, clad in nondescript clothes which faintly suggested British battledress. "What luck!" he cried, almost dancing with delight, "Anna darling!" And having stopped the lorry he leaped lightly onto the footboard and planted a kiss upon the ugly but radiant face of the driver. Then, thrusting his grinning face forward, he explained himself with breathless elation, his white teeth bared under the dark circumflex of a moustache which gave his face a faintly Kalmuk cast. "My bloody motor-bike broke down: I hoped you'd take this road. And you did. Bravo, Anna, bravo, Naomi! At least I shan't have to spend the night walking to Haifa. Make room for me, will you?" He smiled at Judith and jerked his thumb with the easy assumption of authority. "You climb into the back with the others," he said. Judith felt a sudden wave of annoyance at his tone and opened her mouth to say something, but before she could formulate either a question or a protest he had vanished again, uttering a brief "Wait." While she climbed awkwardly over the back of the seat, surrendering her place and exchanging it for an uncomfortable crate among the other passengers, he had started to race back among the trees. He seemed to do everything at top speed. He stooped down to gather up a bundle and then ran down to the road once more, grinning with pleasure. The doctor moved into the centre to make room for him and he climbed aboard in high good humour, banging the door and crying, "All aboard!" The two women smiled indulgently at him as the lorry once more got into gear. He expelled his breath and mopped his head. Around his throat he wore a blue scarf and, dangling below it, a pair of binoculars; his useless motor-cyclist's goggles he had drawn up on one leg so that he was wearing them on his calf.

"Well," he said, and his tone suggested that of a good-natured autocrat of a small circle, "everything is marvellous; increasingly marvellous. The situation is getting so bad now that we can really afford to stop worrying. Another big trouble this afternoon at the Jaffa Gate with fifteen killed. *Six* British, my dears, and two Jews. All the rest Arabs. Tonight they are going to have a go at the Haifa factory."

"I don't see why you sound so elated," said the doctor with a little shudder. "It's horrible." He looked suddenly chastened, like a scolded puppy, and nodded in agreement, his face grave again. "The horror is not of our making, alas!" he said in a different tone. They jogged on in silence for a while and now Anna turned the lorry northeast upon a road skirting mountain landscape — rude red rock burnished to the colour of dried blood in the sun. "I bet the road will be picketed," said Anna gloomily. "It always is after trouble." He seemed to cheer up. He put his arm affectionately around the doctor and said: "If we get through Nazareth without a block then there will be nothing to worry about. The only other person to stop us might be Lawton — *Major Lawton* — and we can talk him round. But what's wrong anyway? Aren't our papers in order? You girls have your cards?" He suddenly turned a narrow-eyed gaze upon the passengers in the truck, his lip curling. They all nodded. Judith gazed at him with mounting contempt. His manner infuriated her. Their eyes met coldly for a moment. "And you?" he said. "Why don't you answer me?" Judith's eyes ignited rebelliously, but she controlled her feelings. "I have my card," she said. "Good," said Aaron, turning back once more, the curtness of the word softened by a smile. "Then we have nothing to worry about. God, I'm hungry." He groped about in his bundle for a piece of dry bread which he ate ravenously as he talked. Then he tilted a water bottle and drank. His lips were wet with red wine. He licked them carefully and wiped his moustache on the back of his hand. "Anyway," he said, "Jerusalem likes my plans; we are going to get some more weapons if the bloody British don't capture them." He gave a short laugh. "And the valley of Ras Shamir will become a strong point. Good." He rubbed his hands and then scratched his armpits. His buoyant, self-confident rudeness jarred on Judith. She found him one of the most disagreeable people she had ever met.

Nazareth, to their surprise, was quiet and they climbed the winding road into the mountains without incident. "There," said Aaron when they were past the ugly straggle of streets and churches, "what did I say? We are in luck." On they ran and the air turned colder; the sinking sun made the mountains glow like jewels. They passed a few mule-trains on the road, piloted by Druzes, but on the whole the countryside seemed deserted.

The rumble of their engine flapped and boomed back at them through the dark ravines as they turned the last shoulder of mountain and were able to stare directly down on the valley. Here Aaron stopped the lorry and got down to sweep the ranges with his binoculars. "Nothing unusual," he cried cheerily and proceeded with *sang froid* to relieve himself against a tree before rejoining the lorry. As they let in the clutch and began to roll down the hairpin bend of the mountains, Judith sat up straight and gazed at the valley herself. At last, on the shoulder of a high pass, they saw the ugly mass of a concrete fortress pricking the skyline and Aaron remarked: "There is Major Lawton's country house." The doctor turned to Judith and said: "The border starts along there; and just beyond is our valley, only to the right, we have to crawl down the mountain again from this point until we reach bottom again. You'll see it all from the next pass."

In the gathering twilight (for the sun had just sunk behind the mountains of Lebanon) they rounded a steep bluff and came upon a platoon of infantry blocking the road. "What did I say?" growled Anna, delighted as all pessimists are when one of their prophecies proves true. The lorry drew to a halt before the battle-clad figures. And now a surprising thing happened, for Aaron turned in his seat and, with the calmest air of self-possession, slipped a revolver into the throat of Judith's dress. It settled between her breasts, the steel icy cold. Before she could open her mouth, Aaron had opened the door and stepped down into the road. "Ah, Sergeant Manning," he said. The sergeant peered at him and grinned. "I think you know us all," said Aaron with a confident air. "We are getting back to Ras Shamir with some stuff for the farm."

"Well, I'll have to search you," said the sergeant, and a couple of privates barked. "Everyone out. Papers please." Laboriously they climbed down into the road, Judith, confused, almost on the point of tears, feeling the weight of the pistol sagging between her breasts. While a couple of privates searched the lorry, a third examined the identity cards with a perfunctory air; it was obviously a routine gesture. Yet two of the girls trembled so much that Judith wondered how they could avoid arousing suspicion. Meanwhile, Aaron chatted to the duty sergeant in familiar fashion, amiably putting up his arms and allowing himself to be frisked.

"I shouldn't go down to Ras Shamir tonight," said the grizzled sergeant. "There was some shooting earlier on the hills and a patrol reported some Arab cavalry on the crest to the east."

"We'll risk it," said Aaron blithely, "even though we are unarmed as you can see. It's a question of urgency. The truck is needed tomorrow."

"Well, it's up to you. I'm just warning you."

Aaron lit a cigarette as he watched the truck cleared and the girls helped back into it by a kindly private. "You can tell the Major from me," he said, "that if the British are supposed to be responsible for this valley they are making a poor job of it. Things would be perfectly quiet if they patrolled enough and took some interest."

The sergeant chuckled, showing yellow teeth. "The Major knows that as well as you. But they won't give us the men. What can we do?"

"Leave it to us," said Aaron mildly. "Instead of making our lives a misery on the kibbutz and trying to prevent us arming ourselves. You want us to be eaten by the Arabs."

"Personally, I don't care who eats who," said the sergeant.

"That's clear."

"But I'll tell the Major what you said."

"Save your breath — I've told him myself more than once."

The privates had cleared the lorry, and helped the occupants back into their uncomfortable seats. The sergeant sighed. "Okay," he said, "off you go."

And off they went, the rumble of the engine again flapping and booming at them. Without a word or a look, Aaron reached back and repossessed himself of his pistol. "Anna," he said, "just stop at the head of the pass and let me have a look."

The twilight was lengthening into darkness. They were shivering with cold. At the next bluff the cliffs fell away and they saw, gleaming below them, a long diamond-shaped valley which thrust its muzzle deep between two mountain ranges. Light twinkled here and there in it, made furry by the atmosphere. "Ras Shamir," said the doctor, pointing downwards. "The mountains are the border — Syria that side, Lebanon this." Judith gazed uncomprehendingly down across the scarps and foothills into the fading hollow which was brimming now with inky darkness. But Aaron was out on the road, already sweeping the mountain range with his glasses. Finally he seemed satisfied for he returned and said: "No. It looks normal. There are all the lights up. It's probably a false alarm. Anyway, what the hell. Let's get moving." From now on it was a steeply falling gradient, and Anna let the lorry gather speed. Judith was surprised that no one showed any undue alarm, in spite of the warning and, as if the doctor had surprised her thought and read it, she heard the gentle voice say: "All in the day's work." Down they swept round the hairpin bends, their lights cutting a dim path for them. And now, to increase Judith's surprise, Anna began to sing an old Hebrew song and, after the first phrase, Aaron joined in with his deep baritone. It was infectious. The doctor, too, began to hum and one of the girls in the back who knew the song suddenly lent her voice to it. On rumbled the lorry with its freight of singers, and gradually the air became warmer as they descended, until they were once more on the valley level, rumbling across dusty roads lined with tall trees. Orchards stretched away on every side, the leaves of the trees dusted pollen-yellow in the faded gleam of their headlights. Darkness had fallen fully now, dense and deeply scented by flowers. They crossed a number of small bridges and traversed long areas of meadows where the water of the carp ponds gleamed back at them with a dull metallic lustre. Finally, they appeared to have traversed the whole valley, for the mountain range began to rise once more, etched on the sky. It was in its shadow that they turned aside, stumbled and rattled over a long dirt-track and arrived at a grove of trees with a perimeter of barbed wire and a gate. There was an unarmed man on sentry duty who flashed a torch and interrogated them hoarsely. Then the gate swung wide and they drove into the deep tree-grove. And here Aaron stopped the lorry and gathered his belongings together.

"I must be off," he said, "I have a lot to discuss. Thank you Anna dear, and Naomi. Good-night." He stalked into the shadow of the trees, disappearing even more suddenly than he had first appeared. The lorry grumbled slowly on in the dense green and finally came to a halt in front of a large structure which looked like a depot for tractors. Anna kept the lights on until they had all disembarked and then plunged them into darkness. The doctor took charge of the party with a pocket torch and led the way (their steps once more lagged with fatigue) along a number of twisting paths. They were obviously in a settlement of some kind, for here and there they saw lighted bungalows, but they were all deeply surrounded with greenery. Finally great walls loomed up, which later Judith was to recognize as the remains of a Crusader fortress. They entered a courtyard and stood under a long wooden balcony where the doctor called softly: "Miss Peterson!" A door opened abruptly and a tall gaunt figure appeared in silhouette above them, looking down. A deep hoarse voice said "Naomi" and the doctor answered immediately: "Yes, we're back, Miss Peterson." The figure grunted. "We are in darkness for another hour at least," it said in the same hoarse, rather thrilling voice. "There's been a power failure but Tonio is mending it."

"So I see."

There was a long pause and then the figure said: "Is Judith Roth with you?" Judith jumped at the mention of her name.

"Yes," said the doctor, and at once a torch flashed down upon them from the balcony, blinding them. "Which is she?" said the voice and the doctor answered: "Here she is," pointing at her. Judith felt the light exploring her from the top of her clipped head to the soles of her ill-clad feet; it travelled slowly down her, and then once more settled on her face. Then it was abruptly switched off and the voice said, "Good. Now listen." The deep authoritative tones brought the whole party to attention. The figure leaned further and said: "I have a meeting tonight and cannot receive you all as I wanted to. I shall welcome you tomorrow. Meanwhile, among the various other troubles of this settlement, the pump has broken and won't be mended until morning. We can't offer you hot water, but anyone who wants to can bathe in the Jordan. It runs through the end of this orchard."

There was a pause. The Jordan! It seemed the strangest place and circumstance for this odd symbol to obtrude itself. The figure on the balcony stayed quiet for a moment, as if listening. Then it went on: "There is food in the dining-hall and all your quarters are ready for you. Eat well and sleep well. For there is a lot of work waiting for you here." Nobody said a word. Then the voice went on. "And Naomi, I'd like to talk to Judith Roth but I am not sure if I shall be back tonight. Could you bring her back to the office after dinner, just to look in and see if I am?"

"Certainly."

"Then that is all." The dark figure turned and vanished, a door closed. The doctor turned to them smiling and said: "Well, I imagine nobody will want to bathe in the Jordan tonight..."

"On the contrary," said Judith suddenly. "I would."

Two of the other girls after some hesitation also said they would, much to the doctor's surprise. In the case of Judith it was pure superstition. She had a sudden idea that the river might cure the rash on her throat! The idea at any rate seemed to enliven them all, and the doctor, laughing, led them through the darkness of the groves to where they caught the murmur and flicker of the river. Here she dived into a shed and produced towels, before leading them down onto a wooden jetty where they began to undress. Only Judith and two of the others took the plunge into the water, groaning as the cold hit them. A thousand tree-frogs and water-tortoises slithered down from the banks, their eyes agleam in the light of the doctor's torch. The fat woman washed her face and drank the legendary water in cupped hands. The doctor sat on the jetty, watching them and smoking.

Then, when they were dry, she led them once more across the maze of interweaving paths among the dim houses to where a gaunt building stood. As they entered it, the lights suddenly flashed on and a subdued cheer rose from the half-dozen or so late-comers who were finishing their dinners. The girls glanced curiously about them, half-blinded by the sudden illumination. Fifteen or twenty tough-looking men, mostly blonde, were eating their evening meal. They were clad in the traditional blue pants which Judith was to come to recognize as the uniform of these workers. They talked in low voices and smiled a greeting ("Shalom") at the newcomers. It was a typical kibbutz canteen and several trolleys full of food circulated, pushed by girls and boys, some of whom were of another cast of feature with the long sallow faces of Sephardic Jews and their great dark eyes. The doctor took charge of the party, explaining everything in her cool detached voice: they fell upon their food ravenously and earned her smiling approval by their appetites.

Then the little party made its way outside. Judith stood still, inhaling the deep scents of the night and said to herself: "The stillness is the extraordinary thing." The ordinary geography of the camp had now become much easier to comprehend, for with the restoration of the current the bulbs which lighted the curving intersecting pathways among the trees shone out clearly. A faint feeling of recognition came to the tired girls. The doctor led them to their quarters in a clean hut full of small single cubicles, each with a locker, a chair and a bed in it. She said good-night to the others and then, turning to Judith, said: "Would you care to come and see if Pete is back, or are you too tired?"

"No, I'll come. I'm curious to know what she wants of me."

"I don't know, I'm sure."

The two women made their way back towards the tall dark ramparts of the Crusader fort; now, with the light, its outline became clearer. It was obviously used as an administrative block, the houses and offices built cunningly into the ceinture of the ancient wall. She remarked on this, and the doctor said, "Yes, the old walls are still thick enough to stop a bullet." It sounded a somewhat ominous remark. This time, they climbed the long wooden staircase and walked along the row of closed doors until they came to the end one. The doctor threw it open and they walked in. The light was on but the room was empty. Its only furniture was an old desk, a table, some files and a small old-fashioned safe. There was no ornament in the room save a small silver-framed photograph on the desk. Judith found herself gazing at it with amazement, hardly able to believe her eyes. She walked closer and stared. No, there could not be any mistake. She started out of her dream as the doctor spoke. "Well, she's obviously not here and I don't think she'd want to keep you hanging about, so let's go."

Without a word, Judith followed her along the landing and down once more into the courtyard, now feebly lit by a single electric bulb. She turned to the doctor and put an arm on her shoulder. "I can remember my way back to my billet," she said with a smile. "You don't need to show me. You must be sick of the sight of us all by now — and after all you've done too!" The doctor smiled and patted her elbow. "I admit to being tired, if you are sure you can find your way…"

"Of course."

"Then I'll go back to my house; my husband will be there waiting for me, and probably a bit worried about the time."

"By all means," said Judith, "by all means."

They said good-night and separated, and Judith was all at once glad to be alone. She walked, deep in thought, among the dark trees, slowing her pace to a saunter, while one half of her mind enjoyed the deep odours of the night, the smell of blossom. The sky was dark, but with a brilliant velvety darkness and the stars shone brightly. She turned off the track for a moment and sat down at the foot of a tree to savour it all for a few moments before she surrendered to sleep. She had been there for a few seconds only when she heard footsteps upon the pathway to her right and the sound of low voices. A man and a woman were approaching, in silhouette, with the feeble light behind them. Vaguely she recognized the outline of a man who looked something like Aaron; with him was a tall thin figure walking with a deliberate meditative slowness, dressed in some formless fashion which suggested a shawl, a mantilla or a cape. Yes, the man was Aaron. As they approached she heard him say in a sharp authoritative tone: "Pete, you listen to me and stop throwing your weight about. You may run the place as you please, but you are not running me."

"I'm not trying to," said the deep hoarse voice which Judith recognized as belonging to the woman called Peterson. "Not at all. But you are not to take any decisions inside the perimeter without consulting me or I shall have the committee on your neck. Is that clear?"

Aaron sighed with exasperation. "I am responsible," he said angrily, "for the defence of this valley. My decisions are going to be respected and my orders carried out."

"Not unless they meet with the approval of the committee."

"Damn the committee."

"I would be heartily glad to. But I can't."

Aaron stopped and took her roughly by the arm. "Listen, Pete," he said angrily, "if we get this new stuff we shall have to improve the instruction for the settlement. This is automatic stuff, not bolt-action rifles and rusty muzzle-loaders. And everything will depend on it. I have made up my mind to find an extra hour a day for it. I know that everyone is dead-beat in the evening, but what else is to be done? We must turn them into efficient *francs-tireurs* as soon as possible. What's more, I propose to start tomorrow if the stuff arrives."

"I shall tell the committee. You will have my answer tomorrow."

"Stop crossing me, Pete."

"You stop crossing me, Aaron. I know how serious your military considerations are, but so are the crops. We must find a way round both difficulties. But you are not ordering me around, do you see? Not as long as I'm organizing secretary here."

He bit his lip. They glared at each other like angry dogs. "Look," he said at last, "if we get the stuff, I propose to start tomorrow night with a general demonstration... if the committee agrees."

"That's better," she said grimly.

"And if it doesn't, I shall know who to blame and who is responsible — and I shan't forget it, Pete. On my word."

"Good-night," she said gruffly, and turned on her heel. Aaron stood in perplexity, looking after the diminishing figure. Then he shook his head and made off in another direction, banging his leg with a switch.

Judith was once more alone. She moved circumspectly across the path now towards the little hut from which a chorus of healthy snores resounded. The door of her room was ajar. She entered in darkness and undressed quietly before slipping into the hard but not uncomfortable bed. She turned on her side, put one arm under her head and was instantly asleep — a deeper, dreamless sleep this time which carried with it a hint of reassurance and even of a fugitive contentment. In her mind she heard the ripple of the Jordan river and felt its cold waters sliding across her breasts and flanks.

4

Pete

She awoke with a start, and found herself gazing into a pair of enormous black eyes, set deeply under arched brows in the long pointed features of an ancient Greek queen, or a witch. They were eyes with a deep sadness in them and yet at the same time with a hint of something like mischief. The face was oval, the forehead high, the lips thin and aristocratic. It was so close to her own that she had the sudden illusion that it was magnified to twice its normal size, as if seen through a lens. The figure was wearing not a mantilla but a dark shawl which was drawn up over her head in the fashion of a peasant-woman. The dark hair was liberally streaked with grey, though it was thick and curly. It was a head of striking beauty, with its long slender nose aimed justly to compensate for the hardness of the chiselled lips. The hands too, which had been softly touching the girl's forehead in the darkness, were resolute and strong, and ringless. All this Judith took in with a single glance. It was clearly Miss Peterson, and she was kneeling beside the bed with a small candle alight in a saucer. They stared at each other for a long moment, neither pair of eyes so much as blinking. Miss Peterson's, enormous and the colour almost of tar, were focussed on Judith with concentration and a certain air of greedy assessment.

But, seeing herself observed now, she allowed a smile to overflow into them though her lips did not copy it. She put her finger to her lips and said, "Sorry I missed you." Even her low whisper sounded hoarse and strong and peasant-like. Judith propped herself up and said:

"What is my father's photograph doing on your desk?"

"Ah, you noticed it?"

"Yes."

Miss Peterson depressed her cheeks in a smile which hovered on the edge of mischief, before turning to a kind of sadness. She said: "I was his mistress for many years. You could have been my child. That is why I was curious to see you. I only once caught a glimpse of you when you were small."

"I heard he was in love with a woman called Peter."

"I am Peter."

"But she went away. I don't know why."

"There were several reasons. It was for his sake..."

"But, Miss Peterson..."

"Call me Pete if you wish; everyone does."

"Pete. And you brought me here?"

"Well, not me entirely. I knew they were going to try and get you out and I asked for you here; but I don't expect you'll stay long. I imagine that Professor Liebling will want you in Jerusalem."

"The physicist?"

"Yes — he arranged it all. It has something to do with your father's work."

"I see!" Judith lifted her head from the pillow.

Pete stood up now, very thin and tall; even in the rosy candlelight her pallor was striking, giving her a witch-like cast. She whispered: "I'll go now and get some sleep. Good-night, Judith." As she turned to go, Judith put out her arm and drew her face down towards her own. They kissed briefly and smiled. "See you in the morning."

5

The Kibbutz

Next day dawned fine and brilliant, and Judith made her way to the gaunt dining-room for her breakfast, walking rapturously through the green groves of fruit-trees on grass made springy and verdant by frequent watering. Everywhere there were sprinklers at work, spouting a fine hazy parabola of water. She began to accustom herself to the geography of the place, and found her way back to Miss Peterson's office without much trouble. Here everything was bustle and activity. A couple of typewriters chattered; everywhere lay files and rosters and maps in coloured chalk overscribbled with engineers' mathematical computations. Pete greeted her and detached herself from the melée after giving a few orders. "You had better come on deck with me," she said. "From there you will see the whole layout of the settlement as well as most of the others." The "deck" turned out to be the flat roof of the tower which they climbed by a wooden staircase. Emerging into the brilliant sunshine, Judith saw the whole valley laid out around them, narrowing and edging into a slot as it entered the single great defile in the mountains, out of which the river flowed, to broaden immediately into a wide, smoothly running stream which watered the broad pastures and meadows on either side. "In fact," said Pete, "our valley sticks out like a very sore thumb into enemy territory. It's roughly a triangle contained between these two mountain ranges — Lebanon this one, and Syria that."

"And the border?"

"Approximately the ranges mark it, but it's never completely closed and there is quite a lot of marauding and smuggling. Up there you can see the patches of the seven settlements along the escarpment. They are actually on the border." She named them slowly as she pointed, but each time as she mentioned the Hebrew name, she added, as a sort of pseudonym, the name of a town or a country which characterized the inhabitants. It appeared that these settlements were called respectively, Brisbane, Brooklyn, Odessa, Lubeck.

"No, it's not code," said Peterson. "It's simply that the inhabitants come from those places. Talk about a tower of Babel. But then you see that Israel consists of sixty nations. A patchwork quilt."

"It looks so peaceful."

"Most of the time it is. Sometimes not. See the bullet holes in that wall. Arab fire last year, one night, without warning."

"But don't the British keep the peace?"

"When it suits them. I think they would be rather glad if their Arab friends wiped out the kibbutzim; we are an embarrassment to them. On the Lebanon side we are well protected because we control the crown of the mountain and the settlements are spread out along it — good defensive positions with steep cliffs the other side. On this side, alas, it is not so good because the Syrians are astride the crown and we are down in the valley. They could lob stuff down at us quite easily and we couldn't hit back with our weapons. Luckily, up to now, they don't seem to have anything heavier than machine guns."

At one end of the long terrace there stood an old-fashioned heliograph manned by a couple of girls, one of whom was the taciturn Anna. Seeing Judith's curious eyes on the machine as it winked away, eliciting a similar star of light from the second of the settlements, Pete said: "We've no telephones, alas; heliograph by day and torch signalling by night is what we have to do."

One of the girls, scribbling on a signals pad, looked up and said: "Pete — there was some sniping in Amir last night; nobody hurt. They say they want more apples against apricots weight for weight."

Pete snorted. "The last lot of apricots were weary, tell them. More-over, tell them from me that they are just a bunch of Glasgow Jews thriving on the sharp practice they picked up from the Scots. Tell them, moreover, that we honest lowland Jews from Poland, Latvia, Russia and Brooklyn hold them in massive contempt." Chuckling, the girls spelled the message while Pete took a turn or two upon the deck, looking indeed as business-like as an admiral on his flagship. "You see," she said to Judith, "we have a perimeter round the camp but we've long since overflowed it and put the whole valley under cultivation. It took thirty years and about two hundred lives to drain what was stinking marshland and turn it into the richest valley in Palestine. The Arabs never did anything with it, and were glad to sell it off bit by bit — now, of course, they would like it back. So you see, we have our problems."

One of the signallers turned her head and giggled as she said: "They've replied, Pete."

"What do they say?"

"They say: 'Tell Pete to stuff it!'"

Pete grunted and turned aside, smiling. "Today," she said, taking Judith's arm, "I'm not going to attach you: just wander around and have a look at everything — orchards, vegetable plots, chickens. We even have a flock of sheep. Do you see where the river turns out of the mountain and gets broad? Those white things are the sheep at pasture. It's the very edge, though; the border starts inside the ravine and if you go too close you are likely to get a bullet through your hat."

Judith took her at her word and spent the whole morning inspect-ing the settlement. The spring flowers were in their first glory — car-pets of scarlet and blue anemones, hollyhock, cyclamen, lupin, rose. She gathered herself enough for a bowl as she sauntered.

At lunchtime she managed to borrow a small pottery jar for her bouquet of flowers and she put them on the window-sill of her tiny room. Looking around her at its primitive simplicity, and its view onto the beds of carefully tended flowers, she suddenly felt an absurd dis-position to cry; and cry she did a little for relief, telling herself that it was "just a reaction", though she could not have defined the word with any precision. She felt rather like a snake about to shed its skin, to slough off the misery of the past and take on the bright hues of a present in this lovely place. Yet, from time to time, the past came back and almost choked one: rounding a hedge by the vegetable gardens she had suddenly come upon a row of smoking incinerators burning garbage — old turnip-ends, newspapers, kitchen refuse, rotten pumpkins. The incinerator was being fed by a bunch of Poles and Americans whom the smoke had turned black as demons. Her memory turned a double somersault and scattered all her self-possession. The incinerators! It was all she could do not to be violently sick.

6

The Long Arm of Chance

Mr. Donner was fated to be a policeman; it was not a question of voca-
tion entirely, though he fitted the part and played it with a certain rel-
ish. He was in fact well cast, for he was a mountainous figure of a man
who used his fat as extra weight when it came to exchanging shoves
or blows with Arabs or Jews. Tall, of a deceptively babyish blondness
and blue of eye, he could, when he chose, look as shy and innocent
and bashful as only a Protestant Irishman can look. He had the brogue
too — that slippery dialect accent which sorts so well with a national
talent for hysteria or wheedling. Donner in his uniform was one
thing — but Donner undressed... for at this very moment he was lying
naked on his bed, enjoying the vague doze which helped him to pass
away the siesta hour and digest a heavy meal, wallowing in the suds of
beer. The Palestinian sun, instead of turning him brown, had only increased his pinkness; his flesh resembled somewhat the celluloid skin
of a cheap doll. His knees and elbows wore large dimples. His legs were
slightly bowed so that he stood awkwardly askew, which increased his
air of apparent shyness. He breathed stertorously through his mouth,
his straggling blonde moustache fluttering with the breaths. Mr. Donner... Inspector Donner, was sleeping the sleep of the just, from which

he would be wrenched at a quarter to four by the silvery chime of an alarm clock. His little villa in the German colony was snug and well appointed for a bachelor. His Arab cook was good and cost little, though he thieved when he could. His office was within walking distance of his house and consequently most conveniently situated. But Mr. Donner was dreaming of himself in other circumstances, and in a more resplendent uniform than a police outfit. He saw himself walking about with modest vainglory, clad in the duds of a Staff-Captain (Substantive); nor was this entirely a dream, for he had, with great skill, managed to lobby himself the promise of precisely such a post on the Syrian Mission, and had that very day received confirmation of the fact that he would eventually be able to kiss his hand to the Force as well as to the Superintendent, who was a thorn in his side. The Superintendent could kiss his arse, thought Donner vindictively, as he lay with closed eyes, hovering between sleeping and waking. A single mosquito droned. He had forgotten to tell Abdul to fill the flit-gun. There! The clock had started to chime.

Donner hurled himself out of bed as if he were about to race the hundred yards in ten seconds flat. He caught up the clock in his great paw and strangled its voice. Then he stepped into his cool shower and slowly rotated his great pink bulk to enjoy it to the maximum.

He accompanied the delicious splashing of the water with appropriate sounds of physical gusto, hissing through his teeth like a grampus. Then he dried his rosy body and slipped into his uniform. He combed and set his moustache with great care, smoothed his eyebrows, and examined the cavities in his teeth. There was no fault to be found with what he saw — or at least he had none to find. Satisfied, he took up his black leather-covered swagger-stick, tipped on his hat cautiously so as not to disturb the parting in his hair, winked at himself in the mirror, and left the house to start walking with that wide bosomy stride which conveyed a certain feeling of charitable benevolence towards the world and its creatures. In his mind's eye it was a military man who passed down the street — not an Inspector of the Palestine Police. It did not take him long to reach the police post. He touched his cap to the sentry and then, as he mounted the long staircase, thought that he might as well get his hand in again and try a real salute   a *military* salute — on his chief. The Superintendent sat brooding over his files, smoking a pipe. He had a long, petty, disappointed greyhound's face and the airs of a churchwarden. He was unprepared for the evolution that Donner performed before his desk, bringing his heels together with a profound percussion and saluting so hard that his huge hand wagged by his ear.

"What the hell's that in aid of?" asked the astonished officer, mildly. Donner grinned. "Military salute, Sir," he said with pride.

"Aren't you being a bit premature? Your papers haven't even come through yet, you know."

"Well — they can't come too soon for me."

"I see your point — with things hotting up as they are," said the Superintendent with a touch of veiled irony, which his subordinate failed to notice.

"I'll really be glad of the change," said Donner in a heartfelt tone.

"If you call the desert a change," said his superior with an acid smile. Donner looked grave. "Of course it will be!" he said reproachfully.

"Anyway, there's little enough inducement to stay. They blew up another post this morning. Macintosh is dead and a dozen or so wounded."

The two men looked at each other and sighed. "Why the hell don't we clamp down on them?" Donner asked the world with an aggrieved air. The Superintendent puffed his pipe and reflected. The question, so often echoed, had become a piece of threadbare rhetoric by now. Donner was heartily glad to be within sight of leaving it behind him with his uniform. He sank into a chair and mopped his brow. He noticed that the Superintendent was holding one of the green Miko files. "Government House just sent in a Miko," he said with an air of mild pride. They gazed at the file with respect, for it was only on rare occasions that the Secret Service asked the Police for a routine check on something. The Miko files suggested high romance to ordinary policemen, as well as a beguiling mystery, for they never saw who sent them. Somewhere in the cellars of Government House there was a mysterious man or men whose habits and interests were singular and mysterious.

"Does the name Roth mean anything to you — Judith Roth?" asked the Superintendent. Donner shook his head and held out his hand for the file: "Let me see," he said. He loved to handle these highly romance-charged documents himself; but the Superintendent ignored the outstretched hand, thus demonstrating his superiority in rank and practically insinuating by the gesture that Donner, as his junior, did not merit the confidence of a personal glance at the typewritten sheet. It was like implying that Donner might possibly be "insecure"; fully aware of the insult, the Inspector frowned and coughed behind his hand. "Roth, Roth," he mused, choking down his resentment and forcing himself to toady. "I can't honestly say it does. Any other data?"

The Superintendent read slowly from the file with a suburban accent: "We have reason to believe that the Nazis are alarmed by the fact that this daughter of a famous scientist may have escaped to Palestine with his papers. Among the unpublished material there are, according to rumours which have been circulating in scientific bodies for some time, plans for a new type of engine. There is no need to stress that such material would be of the greatest interest to the British and American governments and would be worth an immense sum of money to obtain or even to deny to the enemy."

"Money," said Donner reflectively, as if the word was new to him. "What do you know?"

"We have only one rather old picture of the lady taken from the press." As if making a great concession, the Superintendent passed a cutting across the desk to his junior. It showed Isaac Roth receiving the Nobel Prize for Physics the year before his death. A dark-haired, rather handsome and very young girl stood by him, her hand on his arm, her unsmiling eyes gazing into the camera. Donner brooded on this. "It's a very common type," he said. "Must be thousands like her in the world."

He sucked his teeth loudly, and handed the picture back. The Superintendent replaced it, closed the file, and stared at his fingernails.

"I shall tell them that we are keeping an eye out, but if she came in illegally, it's hopeless of course." Donner nodded sagaciously. "Hopeless," he agreed. "Well, we'll keep it in mind."

The Superintendent replaced the file reverently in the safe and stretched himself before re-lighting his pipe.

"See what you can do with your contacts," he said. Donner sat, deep in thought, for a long moment.

"Apparently the young woman is quite a well-known scientist herself."
Donner was only paying attention with half his mind. "Well," he
said, "is that all that's on the cards for this afternoon?"

"Yes."

"I'm glad. I thought I'd go down to Tel Aviv and see what is doing
about the Abdulla case. I think we've got him fair and square this time."
The Superintendent grunted. Donner rose and tugged down the jacket
of his uniform, which had a tendency to ride up over his belly. "Any
objections, Sir?" The Superintendent shook his head and ventured a
mild pleasantry. "Always glad to see the back of you, Donner," he said.
He was smiling, but it was unfortunately true. Donner frowned heavily and coughed behind his hand. "Roth," he said, "I'll bear it in mind."

He would have liked to risk another military salute, but the Superintendent's attitude about the Miko file had nettled him. He stalked
down into the courtyard and purged his annoyance by adopting a bullying tone to the transport officer as he asked for the duty transport
to which his rank entitled him. A jeep was duly forthcoming and he
settled his large frame in it with a portentous air and closed his eyes.
The drive down to the coast was not a long one, and it made a nice
change. Donner was able to spend a pleasant afternoon making his
juniors dance attention on him. Yes, the Abdulla case was tied in a
neat bow. Donner could not resist the temptation of telling his victim
so, and he spent some time in the verminous lock-up, railing at the
old one-eyed Arab who was still wearing the marks of a recent "treatment" — extensive bumps and bruises. He wailed and pleaded and
Donner growled agreeably at him.

It was getting dark when he left the police post and made his way
swiftly across the town towards the little villa on the outskirts which
they used as their interrogation centre. It was set apart from other
habitations in a grove of trees. This was useful as there were no neighbours to be bothered or made curious by the sounds of beating, or
the more refined types of ill-treatment which were so often necessary
in order to obtain information; and victims did sometimes scream in
the course of a "treatment". The house was deserted now and the way
ill-lit. Donner loosened his pistol slightly in its leather holster under
his armpit. One never knew. In the darkness the tattered garden round

the house looked melancholy in the extreme. But, undeterred by aesthetic considerations, Donner mounted the steps and opened the front door, switching on the lights as he did so. They revealed a large barren room with peeling walls, and an old cupboard empty of anything save scurrying mice. Its only furniture was a pock-marked desk over which hung a dusty unshaded light-bulb. A water-tap dripped obscurely in a dirty kitchen. Donner turned it off, frowning. Someone must have left it on after the last "Water-Cure" — a refinement which consisted of pouring water from a teapot up the nostrils of clients until such time as they decided to tell the truth. Donner seated himself at the desk in a creaky swivel-chair, placed his pistol at hand on the desk, and opened a copy of the *Illustrated London News* which he had thoughtfully brought with him in case his wait should be a long one. He had business of his own to transact that night. The anonymous letter had arrived as usual at his house, summoning him to the rendezvous. His wrist-watch ticked on. He read with concentration, shaping the words with his lips. He had not been at it long before there was a tapping at the shutter — two long and three short. He took his pistol in hand and went to the front door, opening it to admit the little figure of the Jew. "Ah, Abraham," he said with a kind of frowning benevolence. The old man nodded his bearded head and said "Good evening." Donner shut the door and locked it. Then he stalked back to his desk and sat behind it with a businesslike air, rubbing his hands. The Jew came softly up to the desk. Donner allowed his pistol to lie once more before him, moving it slightly to one side in order to make room for the bundle of papers his visitor carried.

"What have we got?" said Donner briskly.

"Twelve identity cards to be signed, sixty pounds." He began to count out money from a slab of notes. Donner suddenly exploded. "Twelve!" he exclaimed in an outraged tone. "You asked for fourteen. Seventy pounds, Abraham. That's my price."

"Two died on the voyage," said the little man in a meek voice.

"I can't help that," said Donner with bristling moustache. "You made the bargain, not me. It's not my affair if they die."

"Very well," said Abraham softly, "seventy it is."

Donner beamed at him. "That's better," he said with subsiding truculence and added "Put it on the table." He watched the counting of the notes carefully, then gathered them up and put them in his capacious wallet. "All right," he said, and detached a fountain-pen from his breast pocket. The little man laid a bundle of identity cards on the desk and Donner began to sign them, his tongue protruding slightly from between his teeth as he concentrated on the task. He signed them in the name of a predecessor of his who had held the post years before and who, being now dead, was obviously beyond recall if there were any questions asked. The cards were all greatly antedated in order to take advantage of the residence laws.

The little Jew said: "As a matter of fact, there were two children born on the trip as well. I suppose you don't want to charge for them?"

Either Donner was too obtuse to sense the contemptuous cutting edge of the remark, or else he did not feel disposed to regard himself as insulted. He raised his great head and took on his most innocent expression, blue eyes wide with reproach. "My dear Abraham," he said, "you are joking. After all, I am British, you know, my boy."

"So it would seem," said the little man, scratching his ear. These subtleties were too much for Donner. He waved a hand and said: "I told you I was being transferred, didn't I? I won't be much use to you in Syria, will I?"

"You never know."

"Anyway, I don't know the exact dates yet — but keep in touch. There may be ways."

"We will."

Donner blew on his signatures, disposing the cards across the desk in order to let them dry the better. Suddenly he got a shock, for the name Judith Roth stared up at him from the piece of pasteboard. There was no mistake. He was overtaken by a sudden feeling of irresolution. Should he ask Abraham directly... it might make him feel suspicious. As he signed the card he thought furiously, comparing the photograph with the memory of the newspaper cutting. It almost seemed the same picture. His brain worked at top speed, exploring the possibilities. Was there any way he might turn his find to his personal benefit? Donner's self-interest was a plant of long and sturdy growth: the old Irish Constabulary had planted it, the war had nourished it. After all, the sale of dispensations is one of the oldest police habits in the world. He had a sudden brainwave. With his head still lowered over his work, he asked casually: "Where are you going to send them all this time? Up north?"

"Mostly to Galilee — the women to Ras Shamir."

Donner almost chuckled at the ease with which he had extracted this piece of information. He finished the cards and watched Abraham gather them up with a whispered "Thank you." They shook hands and Donner saw his visitor out, carefully locking the door behind him. Then he carefully sorted out the money in his wallet, took up his pistol and turned out the lights. He shut the front door behind him and set off down the dusty path towards the lights of the town. He was in the best of possible moods. But there was some hard thinking to do. In a matter as complicated as scientific research he was somewhat out of his depth — the subject was a larger one than he was used to handling. And yet... the echo of the word "money" sounded pleasantly in his memory. After all, there would be no comeback from a mere Jew if such papers were *lost*; and if he, Donner, could possess himself of them... He ordered a large Arab meal at the "Saad" and ate with gluttony.

While he could not form any clear thoughts about his own intentions as regards Judith Roth, he was filled with a pleasant premonitory sense that his luck was holding firm, that things were moving his way. Of course, he would keep the information to himself until he had explored all its possibilities; if the girl had something saleable it might be possible to prise it away from her. Who knows? She might even be anxious to pay him in order to remain "undiscovered". Donner called for his bill in a throaty voice, feeling the fatness of his wallet with satisfaction: apart from the money paid him for the signatures he also possessed a large sum of the office's funds — part of the secret vote set aside for confidential work. He had of course signed the green voucher in the regulation manner, but he had stated that it would be used to pay informers and for "special investigations", and of course no receipts were expected from these tenebrous transactions. As a matter of fact... but why labour the point? Donner turned them to his own uses and quite a lot of his money went to little Coral Snow. It was with his inamorata in mind that he took a taxi now to Jaffa and set the bead curtains of the Montgomery Club swinging with a heave of his huge shoulders. A band played sagging Levantine jazz. Coral was standing in a group of girls at the bar, engaged in the none-too-elegant act of picking her front teeth with her little fingernail. She was clad in a kimono of tawdry vivacity, a Woolworth inspiration based on vague dreams of the summer palace at Pekin. It was very suitable for little blonde Coral with her fox-terrier face and her honest little eyes. "Humphrey!" she cried out with pleasure, and moved to meet him; Donner smiled broadly and rolled towards her with an air of complacent indulgence. "I *hoped* you'd come this evening. I was waiting for you, Humphrey — I was going to give you till eleven."

"And then?"

"Go home, silly. What else?"

"Alone?"

"Oh, cut it out, can't you?"

She looked aggrieved and Donner chuckled with delight at having taken a rise out of her. Actually Coral was a faithful little creature and had given him very little cause for heart-burnings. He would miss her in Syria. He ordered champagne-cup repeatedly and allowed his natural fund of Irish sentimentality full rein. They danced a little — Donner with the capacious, disorganized enthusiasm of a seal or a very large suitcase gone mad. He swayed about and rolled his buttocks heavily. But he did not tread on her feet.

By midnight they were lying in Coral's cheap bed in the southern end of the town, talking in maudlin fashion about partings and forgetfulness and love; Donner, who was pretty drunk now, promised to spend all his leaves with her. Coral appeared both grateful and befittingly tearful. She stroked his paps with her little hand and told him that he would be always in her heart. And it was now that Donner could not resist a little boasting about his virtues as a policeman. The apropos was that Coral herself was not going to be the only person to feel the weight of his absence. No. The Police would never get over it either. What would they do without him? Nobody else was capable of swift thought and action. He would give her a typical example. This morning, the Secret Service asked him to trace a woman called Judith Roth. Within a few hours he knew where she was! Coral dipped into the bedside contrivance which housed the tin pisspot, detached from it a typist's pad covered in doodles and graffiti and noted down the name. She did this with such charming naturalness that Donner noticed nothing. The pad contained fragments of several conversations both with him and with other men, policemen, pimps and patriots, which it was Coral's duty to jot down. Twice a week she visited the Old Quarter of Jerusalem, where a smooth young man, dark and slim with melting black eyes and an Oxford accent, gratefully took jottings. Yes, she sat with her scribbles on her knee and recounted all she had heard, reconstructing partly from notes and partly from memory. This was the only way, as Coral had no means of evaluating her findings, or discriminating between worthless rubbish and real intelligence data. The young man smoked Abdullas and was called Ali. He reminded Coral of the "sheik" of romance and, indeed, he was one and never too proud to stoop and enjoy her on the sofa in the other room. But business first. The note about Judith Roth interested him very much, though he said nothing. Later, as he kissed Coral he told her that she was a clever little puss and she replied, "Oh Ali, you know I'd do anything for the Arabs!"

So it was that Donner found himself bidden to cocktails at the Long Bar of the Hadrian Hotel and to a meeting with Ali which threw a little more light on the question of Judith Roth and sharpened his cupidity quite considerably. Ali was very suave and soft-voiced; he spoke perfect English of great refinement, which suggested an English upbringing. But he had the long yellowish face of a shark with small unwinking black eyes set deeply in it — eyes which regarded Donner steadily and a trifle contemptuously. His cigarette smouldered in a long bone holder. Nor did he beat about the bush. "I know that you are a frank man and I want to be frank with you," he said with an air of pious sincerity. "I know that you do a number of unorthodox things for a policeman, Mr. Donner." Donner jumped, as if he had been pricked with a pin. He looked uncomfortably at his interlocutor. "I don't know what you are getting at," he said hoarsely. "I do my duty."

"Of course you do. We all do. But sometimes you do more than your duty."

Donner got angry. "Look here," he said, "I don't know who you are and what you are getting at. But if you think..."

"I don't think anything — I know," said Ali, unperturbed. "And I want to make you a perfectly firm business offer — that is all. As a sensible man I feel sure you will accept it. After all, who today could afford to turn down a sum like..." He smiled and named a large sum of money. "Just for a few bits of information?"

"Go on," said Donner with an expressionless face.

"There is a girl," said Ali with a sigh, and proceeded to tell Donner all that was at present known about Judith Roth. Donner listened, with his head on one side like a fox-terrier. Had he seen the Secret Service file? It was possible. Donner's mind worked furiously. Was it a trap, perhaps? He sucked his teeth and said: "What is it all about?"

"We would like to know where she is, and if she is in possession of some papers; if she is, we would like to offer a large sum of money for a look at them."

"War secrets," said Donner, staring into his glass. He sat as still as a stone. "More bloody war secrets."

"No," said Ali. "These are *oil* secrets. Nothing to do with the war. I would not mention them if they were. I would not ask you to sell your country, Donner."

"I'm glad to hear it," said Donner piously.

"Certainly not," repeated Ali, spreading his hands. "I represent some very large oil interests, that is all. Set your mind at rest."

"Well, what is it then?" said Donner with a touch of impatience. "I must say you've come to me rather late in the day."

"I know. You are being posted to Syria."

"You seem to know everything."

"Not everything. That is why I am here. I want some general information about where the girl is; and then, if you can find a way of supplementing it and finding out if she has any such papers... After all, as a policeman you could raid the place and impound what you found; all we would ask is a photographic copy. You see my line of reasoning."

Donner laughed morosely. "I've raided Ras Shamir more than once," he said. "If you want the papers to disappear there is no better way. They're cunning. We never find anything. No, that's no way to start."

"So she is at Ras Shamir?"

"So I believe."

"Is there any way you could go up there and... find out with a little more certainty?"

"I could try, but there's precious little time left."

"But the money is good, Donner."

"Yes, the money is good," said Donner soberly and sucked his teeth. He stood up and thought deeply for a moment.

7

The Professor

One day Professor Liebling materialized before Judith's eyes at the lunch table. He looked like a benign little silver gnome in his shabby dark clothes covered with cigar ash. He carried a mackintosh over his arm and a long leather briefcase. His curly hair was quite white; he looked more like a musician than a physicist. He sat himself down with a self-deprecating smile and said: "As an old professional friend and colleague of your father's, I am going to call you Judith."

Judith smiled into the gentle world-weary eyes and said, "I believe I must have seen you, but I don't remember."

"Time is very wicked," said the Professor. "You must have seen an earnest middle-aged man with a beard. And I *must* have caught a glimpse of you. But... I must be truthful and not gallant. I do not remember."

They talked for a little while as the meal progressed; Peterson and the little woman doctor were at a table close beside them. "Now Pete I do remember," said the Professor. "We are old friends."

It was at the end of lunch that he asked permission to light one of his tall cigars and to talk shop. Judith made a characteristic little gesture of acceptance and took a cigarette from a battered packet in the pocket of his coat.

"I know what you are going to ask me," she said. "And I'm afraid

I'm going to disappoint you. By bad luck I was not working on this device of my father's. I was away lecturing in Oxford and Princeton for some time while he was busy on it. I know what it is — what sort of thing it is — because he talked to me about it. It was a new theory of propulsion based on an electro-magnetic field. But I didn't work on it. His assistant, a man called Kalman, had all the data."

"I know," said Professor Liebling quietly.

"Well, it was pretty far advanced because my father actually published a paper on it — and he never did that unless he had the whole thing finished. In fact, they were about to go into prototype and build this new kind of turbine when... he died."

"And a new world was born."

"A new world was born. When I got back, Kalman had disappeared with all the materials, and all I knew about it was what my father himself had told me, early on in the experiments. Oh dear!"

"Why do you say 'Oh dear!'?"

"I am sorry not to be of more use. And yet, in a way, it was perhaps lucky. The Nazis had wind of this and were most anxious to find out about it. It was impossible to convince them that I knew nothing about it. They sent me to a camp to punish me and then let me out, thinking I knew where the papers were hidden and would lead them to them."

"Everyone thought that — everyone feared that."

"Alas. But luckily I was kidnapped and managed to escape. But as for the papers... I have never seen them!"

Professor Liebling exhaled a violet stream of smoke and considered her gravely for a long moment. Judith stubbed out her cigarette and pondered before continuing. "As far as I remember from what my father said, he came upon some equations by Gauss in the Collected Papers. They had been completely discarded and set aside. He saw a connection with other work he was doing on electro-magnetic fields and began to turn them to use. The idea of this thing, device, grew out of his studies. But just what the data were I cannot say."

"Could you identify the equations again?"

"I might. Why do you ask?"

Professor Liebling sighed and rubbed his chin.

"Here's a strange part of the story. Kalman's papers (I suppose they are your father's) actually did get out here to Palestine, though we have never heard what happened to him. As a matter of fact, I have brought them with me today. We can't make very much of them; the drawings don't match the schema. I have had two of our most brilliant young men working on them. I was wondering if you would care to have a look and see whether you can unravel the whole thing. There may be whole chunks missing from the materials. It looks like a new sort of turbine."

"It was. Oil, he had in mind."

"Oil is what we have in mind," said the Professor. "It is also what the Nazis had in mind; they had plans for the Rumanian oil-fields which would have been helped by this idea. By the same token, the British, Americans and Arabs would all be profoundly interested. Do you understand? Meanwhile, the data we have all seems pure gibberish. I came here to ask you if you would work a while on it and try and reduce it to some sort of shape. Look."

Judith watched him zip back the briefcase and extract a couple of stout folders. He put them down and said: "There. Have a riffle." She turned the papers over slowly, and read them like a musician thoughtfully reading a score. Then she sighed. "I can't do it all at once of course. I should need time to really study them."

"You have all the time in the world. Months if necessary. I only wanted to ask you for your help. In fact, you could come up to Jerusalem if you wished, and work there at the Institute. Why not do that?"

She was silent for a moment. "I mean," said the Professor, "there at least you have a library and reference works to look up, but perhaps there is a special reason? Perhaps..."

"May I be frank?" said Judith at last. "I am still rather shaken and upset by the last few months — indeed longer than that." She smiled. "Look, Professor." She held out a hand in which a newly-lit cigarette smoked. It trembled like a leaf. Suddenly the Professor caught it in his own small hand and kissed it. "Of course," he said, "of course."

"I would like a little time to collect myself; of course I will look over these materials in my spare time, and tell you if there is anything that can be done with them — and perhaps you could send me a few books if I gave you a list? Or would that pose problems?"

"Of course not. And I perfectly understand."

"I like it here so much — what I have seen of it — it is really most interesting as a community venture, and somewhat unlike the last community in which I found myself!"

"Yes, the kibbutz is an odd form of voluntary organization. We have every type, you know, collective, cooperative and so on, and then when you think that there are seventy nations babbling on this strip of land you get quite dazed! Yes, I should stay if I were you, and work here. Take your time. Besides, things are not going to be very pleasant up there."

"Why do you say that?"

"I know it. We Jews are going to make a supreme attempt to bounce the British out of Palestine and into the United Nations — if we have to drag them there by the scruff of their thick necks. I think there is a very slim chance that we might emerge from such an affair with a mandate to create and run our own state — a new state — Israel! But of course you can judge what the Arab reaction would be. Egged on by the British, of course, as always. Yes, we are planning extensive operations shortly. Stay here. Yes, give me your list and stay here a while."

He chattered on amiably for some time, and they were again joined at the long table by Miss Peterson and the doctor, both, it seemed, old friends, if one could judge by the fact that they teased him unmercifully about his shabby clothes and the amount of cigar-ash which covered them. Professor Liebling took all this in good part. "Well," he said, "I came to kidnap Miss Roth, but she has decided to stay on awhile here, though she will be working on something... Pete, you know about it. Make the girl a little leisure time for study, will you?"

Judith said, "I want to do my full share — no special favours."

Miss Peterson shook her head and said: "There's no time for that here; but we'll see. Between teaching the children and digging potatoes..."

Liebling made a protesting sound and spread his hands wide. "Now listen, Pete, be reasonable."

"Leave it to me," said the decisive Miss Peterson, and the doctor wrinkled her nose and smiled.

"Don't fear, Herr Professor!"

The old man pretended to register a resigned exasperation. "Well, give me my book list, and I'll go."

He lent Judith his fountain-pen and she made a thoughtful list of books, tables and instruments. Then they all walked out to see him to his car across the meadows. Judith still held the briefcase as she took his arm.

"I shall send you the materials as soon as may be, and if and when you see the light please let me know. Either come up to Jerusalem or signal me and I'll come down. But don't lose the stuff, will you?"

"You can keep it in the safe in the office," said Pete, and Judith nodded.

They paused for a moment by the car, and the Professor peered around him at the brilliant sunlit landscape.

"Hm," he said, "it's a good place to be living; when Israel is free one day I'll come here and retire for good. Eh, Pete?"

"You'd have to work."

"Ach, work!" He made a vague gesture at the sky and stepped into the car after a final handshake. "Well, good luck and good industry," he added as the clutch was let in and the car slid off down the dusty road.

Judith walked thoughtfully back to her room and took a preliminary look at the documents before going over to the office and surrendering them to Miss Peterson, who put them in the safe with the other archives of the kibbutz. Then she walked for a while by the river, watching the children swimming. How purposeful everything seemed, how industrious! There was a contagious happiness in the air. Happiness! The word had an old-fashioned ring. She sat down on the bank and was deep in thought, when a thin woman with grey eyes came along and called her by her name. "I'm Rose Fox. I've come to ask if you need Hebrew lessons? No? Good. Then can you shoot?"

"No."

"I'll put you down for the course then tomorrow."

Judith looked wryly at her hands — she could not visualize them holding anything as unacademic as a rifle. And yet, why not?

"Lastly," said the girl, "will you do a turn tomorrow night on duty at the children's house — ten o'clock to six?"

"Of course."

"Well, I'm on with you, so I'll call and get you after dinner. You know where it is — right in the centre of the grove by the schoolroom. Never mind, I'll fetch you anyway."

"Thank you."

8

Daily Bread

She carried her reflections upon the Liebling visit as far as Peterson's office, feeling a little guilty that she should so much want to stay on in this valley, rather than risk the distractions of town life. But Pete was delighted.

"It's exactly what you need," she said, "a few months here before you decide what you want to do. Besides, you could quite well do your share of the kibbutz work and still have the mornings free for your own. Look — why don't you take your papers and go out with the shepherds? There are lovely quiet spots where you could sit and work with nothing to disturb you except the gossip of old Karam and an occasional tune on his flute; and those two imps of his could easily carry you a cushion." It was an idea worth thinking about.

"From tomorrow," she agreed, "I'll try it, Pete."

In the evening Rose Fox came for her after dinner and the two women sauntered in the darkness across to the childrens' rooms where they were to take over from those who had put the children to bed. They traversed the little gardens where the future farmers of the settlement were making their first humble experiments with flowers and vegetables. They entered the great dormitory, with its soft buds of night-lights and heard the gentle susurrus of the sleepers, each building and rebuilding in fantasy their private worlds of happiness or terror. Rose said in a whisper: "A lot of them belong to us — their parents are here — but very many we have inherited as orphans: you can guess why. A lot are fearfully disturbed. We try to mix the healthy ones in amongst them, to help them get their balance again." Slowly they made a tour of the beds and the girl gave a brief sketch of each child; and in the silences the sleeping whisper welled up around the words. Here was Anita who woke imploring "Don't! Don't!" in the voice of a seagull; there Dov whose tears all but strangled him; Martin who shivered at the sound of boots marching about in his dreams; Abe whose fingers picked at each other or wove elaborate and invisible tapestries all night; and Solomon who wet his bed, and poured with sweat and never said a word. Judith listened, deeply moved. She remembered the three visits of the old scientist to her father. The first time, her father saw him to the door and came back into the room saying: "The man's a crackpot"; the second time he was silent and thoughtful; the third time he said, "I did him an injustice. This man Freud has something of genius in him." She scraped about in her mind to remember as much as she could of the lore of psychology, in order to give her sympathy and emotion a tool, a weapon that might help her to aid the sleepers.

They sat for a while, listening to the soft echo of the children's breathing in the cavernous room. Then Judith took paper and pencil and seated herself in a corner. "Going to write a love-letter?" whispered Rose with a smile. Judith smiled back and nodded. "In a sort of way," she said and, as the long equation formed under the point of her pencil, she reflected that it was perhaps the only sort of love-letter her father might understand. Had Pete written love-letters to him? She bent her head over the long chains of symbols and figures and found they brought her calm; the great abstractions of weight, velocity, field, magnitude were full of poetic echoes. She worked on them slowly, touch by touch, like a painter working at a picture...

≈

Within a few days' time she had begun to have an entirely new feeling and meaning: absorbed in her kibbutz duties, she felt for the first time her self-confidence and self-assurance coming back, together with her physical health. Her skin infection disappeared, her hair had begun to grow again and bring back not only the fine shape of her head but also meaning and expression to her dark, thoughtful face. Not all the work was easy and, if she had had to confess to a partiality, it would certainly have been to her teaching duties with the younger children. Her subjects, by common consent, were arithmetic, geometry and algebra, and she enjoyed exploring these mysteries with them in the cool evening hours. The little school-room with its bright maps and amateur frescoes was a pleasant place to sit and work, and the blackboard was big enough not only for diagrams but for an occasional cartoon with which she helped rouse interest in the subject — an interest growing out of the delightful care-free laughter of her charges.

"How many ducks make five? Hands up."

A forest of hands would rise, among them many a grubby one.

"You, Esther — come and draw them."

Painfully, the five ducks would come to life on the board, accompanied by many an argument as to how many beaks, tails and feet a self-possessed duck should own.

"Now, if five ducks have two each, how many…"

~

Other duties were just as absorbing, though far less easy to master. In the enormous underground cellars which they had inherited from some order of Crusaders long since disbanded, there was a small-arms range, presided over by the gloomy Anna. Here there were moments of exasperation as well as panic.

"Now listen to me, Roth, for the tenth time, if you hold her too loosely she'll kick much worse. Hold her hard. AND OPEN YOUR EYES FOR GODSAKE. It's no use just spraying the universe! On the sandbags. Go on. Open up."

Inside the high vaulted cellar, the crackle and swish of the Sten sounded as loud as a hurricane at full velocity; yet from the outside there was little to distinguish it from the other sounds of the kibbutz, like the screaming of the circular saw and the throbbing of the pumps which fed both human beings and their animals and crops.

"Judith, you are not trying."

"I *am* trying!" cried Judith, almost in tears with exasperation. "You are not very helpful, Anna..."

"I'm doing my best for you. Now try again. And *train* the bloody thing. Remember, the balance is altering as the magazine is expended. *Train* it and *look*."

"It's worse than a fireman's hose at full pressure."

"In a week you'll be O.K."

"*Thank you*, Anna. That is the first kind word today."

But Anna was right, and soon Judith found herself actually enjoying arms drill, with its challenge to the sure eye and steady hand.

∾

One day Rose Fox, the psychologist, said to her:

"The Agency has told us to mount an operation. There is to be a large-scale landing — illegal — in ten days' time. They're asking for volunteers from several of these camps. I was wondering whether you would put your name down. I have. It will mean perhaps two nights on the beaches south of Haifa, and perhaps the danger of being shot at by the British. The boat is coming in from Salonika. At least — we hope it is. There will be a lot of children aboard. How do you feel?"

"I should like to be of use," said Judith slowly. "Yes, put my name down."

"Very well," said Rose, "I'll send it up to Aaron with my own. He is organizing it with the Central Committee."

Because she had arrived so recently, and presumably lacked experience, the committee were doubtful, but agreed to put her candidature to the vote. Sholem scratched his hairy ear and said in a growling voice:

"Well, Aaron, though you *are* the operational commander, it is, after all, the Committee that decides."

Surprisingly, Aaron stood up and set his jaw.

"The Committee will give me the opportunity of choosing my own troops from among the volunteers or else accept my resignation."

Peterson looked sardonically across the table, cocking her eyebrows.

"A declaration!" she muttered, and on her pad drew a heart with an arrow through it.

Aaron stood like a cornered bull with lowered crest.

"Well, shall I go or do I stay?" he said gruffly.

Sholem's face broke into a sudden grin. He rose, pulled in his drooping boy-scout belt around his sloppy waist and, putting his arm around Aaron, coaxingly said:

"Aber, habibi, mein kleiner Aaronchick, let us not quarrel. You will get your Miss Roth…"

It was Pete who later recounted the scene to Judith, who listened in incredulous silence. But as she went down the staircase and across to the children, she had a sudden new feeling of belonging and of pride. Astonishingly, she found herself humming a tune as she walked.

That evening she found herself among fifty or sixty others assembled in the gaunt refectory. She sat in the back, dressed as well as her humble wardrobe allowed, her hair neatly brushed back behind her pretty ears. She listened intently to Aaron giving a precise and detailed account of the operation he planned. He assigned roles to each group and he charged several individuals with precise responsibilities. It came to Judith's turn and he said in a terse, dry, parade-ground voice:

"You will be with me, Roth." She nodded solemnly.

"Yes, yes."

But under the cold, unflinching gaze of his eyes, she felt herself flush.

～

In the interim she worked hard, and learned a great deal about the life of the kibbutz. And for her, too, the rewards of leisure were sweet, as always to those who do hard physical labour.

She had discovered a shady spot up-river, where she could bathe naked. Here she spent some of her scant free time, feeling the sweet river water wash away not only the sweat and callouses, but something more important — the interior stresses and anxieties which were the legacy of her experiences. She had always adored swimming, and indeed swam like an otter, lightly and effortlessly. One day she saw, reflected in the swift-flowing but still green waters, the reflection of a mounted man riding along the bank towards her private nook. He rode lightly and easily on a white Arab and, as he turned his head, she saw that it was Aaron. She took refuge at once in the deepest part of the reeds, in order to let him pass. But he rode up to the tree apparently by design and, noting her clothes hanging from a willow twig, reined up and let his horse lower its head to drink, while he looked about him keenly.

"Miss Roth," he called in a hoarse voice, and she shrank back among the reeds. "Miss Roth!" After a moment she called back:

"What do you want?"

He smiled with relief.

"Oh, it is you. Good. I have a message for you. Liebling has sent the books for you. I also have a note for you from him which he asked me to deliver."

Judith bit her lip.

"Thank you," she said. "Could you please leave it with my things? I'm naked."

He looked surprised.

"Good Lord, I didn't understand. Sorry to embarrass you. I'll walk along the bank until you have dressed. I want a signature for the books."

Judith sighed. "Very well," she said. He dismounted and walked away along the bank, only to be riveted by her wail as she called out: "Oh! Your horse is eating my clothes."

The animal showed every disposition to do so, and he started to run back towards the tree — too late. The clothes had fallen into the swift-running river and gradually fanned out. "Damn!" she cried. Ineffectually he tried to reach them and then to poke them up with a stick. Further concealment was impossible if she were not to be forced to walk naked back to the kibbutz. In a couple of strokes she was in midstream and had retrieved them. She was furious.

"Wherever you turn up there is trouble!" she cried. "Why don't you go away?"

He was abashed and turned his back, saying, "I am dreadfully sorry."

"So you should be." She was struggling into her knickers in the water. "One can't even swim here without interruption."

He bit his lip but said nothing. He had grasped the bridle of his horse, which was showing some disposition to rear and kick. She crawled out of the water and donned her other bedraggled clothes in a silent fury.

"Now," she said, "What do you want me to do?"

"The note asks you to sign for the books and instruments. They belong to the University."

"Very well."

He turned to tender her a slip of paper and a card. Their eyes met, and irresistibly laughter sparked up in his, which she had difficulty not to echo.

"I really am dreadfully sorry," he said, but he was shaking with laughter now; for a moment she managed to remain icily cool and then she, too, could not resist.

"You look so funny and so beautiful," he said, roaring with laughter.

9

Operation "Welcome"

It was an autumn night of no moon when they arrived in different groups at the point of rendezvous on the coast. It was a lonely and desolate place, an area of shallow sand-dunes which supported little life beyond thorn scrub and tamarisk. The first premonitory lightening of the eastern sky had begun, though it would yet be two or three hours before sunrise. The sea was running relatively high, and the waves burst on the shallow sand to form great pools of phosphorescent bubbles which reflected back the stars. There was a wind blowing which chilled them as they crouched among the dunes.

Aaron cursed his inability to smoke. He himself had given the order, for they were only a few hundred yards away from the main road, and from time to time they could hear the rumble and whine as a British convoy passed on patrol. There was some anxiety as the ship was rather late, and Aaron expressed the fear that perhaps the British naval blockade had managed to intercept it. He stared at the phosphorescent hands of his watch and said grimly:

"I can't afford to give them more than another hour. It will be broad daylight soon." But, even as he spoke, Judith pointed out to sea, licking her salty lips, and said:

"What's that?" They stared, tense and expectant, while a frail light was born and gradually blossomed into a beam. Then it sparked four times and four times again, and the parties expelled their breaths in a hiss of relief.

"That's them," cried Sholem, so loud that Aaron had to call out in a terse whisper:

"Silence down there!"

A large patch of low-lying cloud on the horizon had prevented them from seeing the silhouette of the approaching ship, but now they caught sight of her as she turned beam on, and Aaron gave orders for the operation to start, answering signal for signal with his hand torch. For the next hour a frantic though purposeful activity reigned. Boats dotted the phosphorescent water and the lee of the ship. Voices called hoarsely in a number of languages and the reception party at the water's edge worked feverishly but methodically, like postal sorters on the day before Christmas. Bundles of clothes, medical equipment, false identity papers and packets of food had already been dragged into various positions on the dunes among the bushes, and people were directed to the point where they could be either treated for wounds, given first aid, or hot drinks after falling into the sea. Many individuals swam ashore and, later on, Judith heard that several had been drowned, though in the heat of operations she noticed nothing which suggested this.

The only untoward and gruesome side of the business which filled her with a wild exhilaration — because at last she was not afraid — was the sight of Sholem giving artificial respiration to a woman on the beach. She heard the rumble of lorries taking off with the first of the refugees and Aaron, who was everything and everywhere at once, seemed delighted with the progress of the disembarkation.

"With any luck, we'll have them all away before light," he said. "Judith, where are you?" he added. "Could you come with me quickly." He thrust a torch into her hand and led her down to where, among the dunes, there lay an emaciated young man, groaning.

"Give us some light," he said tersely. And in the puddle of yellow glow she saw him deftly slip up the trousers of the man to reveal a long, jagged splinter of wood buried in the thigh.

Aaron grunted and said: "Consider yourself lucky, if you'd had it through the belly…"

The wounded man groaned and said: "I'm sorry to be such a nuisance."

"*I'm* sorry," said Aaron. "I think that should come out. Do you mind?"

"Good God, no," said the man wanly, "I'm just furious to be such a burden at a time like this."

Aaron opened a first-aid kit and covered the contused area with yellow acroflavin, before taking a pair of surgical scissors and snipping the shallow groove of the splinter as one might open an envelope. Then, between finger and thumb, he jerked out the splinter and gazed at the blood that followed it, with a kind of detached curiosity. After a final disinfection of the wound, he set to work and bandaged it up while the young man said sleepily:

"That feels better already. I think perhaps it's the morphia that's beginning to work."

"You'll be alright," said Aaron laconically and, taking the torch from Judith, he turned it upon a nearby group of figures, calling softly: "Stretcher bearers."

To her surprise, Judith found herself standing with her hand in his. She did not stir nor did he make any gesture. They stood like this, pointing the torch on the sick man, until they saw him loaded onto the stretcher and carried away. Then Aaron abruptly dropped her hand and marched off towards the shore.

Now Judith had the chance for the first time of witnessing the different reactions of these arrivals. Some had thrown themselves on the ground, others were laughing and crying, others kissing the wet sand. Most of the refugees were wearing on their backs all the clothes they possessed, which gave them an unnatural walk like blown up balloons as they bobbed around towards the dunes, behind which they were being divided into groups, some of which were immediately pushed onto awaiting lorries and sent to different kibbutzim; others were led on foot to the nearest settlements. One girl she helped along the shore to the waiting doctor was yellow-haired and blue-eyed. Her delicate features were drawn and pale, her voice muted as she answered Judith's brief encouragements, in German monosyllables. Her name was Grete Schiller, she said, and Judith thought fleetingly how completely Aryan she looked — they were to become friends in an undemanding, non-intimate way, but neither of them suspected it at the time. There was too much to think about and to act upon… and so little time.

Aaron and his men were still going back and forth with the last immigrants, when suddenly, ominously, the buzzing of the helicopter and pencils of white light pierced the darkness and began to move laboriously like the feet of a daddy-long-legs along the beach. Almost at the same moment there came the boom of the ship's siren which made Aaron exclaim: "Oh, no, I hope that's the last of them. The ship's pulling out."

The relentless glare approached them and they instinctively threw themselves face down on the dunes. Judith found herself lying almost face to face with Aaron in this theatrical white light. "Don't move," he whispered but, as the light plunged them back into the darkness, she saw that he was smiling at her.

The helicopter now veered off out to sea, whence the hoot came, and left the prostrate group in darkness once more. Taken by surprise again, they used this opportunity of jumping to their feet and making for the waiting lorries, but not before turning towards the sea and seeing that the helicopter had picked up the stern of the ship.

Four miles to the east, the convoy of jeeps and lorries had been drawn up off the road among the olive trees, where the commanders and their troops were refreshing themselves with what the British Army knows as the "brew-up". The sun had already begun to etch into the mountains and leak into the plains behind them.

Major Lawton, the O.C. of the patrol, fingered the unshaven stubble of his jaw and debated whether to shave there and then or wait until his return to Jerusalem. The hot sweet tea was delicious in the chill of the early morning. Presently, however, he heard the sound of static from the command car and he saw the Signal Sergeant stiffen up, adjust his earphones and start "talking". Lawton turned to his companion, the youthful, elegant John Carstairs, who was sitting on the ground, smoking a cigar, and said:

"John, something is coming through. Probably from the shore patrol."

Instantly Carstairs was all action and crossed to the jeep, returning almost immediately with a signal pad. Lawton knitted his brows and studied the message. Then he banged his knee with the pad in exasperation, and handed it back to Carstairs, who chuckled as he read the message — "Well, what do you know?" — and proceeded to read in the mincing tones which naval officers of the old school allegedly affect:

"Large-scale illegal landing taking place on coast at two miles south of Rasmir, Hayson."

"How typical of the Navy," he said. "First they refuse to co-ordinate or let us know the movements... oh, I'm damned!" and he burst out into a laugh.

But if he seemed disposed to take the news humorously, the Commander did not. Lawton walked up and down with a black scowl on his face.

"This time," he said grimly to his junior, "I will really send a scorcher to Naval Command. You can start drafting it in your mind." Carstairs grinned irreverently and said: "Very good, Sir. Would you prefer prose or verse?"

"Don't fool, John," said Lawton sternly.

"Or perhaps in limerick form," said the young man thoughtfully.

But Lawton had already turned on his heel and was striding away towards his jeep. Carstairs followed him at a slower pace, murmuring:

"There once was a Naval O.C.

Who was rather afraid of the sea..."

He was interrupted by a shout: "John," and he immediately dropped his lackadaisical air, and hurried to Lawton's side, to gaze down with him at the map of the west coast. Lawton's pipe stem was already following the sinuous curves of the coast road. It came to rest tapping upon the name "Rasmir".

"I think we could do this in twenty minutes. We may not be too late yet, in spite of the bloody Navy."

He gave a quiet order which Carstairs transmitted instantly down the long line of vehicles, and with almost magical speed they pulled out from the orange grove and started racing along the road towards Rasmir.

Lawton's gloom and depression were in contrast to the light-hearted irreverence of his second-in-command:

"Why so pensive, *mon général*," Carstairs asked: "why so down-cast? This time the Navy is so plainly at fault... The army has not smirched its escutcheon on this job."

"I'm tired," said Lawton in a dry, weary voice. "I thought this was going to be quite a different sort of job. I did not think that I'd see regular troops-of-the-line used like policemen, simply because the Government is too mean to pay enough coppers. Moreover, it's going to get worse, you'll see, much worse."

Carstairs produced some toffees from his pocket. "Have a gob-stopper," he said. Lawton refused his kindly offer, but the driver of the jeep, as a junior N.C.O., was in no position to disobey orders when Carstairs forced one into his mouth as he drove.

"Thank you, Sir," he said indistinctly.

"Don't mention it," said Carstairs. "And don't let me hear you use the word 'underprivileged' again. The gob-stopper is a symbol of brotherhood."

"Yes, Sir," said the driver seriously. Carstairs pursued the matter further as they drove.

"They may not believe this down in the Sergeants' Mess," he said.

"No, Sir."

"Nevertheless, it is true."

"Very good, Sir."

They drove on happily sucking their sweets while, in the back of the jeep, the scowling Lawton brooded on the iniquities of the Navy. They swept down to the dunes where the landing had taken place and the familiar operation was signalled. Troops fanned out and scattered, while Lawton and Carstairs ran and scrambled towards the nearest high point on the dunes, from which they might train their binoculars on the country round about. Carstairs groaned.

"Too late, by God! Too late!" he cried theatrically. "But have a look down there on the beach, Sir!"

Lawton turned his gaze on the tell-tale marks of the illegal land-ing. Footprints led in all directions, and here and there were piles of personal belongings dropped in the confusion of the moment. An old sweater — bits of cardboard — a woman's shoe — a toy — a many-coloured scarf — soiled bandages — broken biscuits. But it was not only the beach that presented this picture of frantic disorder. A cluster of Carley floats and boats minus their floatings bobbed aimlessly in the shadows, some knocking against the rocks of a narrow spit.

"Hallo," said Carstairs suddenly: "What's that?" as he made off down the hill towards the rocks. "That" turned out to be a vulture which took off with a throaty chuckle as the young officer approached. As he came to the outcrop of rock, Carstairs saw the object of the bird's attentions — namely, a body which floated face downwards. The tell-tale prayer shawl round the shoulders spread out like white wings. Nearby floated the skull-cap. Carstairs turned and shouted sharply: "Sergeant — Sergeant Francis…" before dashing into the water himself to drag the body ashore.

Lawton, by this time, was making a methodical survey of the surrounding terrain with his binoculars. Suddenly, one of the men on the dunes called out to him: "Over there, Sir," pointing towards the west, and Lawton turned his glasses on an olive grove about a mile and a half away, from which the last immigrant convoy was setting forth. He ground his teeth with impotent fury, realizing how narrowly they had missed intercepting them, and was about to give orders for a detachment to comb the slopes at which he was gazing, when, as if by a miracle, a piece of vital information came his way.

Into the range of his binoculars, strayed a man and a woman whose gestures and stance carried a hint of vague familiarity. He held his breath in order to steady the glasses, for, at this extreme range, his very pulsebeats disturbed the field and gave a hazy dancing vibration to the distant figures. Then, for one long second, he succeeded in attaining the desired stillness of wrist, and the faces of Aaron and Peterson printed themselves on his vision.

"It can't be," he muttered to himself. And then, lowering his glasses, he was suddenly sure. "It is, it's them!"

All of a sudden he was a man transformed: he shouted to Carstairs, who was busy loading the corpse into a three-tonner, and his face was radiant.

"John," he cried. "They're heading for Ras Shamir!" Then, taking a whistle from his pocket, he blew two short blasts on it as a signal to the dispersed troopers to reform. By now the sun was warm on their shoulders as the convoy began to race back, retracing its steps in the direction of the kibbutz. The slow plume of dust ahead of them on the road only confirmed in Lawton's mind the suspicion that Ras Shamir would be hiding some, if not all, of the guilty immigrants. He obtained full confirmation of this when they reached the head of the pass and halted for a minute to allow him to get down and to have a further look with his binoculars. Ras Shamir was seething with activity like an ants' nest. Lorries were swerving into the perimeter and disgorging groups of figures which began to run and stumble in different directions.

Lawton's face grew tense and grim as he watched.

"Oh, dear," said the second-in-command, who was also interpreting the same scene through his glasses. "It looks as if we'll have to unstitch Ras Shamir once again."

The two men groaned in unison as they climbed back into the command jeep, and Carstairs pursued his melancholy reflections as they swept down the hill.

"It may interest you to know, Sir, that when I joined the army to fight Hitler, I felt sure that I'd be loved and wanted by the Jews forever after. All this has been a horrible shock to my nervous system."

"Oh, shut up," said Lawton furiously and his junior subsided into chastened silence, and contented himself by slowly selecting another sweet from the apparently endless supply in his pocket.

As they neared the kibbutz, taking the long straight road across the valley, they came upon the human roadblock which had been set up a hundred yards or so from the entry to the settlement to delay them until the immigrants were adequately dispersed and hidden by the inhabitants. Sixty or seventy elderly men, women of all ages and older children in rows five deep had taken up their position across the road, linking their folded arms in the fashion of police trying to contain a crowd. Their faces were bitter and determined. They did not flinch as the convoy moved down upon them, and as the jeep drew to a halt, almost touching the thighs of a bearded farmer, Lawton jumped out with Carstairs and scanned them with a coolly professional eye, looking for someone who might be spokesman for the kibbutzniks and with whom he might parley. As the troops debussed and formed up in ditches on either side of the road, ready to advance, there was a dead silence, ominous and heavy. As Lawton walked up and down the row of dramatic faces, it seemed as if he were inspecting a guard of honour. They regarded him curiously as he walked, apparently in deep thought, and the initial tension of their anger, since it had not been put to the test of battle, began to slacken, to become tinged with curiosity. The oppressive heavy silence continued, seeming immense and pregnant. Nobody moved, nobody stirred.

Lawton finished his quiet walk, up and down, and at last came to a familiar face standing in the middle of the front row. He walked up very close to Aaron, and the two men stood staring at each other. The one face set in an expression of grim insolence, the other hard, determined and yet at the same time with a hint of reserve.

"Stein," said Lawton at last. "I don't have to explain to you what we are doing here. It is rather for you to explain what all this means."

Aaron remained silent.

"It would seem from this demonstration that there is something to hide at Ras Shamir, something that you are afraid we will find out. As I saw you not long ago on the seacoast near Haifa, I can presume that it has something to do with illegal immigrants. Am I right?"

A chorus of gruff "No's" greeted him. Lawton said:

"I am sorry not to be able to believe you. You must let us through."

Instantly the whole line of faces kindled with resentment and determination. Lawton looked at them for a moment, then turned on his heel and walked back toward the first lorry in his convoy, calling:

"Sergeant Gregory, forward please."

As if to a pre-arranged plan, a stretcher borne by two soldiers came forward. On it they had laid the dead man plucked from the sea an hour before. In almost ritualistic fashion, Lawton and Carstairs formed up, one on either side of the body, and walked towards the roadblock, slowly, pensively almost. They set the stretcher down at Aaron's feet and Lawton said:

"You have five minutes to let us through, we don't wish to use force."

The diversion had, however, broken the psychological tension as well as the actual line. Aaron came forward and knelt on one knee to examine the face of the corpse. Others followed suit. And it was now that Lawton was able to give the signal to his troops to advance.

There was no resistance. In fact, both parties mingled now as they walked in open order towards the kibbutz perimeter, the British officers leading the way, the stretcher with the dead man on it being carried by his compatriots. Something of this changed atmosphere was visible also inside the perimeter, where the sight of the dead rabbi aroused the concern, pity and sadness of the women and children. Now Lawton took over.

His troops obeyed orders with a proficiency born of habit. The perimeter of the camp was picketed, and Aaron was told to assemble all the inhabitants in the car park. Meanwhile, the two ponderous and methodical sergeants set up trestle tables and chairs in the open air, at which they dispersed themselves as if for a court martial. Lawton sat in the centre with the two sergeants on his right and Carstairs on his left. But if the inhabitants of the kibbutz showed a sullen indignation, the children showed no fear of them. They raced in and out of the crowd, teasing the troops. Carstairs made a somewhat ineffectual gesture of friendship towards them by offering them a sweet, but the child that reached forward her hand to take it was suddenly snatched away by her father.

"Just as I thought," he said to Lawton. "The natives are somewhat hostile." Sergeant Francis, a grizzled father of six, cocked a disapproving eye in the direction of the children and said:

"It's dumb insolence, Sir, that's what it is."

Lawton looked around him with distaste and weariness, fully aware that this interrogation was only a sort of charade, and that unless the troops actually uncovered something of importance, such as arms, there would be no justification in civil law for penalizing the kibbutzniks. Nevertheless it had to be done.

"Check identities," he said shortly, and his troops moved the Israelis one by one to the trestle tables with their papers to identify them. Meanwhile, the two officers contented themselves with a cursory glimpse at the cards and a routine question ("Who are you?") which elicited a routine answer ("Ben Israeli" — son of Israel). This tiresome interrogation held no novelty for them and Carstairs, still sucking sweets, gazed with a sardonic indifference at the date of entry column on the card. He was not above trying a trick or two during the interrogation, at least in cases where obviously he was facing a very recent newcomer. He was not, for example, past asking what the mountain opposite the camp was called, and it was not everyone who could tell that it was Mount Tabor.

Meanwhile, the less agreeable task of house-to-house searching was going forward, also without result. There were a few anxious moments in the cellar, where the entrance to the secret armoury was almost discovered by a private, anxious to see whether the line of casks against the wall were empty or full. But here the native wit of a lance-corporal saved the day inadvertently.

"You only have to tap them," he said, "to know if they are full or empty." And so, in order to find out, they contented themselves with tapping on the casks and listening to the hollow empty sound they made.

One by one, the sergeants and their platoons drifted back to the officers with nothing to report, and still the long line of faces in front of the table under the weary eyes of Lawton continued.

Bill Ogilvie opened the door of a wooden barrack which was half hidden by leaning farm implements. Two privates waited for him outside. He entered the shack and, opening a second door, came upon a small group of about ten people ranging from the very old to the young. The atrocities of the concentration camp had left a marked imprint on all their features, as if all age, sex and individual differences had suddenly been melted into one unique mask — like a silent gathering of ghosts still hovering over a fresh memory of indescribable horrors.

Sergeant Ogilvie gazed at them in a long silence, then, turning his back and going outside, told the two soldiers that there was no need for a closer inspection, they could go on to the next hut.

A little boy sneaked up under the table to play with Lawton's gaiters and pulled at his polished stick.

Lawton bent down to see the child grinning at him and, without being asked, the boy challengingly shouted the ritual words: "Ben Israeli."

At last Aaron, too, stood before him with an expression of insolent triumph on his face. Lawton tapped on the table with his pencil and looked curiously, almost pensively, at him.

"Stein," he said. "There are at least eight identity cards which look suspicious. I don't want to use a ruder word, but I have taken the names of the people involved and I'll have them checked on."

Aaron's expression showed clearly that he recognized this as a bluff.

"By all means," he said. "You are only obeying orders, after all."

Lawton added a trifle more grimly: "And if they prove to be faked, they will have to be deported to Cyprus. I'm telling you this because I know you are on the Central Committee. I hope you will repeat it to them."

"May I have a list of the names?" said Aaron.

"I'm afraid not," said Lawton. "It's confidential. You may go, Stein."

Aaron walked back to the crowd, muttering: "Trying to get us worried."

And now it was the turn of Grete. The four pairs of blue eyes regarded her with a certain diffident admiration. Her blonde beauty of face and feature was striking in the surrounding darkness. The coloured kerchief around her head only set off to advantage the slender magnificence of her profile and the luminous beauty of her eyes. Sergeant Francis could have kicked himself for discovering that her identity card was so obviously a fake. Her own picture had been glued over that of some previous owner, and it had worked its way loose. He lifted the corner with his fingernail, where the glue had become unstuck, to reveal a passport picture of a bearded youth. He swallowed audibly and said to Lawton:

"You had better look at this, Sir."

Lawton looked at the girl for a moment, leaving the document on the desk before him.

"Name?" he asked. And she told him her name in a pleasant low voice. "Grete Schiller." For some reason, her composure irritated him, and it was with a curl of his lip, almost a sneer, that he said:

"There's no need to ask *you* a routine question. It is obvious you're Ben Israeli too."

Her retort came instantly: "As a matter of fact, I'm not. I'm an illegal immigrant. My paper is forged. And if it's so obvious why are you wasting my time?"

This sudden and unexpected deviation from normal routine caused astonishment and dismay; astonishment on the faces of the British interrogators, and dismay on the faces of her compatriots.

"Has she gone mad?" said Aaron in a loud whisper to Sholem.

Carstairs stopped sucking his sweet, and repressed a chuckle. He scratched his nose and looked sideways at Lawton, whose discomfiture was obvious.

The Major ground his teeth and said: "I'm doing my duty, and as for you, young lady, you had better be more careful in what you have to tell me, or else... I could have you deported to Cyprus, you know."

"I'm not afraid of this petty bullying," she said scornfully. "We are all completely in your power. And you talk of duty and how much longer is this idiotic interrogation going to last. You've paralyzed the life of the camp, the children haven't been fed, we are short of running water and all we hear about is your duty. Duty is all very well, but what about conscience?"

"Conscience?" said Lawton, setting his jaw grimly and out-staring her. "I wonder how many of you would be here if we had no conscience!"

She stared furiously at him but did not speak. Lawton took up the identity card, glanced at the photograph and handed it back to her. "You may go," he said coldly and, in the same breath, curtly gave the order to terminate the operation. Then he called over his shoulder to Grete.

"Miss Schiller," he said, "I think you look much nicer in the beard," and, turning on his heel, strode out through the perimeter to the waiting jeep.

"If you want my opinion, Sir," said Carstairs.

"I don't," said Lawton.

"Well, I'll give it to you anyway, Sir. I think we've lowered our moral standards by not arresting her. It's seldom one has a chance to arrest so pretty a girl. Here we are now, doomed to wenchlessness all the way to Jerusalem."

But Lawton was in no mood for banter. He turned up the car radio full blast and the strains of "Lili Marlene" enveloped them.

10

The Cipher

Judith took Pete at her word and, claiming her papers, set off with the flock of sheep, having been formally confided to the care of old Karam, the Yemeni shepherd, and his two small grinning sons. Karam was a story-teller, a fortune-teller and a singer of old songs. He had a splendid great winged moustache and a small brass flute. They followed the flocks slowly along the verdant meadows and into the shadowy defile from which the river emerged. The pasture was rich hereabouts, and there were shady trees in the shadow of the cliffs. The pleasant noise of rushing water punctuated the silence and the shrill voices of the two boys who clambered about as active as goats. Somewhere up the mountain, invisible to them, there were Arab sharpshooters guarding the unmarked border. More than once they had been shot at, while the boys were always scaling the cliffs, much to the annoyance of the old man, who was always afraid that one of them, or both, might be shot by the sentinels on the Syrian side. But it was hopeless to try and control them; besides, once Ali had come slipping and slithering down the ravine among the loose stones with bullets chipping off flakes of rock all round him. He was bursting with laughter as he gained the shadow of the cliffs again. He had been snooping in the Arab camp and had even stolen a dagger which, still bursting with laughter, he threw in his father's lap. Apparently, immediately behind the ramparts of stone, the desert began, and here lay an Arab force of some size, belonging to the tribe whose chief was Prince Daud, and whose advisers were rumoured to be British. It was hard to imagine this abrupt change from the desert to the encampment when one looked across this verdant and peaceful valley.

Midway up the cliffs were a number of gloomy-looking caves, which Karam very firmly declared out of bounds to them all; they were called the Whistling Caves by the Arabs, he said, and they were full of djinns which haunted them. While he himself was no Muslim, it was clear that he was quite superstitious, as befitted a star-gazer and teller of fortunes. He told Judith that there was a dark man in her life and the information amused her; pretty soon this man was going to threaten her. Later still he was going to die or be very badly hurt, Karam could not see which as yet. Or else, triumph over his enemies… Judith was a thorough-going sceptic and paid no attention to these sallies. But she worked and rested, and began to adore these apparently lazy days spent by the water. Then, one day, old Karam was unwell and the sheep went out with only the two boys for shepherds; as usual they wandered off on some expedition — it was to try and get a golden eagle nestling from the crags — and she was left alone. Some little flutter of emotion dispersed the sheep and two of the small lambs, much to Judith's horror, made a bee-line for the Whistling Caves. She called for the boys, but they were nowhere to be seen. There seemed to be nothing for it but to follow them and try to drive them back. It was with trepidation that she entered the gloomy corridors of the first cave, in which she could hear the frightened bleating. She entered hesitantly, calling to them. She had hardly gone ten paces when a hand closed over her mouth and she felt a pistol pressed into her back. Terror rendered her speechless — had she been in a position to speak. She was turned round by strong hands and a torch was flashed in her face. Then she was released and found herself confronting a very angry though familiar figure. It was Aaron. He was in a towering rage.

"Fool. You have probably given away my position, wandering

around with your blasted sheep. Why can't you do as you're told and keep them down by the river?"

A mixture of rage, fright and a sense of injustice brought her very close to tears. Besides, his grip had bruised her. She flew out at him:

"You have no right to treat me like that. To speak to me like that."

Aaron said grimly: "I have. I am supposed to be in military command of this valley. Look."

In the light of his torch she saw the reason for his concern, for a man sat bowed over a wireless set, jotting furiously on a pad. She heard the tittering of static which satisfactorily explained the djinns which haunted this forward observation post. She apologized, and his temper cooled.

"I am sorry too," he said coldly, "but you can't leave this cave until dusk. I'll arrange to get the sheep back to the shepherd. You had better sit down somewhere."

She did as she was told, and sat down on the cold rock. The operator worked furiously for a while and then took off his earphones. He handed across a sheaf of paper covered in block capitals and Aaron groaned. He sat down and clasped his head; then catching her eye, he smiled ruefully.

"We have been listening in to the British talking to their mission. Vital information. But now we are really stuck. With the new military mission they've changed code and we can't break it — even Jerusalem is stumped. We are getting pages and pages of gibberish. And it might be of vital interest. They were talking of giving Daud armoured cars..."

His despair made him for a moment seem almost sympathetic. She saw the long ribbon of paper hanging from his fingers and said:

"Can I see?"

He handed it to her without a word, and lit a cigarette. She gazed at the long lines of capitals. She said:

"Would you let me have a big piece of this? I might be able to do something."

Aaron blew a dispirited streamer of smoke in the air, and said with contempt:

"What do you think you could do?"

Judith felt the sting of his manner.

"Perhaps nothing, but I could try."

In her mind she was already turning up the laws of recurrence and probability, like a spade turning up earth.

"At any rate, nothing would be lost," she said, almost humbly. "I could leave these for you in Pete's safe. Tomorrow."

Aaron sighed once more.

"If you wish," he said with indifference.

When dusk fell he allowed her to leave the cave and descend to the river-bank. The rest of the sheep had already started for home with the two boys. She could hear their shrill shouts. Aaron stopped and said:

"Whatever you do, don't repeat this little excursion, or you are likely to get shot. And keep it secret."

Then he turned on his heel and strode off. She swore with rage under her breath:

"The bloody self-importance of men!" she said; but then, looking at the papers she had been loaned, her lips set in a grim line. She stayed up until after midnight that night, covering sheaves of paper with calculations until a smile of triumph dawned, for the code yielded. This was to be her answer to the self-important young man. She copied out the scheme neatly in an exercise book, bundled the papers together and turned in. The next morning she gave them to Pete. She explained what they were and spent a quiet morning by the river with her own work. Towards noon, she saw Aaron coming along the river-bank with great excited strides. She watched him with a cool contempt. He was ugly, she thought, and his self-possession had a disagreeable habit of foundering under rebuke, so that he looked like a chastised puppy. He stood before her at last, with his hands outspread apologetically, but smiling.

"Well," she said at last, "what do you want?" Aaron said:

"I came to apologize and to thank you."

She looked at him seriously for a moment. Then:

"I accept both." She grinned.

"I have never been more surprised," he added.

"You don't think much of women's brains?" she asked ironically.

"Most women have none. Admit it."

"Have most men?"

"Of course, and am I not among the have-nots myself?"

"You are very modest today."

"I am very grateful indeed."

He turned abruptly and started to go away. Then a thought struck him and he came striding back.

"Do you ride?"

"I have ridden," she said.

"Do you like it?"

"I used to."

He frowned in thought for a moment and then said, with a touch of hesitation:

"Would you ride with me this afternoon? I have to go up to the other end of the valley — couple of hours…"

"With pleasure," she said.

"Good," he said softly. "Good."

So it was that she found herself mounted on a fleet white Arab horse, galloping across the greensward of the upper valley with Aaron beside her on his own. They crossed the maze of green rides and climbed to where the silver olive trees began to grow more dense. Here there was a deserted shack of boards in an untended garden, where he dismounted to gather wild flowers.

"This is my country house," he said with mock pride. "My grandfather built it and lived here for many years. It belongs to me."

"It is beautiful," she said.

"When I think of all the work I put into this garden," he went on ruefully, "as a child. Look at the damn place now. Nothing but weeds."

"It smells of thyme."

She rolled over luxuriously in the sunlight and pillowed her head, chewing a blade of grass. He looked at his watch.

"Another five minutes," he said, and frowned. She groaned.

"Really so soon?"

Aaron sat with his arms round his knees, head bent in thought.

"There's always too much to do," he said, "especially for a general without an army — or rather with an army I shall have to borrow."

"Why don't you come and live here?"

"If ever I marry I shall." He laughed. "*Après la guerre.*"

"If there is any *après* about it."

He lit a cigarette.

"It will end this year or next, I'm sure. But then we shall have to face the music here unless I am mistaken. Somehow we must get Israel born."

"Haven't you had enough of this war?"

"Yes."

"So have I. Too much. Can't we think about peace a little? I have so much work to do as yet..."

"That is just the point," he said angrily — almost angrily. "You don't really believe us when you hear our plans for a free Israel."

"It sounds so problematical. You are so weak. The British are strong, and with their oil interests to worry about..."

"You will see," he said.

"I hope you are right."

"Israel *must* get itself born — it must."

They rode back in silence to the kibbutz. As he reached her down from the saddle he stood for a brief moment with his hands on her shoulders, looking deeply into her eyes.

"Thank you, Judith," he said softly. "It was a memorable day for me."

Then, as if of a sudden abashed by his own frankness, he stepped back a pace and added:

"And it was particularly splendid, as I am leaving tonight."

To her own intense surprise she felt a sudden pang, like a pain; it was as if she had allowed the thought of him to lie neglected and unevaluated in a corner of her mind. It had somehow never occurred to her that he might go away. But why, she asked herself, should such a notion surprise, almost shock her? Aaron was nothing to her. She had come to accept him as part of the landscape, as part of the furniture of her new life here in the kibbutz. To her own amazement, and indeed vexation, she felt herself turn pale, and her voice when she spoke was very far from calm.

"For good?" she said, astonished that the very phrase should weigh so heavily on her tongue.

"For at least a year," he said. "I have to go south on an Army course. Sometime I'll be posted back, I suppose, since I belong to this valley, but... I can't say when at all. I wanted to go and say goodbye to my country house today. That is why I was so pleased you let me show it to you."

"Oh, Aaron," she said, still struggling with this new unfamiliar sense of disappointment, "I wish I had known!"

"It was perfect," he said. "Goodbye."

He climbed into the saddle and grabbed the reins of the second horse. She stood irresolutely before him as he smiled down upon her. Then, as he turned his horse, she cried, "Good luck!"

But he was trotting away from her and without a single backward glance.

That evening she worked late on the papers which the Professor had left her; light was slowly beginning to dawn on her as the tangle of formulae gradually began to take coherent shape under her swift pencil. The kibbutz was silent and everybody was long in bed. She worked now in the deserted school-room. It was pleasant and cool with its deep hedges and green outside. As she worked, she heard the soft sound of footsteps on the gravel path outside. Something flew through the open window like a moth and fell with a soft plop upon her papers. It was a white rose.

But by the time she reached the door and opened it there was nobody to be seen on the dark path outside.

11

Grete

There were other things too, to keep her constantly interested and active, not least the observation of the camp's inhabitants, their reactions to the life which, for so many of them, was utterly new and not always entirely pleasant. Despite the comparative bliss of freedom from torture and suffering, few were able to adapt themselves at once to the curious atmosphere of discipline without unkindness, ample food without luxury and, above all, the integration into group-life which only boarding-school children normally know, and soon forget when they leave. Some felt uneasy and slightly on the defensive, as if there was some catch in the whole thing. The blonde girl, Grete, who had so startled them by her scornful declaration of illegal entry, was one of these. Though they never became close friends, her life and Judith's in the kibbutz ran along fairly parallel lines, and, perhaps because they were so different from each other, a certain liking sprang up between them, and they often talked for a while during their free periods. There was something in the dark, serious eyes of Judith which attracted confidences, and Grete found herself telling her of her experiences only a few days after her arrival on the dark beach.

"When we reached the kibbutz," she said, "I was handed over to a very ugly girl with spots who seemed to be one of the duty nurses. But I don't know now: everyone seems to take turns at doing everything. She was brusque and it made me feel rather weepy. She told me to wait for the doctor, and took down my particulars. Horrid performance. Name, age, profession. I nearly fainted, but she gave me some water, and that awfully nice woman doctor came in. She was much more helpful. She had my dossier, from the Agency, and she was sympathetic. The wretched nurse-girl took me to the showers and gave me a hot drink and a sedative. Funny — while she read my dossier she said — the doctor, I mean — 'You've had quite a time haven't you?' It seemed such an understatement! When they were unpacking my small bag, they found my child's photograph. I don't know what got into me. When the doctor handed it to me, saying she thought he had my eyes, I went berserk and tore it up. She didn't say a thing for a moment, and then just 'Tell me.' I did, I filled up the gaps in the dossier, without a murmur. At least she already knew where I had spent the last eighteen months — I didn't have to go into that."

"Where?" asked Judith simply. Her large eyes were kind and not curious, and Grete told her the rest. About the officers' brothel and, before that, about her marriage to the Nazi Colonel of impeccable Aryan descent. "When Hitler came to power the party learned that I was a Jew, and faced him with the choice of surrendering his position or his wife. That was how I found myself in Auschwitz. For ages I believed that my son had suffered the same fate. My husband, whom I have never seen since, was posted to the Russian front. For all I knew, he was dead. But a year ago I met a man who knew him, and he repeated a conversation with my husband which suggested that the child might still be alive, with foster parents in some neutral country. But I don't know where — I don't know where."

Judith nodded in silence.

"I told the doctor of my confusion of mind. Perhaps you can understand. I should love nothing better than to find him again, and yet, with half my mind, I do not want to find him because… well, you know why!"

She stretched out her arm, bared it and lifted it up to Judith's face. On the smooth flesh, a neat seven-digit figure in blue was printed gro tesquely along the arm, next to another shorter row of figures with a perfectly straight line through them.

"She said she understood," went on Grete, "but that time would change it. That what I needed now, and what they could give me, was hard work here in Ras Shamir, manual labour. I nearly laughed."

The two young women looked across the river to where a group of girls was busy washing clothes in the clear water and hanging them up on the bushes. As they thumped the clothes on the flat rocks, they sang *Ushavtem mayim besason*, their voices sounding gay and innocent over the murmur of the stream.

"Can you follow the words?" asked Judith.

"More or less. 'You will draw water with exultation'?"

"And then?" asked Judith.

"Well, then I met Pete. She knows all about everyone and everything, I think. All about me, certainly. We walked through the kibbutz in the shade of the willow trees. There were roses and sprinklers and it felt rather unreal. We came to the place where they park the tractors, and there were a few new machines. There was a young man — David — the second in command — you know him? Yes, well he was servicing them. He showed them to Pete with enormous pride. And then he said he was glad to see me looking alive. He said I looked quite dead when we arrived — strange that he should notice, don't you think?"

"Very," said Judith with a straight face.

"Well, then he turned to Miss Peterson and reminded her of the small arms drill. And he told me to report at the armoury in the morning. Just like that."

"I know," said Judith sympathetically. "Ugh!"

Grete told her how Anna had suddenly bandaged her eyes and walked her blindfold to a staircase which led deep underground. She had said, "We have one of the largest and most skillfully concealed armouries of all the Palestine kibbutzim — even a small arms range. The fewer people who know where it is and how to get there, the better." Then, after a sound of closing doors and some heavy pushing and shoving, her bandage was whipped off and she found herself face to face with David. The armoury was a strange subterranean building with enormous vaulted bays, which showed a tremendous wall thickness like the crypt of a medieval cathedral. The walls were damp and covered in a soft cocoon of verdigris, such as one might see in a choice wine-cellar in France. Long racks of weapons stood against the side walls and a dozen girls were busy oiling and proving them. The extent of this building was immense, and at the far end there was a miniature range perfectly adequate for small arms and tommy-gun practice.

"Come along," said David, "and try your hand. There are no prizes, I'm afraid."

She wondered how the infernal racket of rifles was not audible outside and, as if he had read her thoughts, David said: "Partly because we're deep in the ground, and partly because of the thick walls. During the last arms search we carried on throughout down here and if they heard anything they might have thought it was a couple of typewriters." He seemed to say more, but at that moment a burst of gunfire broke out at the end, and the cloth and cardboard dummies wavered and danced grotesquely under the hail of shot, like wet shirts hanging on the line in a high wind. David motioned her forward and Grete obediently took her place in a line of girls. He brought her a Sten gun and said: "Before I break it down, I'd like you to try it for weight and for kick. Take a shot at those targets."

"I started trembling violently. The targets had turned into the frightened and bewildered faces of Jewish families standing in the snowlit square of a German town, hands above their heads, waiting to receive the sweep of steel bullets across their chests. I threw down the weapon with a cry and, putting my hands over my ears, I ran in a blundering attempt to find the way out. David watched me for a moment in surprise, and then in apparent pity. I suppose I was rather like a wild animal in a trap, yelling 'Let me out! let me out! I want to *go*!'"

Judith remembered her own first experience of arms drill at the kibbutz, and mentally compared her own irritation and frustration to the other girl's terror. Neurotic, she thought, but thought it kindly. She nodded as Grete continued her story. David had come towards her with outstretched arms, saying, "Calm yourself, please..." but she had run round the walls, from point to point, bay to bay, as he followed her, speaking in a cajoling voice. When she could go no further, and he had her cornered in an archway, he put his hand on her arm. "Listen,

Grete," he said, "if we are attacked here, there is nowhere to go except into the sea. There is no choice. We must learn to defend ourselves."

But with quivering lips and pale face she repeated, almost beseechingly:

"I can't do it! Don't you see, I can't do it! I have seen so much of it. Don't make me!"

Then he made the mistake of saying:

"Lives were risked to bring you here. Doesn't the existence of Israel matter to you?"

"Nothing matters to me!" she screamed. "Please let me go."

"Very well," he said coldly. "Anna, bring the bandage." He motioned Grete gently forward and tied the bandage round her eyes. "I'll send you back to your room," he said softly, but there was a deep note of disdain and chagrin in his voice.

She turned her pale face to him and said:

"Listen, I'm sorry if I..." but he cut her sentence short abruptly, saying:

"There is no need to be sorry. You're clearly a very egotistical person, and we don't want people like you. Ours is a voluntary organization, so please don't imagine that I'm going to press-gang you. Anna, take her."

And as he turned away, she heard him call:

"Cross Grete Schiller's name off the roster."

It seemed like a black mark against her, and she bit her lip furiously and said nothing.

A few minutes later, she found herself standing on the river bank by herself. The figure of Anna, foreshortened by distance, stumped off into the surrounding field. Grete made a half-gesture, as if to restrain her or to call her back. Then, a sudden impulse overtook her. She turned and ran towards the administrative building where Peterson sat doing accounts. Grete burst in on her breathlessly.

"Pete," she cried, "I'm no good, I'm no use to you at all. You must send me away somewhere. I shall only disgrace myself and prove my uselessness if I stay. Already they are beginning to hate me."

"Pull up that chair," said Peterson sternly, after a pause. She pushed a box of cigarettes across the table. Grete refused. She burst out vehemently:

"Oh, I wish it was different! Perhaps I am an egotist, perhaps that's what it is! David is probably right."

"Of course he's right! You couldn't be a woman without being an egotist, any more than you could be a man and not be an opinionated ass. David's a fool. What's he been saying to you?"

Grete shook her head. "No, he's right," she said. "I care nothing for Palestine. It means nothing to me. All I care about is to see my child again."

A girl came in and brought cups of tea. "Drink this," said Peterson and, taking a little tube of pills from an attaché case beside the desk, she dropped a couple into Grete's cup.

Peterson stared at her for a long time without saying anything. Then she said:

"Of course I can send you away, and perhaps I shall have to. We can't carry too many pairs of idle hands and large appetites around here. We already have a share of old people whom we look after and who contribute nothing to the work."

"I'm ashamed of myself," murmured Grete.

"*That*," said Peterson, "is the final egotism. I'm going to give you one more chance before sending you away. If you can't get on with the grown-ups, we'll see if you can help with the children. How do you feel about that?"

Grete stood up and said: "Thank you, I will try again."

"Good. Then you can take night duty, tonight," Peterson said. "I'll have you called."

As Grete turned to the door, Peterson added:

"Grete, the worst of all our weaknesses is self-pity."

Grete turned to her and replied:

"I see, you are beginning to hate me too."

"On the contrary," said Peterson. "You can count on me."

But Grete shook her head sadly, and went down the staircase in a deep despondency, head bowed. Halfway down, she met David coming up. He hesitated and opened his mouth as if he were about to say something, then changed his mind. He looked away, and passed her without a word.

He found Peterson standing at the window and smoking. She did not turn round when he came in.

"Pete," he said, "we've done our shoot, but I've had to cross that wretched Schiller girl off the roster. She's an uncooperative prig and a true-blue hysteric. It is infuriating that she is as attractive as she is."

"She also happens to have spent her last eighteen months in a German officers' brothel." She turned and faced him, and they stood staring at each other for a long time without saying any more.

Peterson was as good as her word, and that evening Rose Fox came over to Grete's table at dinner.

"I hear they've posted you to night work with the children. I'm glad and I hope you are too. There is a lot to observe and a lot of them who are sympathy-starved." Her own two boys were among the inhabitants of the children's camp. Grete liked her immediately, and together the two young women finished their dinner, gossiping lightly before traversing the gardens which the children themselves had planted and were working, as part of their education.

"Here," said Rose, "the future farmers of the settlement are making their first experiments with flowers and vegetables. As you see, some are lazier than others. But no one could accuse David's son of laziness."

"David's?" asked Grete with surprise.

"You know David," said the girl Rose. "David Eveh…"

"I had no id… idea…" stammered Grete, "that he had a… child."

"Well, all these trees are his work," said Rose, pointing to a clump of eight young peach trees.

Rose whispered about the sleeping children; they came to a cubicle with four beds in it. The psychologist pointed a finger and whispered to Grete:

"That's David's son." An exceptionally handsome boy about eleven or twelve years old, bearing a marked resemblance to David, lay asleep. One hand protruded slightly from under the pillow. It held an imitation pistol of wood. The doctor quietly removed it and put it on the shelf.

"Like father like son," she said, and added: "Now I'm going to leave you. Call me if there's any need. This bell rings above my bed."

But neither that night nor on the succeeding nights of that week did it prove necessary. For the first time, Grete began to feel that she had found a sphere in which her efforts could prove useful. The work was not only rewarding from the point of view of psychological interest, but because the hours were long and her duties tired her sufficiently in order for her to sleep well.

The children were very various in background and education and temperament. They were treated already as budding farmers and, apart from tending their personal cottage gardens with a fervour bordering on religiosity, they played quite a part in the adult settlement. They sometimes stood in for old Karam, the shepherd from Yemen, and grazed the settlement flocks on the rich water meadows by the border. They harvested the apples and the potatoes with the grown-ups. All this activity was quite apart from their regular school hours, and Grete played a role in most of these activities with them. Though the night duties appealed to her most because of the silence, and the time to reflect, in the practical field she found she had a lot to learn from the children themselves. They proved kindly and spirited instructors. They treated her a little patronizingly, and at the same time took an almost paternal pride in her achievements through their teaching. Paul, David's son, a mischievous good-looking small version of his father, a self-appointed teacher in matters military and agricultural when it came to showing off either to her or to her charges, found her one day digging in the vegetable patch. He approached her nonchalantly, his wooden pistol tucked in his Arab belt and his American tee-shirt emblazoned by a sheriff's star.

"What's wrong?" he asked, seeing her standing with both hands on her haunches, massaging them ferociously with an exasperation bordering on tears. She had never had to contend with an ordinary pitchfork before, and the experience was a bitter one. "Broken your spine again?"

"Just about," said Grete angrily. "This is real work, Paul!"

"Of course it is."

"Yet you kids manage. How is it?"

"Technique," he casually said, imitating a grown-up. "You are wasting your energy and working the wrong way. You look as if you were going to play golf."

"No," she said half-humbly, "*that* I could probably teach *you.*"

"Everything has its technique." He used the word "technique", which he had lately picked up, as often as he could get it in.

"Well, show me again."

"All right."

In his good-natured, enthusiastic way, he showed her and then thrust the tool into her hand with his grubby paws and said:

"Now let's see you try."

Laboriously she followed his example. "Better," he remarked after a critical pause. "I reckon in about ten years we shall be able to trust you with the middens."

But though, superficially, she was leading an idyllic pastoral existence, her period at Ras Shamir was not to end before she had come up against some dangers as well.

One day, while the children were looking after Karam's sheep on the river bank, they strayed up rather too far and, all of a sudden, out of a clear sky, they saw the Jordan water being threshed by bullets and heard the crisp rattle of machine guns. The flock scattered, and Grete managed to get the children into a bunch and race them to the shelter of an overhanging rock where they took refuge, both excited and a little shaken. The machine-gun fire had alerted some of the tractor drivers, and they saw two tractors racing towards them, one driven by a man and one by a girl. Both were armed with Sten guns and kept up an answering volley in the direction of the target which, from her own position, Grete could not see. The panic-stricken flock of sheep had made off towards the kibbutz, but it had left a lamb kicking and moaning on the grass, and this sight was too much for Paul, who dashed out of cover and brought it back. He acted so swiftly that Grete was not able to restrain him, and it was lucky that the child was not hit.

By now the tractors were approaching, and while the girl on the one vehicle turned eastward towards the frontier, still firing, the second tractor stopped and Grete saw that the driver was David. He ran with great strides across the intervening field, calling out anxiously whether anything or anyone had been hit. Luckily the only victim was the lamb, which was still alive but bleeding profusely. Grete held it in her lap and David knelt down to examine it in his swift authoritative way.

"We'd better take it back to Naomi," she said. But he shook his head. "It's too far gone," he replied. "I'd better put it out of its pain."

Swift as a thought, without waiting for anything further, he picked it up in his arms, took ten long paces away from them, and, placing it on the ground, shot it through the head. It quivered and lay still. He came back to the horrified group of children who surrounded her in her now bloodstained skirt, and said with a smile:

"We're lucky. It could have turned out much worse." He then listened with his head on one side like a dog. The firing had stopped.

"Stay here five minutes more and then return as fast as you can with the children." And then, turning to Grete, he said: "You carry back the body. I'm going up to the border to see if we need any covering fire." Without waiting for any reply from them, he ran with great loping strides back to his tractor and set it into gear with a roar.

Grete obeyed orders, and in five minutes the party set off with all speed for the kibbutz, Grete holding the still-warm and bleeding body of the lamb in her outstretched arms. She walked in a kind of speechless daze, and when one of the smaller children asked: "Isn't David brave?" she only managed a nod, though she saw his son's eyes kindle with pride.

At long last they got back to the camp, and Grete surrendered the lamb to the kitchens and the children to the school-room. For her part she still felt numb and a trifle dazed. She went down to the river instead of going to the room to change her clothes and, kneeling, washed the blood off her hands and from her frock, gazing as she did so at the pale white face which stared back at her from the water.

She was kneeling thus when she heard the rumble of a tractor and on the opposite side of the river she saw David riding into camp. He stopped the tractor opposite her and turned off the engine. She paid no attention but went on scrubbing the hem of her dress, sitting there like a mute child under strict orders to finish her task. There was a long silence during which she was conscious of his eyes upon her.

"Grete, you are very beautiful… I came to thank you."

Receiving no response, he leaped back into the bucket seat of his tractor and switched the engine on with a roar. He disappeared without looking back and left her there, gazing at her own pale features rippling in the water.

Listlessly, heavily, she pondered as she stared, wondering what the word could now mean, if anything. She turned it over awkwardly in her mind and even repeated it aloud in a sardonic voice as she looked into her own floating eyes:

"Beauty!"

12

David and Grete

Now the work of the kibbutz engulfed her, and she found herself enjoying its strict routines; even its privations were welcome. The fact
that she had acquitted herself honourably, if recklessly, after the illegal
landing, gave her a new measure of self-esteem and confidence. David
made no new move towards her, but she could not help thinking about
him with anxiety. The old nightmare of the past had not been excised,
and she thought herself to be a woman whose emotions were prema-
turely exhausted, a woman incapable of love.

A sudden twist in events disabused her of this idea, and replaced
it by an even more alarming one, namely: that she had no right to
meddle with the affections of David. It came about in the following
manner — preceded by an hysterical attack as unexpected as it was
unwelcome.

One of the smallest of the children fell out of an apple tree and
hurt itself. This type of incident was common enough, and her reaction seemed out of all proportion to its seriousness. Or was it simply
the desperate screaming of the word "Mother!" (Hebrew: "Imma!"). At
any rate, Grete took the sobbing child in her arms and found herself
cradling it, to still its crying, murmuring as she did so her old German

nurse's lullaby, the words of which she had last recalled singing to sleep her own child: "Schlafe süss…" Gradually, as she cradled the child, the swinging movements became mechanical. Her mind seemed to have left her with her feelings alone. The child was quiet now, gazing at her curiously. She stared open-eyed into the void with unfocussed eyes. She continued like a monomaniac, rocking and staring, rocking and staring. The child in her arms suddenly took fright, aware in an obscure way of something abnormal in her behaviour, and started to scream out in terror. Instantly, the fear was communicated to the other children around her, and the panic spread. Some babies began to cry too.

There is no knowing how long Grete would have gone on, fixed in this posture of mad concentration. She suddenly felt the hand of Rose on her shoulder, and heard the firm voice admonishing her. Rose gently released the child and took Grete's arm:

"Come along," she said softly, under her breath, and Grete obeyed like a sleepwalker. Once in her room, however, she broke down and lay on her bed, crying convulsively. Rose watched her compassionately for a moment or two, and then forced her to take a tranquillizer.

"I'll go and tell Pete."

But in fact it was not Peterson who next appeared beside her bed, but David himself. Unbelievably, she heard the concern in his deep voice as he came to the side of her bed.

"For God's sake, Grete, what is it?"

She glanced wildly at him, and then turned her face to the wall, ashamed that he should see her at a disadvantage, weeping. He knelt down beside the bed, quietly and purposefully put a hand upon her shoulder, turning her towards him. He spoke now in a whisper:

"My goodness, how little you understand," he said. "Grete, Grete, wake up," and he shook her softly, like a doll.

She gazed at him with a wild beseeching fear in her eyes.

"Please go away," she said, but his only answer was to draw her towards him, and start stroking her, as if to soothe her. Somehow a barrier had been crossed. She lay in his arms without defence, helpless, broken and incapable of response. For his part he was astonished by the depth of misery and confusion into which she was plunged. He stared into her wide eyes and whispered once more:

"What is it?"

"Don't you pity me!" she cried out, pushing him from her.

"I'm not, you fool!" he almost shouted, shaking her with both arms and pinning her down. She did not move, but still stared at him as if she were trying to drag every shred of meaning from his face. Then, with a sudden low moan, she pressed her mouth to his, kissing him almost brutally, as if each kiss were a stab wound delivered or received.

The act of becoming lovers, the thought of which had so terrified her, was quite different from anything she could have imagined. All the pangs of conscience, all the confusions and disorders of her psyche, were suddenly purged by his deliberate passionate embraces. It was only when they once more lay side by side, eye to eye and mouth to mouth in the darkness, that she was overwhelmed by terror and her mind threw up once again the frightening gallery of human portraits which had tormented her for so long. Like a masquerade they came and went, those brutal denizens of the Lager. She suddenly realized that she had taken an irrevocable step, and the thought was like a pistol shot fired in her brain. She sat up and said in a tone of surprise, almost:

"I must go away."

He did not hear the words, but turned lazily on his elbow to study her face, touching its features with his forefinger, studying it with a passionate intensity.

All at once they caught the noise of footsteps on the asphalt outside the house, and they heard the familiar cough of Peterson. In a flash he was at the door. Peterson stood on the threshold outside.

"What are you doing here, David?" she asked in a low voice. But he passed her without a word, and walked away into the dusk.

Peterson took one step forward and tapped with a knuckle on the door. If she suspected anything, her features did not betray it. She stood smiling at Grete, who looked up at her with a new intensity on her face, hugging her knees with her arms.

"I'm going away, Pete," she said. "I've come to a decision."

Peterson seemed quite unmoved by this declaration. She groped for her cigarette-holder and fitted a cigarette into it, asking with elaborate casualness:

"Are you going because you are in love, or because you're not in love?"

"This evening has decided everything. I took a step against my better judgment. There is no going forward for me now."

"Has David no stake in the matter?" asked Peterson dryly.

"He does not know anything about me."

"Well, he knows all that I told him," said Peterson. The girl turned her troubled eyes on the older woman and asked:

"Even about…?"

Peterson nodded curtly.

In a sudden gust of shame, Grete put her hands to her cheeks.

"Oh, Pete!" she exclaimed. "Can't you see that it wouldn't work! And besides, David himself is a married man with a child!"

"On the contrary, he's a widower."

Grete paused for a brief moment, refusing the immediate delight of that knowledge, then suddenly flung herself on her knees beside Peterson, and said:

"Oh, don't try to talk me out of it. You know I must leave, so please help me go. I suppose Rose has told you what happened."

"Well," said Peterson. "If that's what you really want, I could help you if you wish. I could try and find you a job in Jerusalem. When do you want to go?"

Pete reflected for a moment. "Jerusalem is not very far, you know," she said. "Which may be all to the good in the long run. I mean if David should wish to get in touch with you."

Grete made a gesture of furious impatience.

"I would like to go back to Europe," she said. "Oh why were we Jews born so unlucky!"

"Speak for yourself," said Peterson. "As for me, I'm not a Jew but I can't say that I've been conspicuously luckier than one."

"Then what are you doing here?" asked Grete.

"I have become one by choice," said Peterson with a grin. "I was in love with one, once. He was a great man. He always suffered from a feeling of persecution, of self-contempt, and yet was proud of his country. When the real persecution started in Germany he was dead. By the way," she went on, "this is in confidence. Only one other person knows this here, and I don't want it to spread. Like you, I dislike being pitied."

Grete touched her hand softly and gave it a sympathetic squeeze.

"Now sleep," said Pete, "and tomorrow you will be in Jerusalem. We'll try and find you a job to do."

They parted, and Grete lay for a long time with her eyes wide open in the darkness, her mind full of plans and self-reproaches. She was afraid that David would come back and weaken her resolve, and she was genuinely grateful, when she heard the clock strike four, that he had not put in an appearance.

At first light she had an early morning swim in the Jordan and packed her exiguous belongings in the cheap fibre suitcase.

The first bus to Jerusalem passed the cross-roads near to the kibbutz at eight o'clock. She did not intend to miss it. As to finding a job, she decided to find one for herself, starting from scratch, if necessary.

13

Jerusalem Interlude

In the spring sunshine Jerusalem was looking its best, the honey-coloured tones of its buildings giving back the light of the sun as if filtered through the heart of a honey-comb.

It was in ironic contrast to the mood of the girl herself, as she sat, operating the wooden STOP/GO signal which alone enabled traffic to flow on a narrow road. She was surrounded by cement mixers, pneumatic drills, asphalt barrels pouring out their contents, and hissing steam rollers.

She was tired and grimy. Moreover, her inefficiency at this simple task was already patent. The hooting of cars stabbed at her nerves. Their impatient drivers volleyed abuse at her. Too soon she found herself reversing the STOP/GO signal, with the inevitable result she had been dreading all that morning. The two streams of traffic drifted together like glue and halted in an inextricable confusion. Panic-stricken, she abandoned her signal and tried to restore order by a little amateur point-duty, but in vain.

She was aware of a pair of steely blue eyes fixed upon her embarrassment, her utter ignominy. Lawton gave her a smile of amused malice as he sat in the front of his jeep. His driver showed some disposition to add to the noise by hooting as well, but the Major put a hand on his wrist and said something in a low voice that made him stop. Finally, with the help of the foreman and several hirsute navvies, the damage was repaired and traffic began to move again. As Lawton's jeep passed, she saw that his face still wore the ironical and rather malicious smile which she took as the unkindest masculine criticism of her competence. She went back to her signal post with burning cheeks, pressing her lips with determination as she resumed her task. She *would* get it right this time.

Meanwhile, further down the road, Lawton had made the jeep pull off on to the grass verge to allow him to get down. He made his way unhurriedly back to where the girl stood, and now the malicious insolence on his face had given place to an expression of sympathetic interest.

"Miss Schiller," he said, "forgive me for intruding, but may I ask you the meaning of all this?"

She looked up for a minute, as if about to respond with something harsh, but one glance at his face was enough to establish that his interest was well intentioned.

"Have you left Ras Shamir?"

She nodded. "A month ago."

"And is this the best you can find in the way of work in Jerusalem?" he asked.

"So far," she gazed at him proudly.

He felt suddenly a little out of countenance and stammered: "You must be capable of something better than this."

"It is all I could find," she said shortly.

"Would you resent as interference an offer to help?" They looked at one another and, without waiting for her to say anything further, he took out a card case, scribbled something on a card and handed it to her.

"Go and see our Chief of Personnel," he said. "You probably know some languages at least."

She stood looking at the card while he, saluting her punctiliously, turned on his heel and made his way back to the jeep...

~

Her translation from a job so ignominious to one of relative ease and respectability could not, she realized, have been achieved so easily without a helping hand. She caught sight of herself reflected in the sunny shop-windows, no longer the ragged and stained kibbutz field worker, but a young woman personably groomed and dressed. It was almost unbelievable. The kindly personnel chief had advanced her a month's salary and even found her a flat.

"Mind you," he said, "three months' probation is the custom."

She sighed and folded the file which lay on her desk, the slip cover of which bore the words: "ARCHIVIST TRANSLATOR SECOND CLASS — HUNGARIAN, RUSSIAN, GERMAN." She picked up the phone and asked:

"Is the Major in yet?" Then, reassured by the response, she walked down the maze of corridors to Lawton's office. Coming down the corridor, she almost collided with Carstairs, who was overwhelmed with astonishment. He opened his mouth as if to say something, but she sailed past him like a galleon in full sail, and he stood staring after her, inhaling the rather too successfully applied Chanel No. 5. He watched her like a man in a trance as she entered the door to Lawton's office, and closed it softly behind her. His face was a study.

Re-entering his office in a daze, he found his solid secretary, Brewster, tapping away at a service message. It was Carstairs' custom to ramble on and Brewster did not stop his typing. It was his private conviction that nothing but utter gibberish escaped Carstairs' lips.

"At what point, Brewster, does a man cease to believe his eyes?"

"I wouldn't know, Sir," said Brewster without pausing.

Carstairs reflected deeply at the window, and said, with an appropriate gesture:

"Ah, but one bite, Brewster, from the peach of immortality, is worth a whole basketful of apricots."

"Very good, Sir; if you say so, Sir."

Meanwhile, Grete stood before Lawton's desk, transformed out of all recognition, smiling at his obvious confusion. He looked staggered, even awed.

"I've come to thank you," she said.

He stood up nervously. "Thank me," he stammered. "Thank me for what?"

"For sponsoring my application," she said. "Without it I would not have got this job, and you know it."

"It's not strictly true," he said. "You could as easily not have got it, but I'm glad to have been of use. I'm sure you'll be happier." An indecision had seized him. He did not know whether it would have been appropriate to invite her to sit down in one of the leather armchairs and accept a cigarette, but he rejected the idea, as not sufficiently official. The infuriating thing too was that, while he had recognized her as beautiful, he had had no idea that she was quite as beautiful as all this — a veritable Pygmalion's image. He cleared his throat nervously and said:

"If there is anything else I can ever do..."

She turned to the door with a docility which was tinged ever so slightly with disappointment.

"Miss Schiller," said Lawton impulsively in his cold voice: "Would you consider dining with me tonight?"

He looked as if he expected an explosion of some sort. Her docility was the most surprising thing about her.

"With pleasure," she said in a low voice.

He sighed with relief. "Thank you," he said. With returning self-confidence he said:

"I'll send a car for you at eight."

The door shut behind her and Lawton folded his arms, and lit his pipe, to muse on his own good fortune. It was not long before it reopened to admit Carstairs.

"Oh, what is it?" he cried irritably.

"Nothing, dear old spy-catcher, nothing. I only wanted to look at you. I'm beginning to see you in an entirely different light..."

Lawton's dinner invitation marked a new epoch in Grete's life. Picnics by Lake Tiberius, swimming at Caesarea by moonlight, dancing and dining in the sparkling summer air at Tel Aviv. While these occupations were valuable, in that they provided a total contrast to the hard and rather arid life of the kibbutz, they did not offer any final cure for her inner malaise. From time to time the old obsessional nightmares returned and, more than once, she found herself drinking to still them.

As for Lawton, a man both purposeful and wise, the new epoch was both intoxicating and equivocal. He felt himself slipping into a hopeless infatuation and even Carstairs, who was so frequently in their company, registered his disquiet by forgetting to tease him. Some of their conversations stayed in his mind as disturbing and touching.

One evening, at a cocktail party, Carstairs had plied her with drinks so strong that, when they left the hotel, Lawton saw she was reeling. He took her by the arm and walked her in the garden for a little while, debating whether she would be able to carry out the planned programme for that evening, which included a midnight swim.

"I think," he said, "I'd better take you home." She glared at him unsteadily and sat down with a bump on a marble bench. Smiling wanly she said: "How lucky you people are, Hugh; tonight I suddenly felt so lost, just looking at you all at the party."

"Looking at us all?" he echoed.

"You belong somewhere. You are substantially yourselves. It made me feel all over the place, German, Jewish, Hungarian... *nothing*."

"Is that really a reason?" he said gently.

"No," she said, "but it is part of a reason. All the other things about me you know... or nearly all. Except one."

He kissed her hands and put them back, folded, into her lap. "I'm going to fetch you a black coffee to sober you up," he said. "Promise you will stay here until I get back?"

"I promise."

But no sooner had his tall figure disappeared into the lighted entrance of the hotel than she rose and, still walking somewhat unsteadily, crossed the garden and slipped through the gate. Though she was in evening dress, her appearance did not arouse much comment or interest in this part of the town, which was very European; but presently, in order to reach her apartment, she had to traverse a maze of twisted narrow streets with flaring stalls of market-vendors — a corner of the Arab quarter. Arab music sounded everywhere with its shrill quarter-tones, and she was jostled and shoved by the motley throng as she passed, no longer so obviously drunk, but still apparently in a trance. On a sudden impulse she entered a low-roofed Arab tavern and sat down at a sanded wooden table to order a glass of arak; but the eyes of a misshapen Arab youth in the corner rested upon her with a kind of calculating insolence and she sprang up once more, spilling her drink. She threw down money from her glittering evening bag upon the table — a rash move — and walked faster down the twisted streets towards her flat, aware that now she was being followed.

She heard the steps behind her but did not dare look round, for fear that the last of her courage would desert her if she did so. At times she stopped dead, and the steps behind her stopped dead as well. Once only, as she crossed a lighted street with a few shops in it, and feeling more courageous because of the lighted shop-fronts, she turned about. But the street was empty. Down the last long dark street she broke and ran, slamming the heavy front door of the apartment block behind her at last, panting with relief. Then through the frosted glass she saw the shadow of a man standing, as if in deep thought, on her front porch. It was Lawton. She opened the door once more and they stared at each other for a long moment.

"It was only to see you safely home," he said in a low voice, apologetically; and now suddenly she was reeling with fatigue, once more overcome by the incoherence and drunkenness of the earlier part of the evening. She fell against him, and he stooped to pick her up. He walked softly, circumspectly up to the first floor with her and, pushing open the door of her flat, walked into it with his burden.

"You are tired," he said.

He crossed the dark room and laid her down upon the sofa; a street lamp shone with an unearthly glow-worm light through the pane of glass, lighting up her sad and vague expressions.

"I haven't been fair to you, Hugh," she said indistinctly and, as if the thought had stung her, she said:

"Come here, oh come here and sit beside me." And when he obeyed she reached out her arms and put them round him, saying incoherently: "You know how much I think of you, don't you?" With her lips she searched his, but he evaded her embrace, all the while staring at her with a fixed and melancholy stare.

"Don't you want me?" she whispered at last, gazing at him, with a bemused and repentant glance. He nodded grimly.

"But not out of gratitude," he said, and his cold harsh tone cut across her indecision like a knife.

"Gratitude," she said, genuinely aggrieved.

"Yes, or perhaps boredom," he said grimly.

"My God, what a prig you are."

"Perhaps I love you Grete, and I would be mad with happiness if I thought you could love me. But can you? I don't know. Can't you see that anything less would be an insult to someone who loves you?"

She groaned and made a little sketch with her hands of someone tearing out her hair in a pantomime of exasperation.

"Why do men complicate everything?" she cried out, suddenly falling back on the cushions with a wail of despair. "Oh why? You are like all the others."

"Good-night," said Lawton. He leaned forward and suddenly took her in his arms, hungrily, angrily. He kissed her until she was breathless. It was truly like an act of aggression, as if he were trying to prevent her breathing. And after each bout of kisses he stared at her with his crooked grin. Then, without another word, he smacked her across the face and the white light splintered into a thousand stars.

"Some people can think of nothing but themselves," he said from the door and she heard his feet run lightly down the stairs. The front door closed behind him with a faint jar, and she heard the distant sound of his hurried footbeats in the silent street.

She rose weeping, and staggered across the room to put on the light. Then she examined her own face in the tall steep glass of the bedroom. Her reflection disgusted her and she turned aside to the kitchen, where she unearthed a glass and a bottle of gin. She poured herself a dose of the spirit and filled up her glass with soda. Then she turned off the lights and took herself back to her dark sofa once more; here she lay, drinking, thinking deeply, and from time to time muttering aloud.

The next day she woke with a heavy sense of gloom and despondency; she was late for the office, and she wore dark glasses to disguise the havoc which sleeplessness and tears had wrought with her complexion. She was overcome with remorse, and at the same time with exasperation, at Lawton's determination to complicate matters, to make feelings explicit. After an hour of hesitation she walked along to his office to find Carstairs in possession of his desk.

"Hello," he said gaily, "are you looking for the Major? Didn't he tell you he was going on leave today? How strange. He didn't tell me either. He phoned just after breakfast to say he was flying out to Egypt for a week's leave; by now he must be over the Canal."

Grete sighed heavily.

"Come. Come," said Carstairs. "This is no way to take it; besides he spoke words of winged wisdom unto me and said that if I was to invite you to dinner he would not be sorry. Nay, he would be glad knowing you were in such safe hands. Will you?"

"Will I what?"

"Dine and dance with three waggish second lieutenants at the King David tonight? Please say yes."

"Very well," she said, "though I'm not in the mood."

"We will cheer you up with our polished banter," promised Carstairs: "Besides, we all dance well."

By the time the evening came, she was glad that she had accepted the invitation, for the thought of spending a long solitary evening in her flat was oppressive. Besides, Carstairs' promise of good company was amply fulfilled. The three young subalterns went out of their way to amuse and divert her — and all three of them danced well. Once, as she was leaving the floor after a dance, her eye caught sight of a familiar figure — or so she thought — standing at the bar and watching her. But before she could verify this first impression, the crowd had closed in on her. She made her way as quickly as possible to the bar but the figure — it had seemed to her to be that of David — had disappeared. She shrugged away the impression and continued to dance until long after midnight. All three of her hosts saw her home in the command car, and she was in a happy and self-confident mood as she closed the door on their smiling faces.

She walked into the dark flat and was instantly aware that there was somebody there, waiting for her in the darkness. She paused, every nerve alert, her finger on the switch. Opposite, on the dark couch by the lighted window, she could see the outline of a figure.

"Who is it?" she said in a low voice. The answer, in David's deep quiet tone, came back across the silence.

"A friend. Don't be scared."

She switched on the light with a click and confronted him.

"Scared?" she said. "What have I to be scared of?" David laughed softly. "Nothing," he said shortly. "I thought I was being followed, hence my rather theatrical entry. I apologize."

Grete gazed at him curiously. "So it *was* you at the Hotel?"

"Yes."

"I thought so."

David got to his feet and said: "You were not supposed to see me. I was rather clumsy; but I had dinner there before coming on here to..."

"To what?"

"To see you. To talk to you. May I have a cigarette?"

"Yes. Will you have a drink?"

"Thank you."

She poured him a whisky and he lit a cigarette with none too steady a hand. They both felt confused, ill at ease. She sat down opposite him and said sharply:

"If you have come to ask me to return to Ras Shamir..."

"I haven't," he said shortly. "This is business."

"How business?" she said.

David inhaled deeply and expelled a long column of blue smoke which hung in the air between them.

"Haganah business," he said. "I was ordered here to Jerusalem by the resistance. The build-up of arms is almost complete. It won't be long before the balloon goes up..."

"Balloon?"

"Well, we'll have to take our case to UNO, since the British do not seem to want to pay attention to it. We are planning a few demonstrations in order to reach the headlines."

"Demonstrations?"

"I was using the politest word I could find. There will be quite some trouble here."

"David," she said. "This sounds mad."

"It may," he said setting his jaw in a stubborn jut.

"But if you get rid of the British you will be facing the Arabs without their help. They will march in."

"They must be faced too. Israel must become a reality, a sovereign state, not a rest camp where the victims of anti-semitism can live on the sympathetic handouts of the world. A place of our own is what we want, we must have."

"But the British were prime movers in this business. You will have your sovereign state; but must you have it this weekend?"

"They are hesitating, placating Arab opinion."

"They have to; think of the oil. In the long run this will concern you also, no?"

"Israel must be born," he said obstinately.

She sipped her drink. "You men are all the same," she said at last.

David stubbed out his cigarette and smiled wryly. "Did you come here to give me a political lecture?" she asked.

"No. I'm sorry," he said. "I came here on behalf of the Haganah to ask you to — co-operate."

"In what sense?"

"Provide us with information. You are admirably placed to do so, in fact at the heart of the cobweb — British military intelligence. I was asked if you would keep us informed of everything you hear and see."

"Of course not," she said equably.

"You don't care," he said.

"I care," she said, "but I think you will get what you want in the long run thanks to the British; why jump the gun?"

"You don't believe in Israel."

"I don't believe in fanatics," she said. "The last experience I had of the jackboot brought me here; I don't want to see us Jews inherit the fanaticism from which we have been trying to escape."

He drained his drink and stood up. "I see," he said coldly.

"I wonder if you really do."

"I think I do," he said sadly. "I wish it weren't mixed up with my own feelings for you — but it is. It is the old difference, of course. I am a sabra, was born here, belong here, will die rather than be thrown out of here. This is my land, not only in the religious and historical sense but in the sense of contemporary politics. But you, like so many others, are only here to evade persecution; you want to hide; but you don't want to throw off the whole complex of Jewishness to escape from your past, to start a new world. At the first opportunity you would be off to Germany again."

"Only for one reason," she said. "If there were a chance of my child being alive still, yes, I would go. I care more for that than for all these windy theories. You will end by sickening your British friends and being abandoned by them to the Arabs. That is not a pretty prospect."

"But that is precisely what we are preparing for," said David. "I like the British as much as you do. It hurts me to go against their wishes. But we must. Our policy dictates it, and it is right."

"I think now," she said, "I've had enough."

He sighed heavily. "I am sorry," he said again. "It turned out so completely different from my original idea of it, this conversation; you know how one plans conversations in one's mind — the questions and answers fit so beautifully. But this time we are all at odds. Nothing I say matches anything you think." He looked at her intently, sorrowfully, for a long moment. Then he took a step forward and clasped his hands, pressing them together until the knuckles stood out white against the sunburn.

"I'm so deeply sorry," he said in a low voice full of emotion. "I had so much to say to you and now it is all unsayable. I feel that I've lost you forever, Grete."

He walked slowly to the door and she heard his weary steps on the stairway outside. It was only when she heard the front door bang shut that she suddenly cried "David," like someone wakening from a bad dream. She ran lightly down the staircase, but by the time she reached the front door it swung back to reveal an empty street.

14

A Visitant

The visitations of Donner always occasioned the sinking feeling which Bovril was invented to prevent — for, during some years before he reached the dizzy eminence of his present post, he had been in charge of the arms raids; these enabled him to pay off any number of petty scores or imagined slights, purely in terms of the destruction of kibbutz property. Consequently, his appearance at Ras Shamir early one morning came as something of a surprise, as he had not been seen for some months anywhere north of Galilee.

Pete saw the self-assured figure from the roof parapet, where she was busy discussing a deal with the two settlements at the end of the line — the ones they called "Glasgow" and "Brisbane" because of the nationalities of the overwhelming mass of their inhabitants. She went down to meet him, muttering "Here's a bird of ill omen. I hope it isn't a raid." But Donner was alone, walking with an air of preoccupied nonchalance and tapping his knee with his swagger-stick. He was even disposed to be waggish in his earthbound way, spreading out his hands as he saw her and saying: "This time I come in peace, Miss Peterson. Honour bound. Cross my heart." He crossed his heart and cast his eyes up to heaven like some grotesque doll. Then, nonchalantly, as if to assert his official power by a calculated rudeness, he picked himself a fine rose. She watched him stonily. "I am glad to hear it," she said. And truthfully she was, for recently they had received quite a lot of automatic weapons and some boxes of industrial dynamite, out of which Aaron had plans to build... "I am very glad." The last time Donner and his party, with a lot of infantry, had spent four hours going over the settlement with a fine-tooth comb in a hunt for arms, they found nothing; but it was really a miracle that they did not. Old Karam had put their hand-grenades under the chickens in their boxes; now he claimed that the hens had tried so hard to hatch them they had become neurotic. With these thoughts turning over in her mind, she shook hands gravely with the policeman.

"I came," said Donner, "more or less to say goodbye, Miss Peterson, as I am going for a soldier shortly — a Syrian posting. You won't see my ugly face around here any more."

"I am glad," said Pete absently, "of course I mean sorry."

Donner gave an awkward laugh, rather louder than it should have been, and not as self-assured as he would have liked it to sound.

"You must have your little joke," he said.

She nodded. They walked side by side back to the office where, dismissing the supernumeraries working there, she placed a chair for Donner and settled behind her desk with the air of one who awaits the oracle. But the oracle did not know quite how to begin; it was difficult, like trying to pick up a crab. He cleared his throat and said:

"And there was one little routine matter I wanted to ask you about. Have you a girl here called Judith Roth? I think you have."

Pete did not quite know whether to bluff or tell the truth. She hesitated and then said:

"Yes, of course we have."

"Do you think I could have a quiet word with her?" asked Donner with an air of humble sincerity, tapping his knee with the rose. Pete got up and said:

"Yes, let me see the roster." She consulted a wall-sheet full of names. "She's not on duty now. She must be in her room unless..." If Judith were at the river, her papers would not be in the safe. She swung the heavy door and peered inside. No, there were the yellow folders and the writing-case. Judith must be in camp somewhere.

"If you will wait a moment," said Pete, "I'll go and find her and send her up here to you."

Donner had not missed the slightest move in this little ritual of looking in the safe. But of course! Where else would one keep valuable documents in a kibbutz? There was no privacy in the huts — he knew that only too well from his frequent arms hunts. If plans there were, they must be in there.

Pete left the room, closing the door behind her; for some reason or other she did not lock the safe again, contenting herself with pushing the door shut. Donner rubbed his chin thoughtfully and then fingered his nose as he thought deeply. Then with an agility unusual for a man of his build, he tiptoed across the room and looked inside. There was a stack of purely administrative papers on the top, and on the bottom the folders with the words "Liebling: Physics Dept. U. of J." printed on them. A large yellow envelope, the fatness of which promised well, was marked with the initials "J.R.". Donner gave a low whistle. What luck! On the other hand, was it luck? And if it was, what should he do to turn it to profit? He could not risk a direct theft — that would be obvious. Still pondering, he examined the lock. It was a primitive little safe with an ordinary type of lock turned by key. He took out the little ring of skeleton keys from his breast pocket and soon found one to fit it. He had hardly replaced them and regained his seat when the door opened and a dark good-looking girl came into the room. She was, he repeated to himself, a good-looker all right.

"Miss Roth?"

Judith nodded and shook hands. "You wanted to see me?"

Donner put on a false heartiness of manner, swaying about like an avuncular clergyman and saying:

"I did, yes, to be sure I did." They sat down and Donner cleared his throat, smiling at her in his most seductive fashion. "I wanted to ask you if you had a pleasant journey?"

"I don't understand," said the girl.

Donner wagged a playful rose at her and said:

"I suppose you wouldn't be another illegal, would you? I know plenty of young ladies who are."

Judith coldly recited the cover-story which had been invented for her and which she had been told to memorize. Donner waved this away and said:

"My dear little lady, of course, of course. I don't doubt a word of it."

Judith said: "Then what do you want?"

Donner leaned forward suddenly and allowed his moustache to bristle, in a minatory fashion.

"I'm not *saying* I don't believe you," he said, "but of course you know the penalties for forging identity cards, don't you?"

"Am I under arrest?" said Judith. Donner protested at once.

"Of course not. Of course not."

"Then you have no right to talk to me like that. My papers are perfectly in order."

"Now don't get angry," said Donner plaintively. "I didn't come to make any charge. I simply came to…"

"To what?"

"I came to help you, to offer my services…" He sounded positively hurt at being so misjudged.

"How?"

Donner drew a deep breath and took the plunge.

"These papers, these plans…" he mumbled vaguely, watching her face carefully. Judith's face cleared and she smiled.

"You mean my father's plans?"

"That's it," he said, much relieved.

"I see. The British Government wants to buy them? But I'm sorry, you will have to talk to Professor Liebling about that. I'm only doing the mathematical work on them."

"Liebling?"

"Yes. As soon as my work is finished I shall deliver them to him. But that won't be for a month yet."

Donner looked confused and uncertain.

"I thought," he mumbled, "that you might like them locked up for you under official seal. This is not a very safe place…"

"Thank you, no."

Donner laid his flower on the table, extracted a cigarette case and offered her one which she refused. He lit up and smoked in a laboured fashion.

"I know a good many people of influence," he said at last, with clumsy amiability, "who have nothing to do with the British Government…"

But she let the hint pass without comment.

"You may address any of your questions to Professor Liebling," she said sharply. "Is there anything further you wish of me?"

"It was just an informal visit," said Donner reproachfully.

"I have work to do."

"Don't let me keep you then."

She banged the door so rudely that Donner's lips twisted in a grimace of annoyance. However, he sauntered down to make his good-byes to Pete and took himself off slowly, walking with that swelling, swaying walk which was intended to convey power.

He started the engine of the police car, but before slipping it into gear he took out a notebook and jotted down the name of Liebling. The journey had been worth it on the whole.

That evening at the Long Bar he accepted a fattish envelope from the hands of Ali in exchange for an account of his visit. Ali smoked very thoughtfully over what he had been told, silent as a chess-player.

"We must not be too hasty," he said at last. "What about Liebling? Could you manage with your official net to cover him — then, when she brought them up to Jerusalem, we might… find some way? I am only calculating."

Donner was pondering heavily. "Yes," he said at last. "I could certainly arrange that. Provided I'm still here. I've got this posting to consider. It might come suddenly." Then his face cleared. "But I could always go sick, couldn't I, and delay it? And it's worth it."

"If we could get a look at them…"

"You leave it to me. She said about a month."

"And Liebling?"

"I think that can be looked after too."

They signalled the waiter for another drink, and pledged each other smilingly.

15

The Paper-Chase

One night Judith woke Pete up by tapping on her door and exclaiming:

"Pete! Please forgive my waking you! I've done it. I've finished it. All the data are complete and in the right order and the little toy is in existence."

Pete rubbed sleepy eyes and said:

"Heavens, Judith, it is the middle of the night. What toy?"

"My father's toy — Professor Liebling's toy."

"Really?"

"Yes."

Pete struggled on to her elbow and said:

"This calls for a celebration."

"No, not yet. Later. But I wondered if I could go up to Jerusalem tomorrow evening and deliver all the stuff to Liebling. Anna is driving up and could take me."

"Of course you can. You must. But you will have to ring Liebling and let him know — and you can't do that from here."

She sat up and thought for a moment. She gripped Judith's hand and said:

"Tomorrow morning you can go up to Yeled with Tonio when

he goes to collect the beets and telephone from there. You have Liebling's number?"

"Of course."

"Good."

Pete lay back and composed herself once more, hands folded over her stomach. "And now, my dear, bed. Look at the time!"

"I'm so excited."

"Of course you are."

"Good-night, Pete."

"Good-night, dear Judith."

Judith walked about in the darkened gardens for a while before she went to bed herself. She was puzzled to find herself thinking: "I wish that Aaron were here to share this sense of success, this sense of a difficult job well done. He would be pleased too." She had a sudden and vivid picture of him smiling. But she frowned reprovingly at herself for the thought and, entering her little cabin, snapped off the light.

In the morning she struggled up in time to catch Tonio and cadge a lift to Yeled, from which she got through to Liebling after the wait of an hour or two. His voice crackled on the wire with delight.

"Marvellous!" he said, and the word was like a sip of honey. "I felt you would do it."

She gave him a rendezvous in Jerusalem for that evening at seven o'clock. "In the old lorry," she said. "Anna will be driving." The little Professor was so excited that he could hardly articulate.

"I shall meet you," he said. "I shall meet you myself. Bravo, Judith — bravo, bravo!"

Bravo, Judith! But the denouement was not exactly as planned. As they jogged along over the curving slopes of the main road beyond Nazareth, they saw a little group of soldiers and policemen manning a road barrier some way ahead.

"Now what the hell is this?" said Anna, the professional pessimist of the kibbutz. "Thank God we aren't carrying anything illegal and that our papers are in order."

The routine was so familiar that they had even lost a sense of ignominy in performing it. It was easy to stop the truck and get out with hands up. The soldiers and policemen examined everything with attention, but not very closely. They had the impression that they were going to escape from a mere routine check when a bulky figure emerged from a hut and pointed a finger at Judith.

"Miss Roth," he said with a majestic self-assurance, "will you please bring your papers and come this way?"

Judith was not too surprised to recognize, in the tall figure, the person of Donner. However, though annoyed and put out of countenance, she obeyed. The barrier was removed at a signal from Donner and the puzzled Anna was waved on. The whole thing took place so suddenly that they had hardly time to think of possible explanations. Judith herself stood irresolutely on the doorstep of the shack, holding the old briefcase which she had borrowed to house her papers. Donner was in a most masterful mood. He kicked the door shut behind him and took his place at a desk, where he busied himself with some papers, not looking up. Judith began to recover her self-possession in the face of this behaviour.

"May I ask…" she began; but the great man was busy. He raised his head and said:

"You may sit down." She did so, watching him. Finally he gathered up his papers and went to the door. "Sergeant," he called, and a voice responded. "It's O.K. Release the roadblock. The job is done."

"Very good, Sir."

"What job," wondered Judith idly. They sat in silence as the noise outside gradually diminished. The barrier was raised and the troops took off in their various cars. Donner sat absolutely still, with a faint smile on his face, listening to these sounds of departure. Presently, as the last car rumbled off down the road, he said:

"I have a warrant for you, Miss Roth. But it's a mere formality, of course. I want you to answer a few questions."

"What questions?"

"I have my orders," said Donner, serious with an almost religious air. "You will be released very soon, I can promise you."

"Am I arrested then?"

"For questioning, Miss. That is all. We have that right."

"But I can answer any questions here!"

"No, you can't, bless your soul." Donner chuckled comfortably. "All in good time. Besides, we have to have a look at your papers."

"But my papers... Just look!" She opened her briefcase with an air of despair. Donner shook his head.

"You will get them all back tomorrow, I can promise you that. On my honour."

"But — where are we going?"

"To Jerusalem," said Donner with exasperation. "Where else?"

Dazed, she stood irresolutely before him. "Come on," he said. He led the way out of the hut, snapped off the light, and opened the door of a saloon car. "You have nothing to fear, Miss Roth," he said. "It's a pure formality. You'll be free — perhaps even tonight."

The car swung into the main road and headed for Jerusalem.

~

Anna made poor sense at the best of times, but she was so incoherent on her arrival in Jerusalem that Liebling could have knocked her down. "That's all I know," she kept repeating stolidly. "That's all I know. This chap Donner comes out and takes her off."

Liebling hopped with rage. "But where?" he cried.

"In the hut. I was waved through."

"And her papers? Surely she had something with her?"

"A briefcase. She took it. He told her to."

It seemed for a minute that the scientist was going to drag out his remaining silver hairs. He tugged at them with both hands.

A whole string of Yiddish expletives flowed from his innocent-looking lips. He staggered away across the cobbled street like a man in a nightmare and sat down at a café table. His mind, so competent with abstractions, found itself incapable of determining what all this might mean; but one thing was certain — the plans were compromised if they once got out of Judith's hands. He swallowed a glass of arak and shuddered, pulling himself together. "I shall have to speak to the underground," he said at last under his breath. "It is the only way."

He ran with strange hopping steps along the footpath towards the centre of the town. It was quite a walk, but finally he arrived with beating heart at an old tumbledown house in a quiet side-street. It was apparently a cobbler's shop, and it was locked. He tapped at the door and was challenged by a voice; he gave his name in a whisper and was admitted. On the third floor three men sat round an oil lamp, playing cards at a table, while a fourth in the far corner was copytaking from a small transmitter whose chattering and chirping made the only sound in the room. The three men sat quite absorbed in their game by the yellow light. Only one of them looked up and greeted the Professor as he stumbled into the doorway. He stared more closely, recognized the Professor, and got up to welcome him.

"Ben Adam," said Liebling, "I come to ask for your help." The second man shuffled the cards and stacked them. Then he and his companion rose and placed a chair for their visitor.

"The plans," said Liebling incoherently, "we must not let them out of her hands."

A gruff voice said: "Come, Professor, explain."

Liebling took a very deep breath, fetched up from his shoes, and concentrated for a moment; then he began to explain. They listened intently, with their dark faces turned unsmilingly towards him. Only at the mention of the name Donner did their faces register any expression. They turned to one another and exchanged a glance of recognition. At the end of the recital Ben Adam turned to the second man and said:

"Aaron — this is your part of the world."

"Yes. I know the girl."

They all thought heavily for a moment. Then Ben Adam went to a telephone and asked for a number. "Hullo, is that the Central Prison? May I speak to Faber, please?" There was a long wait while Aaron said under his breath to the Professor: "A contact in Central."

Ben Adam motioned them to silence. "About Baby, Faber, it was about him; what is he doing these days? Is he at home? No. Off duty? Thank you."

He replaced the phone carefully, caressed it like a pet parrot, and came back to the table. "He's not there; he must be at his villa. But he might be anywhere at all. Shall I try and ring him to see?"

He went back to the phone and asked for a number. It rang and rang and he held the receiver away from his head as he shook it with a gesture meaning "Nobody at home" — suddenly there was a click and Donner's voice said: "Hullo?" Ben Adam replaced the receiver.

"Aaron," he said, "get going." But already Aaron was slipping a magazine into his Luger and putting on his tattered overcoat.

~

It was with something of a flourish that Donner unlocked the front door of the little suburban villa and ushered his captive inside. He had solicitously taken charge of the briefcase by this time, with the gesture of a man putting it under arrest. As he opened the door the telephone was ringing. He lumbered across to the hall table and took it up, calling "Hullo" in a peevish tone. The instrument went dead as he did so. He shrugged his shoulders and came back to the girl as she stood by the front door.

"Now, Miss Roth," he said, with an attempt at genial gallantry, "if you follow my advice you will be free and in full possession of your papers in a few hours. Meantime you will wait here." He showed her into a shabby little sitting-room and indicated a sofa; from the sideboard he produced a bottle of whisky and a bottle of gin and some glasses. "If you feel like refreshment…" he said, "you needn't ask. Just act. This is Liberty Hall."

"Why am I here?" she asked.

"To check your papers."

"But you have seen my identity card."

"Oh, that!" said Donner, pouring himself a whisky. "It's the other stuff in the briefcase; how do we know it isn't some secret stuff for the Germans — some code?"

"Do you know my history?"

"More or less."

"And you think it is likely at this stage — and above all with Germany just about to crack?"

Donner put one hand on the side of his nose. "I'm not saying it is so," he said. "But my orders are just to check."

"And do you do mathematics?" she asked acidly.

"No. But we have experts in everything. But let's not waste your valuable time. I'll ring my man now."

He picked up the briefcase and took it back into the hall with him to telephone; she saw him place it on the stand beside the instrument. He asked for a number and was connected fairly soon. His voice had changed. It had become charged with a new kind of excitement. "It's your old friend, remember? Yes, it's me. I've got it all here. Or you could send him round to collect — I'll wait for the vetting. How long would it take? I have the lady here and I don't want to inconvenience her more than necessary. In an hour then."

He came back into the sitting-room with great good humour. "At most a couple of hours," he said, "and you are free as the wind."

Judith bit her lip and stared desperately through the open door to the briefcase; it seemed miles away now, at the end of a long avenue of work and despair. Moreover, it was so puzzling, this strange encounter with this unorthodox policeman; nothing that he said sounded truthful or reasonable. Surely the British would hardly steal unpatented plans; or if they did, surely they would be a bit more subtle about it.

"When I get out," she said, "I'm going straight round to the central station to find out if you have been acting with authority or not."

Donner jumped and his eyes widened. He gave an uneasy laugh and an ugly expression came over his face. He came close to her and said:

"Listen to me, young lady. I'm trying to be nice to you. But if you play any funny tricks, you know..." She stared at him, smiling grimly.

"You are acting without authority. I can see it in your face." Donner flushed and struck her across the cheek. She staggered back and sat down on the sofa with a thud.

"Now," he said quietly, "just don't give me any of your lip, or I'll really start to interrogate you. Authority! I have the authority to use any means to drag the truth out of criminals. It's my job. Just you go round to Central and ask them. They'll tell you all right." His bluster was unconvincing, but she sat nursing her bruised face and feeling the taste of blood from the cut inside her lip.

"Now listen," said Donner plaintively, "be a sensible girl and cut out the rag; I've told you you'll go free quite soon with all your papers. Here, have a little drink and be friendly."

But as he reached forward, the lights went out and absolute blackness engulfed the little flat. Donner groaned and grunted with surprise. "Another power cut!" he said.

She heard him stand up and walk to the window cautiously, where she saw his huge bulk outlined in vague silhouette against the night.

"That's funny," he muttered. "The other houses are lighted all right."

There came a faint sound from the pathway outside the house and a vague alarm filled Donner's mind — but why he could not say. "Stay quite still," he said hoarsely, and crossed to the doorway into the hall on tiptoe. The front door had a wrought-iron frame on hinges, which during the hot months of the summer could be swung back to admit the air. The grille was now shut but, as Donner walked towards it, there was a scratching movement and it swung softly open.

"Is that you, Ali?" said Donner, in accents of hope and uncertainty, peering out at the night; but an arm came through the opening and fastened itself suddenly and brutally upon the collar of the khaki bush-jacket, twisting and knotting itself round in an unbreakable hold. No word was spoken, but Donner's knees suddenly weakened under him as he felt himself choking. His anguished gasps sounded like the bronchial coughing of an animal.

"Let me go!" he gasped as he sagged.

In the darkness Judith crossed behind him and took possession of her briefcase. Donner was sagging now, almost on his knees, but the door was still locked. Judith closed her eyes and mentally made a map of the place — trying to think of something with which to hit the policeman. Then she recalled a heavy metal vase in the sitting-room. She picked up the object and returned to find that Donner had managed in the interval to draw a gun, though his present position, half on the floor, made it difficult to bring it to bear on the possessor of the arm who stood on the doorstep silently strangling him. She brought the vase down as hard as she could on his head and Donner spread-eagled himself on the floor, cursing and whining. The hand released its hold and groped for the latch. The door swung open and a voice called:

"Judith Roth?"

"I'm here," she said and slipped through the doorway. "Have you got…"

"Yes."

Donner's pistol with its silencer made a deep plushy sound in the silence of the night; they felt the grooves the bullets cut in the air as they bounded down the stairs into the garden. The rescuer was wearing a handkerchief tied over his face like a desperado from some ancient print of a hold-up in America. As they ran down the path, a car was drawing up and two men were getting out, apparently bound for Donner. Aaron dragged Judith to one side and they waited behind the bush, panting until the men had passed them on the drive. Aaron had whipped off his mask now, and she stared at him with a surprise and delight that would be difficult to exaggerate.

"Darling," he said. He kissed her breathlessly and they both began to run through the dark streets of Jerusalem until they reached the University quarter, when they slowed up a little.

"That was a bit of luck," said Aaron with a laugh. Judith was trembling and breathless still — she had a pain in her side.

"Aaron — where are we going?"

"To the Professor."

"But it's late!" she cried, for she saw they were entering the dark doors of the Institute itself. Aaron took her arm.

"He said he would wait up all night by the telephone in his office."

But the Professor had fallen asleep at his desk by the telephone, overcome by anxiety. They tiptoed into the room and watched him smilingly. Judith put a finger to her lips and, opening her briefcase, disposed the documents it contained quietly upon the broad desk before Professor Liebling. Then they sat down in chairs facing him and Aaron mimicked a cough and indicated with his hands that he was asking permission to wake him thus. Judith nodded and the cough was well and truly coughed. The Professor woke with a jolt and stared at them speechlessly; then he looked at the documents on his desk incredulously, and back at them.

"Well I'll be damned!" he said querulously.

≈

An account of her passage at arms with Donner made the old man almost incoherent with rage. He talked of going straight away to lodge a protest with the British authorities for this gross violation of common Mandate law. Then he grew thoughtful as Aaron said: "Let us not be hasty. Our own impression is that Donner was not acting officially but on his own account — illegally."

"Mine too," said Judith.

"And if he actually were trying to steal them on behalf of the British, you'd get small satisfaction anyway; they would muffle the news of the incident in the press and produce some excuse. Ben Adam knows Donner's habits well. He takes bribes; someone may have offered him money for the plans."

"But supposing he arrests Judith again?" said Liebling.

"Now the plans are safe he would get no satisfaction," said Judith. "It was obviously the plans he wanted and not me."

They discussed the matter in desultory fashion, and at last the Professor jumped up apologetically. "My goodness me, it is so late and here I am keeping you talking. Judith, I have your bedroom ready in my house. You will come and stay the rest of the night with us. My wife will be quite worried at the lateness of the hour. Come along."

Aaron walked with them across the dark town and said good-night. "There's been no time to talk," he said in a low voice. "I'll see you tomorrow, Judith."

He turned and disappeared down the dark street.

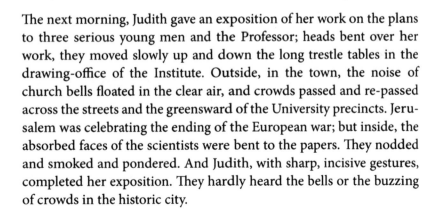

The next morning, Judith gave an exposition of her work on the plans to three serious young men and the Professor; heads bent over her work, they moved slowly up and down the long trestle tables in the drawing-office of the Institute. Outside, in the town, the noise of church bells floated in the clear air, and crowds passed and re-passed across the streets and the greensward of the University precincts. Jerusalem was celebrating the ending of the European war; but inside, the absorbed faces of the scientists were bent to the papers. They nodded and smoked and pondered. And Judith, with sharp, incisive gestures, completed her exposition. They hardly heard the bells or the buzzing of crowds in the historic city.

~

She had elected to return to Ras Shamir that afternoon, and they had hardly finished lunch at the Liebling house when she was called to the telephone. It was Aaron. "I have a surprise," he said. "I hope it will be a pleasant one. I've been given permission to drive you back. It took some wangling as I'm attached to HQ here, but I've done it. When shall I call?"

So it was that she found herself sitting beside him in the late afternoon, as they rumbled down the curves and inclines away from Jerusalem. A newspaper lay on her knees and the empty briefcase at her feet. But her eyes were on the curves and tangles of the foothills they were negotiating. Aaron smoked silently, casting sideways glances at her from time to time. "Penny for your thoughts," he said at last, with a hint of banter in his voice. She gazed at him for a moment, smiling absently. "You are miles away," he said. She nodded. "I was thinking of Germany," she said.

"Germany!"

She nodded again. "Now that the news has come, I suddenly feel that I am homeless in a new way." He frowned but said nothing.

"I mean," she said, "that even if Germany were ever to become her old self and welcome one back, it would be impossible to go. Something very vital has perished in all this train of horrors — a confidence, a trust."

"But you wouldn't think of going back," he said sadly.

"No — I couldn't."

"Well, then."

"But I see I shall have to go somewhere with a future for my sort of work, I don't see myself being of any use here."

"You shock me," he said. "I thought by now you had begun to *feel* the place — the necessity for us founding an Israel here."

"I think you are right, Aaron, but as yet I don't feel anything. I am quite numb. I also see the difficulties. You may be obliged to use force."

"Well then?"

"You may raise more devils than you can conquer." Aaron groaned and was silent again. They were racing along in open country now;

somewhere on the misty sea a warship's gun was firing a salute. "So it's London or New York for you, I suppose," said Aaron. "I can't blame you. You have a career ahead of you. But I am a sabra, and I'm going to stay here and watch a dream come true."

With sudden penitence she turned and touched his shoulder. "Oh, Aaron, I've made you sad with my silly talk."

He shook his head but his smile was unconvincing.

"I have. I'm sorry."

"No. It's simply that I felt sorry that you would not stay with us and share the dream — perhaps a crazy one. Things are going to get harder for a while — not easier. We shall be passing through the eye of the needle."

"Damn," she said. "Let's stop a moment and have a cigarette." Obediently he drew the car off the road under the olive trees and lit a cigarette for her. "Now," she said, "I shall show you that I can still be of some use." She took a piece of paper and began to draw a design on it, swiftly and fluently.

"Perhaps this will interest you," she said. He looked at it curiously. "It's a map of the Arab dispositions opposite Ras Shamir," she went on.

"Good God, how did you get that?"

She drew a breath and said: "You know those two imps of Karam's? In spite of his beatings they can't be stopped from crossing the border. They spend half their time up there playing around, and Yehudi says he has found three paths on the cliffs which are unguarded. I drew this from his description. The crescent of tents there is the British Mission camp; here to the right the Prince and his entourage."

He laughed. "Well I'm damned."

She said very seriously: "I thought you might like to send up some of our people and cut all their throats."

He jumped. "My God!" he said, looking at her with wide eyes. "Cut poor Daud's throat? What next! He is a childhood friend of mine. I've known him since I was ten." He seemed absolutely amazed at her tone, opening his mouth to speak, and then closing it again. He put one hand to his head and gave a hopeless laugh. Then he became very serious. Joining his hands together in supplication he said: "You must let me explain something to you; you *must* understand, Judith." She stared at him with surprise ever so faintly tinged with contempt. He rose and walked a few paces away to another olive tree and laid his face against its trunk for a moment — then he turned and came back, starting to talk, his hands spread out. "You see, the overwhelming problem for us is the question of our legal right to be here, to found a place we can call our own; this is not simply another D.P. camp for us. We want it to justify itself as a permanent reality. But never can this be achieved by force of arms. What we want is for the world, which has made the half-hearted gesture of letting us settle here, to confirm our existence, to ratify our sovereignty. That is why we are trying to bounce the unwilling British into UNO; we believe that we could win our right to exist peacefully and not by force. We believe that our case and our cause are such that the right of Israel to exist as a State will be granted to us. We do not want to take it by force. You must stop thinking of this land in terms of an expiation for the guilt of past persecutions; it is not an expiation — it is a *world commitment*. We Jews have seventy nations represented here already."

He paused and stared at her. "I know what you are going to say," she said. "I feel it coming."

"I was going to say that you do not understand because..."

"I am not a sabra."

"I knew it."

She got up furiously and walked up and down. "And what of the Arabs?" she said harshly. "They will torpedo your vote. You know they will. Who is going to sacrifice good oil to their displeasure?"

"The risk is there — we must take it. It is the only way."

"It will end with a massacre."

"That we can face up to as the worst extremity; but we sabras are not going to stretch out our little white throats to the Arab's knife. But we know that in the longest run we must live with them, cooperate with them. At the moment British oil interests won't let us. That's the point."

They returned to the car and resumed their journey in silence. What followed immediately gave some point to his words, and also made him regret fleetingly that he had chosen, for his own pleasure, the longest way round to reach the kibbutz, for the road ahead suddenly seethed with infantry and command cars. It was a checkpost.

They were searched and re-searched. As they stood under interrogation with arms raised, he grinned at her and said: "You see?"

She looked at him seriously and said: "I'm glad you didn't bring your pistol on this trip."

Once cleared, he drove on but downcast. "Is anything wrong?" she asked at last, almost timidly.

He sighed. "Tales of murder and sabotage," he said. "The situation has become black for the British. It is a matter of time before they throw in the sponge and hide behind the Arab vote." She sighed. "But isn't that part of the plan, to make it black?" He nodded. "I've lost two of my oldest friends. They were killed in a raid last night." She said: "I see." They drove down the winding roads towards the sea in silence.

Once they reached the coast road he said: "I apologize for my gloom. Look, let's have a glass of wine, shall we? And then a few minutes' rest. We shan't get back before midnight anyway with these checkposts. What do you say?" "If you wish," she replied. "Good," he said with false heartiness, and turned down a curving dusty road among the dunes. In the little Roman harbour there was a small restaurant with a dance-floor. They sat under a vine and he ordered wine. With the first glass she felt its warmth. The soft Levantine jazz mixed with the sounds of the sea.

"Come, let us dance once — we don't get much of this at the kibbutz or at training camps." She was undecided.

"Dancing?" she said, "It belongs to the old world, the past. I think I have forgotten how." He smiled. "I'll remind you," he said. He took her softly in his arms and they danced awhile without speaking. Back at their table once more she sipped her wine and said, "Good Lord!" "What?" She laughed. "It's going to my head." He gazed at her with a sorrowful grin. "So you can actually smile," he said. "How marvellous. Thank you." He stood up and once more they danced. Then abruptly he took her hand and led her down to the beach among the dunes. "There are such lovely shells on this beach," he said. "I must gather some for the children."

There was a little Arab cemetery, long since abandoned; she sat among the tombs and smoked while he wandered about for a while. At last he came back and said: "You know what?" "What?" "The sea is as warm as milk." She lay back, gazing up at the dark sky. Suddenly he sat down beside her and took her elbows in his strong hands, pinioning her, and began to kiss her. She tried to resist and turn her face away, but it was no good. She felt his hands on her body, fumbling with her clothes, opening them. "Aaron," she said, but he had covered her body with his own now, and all she could see were his dark eyes staring into her own. A thin misty drizzle had begun to fall. She lay as if doped, and when at last he raised himself on his elbow to look at her, he saw that her eyes were full of tears. She turned her face away with a groan. "Oh, can't you see," she cried, "that I'm exhausted — finished!" He shook his head. "No, you'll come awake. It's only shock and fatigue — and probably mathematics."

She struck him wildly across the face and he sat up, nursing his cheek, but without anger. He considered her for a moment, then, taking her hand, pressed it to his cheek. "I am going to swim," he said. In a flash he had disappeared into the glimmer of the beach. She rose in a fury and found her way back to the car. In a little while he came, his mop of wet hair standing upright. He had unearthed a towel from somewhere and wore it round his neck. He entered the car and turned to her.

"Judith, darling," he said in a low voice full of self-reproach, but she turned on him and shouted: "Oh, if you are now going to be apologetic and penitential I'll hit you — I can't stand stupidity as well as mawkishness." He bit his lip but said nothing. "Well?" she cried, "What are we waiting for?" He started the engine and switched on the lights. They drove in silence down the bumpy tracks to the main road and turned northwards for Haifa. At night the checkposting was even more elaborate and infuriating. They submitted with expressionless faces. Only after Nazareth, where the hills started to climb away northwards, did things begin to thin out a little.

The mountain air was good and keen. Aaron drove in thoughtful silence, gazing at her from time to time, darting little enquiring glances from under his dark eyebrows. But she felt weary and upset and her whole body trembled with nervous fatigue; the sudden sexual intimacy had burned up inside her like a torch, irradiating not only her body but her bruised mind. All the old melancholy phantoms she had been fighting throughout these long months of lonely reflection and hard work rose up from the dark recesses into which she had driven them. How could he not understand that she was still not free from the dreadful shock and melancholia of the death camp? In the shadow of her memories she felt old, used-up, exhausted. She leaned her head on the sidescreen of the car and slept as they rumbled through the night together.

As they reached the head of the pass he slowed up a little and studied the dark contours of the valley below them, bathed in its violet mist. Here and there faint lights shone. But the two great escarpments to the north and south of Ras Shamir were pricked out by the tiny star-clusters of light which marked the settlements lining the dark border: "Brisbane", "Brooklyn", "Cape Town", "Soho", "Naples", "Odessa". He repeated their nicknames, smiling to himself at their old familiarity, and remembering scraps of banter passed backwards and forwards through the old heliograph.

At last they came to the camp perimeter and were challenged by a sleepy figure with a torch who grunted his recognition as he examined their faces, before pulling back the gate and letting them drive in. The car rumbled slowly along the tree-lined darkness of the road and drew up at last near the first faintly etched shadow of a house. She was awake now; as soon as he had turned off the engine, the silence had nudged her fully awake. He went round to her side and opened the door. He seemed to be disposed to say something, though what it was she could not imagine. For that matter, neither could he, he simply could not formulate a phrase to express the mixture of ruefulness and concern which he felt. "Judith," he said at last, but she was fastening up the old briefcase and smoothing down her crumpled frock. Then she said "Good-night" and turned on her heel to walk slowly away from him down the feebly-lit path.

He stood and watched her, sighing and rubbing his chin. The tall slender figure was slowly swallowed by the velvety darkness. He could hear her footsteps still as he turned downcast to the car. Then they stopped — the footsteps — and he heard her call his name suddenly, with a note of urgency.

"Aaron!"

Instantly he strode towards her and plunged into the dark with arms outspread, for he could see nothing. Suddenly he felt her arms around him and her warm mouth searching for his. It was as if all her reserves and terrors had been shed like a cloak, freeing her body and her mind for just such an embrace. "I am sorry I have been such a bitch," she said incoherently, "But I am still all tangled up inside." Aaron's kisses prevented any further analysis of her feelings. She subsided slowly and luxuriously into the deep soft grass under the trees, feeling his arms tighten around her body. "I have come awake," she told herself with joy, "I have come awake."

Much later, at the door of her little cabin, Aaron said good-night with the traditional reluctance of the lover. But his parting was made much less sad for the news he had to give her. "In three months I'll be back here at Ras Shamir." Three months only, instead of that fearsome year!

16

Lawton and the Ambassador

Lawton returned from Egypt at the end of his leave. Grete looked up from her desk and found him standing before her one morning, gazing down on her as if uncertain of his welcome.

"I came to say I was sorry," he said.

She sprang up in ready sympathy and gave him her hands. "Let us rub it all out — forget it all," she said.

And his face broke into a smile. "God bless you," he said. "You have no idea how much I missed you. It ruined my leave. I tried hard not to think about you, but it was useless. I climbed all the pyramids and went to all the night clubs but whenever I was near a telephone the temptation to ring you was almost irresistible."

"I missed you too," she said truthfully.

"And as ill luck will have it, I can't dine with you tonight, I have to go to Government House."

"Never mind. There will be time."

"All the time in the world."

Back in his office once more, Lawton set about expelling Carstairs and his files.

"I thought so."

"Thought what, dear old skipper?"

"I thought you would muck up my files and litter my room with copies of *Vogue* and the *Ladies' Home Journal.*"

"I only get it for the crosswords old chap. I don't knit, as you know. At least not yet, I don't. But I cannot guarantee anything. Another month or two working for this unit may bring about a change of life."

"Get out," said Lawton.

"I wanted to ask you something."

"Then ask and leave me."

"I see you are dining with H.E. tonight."

"Yes."

"Can I dine with Grete?"

"If she can bear it."

"Oh yes, she loves it. Prefers it in fact. Only accepts your invitations for fear of losing her job."

"Go away."

"Well," said Carstairs, "You can tell H.E. from me that I think he is a vexatious old pontiff and ripe for the ducking stool."

"I will."

"And that his ADC is a sycophantic slyboots."

The weighty Oxford Shorter flew across the room but Carstairs, with the celerity of long practice, had vanished and it banged uselessly upon the door panels.

The vexatious pontiff, alias His Majesty's High Commissioner in Palestine, ran true to form; once more Lawton found himself sighing with boredom and irritation as he listened to conversations which so perfectly mirrored the official mind. The conversation was kept superficial and trivial in deference to H.E. who, though a man of "fine presence" as it is called, was fundamentally a vague and limited man, who rapidly wearied of anything which suggested thinking or reflecting. By the time they reached the port and cigar stage of the dinner (the service wives having been shepherded out onto the terrace) H.E. was in fairly good spirits, and disposed to make some concessions in the direction of moderately intelligent conversation. Lawton tried to be responsive.

"Had a good leave?"

"Thank you, Sir."

"I suppose you picked up a good deal in the way of rumours."

"Inevitably, Sir."

H.E. sighed, and stared at the end of his cigar. Then he smiled at the end of the table where his lanky ADC sat and said: "Birds of a feather, eh Roland?"

"What does that imply, Sir?" asked Lawton, quick to be wounded.

"It's just an office joke. Both you lot here and your opposite numbers in Cairo take a very grave view of things. Very grave indeed."

Lawton flushed. "Yes, Sir. It is true. I think our view is justifiably so. The situation is... like that; balanced on a hair."

He reached out his hand with spread fingers and wobbled it like a see-saw. H.E. looked at him indulgently and stroked his moustache.

"My dear boy," he said — Lawton loathed being called so — "I myself am quite impartial in the matter. I am prepared to believe you. I only ask you, when you speak of arms, to show me some, not to repeat rumours only. Do you follow?"

"Yes," said Lawton. "And there you have me, Sir. I admit we've been singularly unsuccessful in capturing the dumps which we have heard about... But I'm convinced our information is correct — that a big build-up is taking place, and that one fine day in the near future..."

He paused and, as if to illustrate his sentence, there came a dull bang in the darkness over there, beyond the garden. They looked at one another and turned to peer out of the window in the direction of Jerusalem. There was a patch of flame which flapped red and then white.

"What the devil..." said H.E. The ADC went to the telephone in the corner — the red Government House line — and said:

"Give me the police call desk, please."

They watched in silence, noting that the flame in the darkness grew and waned, moving from left to right. The phone crackled.

"Police desk? This is Government House. There was a bang... yes I know." The ADC turned his flustered face to Lawton and said: "It's your office. It has gone up, Major."

Lawton turned to H.E. and sketched a gesture in the air which asked permission to retire and, without waiting for an answer, raced for the gardens. He found his car and driver after a brief search and rushed down the hill into the town. Sirens were blaring now and police in lorries were closing in on what at first seemed a shapeless white cloud among the houses — a cloud of cordite and brickdust. Lawton plunged into it, choking and swearing. He came upon a little group of firemen emerging from the doorway. They were carrying, with infinite precautions, the limp body of Carstairs.

"He's dead, Sir," said one of them, recognizing him. Lawton shook with suppressed rage at the thought. "He's the only casualty," added the fireman.

Outside the radius of the smoke he found Brewster nursing a head-wound as he sat on a pile of rubble waiting for the ambulance. "What was he doing in the office at this time?" asked Lawton incoherently, still full of a sense of outrage.

"A service message came over WT and I phoned him, Sir. I thought it might be urgent. No sooner he came than it went off between our teeth, Sir." He shivered and his teeth began to chatter.

An ambulance raced towards them with its bell jangling. "But the safes all held out," said Brewster as an afterthought. "I made the firemen check."

"Damn the safes," said Lawton as he walked slowly down the street to his villa.

17

Enter Schiller

For forty-eight hours after the explosion they worked at top speed to extricate and re-site all the equipment which had not suffered damage from the blast. Their offices they moved to the southern wing of the building. Carpenters and masons crowded them out for a while, building bookshelves and filing cabinets and walling-in safes. Yet at last they brought some order out of chaos and were able to resume the average routine of the normal working day. In all this excitement there had been no chance to see anything of Grete, for Lawton had worked until the small hours each night. Finally the work was done, however, and he was on the point of telephoning her when his door burst open and there she stood, newspaper in her hand. She looked strangely pale and moved, as if some experience had dazed her into speechlessness.

"Grete," he said. "Come in." Then he caught sight of the expression on her face and rose to his feet anxiously. "What is it?" She handed him the copy of the *Jerusalem Post* and pointed to an item. It read:

NAZI WAR CRIMINAL ADVISING EGYPTIAN ARMY?

Unconfirmed rumours circulating in Cairo suggest that Nazi General Günther Schiller, who could not be traced at the end of the war, is to be found in Egypt, where he holds the post of adviser to the Egyptian army in tank warfare. Schiller, it will be recalled, was one of the senior tank experts of the German command and at one time acted as Rommel's Chief of Staff during the desert campaign.

Lawton read slowly through the message and then raised his troubled eyes to the girl.

"What is it all about?" he asked.

"It is my husband," she said, and gave a cracked laugh which turned suddenly into a sob. She put her hand over her mouth and stared at him.

"I thought he was dead. Can it be him?"

"Your *husband*?" said Lawton, still struck dumb by the idea. She nodded.

"But how?" he asked.

"The Party found out I was Jewish and ordered him to surrender me to the S.S. He obeyed. It was either that or disgrace. He was a professional soldier, you see."

"He let you go?"

"He thought Hitler was a god."

"Wait a minute," said Lawton. An idea struck him. "I think we have a file on him." He went to the wall safe and extracted a yellow folder from the "top secret" file. He riffled the pages for a moment, looking for what he wanted, and then gave a grunt.

"Better still," he said. "We have a picture. Would you recognize it?"

It was not too clear a photograph, but it showed a man in civilian clothes walking beside an Egyptian army officer along some street in an Arab town.

Grete gazed dully at this with an air of stupefaction. "Yes, that's him all right. He could never disguise those duelling marks." She raised her head and stared at the blank wall before her in a fit of abstraction, while a million ideas collided with one another in her mind. Then she said, with a sudden fire but as if speaking more to herself than to Lawton:

"The only living soul who can tell me if the child is alive or dead." She turned to Lawton then with blazing eyes:

"I must find a way to see him. Don't you see, he's the only one who knows."

Lawton reflected for a long moment. "You could hardly go there, it would be too dangerous, and besides the Egyptians would never let you in."

"Couldn't you get him brought here through the office — extradite him?"

Lawton shook his head slowly. "Egypt is a sovereign territory," he said. "The most we could do would be to deal diplomatically with them about it. Send them an aide-memoire telling them that he's wanted in Germany and asking them to return him there. But you know the Egyptians as well as I do, he's too useful to them. They'll deny his existence altogether. Then what could we do? You see, from the file it's obvious that he's masquerading under the name of Schmidt and has a valid Swiss passport."

"There must be a way!" she cried. "Please think of something!" Her voice rose hysterically, and he took her arm sympathetically, saying:

"Let me think it over." He paused. "… If only he were here, it would be easy. I could get a warrant out for him in no time."

He stopped, drew a deep breath and went on. "What I will do is this, I'll send a signal to Cairo asking for more information."

"What good would that do?"

He tried to sound cheerful. "You never know, we might unearth something new about him."

"But I must see him, don't you understand?" She burst out: "I must know about the child!"

He lit his pipe, saying nothing, and then, taking the file, he returned it to the safe. She watched him absently with an air of sullen resignation, but the faintest germ of an idea had already formed in her mind. Furtively she watched the fingers as they spun the lock of the combination safe. Five, six to the right, eight, seven to the left… it was not impossibly difficult to memorize. As the combination clanged home and the safe handle clicked into its socket, she turned and rushed from the room back to her own office. Breathlessly she jotted down the safe combination while it was fresh in her mind, and then sat very still for a while, thinking. Then she rose and crossed the room to examine her face in the mirror. She had gone suddenly very pale. "The news has aged you all at once," she told her reflection. She left her office and walked down the long stairway, briefcase in hand; the door of the registry stood ajar and she put her head through it to ask a question of the duty janitor.

"What time does the post office shut?"

He looked at his watch and said: "Six, dearie. You'll just make it."

It was eleven o'clock that night when she put on her dark mackintosh and gloves and made her way down the winding streets towards her office again; but this time, instead of going to the front gate with its sentry-box, she took another route. She had a key to the back door; she reached it through an unguarded wicket gate, crossing the grass on noiseless feet. The building was deserted — she had picked her time. The night watchmen made a round of inspection every hour, and the patrol had just passed down the corridors of the annexe, testing all the door handles. She slipped down to the janitor's office and possessed herself of the tagged keys to Lawton's room. Quietly she walked into his office and turned on the desk lamp. The safe opened to her skilful fingers and she groped about in it until she came upon the dossier of NAZI WAR CRIMINALS IN HIDING. Then she sat down at the desk and copied out the contents of the file in long-hand. It took her almost an hour. Midnight was striking from the clocks of Jerusalem when she made her way back to her flat down the deserted street. It was too soon to expect David, for the drive from Ras Shamir was a long one; nor was she quite certain whether he would act swiftly on her telegram. He might, for example, be absent. She poured out a drink and sat down to wait a while; suddenly the phone rang.

It was David's voice. "I was here in Jerusalem," he said, "and your message was relayed back to me from the centre. Are you all right?"

"Yes," she said, and he sighed with relief.

"I'll be round in ten minutes."

At last he stood before her, staring at her with concern and curiosity.

"David," she said, "I've changed my mind. I have decided to work for you."

He stared at her. "How pale you are."

"Am I?" She shrugged her shoulders and lit a cigarette. "And why have you suddenly changed your mind?" he asked doubtfully.

"I see you don't quite believe me," she answered. "Here, this will prove my *bona fides*. It is a secret MI file copy."

David looked it over hastily, greedily, and laughed incredulously.

"What a coincidence," he said. "Just the man I had been told to capture."

"I heard that the Haganah were busy catching war criminals."

"It's true. I had been told to pick a mission to get this particular one. But alas it is not going to work." He shook his head sadly.

"Why not?" she said sharply.

"Identification," he said. "We are not absolutely certain as yet that he is Schiller. We can't afford to make a mistake — carry off some innocent Swiss and cause a diplomatic incident. We must be sure."

"Well, *I* am sure," she said. "He is my husband; and I must find a way to get to him. If you won't help me I must go alone."

David stared at her with open mouth. "Husband!" Then his face fell. "Do you... are you still... in..."

Her harsh laugh surprised him. "He has some information which I must get out of him. Will you go, and will you take me? And when?"

"You must give me time. It's not my decision, you know. And besides, it will be dangerous. Port Said is seething with spies."

"I will identify him for you; the rest is up to you. Bring him back here where I can talk to him. Please, David." She squeezed her hands together so violently that the knuckles went white.

"I'll ring you first thing in the morning," he said. That was all. But he still stood looking her over with sorrowful attention.

"It isn't what you think," she said. He left without a word.

~

The decision having at last been taken, and the raid planned in detail,

Grete took a week's leave from the office, telling Lawton that she was going to spend a few days on the Dead Sea with a girl friend.

"Well," he said, "there at least you can come to no harm. I understand you can't sink even if you try; and poor old Carstairs used to quote a rather sinister epigram about the place which ended:

'Here the Sodom sunlight blisters

Queen Alexandra's nursing sisters'.

So watch your step."

"I promise," she said.

"Everything may have changed by the time you get back," he said gravely. "We have an Immediate from the Secretary of State this morning. They are going to take the Jewish case to UNO."

"Are they?" she cried. "What a relief."

"Misguidedly in my view," he said. "We shall lose the vote, and lose Palestine as well."

"Then what?"

"Happily for me we shall be withdrawn from here; and the Jews will be left to the tender mercies of the Arabs. Grete, I'm going to ask you something when you come back. Something personal."

18

Exit Isaac Jordan

Once more back in the comparative isolation of Ras Shamir, Judith
threw herself into the ordinary work of the kibbutz with a new energy
and delight, due partly to the knowledge of Aaron's return and partly
to her own returning physical health. Of the future she did not wish to
think in any detail, so perfect was the notion of a present in this quiet
valley. Once she managed to spend the day in Jerusalem, engaged in
consultations with the physicists at the Institute: she telephoned to
Aaron but he was away in the desert, and she had to be content to
return without seeing him. Nor did he ever write. The three months
until his return seemed an eternity, but in the end they passed, and
once more she saw him riding his little white horse across the valley, and once more they were free to visit his tumbledown shack of
a "country house" to pick the wild flowers which had taken possession of the abandoned garden. As if by common consent, they did not
speak of the future, did not try and peer into the mists ahead. They
were content to inhabit the sunlit present, to enjoy each other without
premeditation.

But the country was changing around them, and even here, in this
sleepy valley, they could not fully escape the pressures of history. A

new and bitter purposefulness had begun to grow up. Even Aaron had become harder, more masterful, more self-possessed. New faces appeared at the kibbutz now — the weary but determined faces of the soldiers back from active service with the Jewish Brigade. Their features were engraved with a new determination — a new purpose. The secret preparations for defence of the kibbutz also altered with the influx of better weapons, sterner training. Aaron had begun to think professionally now of times, dispositions, tactical arrangements. He was still a general without an army, but the force he would dispose of in case of trouble had now become a considerable one, for each of the mountain kibbutzim had set aside a promised task-force to come to the aid of Ras Shamir if it were attacked; and of course the kibbutz in its commanding position was the valley's key and central prop. Situated where it was, it was terribly vulnerable.

New activities pressed upon him; small groups of young men from the underground came in from time to time to visit him with news. There were long confabulations by lamplight. News was exchanged in conspiratorial tones now. The country was full of British troops whose task it was to smother the smouldering unrest in both Jewish and Arab hearts. "We are slowly passing through the eye of the needle," Aaron would say. Though it made her sick at heart, she too began to feel the thrill of a new purpose. It was infectious, it was in the air. Was the idea of Israel then a realizable reality? But side by side with this was also a fear for his physical safety. New operations were being planned. Day by day the toll of sabotage mounted.

One morning she saw Aaron talking to an elderly man who seemed vaguely familiar; she recognized the old sea captain who had brought her through the blockade in the "Zion". It was Isaac Jordan. He, for his part, hardly recognized her, so much had she changed, but it did not in the least qualify his delight at seeing her. He was driving about the country in an old car, whose sides bore the legend "FRESH FRUITS AND VEGETABLES LTD." The old "Zion", he said, had sprung a leak and was being docked for overhaul. "But bless you," he said, "I can't sit idle at my time of life. My mother always told me that Satan would find work for idle hands to do. So I've gone into market-gardening. Look." He pulled aside a tarpaulin. The whole of the back was indeed full of crates of vegetables. Isaac winked and, puffing at his pipe gingerly, removed one of the crates as one might remove a brick from a wall. "Peek through," he said airily. Aaron did so and whistled. "All for us," he crooned, and Jordan waved a great paw in a gesture of liberality. "All for you," he said. "Hand-picked stuff with the dew fresh on it."

Aaron produced a pad and pencil and Jordan recited in a low voice: "Thirty Tellers Mark 4, twenty cases of industrial dynamite, four drums of signal wire..."

She moved off to allow them to talk privately, and presently heard the truck rumble away towards the underground arsenal where Anna, bright-eyed and chuckling, would doubtless be delighted at this offering.

That afternoon Aaron seemed preoccupied and thoughtful, and she sensed that something was going forward which concerned him. At last he told her. "There's an ammunition ship in Haifa harbour which they want to blow up. The job has fallen to me. Isaac is arranging the details. It's apparently very sketchily guarded and he thinks we could get aboard as a ration party with a few cases of fresh vegetables."

"When?"

"Tuesday."

She thought wildly for a moment. "You need not worry," said Aaron. "Isaac never makes foolhardy gestures. He says it is as safe as houses. They have the uniforms and the passes and everything."

"I'm coming with you," she said.

Aaron looked at her searchingly for a moment. "I can't take you. It's not my op. Isaac is chief on this one."

"Then you just tell him from me I'm coming and to find something for me to do."

"Are you serious?"

They stared at each other for a long time.

"What do you think?" she said at last.

"I think you are — I know you are," he said and took her in his arms.

Next morning he told her that Isaac had agreed and had allotted her a part in the operation. She sighed deeply, with a mixture of regret and elation. For the first time she felt fully committed.

Their rendezvous was a rather desolate hut on the outside margins of Haifa, in a sort of *terrain-vague* where once some long-since abandoned company had tried to quarry stone from the cliffs. A battered sign board still stood on the main road, with its worn letters proclaiming that inside the barbed wire was a territory belonging to the Kapa Mines. It was a desolate enough place, but easy to find; there was a bus-stop in front of the main gate. Judith arrived at dusk and found it without difficulty. She obeyed instructions and walked along the deserted paths until she saw a Nissen hut with a pale gleam of light inside. She knocked timidly at the door and was admitted to the company of four British soldiers. Isaac himself, clad incongruously as a warrant-officer, was playing cricket with his Bible. Two blonde Poles sat beside him smoking, while Aaron, also in British Army uniform, was occupied in a corner winding up lengths of fuse. "Good," he cried when he saw her, and Isaac raised his grizzled head from his notebook to announce that if things went on this way there was no doubt that Surrey was going to win. Judith was given an ATS uniform, and her papers; her task was to drive the "ration" lorry. There was a large bottle of gin on the table and Isaac poured them all liberal tots while she changed. He was in a pensive and rather melancholy mood, which he explained by saying "I'm rather sorry to send up the old 'Minerva'. She was a good old-fashioned ship and her skipper was a pal of mine. He kept a very good table indeed. However, they've filled her with delicious vegetables and left her there. A sitting target. Moreover, being a man of peace myself, I hate loss of life, and I think we can pull this off, and make one of the nastiest bangs ever heard in the universe, break all the windows in Haifa, without actually killing anyone. That would be wonderful, would it not?" He beamed at the assembled company.

Aaron was still preoccupied in the corner with some technicality. "Isaac — this bloody fuse-wire," he said. Isaac nodded and pursed his lips. "I know. It's a new type. It seems to be slow burning, but it was very damp when we got it. Myself I ordered a couple of time-pencils but they couldn't steal them for me in time, so we shall have to make do. Judith Roth!"

"Yes?"

"Does that uniform fit you?"

"Well…"

"I'm afraid it is too late to have it taken in here and there. In twelve minutes thirty seconds you have to drive us."

"It'll do," she said. "It'll do."

"Good."

Jordan closed his Bible and said: "Now let us just run over the details for a moment." They all came and sat around him while he talked, puffing at his pipe and taking an occasional nip of gin to round off remarks. "As you see," he said, "it is theoretically simple. Agreed?"

They all nodded.

"Twixt cup and lip, however," said Isaac prophetically, "you know the proverb."

It was well after dark when they set out in the stolen three-tonner. Judith and Isaac sat in front with Judith driving, while Aaron and the two other youthful soldiers were accommodated behind, with their four or five large crates of vegetables. As they rumbled down the hill towards the ill-lit town, they felt the tug of anxiety and danger ahead. Haifa was under curfew, and only the dock area appeared to be normally lit up. On the outskirts they passed through their first checkpoint with an ease which struck them all as a very favourable omen. A young and tired-looking corporal took a perfunctory look into the back by torchlight and signalled them forward. Isaac chuckled as they moved on into the town and took a swift puff or two at his pipe before putting it into his pocket. He directed Judith in a low voice. So they arrived at the main gates of the harbour with its little cluster of pickets on duty under an arc-light — naval and military. The sentry who examined their papers winked at Jordan for a brief moment as he busied himself with an air of professional concern. "Rations, eh?" he said. "Okay then."

The lorry rolled across the great network of open stages and warehouses at a sedate pace; it was the only thing moving on wheels in the great no-man's-land of asphalt. The harbour was fairly full of ships which spread the dull yellowish bloom of their landing lights upon the water, as well as across the landing-stages. Somewhere a siren boomed and throbbed.

"Now there is only one picket," said Jordan with pleasure, rubbing his hands. The "Minerva" lay at the far end of the harbour, tied up alongside. She was well lit but apparently deserted. A single gangway linked her to *terra firma* and beside this a naval picket stood under a lamp. They drew up and Isaac climbed out in leisurely fashion, banging on the tarpaulin-covered truck with his hand and calling: "Show a leg you duffers!" Meanwhile, Judith too climbed down and turned her bright eyes upon the young sentry. She began to grope for her papers, but Isaac called out in jovial fashion: "Number three ration fatigue. Father Christmas is here, mate!" The sentry grinned and said, "Okay mate! Make it slippy then."

It was breathtaking, the ease of the whole thing.

The forage party, led by Isaac, unloaded its crates and made its way in leisurely fashion up the gang-plank of the "Minerva", while Judith turned the truck round and brought it back to the sentry-post. She switched off the engine and yawned.

"Been out here long?" asked the sentry sympathetically. "You looked pretty browned off!" Judith nodded. "Too long. I'm sleepy," she said. "Been on duty since three." The sentry tapped a bored foot and sighed. "My relief will be along soon. And right glad I'll be for a kip!"

It seemed an eternity, the five or so minutes she spent there on the deserted landing-stage talking to the sentry under the yellow arc-light. Then the little party appeared, grinning and talking in low tones. Judith switched on. Aaron and Isaac both climbed into the front with her. She let in the clutch and the lorry started slowly along the quays. "I'm still not happy about that fuse, Isaac," Aaron was saying in a preoccupied way. "I gave it another forty or so for good measure." Isaac grunted and said: "I don't know. We have to make do with what we can get these days. I think it will be…"

As he spoke they heard behind them a series of heavy but muffled jolts. They were not bangs in the accepted sense of the word, but as if someone had taken a blacksmith's hammer and delivered a couple of tremendous blows at the earth's axis. Both men moaned simultaneously as they stared at each other with a wild surmise. They both opened their mouths to speak, but before they could articulate the phrase which was uppermost in their thoughts, the dark sky behind them was suddenly split by a long pencil of light and the sound accompanying it lagged for half a second behind this phenomenon. Their ears were assailed by a great detonation like a sudden roll of drums, which threw up streamers of tracer on the dark sky. The entrails of the "Minerva" heaved and gushed smoke and flame. Involuntarily, Judith pressed the accelerator and the lorry rumbled towards the main gate. The night was full of the noise of smashing glass. It was as if the whole town jumped up in the air and landed suddenly, awkwardly, on its knees with an agonizing bump. Jordan was uttering a string of very choice oaths in a sort of litany — the whole of his naval culture was expressing itself in a riot of poetic licence. But meanwhile, the blast from the first series of explosions, almost palpable, roared across the deserted quays like a whirlwind. Judith aimed straight for the dock gates, where a single sentry stood on duty now; but the night was becoming full of other kinds of movement. A large naval picket was running towards them from the middle distance — a fleck of white on the asphalt grey of the yards. Whistles began to blow. It all began to happen at once. The blast stripped the tarpaulin from the lorry with a single gesture, like someone peeling an onion. Its pressure on the vehicle drove it into a long skid. The sentry slammed the gate to and raised his rifle. With a sickening crunch, the lorry buried its nose in the iron railings and stuck fast. Aaron leaped down and called out to the sentry, who, confused, stood in an attitude of vague menace. He made the mistake of allowing his quarry to approach too close and found himself lifted off his feet and dashed to the ground with a clatter. "Run for it," said Isaac and, as if in a dream, they found themselves running like hares through the main gate and into the darkened town. Behind them the horizon seemed to be on fire. Faint and shrill came the cries of the naval picket racing towards them. Even in the crackle and boom of the "Minerva's" explosion they heard the wicked small stammer of automatic weapons.

They got across the main square safely, only to find that army pickets were racing down to the harbour area along the main streets. They ducked aside into a narrow warren of unlit streets, running and halting in doorways to catch their breath. Running thus, it was some time before they noticed that Isaac was no longer with them. Yet there was nothing to do but press on, for behind them the patrols had multiplied and everywhere lights and sounds had begun to flower against the tapestry of flame in the western end of the harbour. One of the blonde boys said: "I'll go back and see what has happened to him. You carry on."

But it was not merely the pain of the traversing bullets which had halted Isaac in his clumsy run across the square; he felt little pain. Only an enormous sense of weariness came over him, of lassitude. He stood in a doorway shivering, his teeth chattering, to recover his breath. Everything had become vague and incoherent: it felt as if he had been drinking. Almost absently he opened the tunic of his battledress and saw the dark stains on his white sweat-shirt. Something had gone wrong with his breathing. He was overcome by a desire to sleep. He groped for his pipe. It was still alight. He puffed at it once or twice in drunken fashion. Then, still walking like a drunkard, he turned away to the quiet corner of the harbour where "Zion" lay on the slip. Here there was no sign of life at all. All the movement and noise was at the other end of the harbour. He walked softly, imprecisely, but with a sense of purpose. Yes, there she was in the darkness, alone and unguarded. With an effort, he hoisted himself aboard and into the familiar wheelhouse. Here he sat for a moment, getting his breath. Then he reached for his old dirty naval cap. Carefully and patiently he stripped his battledress top and absurd forage cap. In them he carefully wrapped his faked papers, together with a large and heavy spanner. This he tipped overboard and watched it slowly settle and disappear into the murky harbour water. Then he sat down with his head on the wheel of the "Zion", puffing a pipe and listening to his own heartbeats which now seemed to be coming from a long way off; a very long way indeed.

~

Once in the dark hut they lit the lamp and divested themselves of their carnival clothes. The silence was oppressive. They felt an enormous sense of fatigue. There was a loaf of bread and some gin left in the bottle. They divided these in silence and ate like wolves. Isaac's Bible lay on the table. Presently there was a sound of movement outside, and the weary face of the young soldier came into their angle of vision.

"I couldn't find him," he said. "There was a trail of blood back toward the harbour."

It was a day later that they heard of Isaac Jordan's death. Ironically enough, he had not been connected with the act of sabotage on the "Minerva". It was deemed an accident by the military authorities, and in default of any other explanation the Navy, always jealous of their own, decreed that he should have a naval funeral.

19

Across the Border

When Donner's papers finally came home to roost, together with the
signal and Movement Order which made him shake the dust of Palestine off his feet, he was vastly relieved; nor did he disguise the fact from
his superiors. "It's a bloody relief, I can tell you," he said, mopping his
brow and staring out unseeingly at the apricot-coloured walls of Jerusalem, shining softly in the afternoon sunlight. "A really bloody relief." The
Superintendent nodded. "The place has changed for the worse," he said.
"We were better off in the old days." Donner smiled gloatingly. "The
old days are gone," he said prophetically. "This week I've been stoned in
Beersheba, shot at in Nazareth, and found a microphone in a vase. I tell
you, it's getting hot." He rubbed his chin and thought too of the casualty
list which was steadily mounting. "Well," he said, "a policeman's lot is *not*
a happy one, and I'm glad to go for a soldier."

In fact the old tune stayed in his head and he found himself humming it on the way to the airport, resplendent in his new kit which had
been lying ready for this great moment for weeks, wrapped in tissue
paper on the chair by his bed. He kept a look-out for senior officers
in order to have a chance of trying his "regular" salute on them; he
carried this new, this military salute, like a violinist carries his cher-

ished instrument, carefully wrapped, so to speak, and ready at hand. His apotheosis was near. "You will report to Prince Jalal at the Palace immediately on arrival at the capital," read the order. It sounded good, it sounded romantic. Yet he had seen too much of the Middle East to feel romantic about it. He supposed that Jalal was just another "bloody wog", some Arab princeling, ruler of a tin-pot state. But his spirits soared with the plane, and the whole journey seemed to pass in a sort of dream. The battered capital was exactly as he had last seen it some years ago on leave; its dusty palms and faded towers drowsed in the exhausted tepid air. A city of dust and disillusion.

But he was a trifle put out to find that Prince Jalal, after letting him cool his heels in an anteroom for an hour, received him without any outward and visible sign of gladness. He was not only a very good-looking man with carefully manicured hands, but he spoke beautifully fastidious English and wore a Rifle Brigade tie. Donner executed his salute and received no response beyond a nod. The Prince was in mufti — the sort of mufti which spelled Camberley. He pulled down the Regency waistcoat and regarded Donner absently. "Yes," he said in the tone of a man classifying an insect, "you are to take the cars up tomorrow. You know the assignment. You will be attached to the Mission under Towers."

"Yes, Sir," said Donner hoarsely, saluting again.

"You know the country, I gather from your report."

"Like the back of my hand," said Donner, and extended the back of his hand, noticing with chagrin that it was somewhat grubby.

The Prince smoothed a carefully trimmed moustache and crossed the room to a great operational wall-map of the western border. "Towers' dispositions are here," he said vaguely, pointing with his chin, as his hands busied themselves with the trimming of a mouthpiece in a slender cigar. "He will explain everything. As you know, our forces are under my brother, the Prince Daud. You will take some despatches up to him from us — my equerry will give them to you. He will also take you to the cars. They are waiting. Better check them over tonight and start early. They must be in good shape for desert work. Towers is always groaning about mobility. Now he'll have some."

Donner breathed hard through his nose. This damn wog telling him his business; moreover wearing a Rifle Brigade tie! The Prince crossed back to his desk and lit up with the huge ornate lighter. As he puffed, he said in a tone of idle reminiscence: "It's a cushy sector and presents few problems. In the event of hostilities — at the moment things look as if they are moving that way — your only tactical problem will be to take and reduce Ras Shamir."

"Money for jam," said Donner.

"So we think. They are not armed, or hardly."

"Perhaps an automatic rifle at most. I have been over the place three times with a fine-tooth comb."

"I know." The Prince puffed for a moment and wrinkled his brow. "That's all, I think. You can take yourself off."

Donner saluted smartly and did a regimental turn. Under his breath he said to himself: "The bastard!"

But if the Prince was a source of disappointment to Donner, His Majesty's Equerry was even more infuriating; he wore an Old Etonian tie and a monocle on a length of black tape. And he lisped.

From the central State Tent of the Prince Daud, with its brilliant hangings and vast acreage of carpets, its forest of inlaid tables and elaborate chairs and cushions all spread upon the smooth sand dunes, came screams of laughter in a high register. They were all seated upon the ground. Daud himself, the Vizier, the three State Councillors and old Abu Taib. The cause of their merriment was the little toy train which Colonel Towers had brought back from his last leave as a present for Daud. It rolled unerringly round and round the skilful cobweb of railway lines until it reached the little red station where it stopped once more. But this time in doing so it had seemed to be about to pass under Abu Taib's robes, and the old man had leaped back with a shriek, like a school-child pursued by a mouse. Hence the merriment. The slim wand-like figure of Daud was bent double. The tears ran down that beautiful and gentle face. He struck his thigh with his palm. It was a capital joke. When the paroxysm had ended, as it always did, in a burst of hoarse coughing — to remind him bitterly of his illness — Daud sprang up impulsively, tears still wet on his cheek. "No, but by God he is right, this Towers," he cried, "It is certainly as beautiful as a poem by Hafiz, this little machine. He is right!" His large benign eyes bloomed with affection and gratitude. His was a face and figure of extraordinary inbred refinement. Daud was as slender as a stag and as emotional and impulsive as a girl. The ivory skin of his features — helped perhaps by the hereditary consumption of his family — was of a beautiful, almost unearthly pallor. Now as he debated, staring at the engine, his long slender fingers picked at the tassel of his belt. "Once more," he said, "and I will go and thank him. Just once more." This time the merriment was even greater, due to an unforeseen interruption by Daud's cheetah, which had watched the manoeuvres of the train in silence up to now; but on this next occasion — as if it could no longer resist the moving toy, any more than a cat can resist a mouse — it advanced in a single bound and stood like a heraldic animal with its paw raised. As the engine stopped, it touched it once, twice, lightly with its velvet paw and then went off to its corner again with a disappointed air. This was a marvellous joke.

Daud burst out of his tent and swept across the smooth dunes to where the little circle of British Mission tents had been pitched. He moved with a flame-like swiftness and grace, still laughing, his lips still moving with unuttered speeches. He threw back the flap of Towers' dusty old bell-tent and cried, "Thank you, Towers, thank you! You are quite right." There was no answer and Daud peeped in.

The old colonel lay snoring on his camp-bed, with an empty bottle of whisky standing upright on the canvas floor beside him. Daud gazed at him with affection, almost with passion. The black patch which normally shielded Towers' right eye had come away a little, to expose the shrapnel-torn socket. His uniform jacket, neatly placed upon a coat-hanger, swung slowly in a corner of the tent, vaunting its long triple row of decorations. His soiled undervest was stained violet at the armpits with sweat. He snored softly and dreamed: he was just driving off the third tee at Lyme Regis into a westerly wind which forced one to bear down slightly to avoid slicing... Daud placed a finger on the wrist of the sleeper and said: "You are a good man, Towers. I will write to your master and have you ennobled."

Then he turned back abruptly and walked slowly back to his tents, his bent head hanging, deep in thought.

Towers slept on softly. He was a most popular figure in his command, not only because of his knowledge and respect for Arab forms of courtesy, but also for an appealing vein of idiosyncrasy in his character, which made him seem to them something of an original. He was the only British officer they had seen carry a chamber-pot on active service — blue flowers on a white ground. Then too, every afternoon when he was off duty, he took a driver and practised swinging for half an hour, as religiously as a Muslim answering a call to prayer. This little ritual always ended by him producing from a green baize bag a number of battered repaints which he drove, slowly, thoughtfully, *majestically* into the desert, where the delighted children fielded them, knowing that he always gave baksheesh to those who brought them back. "I *like* my Arab," Towers used to say sometimes after dinner when he was mellowed by whisky. "And I think he likes me." The Arabs did love him, and paid him the compliment of conferring on him the title of "father". "Not that I have anything against the Jews," Towers would add whenever the vexed question of Palestine cropped up. "Far from it. Fine fellers all. But in next to no time they'll turn the whole country into a Manchester suburb, what?"

It was among such simple formulations that he moved, but of recent months even he had begun to feel the shape and form of things changing around him; new issues with sharp edges were coming to light on all sides. It was consoling in a way to be able to take refuge in his soldier's role and leave all the rest to the invisible politicians who would shape the destinies of the future.

He was awake and dressed now, however, by the time Donner piloted in his convoy of squat armoured cars amidst great rejoicing that evening. He acknowledged Donner's salute briefly, rather admiring its professional finish. "Well, Captain," he said, "come into the Command Tent for a brief drink of welcome."

They transacted their business over a glass of whisky, and Donner handed over his despatches, together with the ornate pigskin pouch in which the Prince's private despatches had been placed. "I don't want to be pessimistic," said Towers, "but I feel bound to confess to my staff that I think things are blowing up. We've made too many promises to too many people. We can't keep them all. I'm no politico, but I'll lay you short odds that H.M.G. will funk it and try and crawl into the skirts of UNO for a vote on the Mandate."

Donner coughed and nodded vaguely. He hardly knew or cared what the issues were, provided they permitted him to earn a living as a mercenary. It all sounded faintly anti-British in tone. He pursed his rosy lips and put on a slightly unwilling expression, as though such trenchant remarks were in some way wounding to his finer sentiments. "And if we do," said Towers, banging his hand down on the *Daily Telegraph*, "in my view we'll lose the day."

He was more explicit that night at a Staff Conference lit by a swinging hurricane lamp. The little group of Mission officers listened to him thinking aloud with various expressions of polite scepticism. "In such an event the place would flare up and I have no doubt that we'd be ordered over the border — ordered to seize Ras Shamir and perhaps move up on the road near us here. Fortunately, the operation would be a simple one against unarmed people; but the cars would give us mobility. However, we can't afford to take it easy; our infantry training is still groggy. A good regiment, gentlemen, matures slowly, like a good wine. You can't rush it. And we haven't had time. So I personally hope that everything will stay quiet. But if they tell us to move we shall have to. Anyway, that's all for now. In the morning Captain Donner is going to give us a shoot; these cars carry quite a hefty pom-pom he tells me..." And so forth.

Later he walked for a while with Donner to examine the cars and meet the crews. "You'd better give the Prince and his entourage a ride tomorrow after the shoot," said Towers. "These little gestures go down very well — anyway, he is nominally C-in-C. Ach!" Donner looked at the colonel, wondering what the expression signified. Towers smiled. "I'm tired, Donner," he said mildly. "That's all. Just tired. I'm within three months of retirement anyway, thank goodness. Got a little cottage down Lyme Regis way waiting for me, and I can't wait. I'm harness-weary."

"Funny old bugger," said Donner later in the mess tent, as he drank a glass of beer among his compeers. "I hope he knows what he's at."

By his standards, Towers was going to be "tricky" — too much of a gentleman by half, and a wog-lover obviously. That evening Daud sent for Towers. He was seated in a veritable sea of papers thrown about in higgledy piggledy fashion. The Palace pouch lay before him. "My brother says there will be war and we will have to take Ras Shamir," he said, his face registering a strange mixture of emotions, joy, confusion and sorrow all at once.

"Your brother may be right," said Towers soberly.

"Come," said Daud abruptly, "come and walk." It was as if he needed to sort out these conflicting emotions. They walked in silence along the rosy cliffs for a while; below them slumbered the silent valley of Ras Shamir, deep in violet mist. The lights of the mountain settlements twinkled like stars across the unguarded border. Daud was at a loss to understand why his heart sank at every mention of his brother's name; it was not jealousy, for he loved Jalal deeply. It was something else. Jalal had been away, abroad, and this had somehow changed everything between them. He, Daud, had always been sickly, confined to his bed for long terms, too ill to risk a life in cold climates. He had never left his country. Indeed, it was much to his credit that he had learned as much as he had from the Palace tutors. His English was good though imprecise, and he could stumble in French. But Jalal! When he came back it was a different sort of Jalal. He was impatient and contemptuous of the old easy-going ways of his own people. He preferred foreign friends and foreign ways; he preferred the life of the court, with its intrigues, to the life here among the tents of the clan. Daud sighed heavily and took Towers' arm. He pointed to the valley below them and said with a sudden little access of emotion: "Ach, Towers! Ras Shamir! We must have it again — we must have it." He bit his white knuckle with whiter teeth. "You know it," he said, almost pleadingly, his fine eyes swollen with a facile emotion. Towers delivered himself of a grunt. "My ancestors were born there," continued Daud with a flowing gesture, "my family and line sprang from there. Now the Jews have it and we are here." With his other arm he described an arc which followed out the contours of the desert, covered by day with their grazing flocks and brilliant tents. It was a surprising contrast: the brilliant moonlit valley below and the bare rufus cliffs on which they stood — stone shaling away immediately into sand and wave-worn rocky foothills.

"It was a swamp before," Towers reminded the young man softly. Daud stood sunk in thought. "Now all the nations will be speaking about it with your leaders," pursued Towers. He had had great difficulty in getting Daud to understand the workings of UNO and the nature of its deliberations. Daud nodded, solemnly biting his knuckle until it hurt him, until tears came into his eyes. "They will understand the Arabs' feelings," he said. "How great we are! Did the Arabs not invent mathematics? You yourself have said so, Towers, and you do not lie." Towers agreed solemnly. But Daud was troubled. "But now they are speaking of a *jihad*, a holy war. The old King has told us to be ready — my brother says so. He has made you give us these wonderful cars." He turned his great sentimental liquid eyes upon Towers. "And the astrologers say that in war I shall be invincible this year. But war, Towers… how could I think of war with them — with Aaron, my friend? That is what troubles me." He hung his head and pulled at his lip. Then his face lit up with a smile. His white teeth flashed under his silky moustache and he struck his knee with his hand. "I have it. I shall ask Aaron to visit me, and we can speak of the matter like old friends. He will understand my feelings, Towers. He above all will understand."

Towers looked quizzical but he did not reply directly. Indeed, there was nothing to say. He put his arm out and touched Daud's wrist; a gesture of affection. They returned in silence.

"Well," said Towers to himself as he got into bed, "I trust that I shall have retired before they start any *jihad* nonsense here. I think H.M.G. must be mad, quite mad. Broken promises on every side and a complete lack of any clear-cut policy. Never seen such a mess in a long career of soldiering. Never!"

～

The shoot the next morning was a great success, as indeed was the triumphal progress of Daud and his entourage by armoured car. Daud was flushed with pleasure and excitement and lost in admiration for these glorious instruments of war. But when, at a signal from Donner, they fired a few ranging shots with the heavy anti-tank guns they carried, he fairly pranced with joy. His clansmen clustered about them like honey bees; and when the machine guns opened up a rapid fire in concert they rolled on the ground with joy. The children fell down like snipe shocked by close gunfire, but screamed with laughter and rolled over and over in the sand. Daud pressed Towers' calloused hand and then put it briefly to his cheek. "What wonders these are," he said with his vivid, innocent smile. "They will make me invincible in battle, Towers."

Then he added with a change of expression: "I have sent them to ask Aaron to come. I must see him, Towers. I know he will understand me."

Indeed, that morning the lean figure of Abu Taib had crossed the border on his elegant black Arab, accompanied by an escort of two horsemen bearing pennons with white flags. They moved with speed and discretion down the defile, surprised and relieved to find that there were no guards and no checkpoints. Once on the greensward by the river, they let their steeds out and thundered across the water-meadows to bear Daud's invitation to Aaron. The escort reined in and waited some five hundred yards from the perimeter, while the old man, with his spiky whiskers blowing, raced on up to the kibbutz. He was in luck, for Aaron happened to be there, and he was able to deliver his invitation couched in the correct terms — neatly turned phrases full of archaic flourishes. Aaron thanked him but hesitated. He looked serious, undecided, doubtful. He stared at the ground. "Well?" said Abu Taib with a hint of disappointment in his glance. "Will you come?" At last Aaron sighed and said he would.

It took a little time to saddle up a horse and accompany the old man back to the defile, a journey which they accomplished in silence. The jingle of harness must have alerted Daud, for he appeared in the doorway of his tent with his dark eyes wide with expectation and delight. The two men stood for a long moment looking at each other, then each cried the other's name as they rushed into an embrace. It was almost like man and wife meeting, so tender was Daud's embrace, so genuine the emotion of Aaron. Arms round each other, they turned back into the tent to complete the civil formalities of their meeting by an exchange of coffee, fruit and bread dipped in salt. Daud was like a child, beside himself with delight. "Oh Aaron,

I knew you would come. I knew it. I knew it." He stroked his friend's arm, pinched his cheek. "So we could speak of everything and settle everything without anger. Before God, how could I have anger for you, my friend? Oh Aaron, you understand, don't you?" And, before Aaron could reply, he placed a sugar-dusted loucoum between his lips. "The nations are speaking of us Arabs," went on Daud incoherently. "They will grant us back... Aaron, the valley I must have once more. Come." Impulsively he led his friend across the dunes towards the steep cliffs which overlooked Ras Shamir. "I am to be invincible in war and games of skill. Oh Aaron, is it not marvellous, my friend? But we will arrange everything in peace and amity. Your people shall go in peace, with presents, and not a hair of the head harmed. I promise you. Do you see, my dear friend?"

It was difficult to know how to reply to this torrent of disconnected phrases, and while Aaron was still hunting for words, Daud clapped his hands and signalled to his servants.

"Now a surprise for you, which will make you smile, give you pleasure. We will play the old game we have not played since childhood. Then you always won, but today, my dear friend..." He squeezed Aaron's arm affectionately. As if from nowhere two big box-kites had materialized, carried onto the scene by grinning Arabs; they were beautifully made, slender and vivid, with long tasselled tails. One was blue and one was black. Aaron smiled as he saw them. "Still the same old Daud!" he said.

"Still the same old Daud," echoed the prince with a giggle, obviously delighted at his own ingenuity. "You have forgotten, Aaron?"

"No," said Aaron, grinning at his friend. "Of course not!" "Shall we play?"

Their horses had been led to them, and mounting now they galloped across the dunes, trailing the kites behind them until these rose gracefully into the air; then, reining and turning about, they began to play them. The mild currents of air drew the kites over the cliffs and they let them out to their full extent now, to swim and tremble in the sky over the silent valley. They were all but knee to knee as they played. Daud chuckled with excitement and pleasure. He began to talk profusely, never taking his eyes off his kite. Aaron's black kite was some way behind. Daud said: "Aaron, when the valley is ours again we shall often play, eh? But this year I shall win every time. Next year perhaps you will, old friend. Did you see the wonderful cars they have sent me?"

Aaron sighed and nodded. "Yes," he said. "Four."

"No, six, six!" cried Daud. "They are so…"

Aaron cut him short impatiently, "Daud," he said, "this can never be, for the valley is ours now and forever will be, for we have worked it with our hands. We bought it lawfully — remember?" Daud pouted and looked at him cajolingly. "Come, friend, be reasonable. You will spoil everything," he said. Aaron said: "I am speaking the truth." Daud said: "But if our King says I must take it, you will have to give it, do you see?"

Aaron, his eyes still on the dancing kites, said: "Think, Daud. My grandfather paid your grandfather money for this valley. Then it was a desolate swamp and dangerous with fevers. With the money he paid, your own clan became rich in tents and camels and wives. Before they were not." Daud nodded irritably. "All this is known and finished," he said, and yawned. "Now we need it again. My brother has said so, it is so. The matter is finished."

"Then it will be war," said Aaron. "I tell you that."

Daud's eye flashed with sudden malice. "Those who want war will have war," he said softly, between clenched teeth. "But not with you, Aaron."

"With me if necessary, Daud."

But the war was taking place in the heavens above them now, for with the old manoeuvre which had won him so many victories in the past, Aaron had allowed his kite to cross strings with the blue kite. They trembled and swayed in the guttering wind, as if they were two brilliant fighting-cocks attacking each other. "No!" cried Daud suddenly. "It shall not be!"

Aaron's kite managed at last to sever the string of the blue kite; it reeled and careened and began to settle, to fall trembling into the valley. A sob broke from Daud's throat. They stared at one another grimly. Aaron dropped the stick to which his own kite was attached. It fell in the sand between them.

"I leave you the omen, Daud," he said, staring keenly at his childhood friend under his dark brows. "Now I will return. Goodbye."

Daud stared after him. His eyes were full of tears now, but they were tears of pique, of rage; so this is how his overtures of friendship had been greeted by his oldest friend!

"You will see, then!" he called incoherently after the receding figure. "You will see, Aaron." He was suddenly overtaken by a fit of coughing. He pressed his hands to his sides.

Meanwhile, Aaron was grimly riding among the tents toward the head of the pass, keenly noticing everything: Two regiments deployed across the sand were practicing open-order advance by sections. As he passed the command tent, he came face-to-face with Donner, now dressed in the traditional Arab headgear of the army to which he had been accredited. It gave him an absurd fancy-dress air, that of a pirate in amateur theatricals. They stared at each other.

"So you are here," said Aaron softly.

"Yes. I'm here," retorted Donner with a scowl.

Aaron rode on into the valley, deep in his reflections. That evening he made his report to the small council of at the kibbutz. They sat at an old deal kitchen table in one of the great underground bays, next to the shooting gallery where Anna plied her trade with the weapons they possessed. In spite of the new emplacements which they had tried to scoop out around the perimeter of the camp, the arrival of the armoured cars presented them with a new problem. Aaron smoked his pipe thoughtfully. He scribbled on a pad. "We haven't got enough mines or enough know-how to lay more than a 20 x 20 field," he said gloomily, "but we can easily lay a fake field carefully marked up for all to see; that might help." Then he had a brainwave. "How about cleaning out those two Byzantine granaries? The ones we filled with stores — remember the time some children fell into them?"

"What are you going to do — catch elephants?" Pete said.

"They'd make a sort of anti-tank ditch."

"But they'd see that."

"Not if we cleared by night and camouflaged them with branches during the day. If your minefields were laid on either side with an enticing-looking fairway between...?"

Everyone groaned. "How much more digging do you expect to get out of us?"

"Think it over. They are full of stones, remember, not earth."

"It would take weeks."

"No, surely — days, perhaps." After a long debate the idea was passed, not without reluctance, and that night they began work; that night too came the news that at long last the British had decided to seek a renewal of their Mandate from UNO. They heard the news as they were humping stones, men, women and children together; it sounded strange to hear the news in darkness, standing in the silence of the fields. Judith shivered with a new kind of anticipation and a surge of pleasure which she could not analyse.

Through his powerful glasses Towers, perched on a crag, carefully swept the perimeter of Ras Shamir as was his wont. Lately there had been signs of movement which suggested something more than the customary work upon the soil of those who planted, sowed and tilled. Those two toy-like tractors, for instance, had for the last week been ploughing out a crude lateral dune in the rich soil. "Outworks," he said to himself, reminded of the shallow Roman barrows he had seen in England as a boy. With the first rain they would be covered in grass and weed — the raw marks of the tractors obliterated. Yet they would offer some sort of defensive position. "I wonder," he said to himself. That evening, as he sat over the chessboard facing Daud, he said: "They are digging in at Ras Shamir." Daud looked at him for a long time, but said nothing until he had made his move. Then he pursed his lips and said: "Aaron is no longer a friend."

But Towers did not notice the careful cleaning-out of the two old granaries, for by day they were covered in branches and the kibbutz carpenter had run supports across them strong enough to enable them to take the strain of human beings.

The autumn came slowly on them as they worked, with its deceptive promises of peace and plenty — grapes and figs to be gathered, oranges beginning to become plump. Now, too, came the first rains, and those sudden unpredictable thunderstorms when, for days at a time, the ragged clouds rolled across the rock escarpments, bursting impartially over the desert and the sown, the valley or the encircling dunes. Torrents burst out and poured for a few hours, the Jordan's waters swelled. And, like heavy gunfire, the premonitory thunder rolled across the ranges.

It was in November that the news of the UNO vote was first broadcast to the world, and there was a night of wild rejoicing in the kibbutz. They lit a bonfire for the children and everyone danced. But on the balcony above, looking down on the scene, Miss Peterson stood grave and preoccupied, gazing at the scene of happiness below. Aaron came and stood beside her, and placed his arm on her shoulder, saying: "What is it, Pete?"

"It's too soon for rejoicing," she said quietly. "We shall have much to go through before we can do that."

"Perhaps not," said Aaron. "One never knows. But it is glorious news; Israel can now emerge at last, and with the sanction of the civilized world... Worth dancing about, my love." But Pete sighed and shook her head. "I fear they will contest it, the Arabs."

"Let them!" said Aaron gaily. The news had made him also faintly euphoric. But next day he too became grave, for there came news that the British were issuing orders to regroup and reform for evacuation. The young man who brought him the news added: "First Army group are off down to Haifa in a fortnight, and that leaves the valley undefended except for..."

"Well," said Aaron with a sigh, "what can we do?"

"Be on your toes."

"We are."

20

Into Egypt

David and Saul turned the black Buick southward in the direction of Beersheba. They must, it appeared, first consult Abdul Sami about ways and means, and his place of habitation was a somewhat flexible one, David explained to Grete as they drove, consisting of large and ornate tents pitched in the middle of the desert. The whole encampment moved with the flocks, with the seasons; and with it moved his two hundred wives and his dozens of impish children. Abdul Sami was a large, prosperous-looking Arab who had had his own teeth replaced by a gold set for sheer boredom, and also to impress clients. His smile was one of the most expensive ever seen. It glittered, all gold. Despite his predilection for the desert life, he was a heavily modernized man, and owned several frigidaires, a helicopter, three Rolls-Royces of different colours, which were always getting stuck in the sand, and a complete womens' hairdressing establishment. Here, in a long line under a marquee, one might see a dozen or so wives sitting under glittering globular dryers, while a French coiffeur walked sullenly up and down the row, and the mere concubines waited their fuzzy little turn.

When they arrived, Sami himself was sitting in the open before his state tent, being manicured by a young girl dressed as a BEA air hostess. He was expecting them, and amiably waved his disengaged hand, ordering chairs to be brought. They sat down and fell to business. It was Abdul Sami alone who could (by what mysterious feat of prestidigitation they knew not) get them in and out of Egypt on an illegal mission. The whole business was second nature to him, as he was a hashish smuggler whose fortune depended on the expertise with which he could get his loads of contraband across the Canal to his clients in Cairo.

"Yes," he said in response to a question. "You could call it dangerous I suppose. My wives tend to worry unduly. But you know, so long as there is hashish in Syria and eager clients for it in Cairo, there will never be a completely sealed border. In the old days it was easier; and since the British installed their X-rays in order to peer into the intestines of my camels at the border, I have had to use less subtle methods. But partly by luck and partly by..." He rubbed finger and thumb together. "I always find a hole in the net. My next trip will be in two days when there is no moon. If you wish, you will come with me. But if I am caught you will go to prison for smuggling, no? After all, fair is fair."

So it was that they found themselves walking along the dark banks of the invisible Canal, accompanied by four Arabs and a heavily laden mule. Abdul Sami led the van, steering in the most professional manner upon Vega, and co-ordinating bearings with the help of an oil compass. He puffed and blew and talked far too loudly in their opinion, but presumably he knew his business. Nevertheless, sounds seemed to carry very far in the still air. The noise of twigs crackling in a distant fire came clearly to them in the stillness. Presently they halted and Abdul Sami told them to sit down and wait, an order which they obeyed with relief, for walking across the soft sand had been arduous and chilly. Even the mule showed signs of intelligence and obedience, for, once divested of its load, it lay down quietly near them and did not stir. It was pitch dark. All that they could faintly discern were the stars.

"Nothing to do but wait," said Abdul Sami with resignation. "Pretty soon he will come."

"Who will come?" said the long-nosed and sardonic-voiced Saul, who fiddled nervously with a safety catch on a Luger.

"The head of the Egyptian Customs, Elfi Bey Hamid," said Sami in a courteous though laconic tone. "Who else? I pay him a big salary — much bigger than his official one."

Saul laughed. "Well, that's good," he said. "Tell him I'll double that." Abdul Sami shook his head. "He would not work for a Jew!" he said. "He is too patriotic. But I am an Arab. For me he will do anything."

They bantered for a while in this fashion, and suddenly David let out a sharp exclamation of surprise and awe.

"My God, what is that?" he cried, and instinctively everyone crouched down. It looked as if a castle of fireflies was advancing towards them across the desert.

"It's a ship," said Sami. "Stay still now."

They could not see the outlines of the vessel itself, so dark was it. Only this colony of lights which advanced upon them without noise, as if running on silent rails. Yes, now it was nearer they caught an oily glimpse of the Suez Canal water, and heard a band playing. It was going to pass so close that they could almost touch it with an outstretched hand. A wall of lights towered up over them now, and they heard a band softly playing Noel Coward's "I'll see you again"; figures in evening dress revolved slowly. Just above them a man and a woman stood deep in conversation at the dark rail.

"I was not talking about love," said the woman's voice. "One does not talk about it, one makes it or not and that is all… When we get to India…"

The wall of soft light sloped steeply away from them now, sliding down the Canal, and they saw the faint outline of a funnel or two from which, like a parting signal, there came now a deep velvety lisp of sound — like the cry of some strange animal on the darkness. The music faded. The lights dwindled. Now they were alone again, with only the dark desert around them.

"Ah, there he is," said Sami; the sound of a small motor-boat engine was growing up from the eastern edge of the Canal.

Sami went down to the river bank and shone a light twice, grunting with satisfaction as the invisible boat changed course. In it sat a solitary figure which did not answer their questions.

"He is dumb," said Sami. "They took his tongue." He added the footnote carelessly as part of the general information of the day. "But he is a very good man, eh Mahmud?" He thumped the steersman on the back and paid him from a wad of notes. It took hardly five minutes to cross and they were in Egypt, walking towards the main road, where an agent was to meet them with a car. Now Sami grew even more confident of their safety, and talked and swore quite naturally as they manhauled the packages along. But they had one more fright in store for them. Suddenly, on a line of dunes ahead of them, they saw, outlined against the sky, a series of figures in silhouette. They were armed men, armed Egyptian soldiers spread out in a line, with about four metres between each one. Instinctively the Jewish party let out a gasp and fell to the ground. But Sami burst into a hoot of laughter and urged them on.

"Come, we will speak to them," he said, still uttering his side-splitting giggle. "They are all my friends."

Still puzzled and disbelieving, they followed him hesitantly towards the figures. As he reached the first one, he pushed it over on to the sand and turned his torch on it. It was a dummy made of wood, obviously manufactured for target practice. Sami beat his chest and laughed. "The nearest soldier is one mile," he said.

They reached the road and bade their guide a tender farewell; his rendezvous was in a different direction, and they heard his laughter dwindle in the darkness. Nor was it long before they saw the slow arc of headlights approaching along the desert road. David lit a cigarette as he stood beside the road, and soon they heard his low tones uttering the password "Galilee". The mission had begun propitiously.

~

Horvatz, their host, and the chief agent of the Jews in Cairo, was a comfortable-looking middle-aged man, a stockbroker by profession, who owned a large and comfortable house in Maadi, outside Cairo. As they sped down the desert road towards the whistling sky he told them, in slow confident tones, what there was to be known about the object of their curiosity — Schiller alias Schmidt. Horvatz himself had been signalled from Jerusalem about Grete's participation, and he showed evident relief that at least one person among them would be in a position to make a positive identification.

"The Office is always so hasty," he said. "I dreaded a mistake — for after all I spotted the man and signalled him *myself*; I wouldn't like us to carry off an innocent Swiss." By the time they reached the edge of the desert road and saw the minarets grow up on the pale-rinsed dawn air, Grete herself was asleep. She saw nothing of the town they crossed; indeed, when she awoke it was to find they had entered the grounds of a handsome white house set by the river. Here they were shown to quiet rooms with comfortable beds in them and allowed to lie down and sleep. It was four in the afternoon before they assembled once more to discuss the business in hand. It seemed absurd, incongruous, to be sitting on a green lawn eating cucumber sandwiches and drinking tea, and discussing something as momentous as the carrying off of a war criminal. Horvatz behaved very much like a banker conducting a board meeting, putting before them proposals which, he felt, must appeal to their intelligence... There was no need for special pleading, for histrionics; his case rested on pure logic. At least, that was what his tone of voice conveyed. His daughter, Eva, sat beside him, smoking.

Horvatz said: "Whatever happens, we must not alarm him and we must — that is to say, you must, Miss Schiller — see, without being seen. Am I right?" He waited for their low murmur of assent before going on. "Now, I think we can arrange for rather a good sighting for you. By a stroke of good luck, one wall of the Abu Sergeh Church abuts onto the garden of the Egyptian officers' club." He started sketching lightly with a fountain pen on the back of a cigarette box. "In these Coptic churches," he explained, "the fenestration of the women's gallery is — well, like it is in a synagogue. The women can see through a thick filigree carved wooden screen, while they themselves remain invisible. One such screen is in the side wall of the church directly over the lawn where our man lunches and dines every day. I have arranged for you, Miss Schiller, to visit the church and look through the screen. I hope you can identify him."

Grete swallowed. "A Coptic church?" she queried in surprise and dismay.

"Yes," said Horvatz. "My daughter Eva will go with you. Abu Sergeh is behind the bazaars and you will have to walk there. I've arranged for you to wear Arab clothes and a face veil. It would be wiser to cross the bazaar as inconspicuously as possible. You will have nothing to do, for Eva speaks perfect Arabic and a few piastres to the sacristan will admit you to the church. He knows Eva, for she has been going regularly all this last week — keeping the place warm for you, so to speak. The sacristan will only see two devout Coptic ladies of Cairo at their devotions. Indeed, the custom of private praying is not uncommon, and there may be another lady engaged in genuine prayers, in which case you will have to wait a while. Do you follow me?"

"Yes."

"Now then," he continued, still sketching away. "As you know, here in Cairo in summer everything takes place outdoors. The Egyptian officers who mess at this club, lunch and dine out on the grass every day. Now, the object of our curiosity is always at the same table. Look!"

His pen roughed out a rectangular lawn, sketching in some palm trees in profile and representing the layout of the tables by a series of circles.

"You will be looking down from this point. This is the table. From your position you should get a good look at him. The rest is our affair."

"Yes," said Grete, feeling her heart beat faster.

The luck which had so far assisted their enterprise showed no signs of dwindling; that night they moved into Horvatz' residence in the capital — a great rambling house, one half of which looked over the river and the other over the covered bazaars of Babalukhan. One frontage was along a narrow street which led directly to the Abu Sergeh Church. They would have to walk only about fifty yards before they turned into its courtyard. So it was that, the following afternoon, two Coptic ladies, well dressed in the Arab fashion, obviously of good Cairo families, slipped into the crowded street from the side gate of the house and made their way circumspectly along the street. They each held a small but richly bound prayer book, and each wore her *yasmak*, which allowed her to reveal no more than a pair of kohl-fringed eyes. They were accompanied by an elderly duenna, imposing and hideous, but she herself did not enter the church. Her duty was to wait for them in the courtyard.

Everything went without a hitch; the old sacristan bowed low before them and accepted the customary *pourboire* with joy. They crossed the cold flags of the echoing church and climbed the musty creaking stairs which led to the womens' gallery. They were quite alone here, and with a swift silent step Eva crossed to the screened window, beckoning Grete to follow suit. With a strange sensation of breathlessness, a choking feeling which made her lips tremble, Grete followed her guide and found herself looking down, almost through the fronds of a palm tree, on to a green lawn covered with tables. She recognized their disposition easily from the diagram Horvatz had drawn. He had not been wrong about the siting, for immediately under her sat a man wearing dark glasses. He was drinking tea with lemon and eating a cream cake. As Grete focussed her glance on him and stared, he removed his dark glasses and — as if deliberately to oblige — looked up at the window. It was almost as if he was looking into her eyes. Instinctively she shrank back, forgetting that the ornamental window was screening her. Panic seized her as she stared down into those grey lustreless eyes of her husband, with their familiar expression of apathy and arrogance. He had changed, yes. He was stouter. He was very much greyer. But there could be no mistaking him. The cicatrices on his cheeks, for example, he had not been able to disguise those — ancient duelling scars of which he had always been so proud and which had always reminded her of the mutilations that African tribes inflict on their youth as marks of ornament. She was terrified of him for a moment, and almost cried out; then her fear left her and was replaced by a cold and scientific hate. How familiar it was — the arrogant set of the head, the small sharp cocksure nose, the circumflex of moustache with its waxed ends.

"Come," she cried to Eva. "It is enough."

They walked down the staircase and across the courtyard again.

"Please take my arm," said Grete; she felt that she was reeling as she walked, drunkenly reeling down the street. But they reached the door without mishap, and climbed the stairs of the high balcony where the men waited for her. Behind them the sunny panorama of Cairo lay with the yellow-tawny line of the Makattam hills down into the desert sands. Traffic roared somewhere out of sight. The river curled green among the flame-touched foliage of the jacaranda. They did not speak, but stared at her in silence. She removed her *yasmak* and stood looking at them with a strange barbaric smile which was emphasized by the heavy kohl make-up around the lashes.

"Well, is it?" asked David at last in a low voice.

"Yes. Without a doubt." She swayed as she spoke, but at once recovered herself.

David heaved a great sigh of relief. "Good girl," he said.

But her eyes were full of tears a few moments later, as she wiped away the kohl in the great mirror which covered one whole wall of Eva's bedroom.

"I thought," she said, "I would feel gladder than I do."

Eva smoked thoughtfully. She had changed back into European slacks and soft slippers. She said nothing, but kissed Grete's cheek. There came a knock at the door. It was David.

"Grete," he said. "Your job is done. I am sending you back tonight. The rest is up to us. There may be a bit of an alert when we kidnap him and I want you out of the way. Horvatz is taking you down by car. I expect we'll be back in a day or three — but we must contact Jerusalem for instructions."

"Can't I stay?" she asked.

"No. It's orders."

Suddenly, without a word, and quite unexpectedly, since neither of them had premeditated such a gesture, specially before Eva, they embraced passionately. Then, almost shyly, they looked at each other.

"Remember," she said, "that I want some time alone with him."

"I promise," he said. "But he will have to go back and face the War Crimes Commission in the final analysis."

"Of course. David!"

"Yes?"

"I love you."

21

Schiller's End

She walked into her office a couple of days before she was expected.

"What is this?" cried the duty janitor. "Are you trying to curry favour with someone? You were supposed to be at the Dead Sea."

"I was. But it proved deader than dead. I began to pine for my little in-tray. Is the Major in this morning?"

Yes, Lawton was in; but he looked somehow changed, diminished. Yet his face lit up when she walked into his office.

"You are early," he cried. "That is a piece of luck for me." Then he added, with a new kind of lameness, a ruefulness, "Grete, I've been posted."

She stopped dead, as if she had been nailed to the ground.

"When?" she asked in a low voice, full of concern.

He made a grimace and said: "I'm posted to India to a military mission. Another fortnight should see me out. For that matter it might see us all out. We've been told to prepare evacuation plans in case the UNO vote goes against us."

"So soon?" she said sadly. It was like the end of a whole epoch; she could hardly envisage Palestine without the British. Lawton stood up.

"I want to take you with me, Grete," he said. "I know you cannot marry for the time being, but perhaps... later when you are free. Would you come, I wonder? Look at me."

She obeyed, looking sadly into his eyes with affection and regret.

"No," she said at last, "I can't. I feel I must stay here. Too many threads still to tie up; too many loose ends." Lawton took a slow walk up and down the room.

"I know," he said. "I know how you feel about that man... and the question of the child."

"Yes," she said.

"But if everything should settle itself finally," he went on with an air of quiet desperation, "would you at least consider the prospect? Time means nothing in such a matter; I would be there always."

"I can't disappoint you for fear of wounding you."

"What does that mean?"

"There is somebody else I care about."

She turned away from him and gazed out of the window, rather than see the misery on his face.

"Very well," he said at last.

~

A few days later, towards the end of the week, her phone rang and she heard the voice of David on the other end of the wire.

"I have some news for you," he said.

Her nerves jumped. "Is everything alright?" she asked, anxiously, and was relieved when he chuckled and said:

"As right as right."

"Come round as soon as you wish," she said.

David hesitated for a moment. "Are you going to be free tonight for your interview?"

She felt her fingers squeeze the phone tightly as she answered in a changed register.

"Tonight? Yes... of course." So the moment had come at last!

"Then I'll be round this evening," said David, and rang off abruptly. He was rather later than she had anticipated; indeed, it was already nine when he at last put in an appearance. It had been a rainy evening.

A freak thunderstorm had burst over Jerusalem. David wore a plastic raincoat and a tweed cap. He accepted a whisky.

"It's to be for eleven o'clock," he said, looking at his watch. "I had some difficulty with the committee; I had to virtually tell them that, unless you could see him alone, you would refuse to sign any evidence against him."

"You shouldn't have done that," she cried, sharply. "They might take the law into their own hands!"

David shrugged. "Frankly," he said, "I wouldn't mind much. He is not a very agreeable creature. And if he has done only half of what they say he has... well... Anyway, you will have your turn with him tonight. At the moment he is very cocksure and proud and protests that he is a Swiss citizen; he thinks that we cannot prove our suspicions true... When he sees you, however!" He sighed and drained his glass.

"Where is he?" she asked.

"We have a small lock-up of our own — part of the old Turkish prison. By Ben Yahmi, you know the place..."

They set off to walk to their destination a little before eleven. As she did her hair in the mirror, Grete wondered to herself: "How will he see me after all this time?" She stared into her own face with eager anxiety. She would wear no make-up for this interview, she decided; but her thoughts were in a complete turmoil. Indeed, ideas tumbled and spilled about at the edge of her mind; she found herself muttering and whispering as she combed her hair and slipped into her black trench-coat.

"What will he have to tell me about the child?" she asked herself, and her heart nearly stopped beating as the thought struck her. She gritted her teeth and drank a final glass of whisky before venturing into the street with David. During these hours of tense activity, they had both forgotten their own personal relationship completely — save for an unstated but ever-present sense of collaboration with no reserves. He sensed something of her anxiety, and out of tact began to talk about other things — about the UNO vote for example, which was expected any day, and which might at last enable Israel to rise like a phoenix from the ashes of past hopes and fears. His eyes flashed. But she listened abstractedly, hardly taking it in. She saw in her mind's eye those greyish oyster eyes which had raised themselves to hers through the wooden screen of the Coptic Church for a moment. She shuddered and set her face.

The rain had stopped. Though it was not unduly late, there were few people about in the streets; they made their way to a street with old-fashioned Arab houses, barred and shuttered. In a dark doorway David stopped and tapped; after a long time a Judas opened in the door with a soft click, and they knew that they were being carefully studied by invisible eyes. Then the door swung slowly open onto an empty hall. They heard diminishing footsteps. David led the way, after carefully bolting the door behind them. They went up a long cold staircase; on every landing a diamond-shaped window cast a lozenge of yellow light on the musty stones. Finally, on the third floor, David tapped at a door, and a little man shot out from behind it like a jack-in-the-box; hardly looking at them, he handed David a huge iron key and waved his hand.

"Not more than an hour," he said in a creaky voice.

They crept along a corridor and confronted a stout door of oak barred with metal. David opened it and entered the prisoner's cell — a narrow and rectangular room. A man sat playing patience at a table in the centre, smoking a cigarette in a bone cigarette holder. For a moment it did not look to her like the same man at all. His rumpled bed in the corner of the room was covered in daily papers. Grete, waiting in the shadows beyond the sill, saw David advance into the cell. The only light came from a single dusty bulb which threw an erratic circle of light on the table with its single occupant. The man wore no collar or tie; a metal stud gleamed in the neckband of his shirt. He looked up at the noise of the key turning in the lock, and then turned back to his game with an air of weary insolence.

David said, "I have brought someone who thinks they may recognize you as Günther Schiller."

The prisoner's face tied itself into a knot of nerves. A pure vexation ravaged him. He shouted:

"I have told you, you are mistaken. Get me the Swiss consul. I am not Schiller, but Schmidt." He repeated the name, making as if to bang the table with his fist, and quietly went on with his game.

David stood for a moment contemplating him and then turned to the shadows.

"You may come in," he said. His voice sounded indifferent — as if this were to be another routine interrogation by yet another prosecutor. He himself passed Grete and she heard the heavy door clang behind her as he went out.

Günther could as yet see nothing; he sat for a moment with eyes screwed up, staring at the darkness outside his little circle of light. Then he gave a grunt and returned to his game. He did not even look up when he heard her slow and hesitant footstep. Grete advanced towards the white circle of light with a strange feeling of confusion, of fear and hatred and disorientation. She walked with a slow, a fatal tread, like a sleepwalker, like an avenging fury — with a slow drugged tread towards the light. Then she felt the whiteness splash all over her features. The prisoner looked up briefly — and was suddenly riveted to his chair. His mouth fell open. Silver drops of sweat started up on his scalp along the white hair. He stared at the white-faced woman advancing towards him with this slow ineluctable tread; she might, for all he knew, be some ghost, some hallucination brought upon him by fatigue and fear. He stared at her and quickly glanced round the cell without moving his head, as if he were looking for an escape route. But his head stayed quite still on his shoulders. Only his little pig's eyes darted about in his skull. Even when she passed out of his range of vision he did not turn round — so like a phantom did she seem. She described a slow circle about him, without for a moment taking her eyes off his face. He licked his lips and stayed rooted to his chair; all his jauntiness, all his bluster had leaked away now, and left him sitting there like some object washed down to the mouth of a river by floods. At last he breathed her name in a whisper — "Grete," and in the same moment she turned aside like a bird in mid-flight and swooped softly down upon the table. She placed her hands on the rough surface and stared into those expressionless oyster eyes. He put out a hand and touched her, as if to verify that she was not a ghost.

"You are still alive," he said in a low voice, and gave a small harsh chuckle. "I wondered."

"Do you know why I am here?" she said, and her voice trembled as she spoke. He looked at her and a small bitter smile played about his lips. His composure was coming back and, with it, anger. A pulse had begun to beat in his temple. The cigarette smoke curled slowly up between them, hanging in whorls in the white light. Somewhere a mosquito droned.

"To trick me," he said. "To revenge yourself."

"No," she cried sharply, stung into fury by his expression and even more by such obtuseness — for he could not imagine for a moment the force of her central obsession. She clenched her fingers tightly and said:

"Günther, where is Otto? *Where* is he?" For a moment the poignant entreaty of her huge eyes seemed to afflict him — they were so deep and blue — so full of long-endured chagrin and despair. He looked hastily away, as if to recover his poise, and when once more he stared at her it was with a bitterly curled lip, a grimness, an obduracy of heart which was quite frightening to behold.

"Otto!" he said with contempt, and made as if to spit on the floor beside the table. "Why should I tell you where he is?"

"So he is still alive?" With a frenzied gesture she leaned forward and shook him, grabbing at his shirt. "You must tell me please, Günther. He is all I have to live for now." With an indignant thrust of his shoulder and a sweeping backhanded blow, he shook himself free and drove her reeling back against the wall. He shouted suddenly:

"Why should I tell *you* anything? Otto! You will never see him again — that I promise you." He stood panting, with the muscles flickering over his face. He stared at her with contempt. Then, with an untrembling hand, he picked up his cigarette holder and placed it between his teeth as he sat down. She stayed quite still, leaning against the wall and watching him with a strange mixture of disgust and hatred.

"Günther," she said. "Günther."

He withdrew his cigarette holder and said crisply:

"You have simply come here to gloat over me and to persuade your Jewish compatriots to put me to death. Well, I am not afraid; you will not have that last satisfaction, Grete. I *am not afraid.*" The last words were uttered in a penetrating whisper which was blood-chilling. Suddenly her reserve broke down; extending her arms and almost sinking to a kneeling posture on the floor, she began to whine and plead with him, almost like an Arab. Her voice had become sweet and shrill.

"Surely you understand; it is not you, it is Otto I am talking about. Günther, you must tell me where he is. I will do anything. For the love of God, can't you understand what it is to have a child, to have a son?"

"A Jew," he said.

"A child, a child," she almost howled, shaking her impotent fists in the air. Then, as so often in the past, the old sense of uselessness welled up in her. She covered her face with her hands and pressed her cold forehead to the wall, breathing deeply, trying to think.

She opened her eyes wide, staring as if into the very stones of the prison wall; slowly her composure returned and her eyes grew dreamy, speculative, thoughtful; she turned slowly and once more confronted the figure which sat upright over its cards, setting them out with small precise insect-like gestures. His forehead was still pearled with drops of sweat; but his expression was set and grim — the two lines running down from the corners of his mouth framing its obdurate mood. She moved slowly towards him again, but this time her face was calm and abstracted, her voice more curious than forceful. It was as if she were now repeating a formula without being sure whether it would work or not. Yet the words were fraught with a new kind of significance to him; he did not look up at her, but he did raise his head and ponder briefly as he stared at the edge of the table, beyond the coloured line of court cards. Her words, spoken with a puzzled slowness were:

"If I could free you, Günther... if I could free you, you would tell me."

She paused to see what effect this new idea might have upon him. He gave a short harsh bark of laughter — satirical laughter which disowned the validity of the idea; and yet... he did not move. He still stared at the table. Then he took up his cigarette holder and drew a mouthful of smoke from it which he softly launched into the darkness around the door, thinking deeply, almost voluptuously — as if the word itself had struck a note of music in his mind. She stared at him with the eyes of a Medusa. Slowly he turned his head, and his cold eyes met hers with their basilisk stare. For a long second neither spoke. She could hear the drone of a nearby mosquito; somewhere in the middle distance there was the noise of a radio playing Arab quarter-tones.

Grete bent her rapt golden head towards him and said, with a queer note of triumph:

"You would, wouldn't you?"

He rose stiffly to his feet and, with his erect military posture, he walked to the further wall, taking, as he did so, a handkerchief from his sleeve. High on the wall there was an object protruding into the room which might have been the metal end of an air ventilator — or some sort of microlink. He slowly and methodically blocked this aperture with his handkerchief. Then he turned and leaned back against the wall and uttered, with an insolent and indifferent tone, a single word.

"How?"

"I have a way."

A single muscle began to twitch with fatigue under his right eye; but he still stared at her carefully. Words began to tumble from her lips more freely now, for she scented her advantage.

"I tell you I have a way, Günther. It is on me that the question of your identity turns. If I refuse to identify you, or swear a deposition to say you are not Günther Schiller but someone else... there will be no case against you, do you see?"

"The Jews know already," he said softly.

"Of course; but I am not talking about the Jews."

"Who then?"

"The British. I could get you into British hands quite easily; then I could convince them that you were the wrong man. Do you see?"

"I don't believe you," he said, simply and without heat.

"But I can prove it," she said in her thrilling tones. "Günther, I can prove it to you."

"You will have me killed afterwards."

"Why should I? Once you tell me what I want to know, the British army would send you to Germany, and there you would be freed for lack of evidence. Can't you see?"

"How will you get me into British hands? One slip and the Jews will kill me, you know that."

"I know that; but leave it to me. All I want is your promise that if I get you into British hands you will tell me. Have I your word?"

He hesitated for a long moment; she waited, trembling with excitement, staring into those cold little pig's eyes. At last he said:

"Very well. I will tell you then."

She heaved a great sigh of relief. "Thank God," she said; and then all her doubts assailed her anew. She turned her face to him once more, scrutinizing his features with an obsessional attention, as if to read the truth on them.

"Swear," she said at last. "Swear on your mother, Günther."

"Ach." He cleared his throat swiftly and made an impatient little gesture with his right hand.

"I swear," he said, "on my mother."

"Swear on Germany."

"I swear on Germany."

"Swear by Adolf Hitler."

"I swear by Adolf Hitler."

He stood looking after her as she turned and went to the door of the cell. His glance was one of thoughtful absent-mindedness, as if his preoccupations had suddenly shifted to a new topic.

"Send me the gaoler please," he said drily and, putting his hands behind his back, began to walk slowly up and down the cell, deep in thought. He stubbed out his cigarette and stood gazing at the smoke for a moment before resuming his walk. He heard the bolts shoot into the wall after she left, then voices, and finally silence. It was some ten minutes later when the same bolts creaked back and he saw the figure of David advance across the cell towards him. David was astonished by the change in Schiller. His face was pale and drawn and deeply lined.

"I want to see a priest," he said. "I am a Catholic. I want to be confessed."

"Tonight?"

"Tonight."

"Very well."

⁓

Lawton's thoughtful grey eyes rested on the young woman who walked up and down on the carpet before his desk, talking with a strange new nervous intensity. He had never seen Grete so pale and tense; yet she spoke with incisiveness and clarity — almost as if she were talking to herself, defending herself against an imaginary tribunal. Her eyes were circled with black, which suggested how little she had slept.

"Of course I have no means of judging the truth of the story, yet I believe it, for it comes from someone I knew well at Ras Shamir, and who is in the underground; why should he want to lie? On the other hand is this man Schiller — is he my husband? I can't tell you that until I actually set eyes on him. That is what I am asking you, Hugh; let me prove it to myself. And then... if he is — you know what I want from him, don't you? I have hidden nothing from you. But do you see?"

Lawton puffed his pipe with maddening composure and stared at her with his sympathetic eyes.

"I am waiting for Cairo to call," he said. "We'll soon know if the abduction story is true."

She bit her lip with impatience and restrained herself on the edge of an outburst.

"If it's true you will?"

Lawton nodded. But he still sat in a pose of maddening inattention, considering; it was as if some aspect of the affair still troubled him. Grete leaned forward and continued urgently:

"You see there is a grave danger that the Haganah will take the law into its own hands and murder him; that is what worries me. They are not concerned with abstractions like international justice. If they are satisfied that he is the man, do you think they would bother to hand him over to the Commission and risk him getting free again? Don't you see the urgency of it?"

Lawton nodded again, obstinately.

"I want to cover myself against a mistake," he said, and once again she was on the edge of giving vent to her feelings by an outburst when mercifully the phone rang. She heard the links snap home from exchange to exchange, and then the hoarse bronchial voice of Bruce Davis crackle in the receiver. Lawton said quietly:

"Cairo, I have you; did you get my Immediate?"

The voice at the other end replied:

"Yes, it's apparently true; they are keeping it dark for fear the press gets hold of it and turns it into a political triumph for the Palestine Jews. Hiding Nazis will reflect ill on them; and then another reason is that no one is really *quite* sure he was abducted. He might have done a bunk on his own, nicht wahr? But he's gone, my boy, and all posts have been warned to keep a lantern in the window for our wandering boy tonight, to coin a quotation."

Lawton sighed shortly and said, "Thank you, Bruce."

"You see?" she said, her face breaking into a smile of triumph. He nodded. His face had gone very thoughtful all at once. He lowered the desk lamp until its greenish arc swung low over the map which he was unfolding with his other hand.

"Show me where," he said, and she stepped to his side, to trace with a nervous finger a maze of streets leading to the short and squalid cul-de-sac, along one wall of which ran the verminous and deserted cells of the now abandoned Turkish prison. He marked this point with a pencil and added the street number. His pipe had gone out.

"I'll get a warrant out this morning and take in a search party at dusk," he said.

"Not before?" she said with dismay.

But he did not answer her. He was already dialling the number of the prison department to ask for a squad of police and a search warrant. She was consumed with a burning impatience. The slow methodical British way of going about things drove her mad.

"Hugh," she said, "suppose they move him."

He re-lit his pipe and shrugged his shoulders negligently.

"That would be our bad luck," he said, and, once more ignoring her, picked up his telephone.

She heard his quiet voice saying:

"A squad under a lance corporal should be enough for this operation. I want both ends of the street cordoned from six to six thirty this afternoon." Then he put down the receiver and stood up. He crossed from behind his desk and took her hands to squeeze them briefly.

"I know what this means to you," he said.

"I'll come with you," she said eagerly, but he shook his head.

"There might be some shooting. One never knows. Besides, it's strictly forbidden to take you on operations of any kind. You'll wait here and I'll bring him back to this office under escort."

This solution did not please her, and she had difficulty concealing her irritation; but, after reflecting for a moment, it struck her that perhaps it was the wisest decision — particularly as she did not want David or the Haganah to feel that she had betrayed their secrets. She stood for a long minute considering. Lawton watched her sympathetically, and made an awkward attempt to cheer her up.

"The only man I knew who took women on active service was Carstairs. In the field his tent was always crowded with veiled ladies."

But she did not smile. Instead she sighed and said:

"Very well, if that's how it must be... but I don't know how I'm going to live through the day until this evening..."

~

The operation, which had been inappropriately christened "Marigold" by Lawton's G.S.O.2., whose interest in botany far outweighed any other, took place as planned with a precision which, to the professional mind, is almost elegance. Punctually at six thirty, two squads of troopers sealed off the cul-de-sac by the Turkish prison, while at the same moment Lawton and a senior police officer stepped out of their cars and walked with slow unhurried but purposeful tread towards the closed door of number 27.

The street was deserted and silent, and their arrival seemed to cause no kind of interest. Beyond the cul-de-sac the traffic roared past on the Jaffa Road. Dusk was falling, and the first faint blossoms of street lamps were beginning to shine.

Duff, the policeman, was a huge insensitive lump of manhood, with a rosy face and a walrus moustache. His portentous air irritated Lawton.

"I think," he said hoarsely, "I'll call the picket and break the door down."

Lawton gave him an impatient glance and said:

"It may not be necessary. Let's try knocking first. We don't want to wake up the whole street."

Suiting the action to the word, he advanced to the door and tapped it twice in peremptory fashion with the muzzle of his squat Luger. There was a long moment of silence. Nothing happened. They waited, feeling rather foolish. Duff gave a windy sigh and looked at his companion with an air of impatient concern. Lawton was about to concede the policeman's right to call his squad and smash up the door when all of a sudden they heard the noise of footsteps within. They had already noted with care the existence of a Judas in the heavy oak door. This now flicked open, and a startled dark eye confronted them. Lawton barked:

"Open up! Police!"

And, to illustrate the matter, thrust his pistol into the aperture until the muzzle rested an inch from the cold forehead of the man inside.

"Don't shoot! Don't shoot!" said the voice.

"Then open," cried the policeman in a sort of snarl.

There was the squeak of bolts and the rattle of keys and the great door swung open on a deserted area of darkness, at the further end of which there could be dimly discerned a dilapidated stone staircase and a cobwebbed window. Somewhere in the darkness about them they heard the diminishing echo of footsteps scrambling upwards and a voice which shouted:

"Police!"

They leaped forward, their pistols cocked, and covered the great hall in a series of strides. The staircase, however, offered many advantages to a hypothetical defence, and they adopted the customary technique of mounting it, their backs pressed to the wall facing inwards, and taking eight stairs at a time before pausing.

The first floor was deserted and in darkness. The policeman seemed disposed to search it thoroughly before continuing to the second floor — and indeed this would have been a very normal precaution under ordinary conditions. But Lawton knew what he was looking for and knew where to find it. He pressed on.

The diagram which Grete had drawn on his green blotting pad was still fresh in his mind and, in spite of the almost total darkness, he felt confident and at ease. Experience, too, had something to do with it, for he knew that nothing is more futile than a desultory exchange of shots in darkness, and that no revolver can be counted upon beyond the range of eight feet.

So far, however, no opposition seemed in sight, and it was when they reached the second floor that he saw a bar of light shining into the open corridor from a half-opened door. His heart sank, for this was the door of the cell in which the captive had been imprisoned.

He quickened his pace, with the policeman at his heels.

"It looks as though they've got him away," he said hoarsely.

The two men hurried — but with circumspection — down the long corridor and peeped into the room. It was indeed the cell as described so painstakingly by Grete, but the scene in it was a singular one.

Attached to the high iron bar which held a radiator in place hung the body of the German, his neck twisted grotesquely on one side. He had died clumsily, by slow strangulation. Two figures were busy with an old sheath knife, severing the cord which held him to the iron bar. Neither seemed armed and, when the policeman barked "Hands up!" they merely turned frightened white faces upon him before ignoring the challenge and continuing feverishly to try and wrest their captive away from the death he had designed for himself. The Englishmen sheathed their pistols, as if struck dumb by this strange scene, and walked slowly into the radius of the light with an air of vague uncertainty.

Günther Schiller's body, in its strange dislocated posture, looked shrunken and twisted — like the body of a bird of prey nailed to a barn door. His face, puffy and contorted, was the colour of cigar ash. The black tip of his tongue stuck out of his swollen lips.

This scene, which to Lawton was merely grotesque, offered the policeman a professional and academic interest.

"Well, well, well!" he cried cheerfully. "The poor bugger miscalculated the drop. A foot and a half isn't enough. He should have waited for me."

This gross pleasantry only added to the grotesqueness of the scene. Now the rope gave, and there was a soft plump noise as the body of Günther Schiller scratched down the wall and pitched forward into the arms of his gaolers. They laid him on the floor and, between them, made a desultory sort of inspection to see whether there was any hope of reviving him. But it was obviously a hopeless task.

The policeman uttered a muffled expletive and turned on Lawton to say:

"Now I'm beginning to wish we hadn't come. I suppose we can't ignore this."

He took out his notebook, sat down at the table and looked vaguely around him. The two Jews, having abandoned their efforts to revive the body, carried it to the low bunk in the corner and disposed it there, crossing the arms on the breast, covering its face with a cloth. Then they turned humbly round to face the policeman, who said with an air of massive reluctance:

"I suppose I'll have to put you under arrest."

Lawton, who had been absentmindedly reflecting on the scene — in his mind's eye he could see the strained white face of Grete hovering near the office telephone — suddenly took a step forward and said brusquely, imperiously:

"Has he no papers? Did he leave nothing?"

He made a gesture of inconsequential exasperation in the air. Was this all that was left of Günther Schiller?

"Identity cards, passports, letters?..." he had begun to shout incoherently.

The two gaolers shook their heads and spread their hands. One of them said:

"He was captured from Cairo last week. All his papers were destroyed."

He smiled a weak, ingratiating smile.

The policeman crooked a huge finger at them and interposed with his heavy toneless voice:

"You come over here, you two, and sit down. Now I want to know your names and 'ow it 'appened."

He had reverted to type — had become a country bobby again. He produced an indelible pencil and dabbed at his long pink tongue with it. The pencil left a purple mark in the centre of it. Laboriously he began to write.

Lawton watched for one second, consumed by an intense irritation and the feeling almost of despair.

"Was it really Günther Schiller?" he asked sharply.

And the two gaolers nodded. Then turning to the policeman, Lawton said:

"Well, Duff, I can leave the case to you, I take it. There's nothing more for me to do here. I'll be back at HQ if you want me."

Duff nodded sagely, and Lawton re-entered the dark corridor, closing the door carefully behind him. When he was halfway down the staircase the dark window suddenly burst into a blaze of coloured light. For one wild moment he thought that someone was firing tracer bullets, and in his mind's eye he saw the searchlights bracketing Tobruk harbour with a stream of molten rocket fire pouring up into the night sky.

"What the devil!" he said, and stopped to look out over Jerusalem. "Who the devil is sending up fireworks?"

Showers of golden drops slowly dispersed on the dark velvety skin of the night sky above the city. It was only when he reached the street that the explanation came to him. He heard the slow murmur of a crowd which was gathering in the street, the low murmur of chanting which was to swell gradually into a tumult of enthusiasm. While they had all been thinking about other things, Israel had been born.

Excited voices passed the news along the street. There was a tapping at shutters, tapping on doors. Voices cried: "UNO voted 33 to 13! We've won!" Some children raced along the street beating on saucepans with sticks, and chanting: "33 to 13, 33 to 13!"

Lawton found his duty driver crouched over the car radio, listening to the tail end of the BBC news.

"That's done it, Sir," he said. "They've won the UNO vote."

Lawton didn't reply, but climbed into the car with a dispirited air and allowed himself to be driven back to his office.

The thought of Grete afflicted him; he dreaded the coming interview. Mentally he rehearsed various ways of breaking the news to her, dismissing them one after the other as foolish or inadequate. Should he perhaps just walk in and say, "He's dead and he's taken his secret with him." That would sound melodramatic. Or should he simply say, "I have bad news for you. Please remain calm."

For a moment, hovering between these various possibilities, he was tempted to turn coward and ring her up. Nevertheless, he found himself at last opening the door of his office and confronting the figure that rose to meet him from the ugly leather armchair. He found that he did not need to speak. She divined everything from his expression. As he stood staring at her, she read his face with its expression of commiseration like a book.

"It's something bad, isn't it? What is it, is he dead?"

He nodded.

"Did the Jews…?" She stopped and bit her lip.

"Suicide," said Lawton tersely, finding his voice. Then she echoed the word on a sharp, plaintive note. She had turned pale now and whispered:

"Did he leave any message?"

"None," said Lawton bitterly. "Nothing. Not a trace."

She swayed and he caught her by the forearm and put her firmly down in the armchair. Here she sat, staring in a dazed abstraction at the further wall, completely still, except that her fingers plucked and picked at a tassel on the chair.

Lawton, feeling all at once clumsy, crossed to his desk and from the bottom of it extracted a bottle of whisky and a siphon of soda. He mixed a stiff drink, and without a word put it into her hand. She raised it to her lips and her teeth chattered against the rim of the glass. Then suddenly she burst out:

"I can't believe it!"

"Drink that up," said Lawton.

He was walking up and down before her on the carpet now, slowly, like a monomaniac. His face looked lined and tired. Outside, the night sky above Jerusalem had begun to hiss and crackle and change colour. He drew the heavy curtains and they found themselves staring out on an extraordinary night panorama of light and smoke.

She did not appear to care enough to ask the cause of this explosion of coloured light. He took the glass from her hand, put it on the desk and said:

"Come, I'm going to take you home."

She obeyed him like a somnambulist, and together they walked down the dark staircase of the office. He had forgotten to retain the duty car, but at the street corner they picked up one of those ancient horse-drawn carriages which still did duty for taxis in Jerusalem. She sat, her arm inside his, but completely silent as they drove through the streets of the old town, which were now filling up with eager and excited people. From the Arab quarter, however, there was a noise of counter-demonstrations and the harsh scratching of Radio Cairo calling for the death and destruction of the Jews.

Now and again in the winding streets of the town, under this canopy of light, the carriage was almost brought to a halt by surging crowds shouting good-naturedly to them, "33 to 13!" And here and there an excited Jew cried to Lawton, "Britain, go home!"

The girl sat absolutely still and white as death, hardly taking anything in, until at last they reached the flat. Her teeth had begun to chatter now and, as they climbed the stairs, Lawton put his hand on her forehead to see if she gave any signs of fever.

Once in the flat she threw herself onto the sofa and, giving one long wretched moan, buried her face in the cushions. Lawton stood watching her, undecided. He felt awkward, helpless, furious. Should he perhaps insist that she go to bed? He lit a cigarette and walked to the window.

"Grete," he said, "will you try and get some sleep?"

She did not answer and, as he was staring irresolutely at her, he heard the crisp note of the doorbell. Who could be calling at this time of night? He threw up the window and strained forward. Outside the block of flats on the pavement stood a small attentive-looking figure in the white robes of a Dominican priest. It did not look up, perhaps because the noise of the fireworks had drowned the sound of the window being opened.

Lawton crossed with swift steps to the hall and pressed the button which would release the front door spring. Then he returned to the sitting-room and said:

"Grete, there's a priest coming up the stairs. Do you know who he might be?"

She did not hear him, and he crossed the room to shake her by the shoulder as he repeated the phrase. She raised her white tormented face and said incoherently:

"What priest?"

And as if in answer to her question, Father Gaudier was suddenly there. He materialized, or so it seemed, in the doorway of the room, his small white hands clasped in front of him. He was breathing rather hard from his exertions. He uttered her name on a note of interrogation with a kind of child-like submissiveness. He was a small and rugged little man, with a round cropped head of the type which is designated Alpine by ethnographers. His dark hair was cut *en brosse*, his skin was brown and tanned. His eyes were of the bright blueness of periwinkles. His manner suggested simplicity without archness, and he darted swift interrogative glances from Grete to the soldier and back again to Grete, smiling his simple smile. It took a few seconds only to register his appearance, but already the girl had scrambled into a sitting posture and made a desultory attempt to arrange her hair.

Lawton stood up and, feeling somewhat uncertain of himself, contented himself with a gruff "Good evening" and a short nod of the head.

The priest advanced with an air of uncertainty into the centre of the room and concentrated his glance upon Grete.

"I have some news for you," he said.

"News?"

"I wonder if I might talk to you," he said. "I was called to confess a man called Schiller late last night."

The words had a mesmeric effect upon Grete. She rose from her seat white-faced and anxious. The little priest still smiled with his head on one side. His presence radiated a sort of doll-like composure. Lawton noticed his dusty little toes in their worn sandals.

"I think," said the little man, "it would be better if I could see you alone for a few moments."

Lawton took his point and instantly said:

"Of course. I shall be on my way. Good-night, Grete."

"Oh, don't run away," said Father Gaudier. "What I have to say will not take long."

But Lawton, despite his curiosity, gave them a cheerful "That's all right" and closed the front door of the flat behind him, to leave the two of them alone.

Grete had clasped her hands in front of her body as she stared fixedly into the blue eyes of the priest. Father Gaudier, as if with a subconscious intention of reducing her obvious anxiety at what he might be about to reveal, came softly towards her and put two fingers of his right hand on her wrist. As if by his impulsion, she sat down once more and the priest took his place beside her, with his fingers still upon her hand.

"What did he tell you?" she managed at last to get out.

"May I smoke?" asked Gaudier humbly in a low voice.

"Of course."

He helped himself to a cigarette from the enamel box on the table before them and thoughtfully blew a streamer of smoke into the air where it hung, slowly dispersing.

"He told me," he said in a small, unemotional voice, "everything he could about his life and about yours. He committed many grievous sins, my dear, and like all sinners was more to be pitied than hated."

"He promised to tell me about the child," said Grete, in a voice which had a hysterical edge to it.

"Almost the only thing he did not tell me," said Father Gaudier with an air of pensive reproach, "was that he intended to commit suicide."

"And even that did not make sense," she cried bitterly. "It was simply to cheat me. I knew the child was alive somewhere."

The priest coughed behind his hand, doubling it up into a grubby little paw.

"That is what I came to talk about," he said. "It is very cruel and very ugly and will cause you great suffering, but from what he told me I know that beyond a shadow of a doubt your child is dead. In fact he asked me to tell you."

The centre of numbness in the middle of her mind gradually overflowed to encompass her whole body. It overflowed like ink or blood on her carpet and she felt spreading through her a slowly expanding stain of something like amnesia. The phrase had turned her into a pillar of salt.

The little priest did not take his eyes from her face.

"If I tell you that he showed remorse," he said, "I would not expect you to believe it; indeed, I hardly know whether to believe it myself. With a man so complicated it is always difficult to determine these things. He himself would not have been able to tell us whether he was play-acting or not. He somehow did not know where to find his own feelings or how to interpret them."

Grete was not really listening, but she was grateful for the sound of his low voice and the cool sympathetic feel of his fingers on her wrist. The priest sighed and went on, almost as if he were talking to himself:

"It makes one wonder whether the consciousness of good and evil is the fruit of instruction or whether it's inherited like an instinct. Nobody can answer this one. Are there people born without souls? I have met a few people who made me almost believe it — almost, but not quite."

"Can a man who believes in nothing believe in God?" she asked bitterly. "Or rather, could a man who believed in the Nazi party do so?"

Father Gaudier shook his head with a puzzled air, as though all these questions belonged somehow to the rhetoric of theology which was outside the orbit of ordinary human actions.

"The human heart," he said helplessly, as if confronting the central enigma of his own profession. "It has no bottom, it has no top, no centre and no sides."

Holding her voice very steady, and wearing an artificial expression of composure, she said:

"You're sure about the child…"

"Completely sure," he replied.

She got up, and very slowly walked across the room towards the window where the night sky still danced and flickered over the newly-born Israel. Her numbness had intoxicated her and had conveyed a kind of slow unsteadiness to her walk, which was the walk of drunkenness or pregnancy. She turned suddenly and looked across the room at Father Gaudier, who still watched her, head on one side like a diminutive spaniel.

"My God, how strange," she said. "After so many years of longing and wondering, all I can feel now is an intense relief. Would you have expected that?"

"Yes," said the priest.

"I feel so ashamed," she said.

The priest stubbed out his cigarette and said in his level voice:

"You'll begin to cry tomorrow — or the day after. Perhaps even next week. Or next year. Just now it is all over and you're free from an incubus. Isn't that so?"

"And yet a door has closed on everything I care about," she said.

The priest stood up and flicked some ash off his soutane with his fingers.

"No door can shut," he said, "without another opening somewhere. Life is beautifully arranged. Or perhaps I should say a devilishly well-organized affair."

"Look," said Grete... "I must know how it happened, where, when. I *must*."

"Typhoid... Dachau," said the little man.

22

Pulling Out

The ADC opened the side door and admitted Lawton to the gallery which ran around the reception rooms of Government House.

"H.E.'s out on the terrace," he said.

Lawton followed him across the long room with its blazing chandeliers and heavy pile carpets. The long mirrors reflected back his lean form with its nervous long hands and preoccupied face.

"I think," said the ADC, "H.E. is going to make honourable amends."

"For what?" said Lawton in surprise.

"Well, for having disregarded all your political analyses of the last year. You'll be able to say 'I told you so' with a vengeance. That will be pleasurable, no?"

"No pleasure at all," said Lawton curtly.

H.E. was sitting on the terrace, staring thoughtfully at the firework display which still burst and scattered over Jerusalem. The aroma of his Juliet hung in the still night air.

"Ah, there you are," he said pleasantly. "Come and sit down."

He vaguely indicated a soda siphon and bottles on a side table and Lawton, according to long-established custom, crossed to make himself a drink, saying as he did so:

"I'm sorry about the rush, Sir. I didn't expect to go on such short notice. The cable came through this afternoon and I'm to leave tomorrow."

"So I understand," said H.E. Then he added awkwardly, "I'm afraid you must think I've been rather a doubting Thomas... I mean, about your Intel reports."

Lawton sat down and said equably:

"Political judgment is a queer thing. I could easily have been wrong, Sir, and you right."

"Yes," said H.E. handsomely, "but it's my duty to be right, d'you see? And I was wrong."

A note of vexation came into his voice.

"What do you see in store for us now?" he said. "You might as well give me the benefit of a parting word, eh?"

Lawton accepted a cigar from the inlaid sandalwood box.

"Well," he said, "since my responsibility's over, I suppose I can indulge in a bit of fortune telling. That's about all it would be."

"This time I'll pay careful heed," said H.E. "What do you predict?"

Lawton considered for a second and then said:

"Within three weeks, at the outside, we'll all be pulled out of here to leave a vacuum into which eight Arab armies are going to get sucked."

"And then?"

"War," said Lawton laconically. "What I can't tell you is whether the Jews or the Israelis, as they're now called, can defend themselves. That will have to be seen. But none of us will be here to see it, unfortunately."

H.E. got up and walked up and down the terrace slowly and ponderously, reflecting. His elegant and discontented face with its handsome head of grey hair was still part-turned towards Jerusalem. At this moment the ADC appeared in the lighted patch by the great French windows and said:

"Forgive me, Sir, London is on the wire. It's the personal line. Secretary of State's office." Lawton finished his drink and rose.

"The Secretary of State?" said H.E. on a rising note.

The two men exchanged a quizzical and ironic glance.

"That's probably *our* marching orders," said H.E.

Extending his hand, he shook hands with unaccustomed warmth

and added with unexpected generosity: "Good luck, Major. I wish we'd made better use of your brains."

The words echoed pleasurably in Lawton's mind as the duty car jogged him back to Jerusalem. Well, even a bloody fool can be a gentleman, he thought, and that was something. His thoughts reverted to Grete as he had last seen her, standing with an air of white-faced uncertainty while the little priest smiled at her from the sitting-room door of the flat. Perhaps this was the best way. After all, there was nothing left to say to her. He would leave without a word. It was idle to continue tormenting himself on her behalf, and of tantalizing himself by seeing her.

He climbed stiffly out of the car at the gate of his private villa and walked slowly up the path to the front door. Jenkins, his batman, had the evening off, so he was forced to use a latch key. The little villa smelled musty and his bedroom was full of mosquitoes. He hauled a couple of dusty suitcases out of the wardrobe and began to pack his few belongings. This did not take him long. Then he went to the telephone and asked the duty operator at the office to call him at four.

"I have a six o'clock flight from Lydda," he explained.

Then he stood for a moment, irresolutely looking at the carpet and wondering whether he was tired enough to go to bed there and then.

Suddenly the phone rang. It was Grete. But her voice sounded changed. It had a queer note in it — he frowned as he tried to identify it. Was he wrong, or was there a suggestion of exultation, of relief, almost of triumph?

"What is it?" he said anxiously. "You sound so different."

"I wanted to ask you if you were doing anything tonight," she said. "I simply must go out. I can't sit at home for the rest of the evening. Are you free?"

"Yes," he said.

In fact, he cursed himself for his lack of resolution. He could easily have made some excuse; and then by morning he would have gone and a whole new cycle would have started. He was beginning to realize that, while he loved Grete, something in him also wanted to be rid of this encumbering, futile, rather sterile emotion which was doomed for lack of a response in her.

"By the way," he said. "I'm off in the morning very early."

The expression of her dismay seemed very pleasurable to him. "So soon?" she said in a hollow tone.

"I've been expecting it," he replied. "We both have."

"India is so far away," she said.

He ignored the remark and said simply, "Where do we meet, and when?"

"Are you sure you're not too tired?"

"Sure."

"Then the Officers' Club, in half an hour."

He crossed the town on foot, noticing the tremendous animation mixed with uncertainty which pervaded everything. The fireworks still went on, and at the Officers' Club they reflected themselves in the lily pond beside which the diners and dancers sat at tables glittering with white napery and shaded lamps. The grass was soft and green.

She was sitting in a corner at a table on the lawn, waiting for him. The rosy cone of light shed by the table lamp with its red shade set off her shining eyes and hair. What surprised him most was the expression of calm on her face — a strange new relaxed expression of maturity which he had not seen before, and which he diagnosed as being relief after strain. It was in his mind to ask her what news, if any, she had received from her visitor earlier in the evening, but a native shyness made him hesitate and smile instead at her in a tongue-tied fashion.

"Hello," he said simply, awkwardly.

"Hello," she replied.

A momentary awkwardness sprang up between them. It was as if all the contingencies of the world which were about to separate them had, in some way, made them strangers to each other. Perhaps it was to shake off his depression that she reached forward and put her hand on his. She felt how deeply the warmth of her touch affected him.

"I must tell you my news," she said, "since you're too tactful to ask about it."

"It was not tact," he said. "I was afraid for you. Did the priest have anything useful to say?"

"He told me everything I wanted to know," she said. "Coming all in a lump like that, it roared through me like a north wind, knocked me sideways a bit. Otto is dead, for example. I keep repeating the phrase aloud to myself, astonished to find it means nothing. Or if it does mean something, I haven't grasped what it can be. And yet, I'm not dazed... I'm perfectly calm. It puzzles me terribly. I don't know whether to accuse myself of callousness, or what."

In the long silence that followed, he looked at her keenly, intently.

"I am dreadfully anxious for you," he said at last. "This country is going to blow up. I wish you had let me take you away before the balloon goes up, as it must. My poor Grete," he added under his breath.

She was silent and he knew why. The shadow of David rose between them. Then he said:

"Why don't you go back to Ras Shamir?"

"I've asked myself that question," she said, "more than once. I wanted to and yet something held me back. Perhaps that something was the mystery of my husband and... you know. Now my way seems much clearer. Yet suddenly I feel as if I'd lost the impulse to long very deeply for anything anymore. I wonder if you see."

He pressed her hand sympathetically and nodded.

"Come," he said, "let's not spoil our last evening with gloomy questions. Everything will resolve itself sooner or later. Shall we dance?"

They moved softly and lightly into the throng of fox-trotting officers and their womenfolk. Donaldson of the Hussars showed some disposition to cut in, but Lawton pleaded with him successfully, saying that he was leaving in the morning and the young man acceded to his request with a lordly and slightly tipsy air.

"Have you heard the news?" he said. "We're packing up. Marching orders came in this evening. Now it'll be dog-eat-dog, or rather, Arab-eat-Jew."

"It might be Jew-eat-Arab," said Lawton under his breath as they circled the dance floor and then left it to continue their slow revolutions on the green grass by the swimming pool. He had never seen her looking so radiant, nor found her so tender, so accommodating. Dancing cheek to cheek, as they were, one might pardonably have mistaken her for a lover or his wife. The subaltern at the bar looked openly envious and Donaldson expressed his own view of the matter by ordering another Scotch whisky and toasting the distant Lawton, muttering, "Here's to a lucky dog," as he raised his glass.

It was long after midnight when they walked arm in arm across Jerusalem through the deserted streets. The fireworks had stopped now, but great clouds of red smoke still hung in the night sky, while a late thin moon cast its frail light across the domes and minarets of the city. The only noises from the Arab quarter were the withering snarls and yelps of the Arab radio, calling for death to the Jews and vowing vengeance on all who helped them.

At the end of the long line of cypresses, Lawton stopped suddenly.

"I'm going no further," he said. "Goodbye, Grete."

They looked at each other for a long moment, then impetuously, youthfully she embraced him… so quickly indeed that he had hardly time to respond.

"We shall meet again," she said.

And in some strange way both of them believed that this was the truth — that this parting was not a final one. She turned and walked on down the long street towards her house, while he stood and watched her until she reached the safety of her front door. Then he sighed and turned about, lighting a cigarette as he walked slowly and thoughtfully homeward. There would not be much sleep for him tonight. Already the eastern sky was beginning to pale.

Later, sitting in the awkward bucket seats of the Dakota as it circled Lydda before heading eastward into the rising sun, Lawton looked out upon the city as if upon a relief map, tracing every feature of it from memory. He was surprised to find that he had fallen in love not only with Grete but with Jerusalem itself.

23

New Dispositions

Lawton's departure weighed heavily upon Grete, though she did not feel its impact until the day when she found a successor occupying his desk. It was something more than a blow to her social life. It was as if it had set in motion a train of other events which were now going to alter the whole circumstances of her life in the city. The office, for example, was closing. Its technical personnel were being transferred to England, while all the local staff, including Grete, were faced with a month's notice and the gratuity of six months' pay.

The political tension was mounting daily, too, and public disorders had now come to mark their everyday lives — the Jews fighting the Arabs, the Arabs fighting the Jews, while the unfortunate police attempted, without any success, to hold the ring. It became dangerous to walk in the streets. Shootings, burnings and lootings became the order of the day. The occupiers of Palestine, relieved at last of the burden they found so onerous, owing to their inability to tell the truth to either of the chief factions, or to honour the pledges given to both, now became almost deliberately slack in the execution of their duties.

The general attitude was well voiced by Duff when he exclaimed to a visiting rabbi, who had come to complain about lack of protection of property and person in the Jewish sectors of the town:

"You wanted us out, old chap. And you're going to have us out."

Peace had become a precarious matter, public safety in the life of the open street a question of sheer hazard; all day long the columns of motorized troops poured down the dust-choked roads towards the harbours. All night now one heard the crash of grenades in the narrow streets around the Jaffa Gate, or the rapid breathless stammer of pistols. By the time the police patrols had reached the spot, even the sound of running feet had died away, and only the victim of the attack lay there on the pavement, crumpled and silent. More often than not he or she proved to be an innocent victim of terrorism, someone belonging to neither side. Night-curfews came down like a lid upon their lives; all the innocent pleasures, such as dining out, dancing, going for midnight swims, became part of the pattern of their loss.

Such restraints sowed resentment in everyone. It was obvious that the British were packing up and pulling out, yet no official announcement to this effect was made, and this increased the fear and uncertainty. One day they would awake to find Palestine evacuated, left defenceless, and with no armed soldier on hand to prevent the entry of the Arab armies which surrounded this pathetic strip of coastal land. It seemed as if all the gloomy predictions of the Haganah Jews were to be fulfilled.

As for Grete, it was a period of indecision and depression. Her life in Jerusalem was coming to an end, and as yet she could form no coherent plan for the future. Once or twice she thought of returning to Ras Shamir, but a sense of shyness, of inhibition, seemed to paralyze her.

It was in one of these moods of dejection that she set out one day for the monastery by the Mount of Olives where Father Gaudier lived and worked. She had some difficulty in running him to earth, but at last succeeded in penetrating to the walled garden where he was busy pruning an apricot tree. He looked down from the ladder with his uncertain smile, wiping his hands in his soutane, and mopping a sweaty forehead with his sleeve.

"I expected you," he said, somewhat surprisingly. "I don't know why, but I did."

Grete held the ladder while the little man climbed down.

"I suddenly felt the need to talk to you," she said.

The priest nodded and said, "Come." She followed him down the pathway with an expression of puzzlement on her face.

"It seemed to me," she said, "that you alone knew all about me — you knew almost more about me indeed than I myself know. Therefore, I might consult you with profit. I'm at a loss about myself. I don't know what to do, where to go, or whom to love."

Father Gaudier did not appear to be listening. He hummed under his breath as he led the way to a small study which he unlocked with a key.

"Well now," he said, "sit down and I'll make you some sage tea."

Grete sat with her hands in her lap and gazed into the blue eyes of the little man.

"I am glad you are not surprised to see me here, though it was only yesterday I suddenly remembered you. But I have been feeling recently that I needed to talk to someone — to talk about the whole of my life to someone, in order somehow to get back my will to live. I wanted, needed, to re-articulate my past life, so that perhaps I could see in it some sort of pattern which would allow me to make a decision, to plan for the future — for clearly I must soon decide, from a practical point of view, what I should do. I have considered every choice without any result — even the more drastic choices..."

Father Gaudier turned off the kettle and poured out the boiling water into the little *tisane* cups. "The most extreme would be suicide I suppose, or entering a convent. I somehow don't see either of them as being suitable for you."

She laughed with relief. "You seem to know everything about me."

"No," he said. "It is just that you are like everyone else. It is pardonable to feel one is original, but you know that in moments of stress or loneliness most human beings react in the same way. I know much, of course — all that your husband had to tell me; but there are also gaps. Some I have filled in with the help of a mutual friend. Miss Peterson of Ras Shamir."

"You know her?" she said with surprise.

"I consulted her about you — before," he said.

"What did she have to tell you?"

"About your experiences in the camps and elsewhere. To me, it seemed most comprehensible that you should still feel the grave shock of all those horrors. That alone would be enough to make you unstable, afraid of yourself. If one is bound in this way by a feeling of guilt, it is practically impossible to make deliberate choices; one tries to force reality, and one pays for it with the wrong decision. That is why I always tell people to wait until reality refines itself down and leaves only a single way out."

"It is easy to say."

"I know it is."

"But you are right. I do feel guilty after what I have been through — guilty because there was *always* a way out. I *could* have committed suicide, could I not? Yes, but I was too much of a coward. I prayed for the courage, but I never found it. But since I endured and did not kill myself, I am indeed guilty, am I not?"

"Of course. But you must stop regarding it as a very exceptional or original matter. The extent of human guilt is boundless, endless, without horizons. I live and pray my wretched life away here, imagining that I am free from it. But I know I am as guilty as anyone, as guilty as you. In fact, from my point of view, your case is a perfectly ordinary one, and it is sheer stupidity for you to allow it to ruin your ordinary life. You are a victim of false pride, Grete, that is all. Your life is not ruined, as you think..." He broke off.

She stared at him, or rather stared through him, through the wall, the streets, through Jerusalem to Germany, to her childhood. She drew a deep breath.

"False *pride*?"

"Yes. This is what has ruined your power of choice, and made you believe that you are worthless, no good to anyone. You said a moment ago that you did not know whom to love — this is why. As a matter of fact it is not life around you which has changed — it is your own angle of vision. You are seeing things through a mist of false self-esteem! Nothing in fact has changed; life is still before you. You have much to offer, much to give in both life and love. But you must make some little effort to understand why you are paralyzed... I apologize for the paradox. But there it is."

"Yes," she said, and suddenly her tone had changed; she half rose from her chair and smiled at him. In some curious way everything felt changed and renewed by this conversation — as if these few words had knocked down a wall which had been preventing her entry into a part of herself, her own heart and mind.

"What insight you have," she said at last, almost under her breath. "It was for this that I came. I am so grateful to you."

The priest made a grimace. He rose and said negligently, "I must be going I am afraid. Will you come back if and when you feel the need to talk to me? I am always available except on Tuesdays."

"I will," she said on a note of calm resolution, but something inside her told her that she would not — that he had given her what she had needed. He grinned as he showed her to the great oaken door and let the dazzling sunlight into the cool entrance hall of the monastery.

"A word in good time is as strong as a blow," he said. "Or so the Arab proverb has it."

He stood watching as she walked down the street. Grete looked about her with new eyes. All of a sudden a strange new elation had seized her; everything seemed pristine, newly created. Jerusalem with its tones of apricot stone, soft green olives and blue sky had never seemed so beautiful. It was as if all the potentialities of life had suddenly been rescued, become viable again. She felt she was on the edge of some new adventure which would decide everything once and for all. And so she was...

It was through the long window of Wagner's Pharmacy that she caught sight of the long sinewy form of Peterson... as if she had been suddenly conjured up by the conversation Grete had just had with the priest. The kibbutz secretary held a long slip of paper, a shopping list, in her hand. She was busy ticking off the items on it. Grete turned aside swiftly and entered the shop.

"Pete," she cried. "What are you doing here?"

Pete grabbed her in her wiry arms and planted a kiss on her nose.

"Aha," she said. "Fancy seeing you. I'm doing a bit of shopping for the camp. Look."

She handed Grete the list — it was composed entirely of medical stores: bandages, surgical spirit, scalpels, morphia...

"For the clinic?" Grete said and Peterson nodded, grinning.

"Yes, but we are getting into position to deal with much more than our normal intake. Have you time for a coffee? I must leave for Ras Shamir in an hour or so."

She turned, and in her brusque harsh voice gave instructions for her battered little lorry to be loaded up with the materials she had ordered and for which she now paid in cash from her old tattered crocodile-skin wallet. Grete was astonished by the sum.

"But this is for an army, not a clinic," she said.

Pete chuckled and pressed her arm as they walked down the street to a nearby coffee shop.

"It is, more or less," she said. Her eyes twinkled; she seemed full of a buoyant self-confidence, an elation which seemed inexplicable to Grete.

"Are you expecting trouble?" she asked.

Peterson nodded. "Of course, you fool; the minute the British go the Arabs will come in in force."

"But you seem so pleased about it."

"The relief, my dear; it's the relief of it all."

Peterson stirred her coffee and wrinkled up her nose in a smile.

"For so long we have been living in insecurity, dependent on the good will of strangers, on the charity of others... Now, all of a sudden, we exist on paper as a place called Israel. This is a momentous step forward, for we have now become a sort of world commitment. But you know as well as I do that if Israel were to be swallowed up by the Arab states, nobody would lift a finger to save her. At last, my dear, at last we are all alone with our own destiny. It depends on us whether the state can get itself born and fix itself among the other small nations. Can't you see how relieved we all are that now things are going to come to a head — after so many years of waiting cap in hand outside the doors of the great nations?"

"Are Aaron and David happy?"

"Radiant. For years they have foreseen this moment. The battle may be a stiff one, but it will decide everything; either we die or get thrown into the sea, or else... Israel, a place of our own."

Pete drank her coffee at a single gulp and got up; she stayed for a moment, looking down into Grete's face.

"I must go," she said softly. "The balloon might go up at any minute — though the British are still in the valley. Aaron has gone up to find out what he can. But I must be back this afternoon."

She paused and smiled into the troubled face of the girl. Then she said softly, "Why don't you come back?"

Grete stared at her silently.

"Right now!" said Peterson softly. "With me?"

Grete rose without a word, and together they walked towards the door. As Peterson opened it Grete said, "I need half an hour to pack and to give the office the key to my flat. Where shall I find you?"

The decision did not seem to be one she had made herself. It was simply that there seemed nothing else to do. Go she must.

~

Punctual to the minute, she dragged her suitcase to the little side street where, the task of loading the lorry completed, Peterson sat waiting for her, a cigarette between her lips. She gave Grete a somewhat quizzical look as she came up, for the girl had changed her clothes; gone now was the smartly dressed young lady living in a fashionable quarter of Jerusalem. The blue work-trousers of the land-worker and the head-scarf and coarse shirt marked the appearance of another Grete — more resolute and more capable, or so it seemed. As they dropped down the winding road towards the coastal plain she said:

"Is it true the British are pulling out? The radio only speaks of regrouping."

Pete gave a harsh bark of laughter.

"Regrouping in order to embark," she said and added: "What we don't know is exactly when. David is trying to find out. Our real problems only begin from that moment."

"Is David...?"

"He is second in command to Aaron, in charge of defence. He is if anything rather over-confident about our chances of survival — I suppose he has to be, to keep morale high. He has been hoping you would come back, you know; but there! It's none of my business. I think he would like to marry you some day."

"What chance would we have?" she said slowly, "with this war hanging over us."

Peterson flicked her cigarette away. "It will not last forever," she said. "There will be some pretty sharp birth pangs and presto... Israel. Once we have shown our will to survive, the nations of the world will decide to honour the mandate they have given us. After that there will be... I hardly dare utter the word. I'm too superstitious. I'll spell it. P-e-a-c-e."

"I'd love to believe you."

"You must. When that comes you'll find a different David."

"Peace!" said Grete, reflecting ironically. Once on the main road, they were swept into a long string of convoys heading for the coast, throwing out a great white plume of dust as they roared along. Lorries crowded with troops of all kinds, sappers, signallers, transport corps, pioneers...

They did not find unencumbered roads again until they climbed the looping road through Nazareth and began to taste once more the fresh hill air. The mountain fortresses — the so-called Mactaggart forts — were still manned by the British troops — and this was some sort of consolation, since they knew the road would be open to Ras Shamir. So they finally came to the last twist in the mountain road and were able to look down across the misty violet sweep of the valley which by now had come to mean so much to Grete. As they neared the encampment they saw what changes were taking place, and that a new kind of purposefulness reigned. Tractors were throwing up banks of earth which looked suspiciously like tactical outworks; the perimeter had been triple-wired, and the whole large circle had been condensed into a makeshift fortress. Every hundred yards or so there was a bunker which suggested a machine gun emplacement. Who could tell whether they were full or empty?

"It looks quite transformed," said Grete.

"It's mostly bluff, alas," said Peterson quietly. "But it might serve. Aaron has gone off to see the British today."

They entered the perimeter at last, and rolled slowly across the grass among the trees; Grete found herself greeting and being greeted by people she had almost forgotten were her friends. "Shalom, shalom"... the words echoed on the sunny air.

Peterson grinned and said, "I'll tell the committee. Meanwhile, by a bit of luck your old shack is empty and you can settle in there; and here is someone to carry your bag."

David's son stood smiling under a tree; in that short time he had grown taller. To her surprise he came shyly forward and kissed her on the cheek.

"I have been thinking of you," said Grete. "You've grown."

The boy flushed and said:

"We have spoken much about you here; the children asked always when you were coming back."

"They did?" cried Grete in genuine surprise.

He nodded and took up her bag; Peterson let in the clutch and moved off in the direction of the clinic. Grete followed the boy to her little hut. It was still there, primitive and shabby.

"There is a letter for you," said the boy.

This was another surprise. The letter bore an Indian stamp and a sender's superscription bearing Lawton's name; so even he had the gift of prophecy! How had he guessed that she would return to Ras Shamir?

David's son stood looking at her. He said rather solemnly, "My father has asked my permission to love you and I have given it."

Grete looked at him musingly and then stroked his hair.

"I know you will make us happy," he said quietly and, patting her wrist with a small protective gesture, he turned and was gone.

Grete sat down on the bed and opened Lawton's letter, smiling to herself. Then she read aloud a phrase from it. "You know that whatever happens I shall always be here; and if ever you change your mind…"

24

A Gift for Ras Shamir

The two men gazed at each other with a kind of grim respect as they exchanged a perfunctory handshake, the tall grizzled colonel and Aaron Stein. Macdonald, the regular, was seated at his primitive desk in the operations room of Fort B — the Mactaggart fort which dominated the pass leading to Ras Shamir and enabled him to keep a tenuous control on the border. Aaron's eye took in the grey hair, the service medals and the missing thumb which made the operation of lighting a pipe a somewhat lengthy one. He himself puffed at a cigarette.

"I asked you to come and see me," said Macdonald with the faintest tinge of a Scots burr in his voice, "because... well, because we are pulling out."

"And we are going to be attacked."

"Exactly. I see you've been fixing up a perimeter down there and I wondered what defences, if any, you had; also what your intelligence was like. Naturally you need not answer any questions, as my duty would be to disarm you. I shall presume you have no arms, eh?"

He got up and walked once round the room before reseating himself, as a dog settles itself down in a basket; it was clear that he was uncomfortable.

"When do you pull out?" asked Aaron cautiously.

Macdonald hesitated. "Day after tomorrow at four ack emma; from then on the road is wide open to be cut, and as for you..."

He crossed to the wall map of the area, which depicted the long appendix of the valley with its two converging gorges through which the river had carved a way. Macdonald stabbed at Ras Shamir with his pipe-stem.

"You are an obvious target — and if you cave in, the whole valley goes. Now I can tell you privately that Daud the Prince is lying back here ready for a push. He's well armed and trained by us. But he will have to come through the pass with the river. No other way. Have you any chance of sealing the pass?"

Aaron shook his head. "I can't spare the men or the rifles."

"Rifles!" said Macdonald with a commiserating air. "What the devil do you propose to do in such a case?"

Aaron took up the pencil and indicated the dotted settlements along the two scarps.

"The kibbutzim will reinforce me at a signal but... it will be mostly men with pitchforks, thanks to your policy of forbidding us arms."

Macdonald made another circle of the room and came back to rest once more at his desk.

"Look," he said at last, after carefully clearing his throat. "You must get the women and children away. I could provide you with transport. What do you say?"

"No," said Aaron stubbornly. "We stay."

"Well, I can but make the offer; if you refuse it, that is your affair. But I trust you will let me at least send the trucks down to the kibbutz. Your committee may think differently."

"The decision is not mine only; everyone is agreed."

Macdonald scratched his head. "Well I see that you are perhaps a little slow to take my point. It's a pity when you are so short of materials and faced with a possible attack."

He rose and took Aaron's arm. "Come with me and have a look at the transport," he said. "I have to do my morning inspection in any case."

Aaron looked extremely surprised at this unheard-of departure from military practice, but something in the Scotsman's quizzical glance intrigued him, and he followed him out into the compound where his transport lay, drawn up in rows.

"You see," said Macdonald, "I've told HQ that I'm setting my MT at your disposal today; it's up to you to reject the offer and send it back to me. In that way *my* conscience will be clear."

As he spoke, he whipped one of the flaps of a lorry and disclosed a load of Teller mines, signal wire, barbed wire, pistols and signal flares. Aaron stared at him aghast. He could not speak. The Scotsman winked at him laboriously and patted his arm. At the next lorry and the next he repeated the performance. Aaron gaped after him like an idiot, looking up hesitantly into his face as each new gesture revealed a load of valuable military equipment.

"All this stuff," said Macdonald *sotto voce*, "has been written off as stolen by marauders. I need say no more."

They walked back in silence to the perimeter, where the guard saluted with a clash and thump of heels. "Very well then," said Macdonald. "I shall send the column down to you in one hour under a colour sergeant. He will know what to do. I hope you will too." Again he winked.

Aaron's handclasp was eloquent. He started his engine and leaned back to wave to the Scotsman. "Thank you," he cried.

And so the defensive plans of Ras Shamir were entirely reshaped throughout that afternoon and evening, thanks to the lucky gift of arms. They could now afford to think in terms of the small shallow minefield; they could mount machine guns on their tractors; they could even afford to envisage a small corps of well-armed grenadiers using Mills bombs...

All the rest of that day they worked, unloading the lorries and sending them back to Macdonald; regrouping their stocks of munitions; digging and plotting and wiring, while Pete sat in her room with head bent to the little radio, listening to the floods of incoherent threats and ravings pouring in on them from the countries surrounding the pathetic little state which had just been born. No one could guess whether this step-child of persecution and intolerance would survive.

David stood in the doorway. "Is it true she has arrived back?"

Pete switched off and nodded. "Yes. By the way, I've told the mountain boys — Brisbane and Brooklyn and Manchester — that we now have flares to signal them for reinforcements."

"Good," he said. "Where is she?"

"On a washing fatigue, as far as I know," said Pete.

David turned aside and slipped down the long staircase into the compound; he set off with long strides towards the river, whence he could hear the clear voices of women singing as they washed the camp clothes by the river and hung them on the bushes to dry.

25

Lovers' Meeting

She saw him from a longish way off and rose quickly, drying her hands; she set off to meet him, feeling shy and uneasy. She did not want to greet him before the other women. They walked smiling towards each other now, their own reflections riding in the waters below them; and as he came closer she saw that it was a different David, for he had changed immensely. Was it simply that men flourish on danger and anxiety? His moustache had gone, and with it the sombre impression of weight, of inner concealed sadness, a well of moroseness. He had become thinner, too, and his features were purer and more clear-cut. He still wore the old jackboots with the ends of his trousers tucked into them. But now he wore a close-fitting jacket and a scarf at his throat. Last but not least, for the first time he openly wore a pistol at his hip. His bearing too was new — purposeful and self-confident; he had lost the old diffidence. He walked swiftly across the tracks between the meadows and muddy pools, with their giant water lilies floating in eddies, moving as if they were alive — taking long, rapid strides towards her.

"Well, you have picked your time," he said and, before she knew where she was, his arms were around her. He embraced her with complete certainty now, and firmly, expecting her response to be as warm. It was. All the inner barriers seemed to have subsided, freeing her. They kissed each other as if all at once they had gone mad. She tried to speak, but even a simple sentence was breathlessly swept away by the chaotic punctuation of their embraces.

"I tried... so much wanted... but I *wanted* so much..."

He paused only to say "Hush" in a whisper, and again "Hush"; and slowly sinking to their knees, they lay at last in the long grass by the river, helplessly at peace though their bodies still struggled for expression. For a long time after making love they lay like effigies. Then David turned on a sleepy elbow and plucked a bit of grass to put between her teeth.

"I knew it would be like this," he said.

"I hoped it would," she replied, her eyes still closed.

He stared at her for a long time, and then bent to kiss her once more; he rose to his feet and stared at his watch.

"Grete," he said, sinking down briefly on one knee. "I have a job to do now. I must leave you. But tonight I'll come to you."

And, without waiting for an answer, he embraced her briefly and was gone, walking swiftly along the river towards the head springs and the narrow valley which led to Jordan. She turned her head to follow his progress for a moment; then she set off towards the kibbutz.

26

Love and War

At the entrance to the first ravine from which the Jordan rushed, blue-green and ice-cold, there was an old ruined mill, built at some time during the Middle Ages and long since fallen into decay. This was to be an observation point and, thanks to the gift of arms from the retiring British, Aaron had now decided to man it with a patrol of three scouts and a light machine gun. Here they would first be in contact with any intruder into the valley; and the kibbutz would certainly hear any exchange of fire.

David climbed the rocky side of the ravine and, with a long sliding run, came to the entrance of the mill in time to hear old Karam shout with a chuckle:

"Halt, who goes there?"

The whiskered Yemeni emerged from the shadows among the ruins chuckling, followed by the two blonde boys from Sweden.

"Everything okay?" said David, and followed them into the shadowy room which echoed the sound of the current thumping against the stone walls. The machine gun stood in an embrasure covering the end of the ravine.

"Good," he said. "Good. Now listen, no heroism from you three; I don't expect any action from you, simply a signal of engagement. Then make your way back. Fire a green signal. But please make sure it is an enemy and not a flock of sheep or something like that."

Everyone grinned, and old Karam permitted himself a raucous chuckle. It was a capital joke. A few more orders given and discussed, a few trials of the little weapon's powers of traverse, and David set off once more for the kibbutz. None of them had noticed the three silent robed figures on the cliff edge above, who, without sound or movement, studied the position and counted the number of its defenders.

∽

Grete had dozed off, despite her intention to stay awake and wait for him; it must have been around midnight when she awoke with a start, to see his naked body outlined against the square of light where the window was.

"David," she whispered softly in the silence and he moved swiftly to her side.

"It has started in the south," he said. "Jerusalem is besieged and they are fighting at the Jaffa Gate and in Gaza."

He had put his Sten gun in the corner and his revolver on the table beside the blue bowl of cyclamen. She sat up and felt his strong arms around her.

"What about us?" she said.

David began to kiss her softly and thoughtfully on the throat, the cheek, the breast. Then he said:

"Our turn will come when the British pull out of the valley; until then we are safe. After that…"

He pulled her slowly down beside him on the bed and said in a tone which was almost exultant, "Think; we have so much time before us; and now everything is coming right, just as I thought it might, thought it would; you, Israel, everything!"

"I can't understand what has happened to me," she whispered.

"You have come back to yourself."

"David, could the child being dead for certain make me change?"

"That among other things, perhaps the most. Kiss me."

In the confused silence of the little room, the spell cast by their lovemaking seemed to spread out tentacles of lassitude around them, but she felt suddenly buoyant, self-confident, able to return stroke for stroke, kiss for kiss.

"I want to see your face," he said suddenly, and before she could move he lit a match to stare down at her, brushing her hair back from her forehead with his hand, tucking it back in order to free her ears, the better to kiss them. Then the match went out and the darkness closed in on them. In the silence of the camp around them their own soft quick breathing seemed to magnify itself, until they had the illusion that it was not they who breathed, but the starlit night-universe itself. Yes, the night was breathing in its sleep.

David said: "Tonight I am going to make you a child."

Her mind had dissolved into smoke, she could find nothing to say in reply; she lay passive under his kisses, like a creature sentenced to death, awaiting the stroke of the headsman's axe.

From the dark nothingness of sleep, was it the thin calling of the cocks that woke them — or perhaps it was the simultaneous sound of bugle-calls on the violet hillsides beyond the valley? A clear-rinsed dawn was coming up. She heard his rapid breathing as he dressed; the faint bugle-calls seemed to belong to the sounds of another world altogether. The smoke would be rising from their fires, he thought. Abruptly he kissed her and was gone. The light was rising at the edges of the eastern escarpments.

"David!" she called out, rising and running to the window, but he was already striding away through the trees in the direction of the fort. Suddenly, a sense of doom possessed her; all the fond fancies of the darkness, of their lovemaking, had vanished at the frail sound of the bugle-calls. She sat down on the bed heavily and said aloud: "I know he is going to be killed; I know it." And throughout the day the weight of this conscious thought pressed on her mind, heavy with a premonition like a child in the womb.

But David shared none of her fears; at this moment he was gazing through powerful glasses at the mill which covered the head springs of the Jordan. He grunted as he saw a wisp of smoke rising. Doubtless that old rogue Karam was making a morning brew of coffee in the

Yemeni fashion. There was no movement, no fires or sounds from the great mass of rock on the eastern side. The world looked so peaceful and so empty in the dawn light that one might be forgiven for thinking that the Arab army which crouched behind the towering cliffs, ready to pounce, was a mere figment of the imagination.

How sound carried in the quiet valley! He heard the distant roar of transport from the British camp, and knew that the convoys were being formed and would soon be on the road. His pulse beat faster with the thought that soon they would be alone, face to face with whatever destiny held in store for them. He waited until he saw the first dust plumes rise from the mountain roads before turning to the business of the day.

Peterson arrived, pale and serious, to convey the committee's compliance with David's first military act as its local representative. He proposed to issue an order of the day; crisply he dictated the first of such documents:

"Distribution of arms is now complete and all section leaders know their places. If we need an emergency muster I will sound the siren. Meanwhile I want the camp to retain an air of complete normality. Remember that, though there is fighting in the south, we may not be attacked at all."

Anna snapped her pad shut and lumbered off down to the cellars where the duplicating machines were; in one of the cellars she caught sight of Grete with a group of children. They had temporarily moved the school below ground, in case of air attack.

Peterson yawned and puffed a cigarette. "I didn't get much sleep," she said. "Nor you, I suppose."

David looked at her and then away. "What is the news?" he asked quietly and she replied:

"A few of the kibbutzim have been over-run or by-passed, but the main points are holding up. Jerusalem seems the toughest place. How long before the great powers step in and order a truce?"

David bit his lip. "I don't know; but we mustn't cede a lot of ground, for the arbiters are likely to work on the 'finders-keepers' principle when the truce does come."

"David," said Peterson, "I'm worried about the men from the mountains."

He shrugged. Peterson wrinkled her nose aggrievedly and said:

"You yourself say that it would take over an hour to concentrate them in the field to help us... Are you confident we could hold out an hour under sudden attack?"

David threw her a keen look and grinned. "Good Lord, yes," he said. "And we can count on Aaron..."

Peterson shook her head doubtfully. "If they brought tanks and rushed our wretched perimeter..."

David walked up and down. "They couldn't; first we'd get a warning from Karam up at the mill. Then, if they did, we have a number of gentlemen among us who have dealt very efficiently with Tigers and Centurions and would certainly not be above doing in half a dozen tanks of an older pattern, which I believe is all they have..."

"Well, it's your war," said Peterson. "Let me know if I can do any thinking for you."

"I will," he said with a grin. "Meanwhile, business as usual please."

So it was that the community life of Ras Shamir appeared to continue with perfect normality; from the viewpoint of a watcher on those rosy cliffs above the valley, there would have been nothing untoward to report. The tractors went out as usual with their armed drivers of both sexes; from the sawmill came the whine and whir of the saws cutting up timber; a team of brawny Swedes, scythes in hand, cut a circular swathe in the green of a square field, moving steadily forward and round in a slow arc. The British had rumbled away from the mountain ravines. The valley, with its small communities of Jews, lay at the mercy of any invader strong enough to wrest it from them. Yet there was only silence, heat and the drowsy hum of bees among the clover.

David did not quit his observation post; he had food sent up to the roof from which he watched, his face turned now towards the northeast range. Once a solitary plane passed over them — a bi-plane; but they could not tell if it was a spotter sent by the Arab forces or the British. The sun was hot; the concrete floor of the look-out post was baking. From somewhere down among the green trees came the oddly reassuring sound of someone snoring, which made the sentries laugh.

The hours wore on, and still there was no sign from the guard post at the head springs, and no visible movement along the escarpment. Only once or twice they heard a new sound, an echoing, snarling sound of motors revving up. David's face grew grave as he listened with his head on one side. The sentries stiffened at their posts, listening.

"What do you make of that?" said David, but he knew only too well. Tank engines!

For about half an hour they listened to that ominous roaring and rasping of invisible tanks moving about somewhere behind the rosy bluffs of the eastern chain. Finally the sound died away, as if swallowed by a ravine, and silence returned to the valley. But there was still no movement, nothing to be seen. Clouds began to form under the sun and its attenuated light began to change the green valley from emerald to rose-violet.

So much for the heliograph — it was out of action without sun. David thanked God for the kindly Macdonald's gift of Verey lights and signal pistols. Up to now they signalled to the mountain kibbutzim only by torchlight — a clumsy method at best, and always with the danger of the Morse signals being miscoded or misread. Now at least they had naval flares, red, white and green, at their disposal.

Thinking these thoughts, he had turned his eyes to where the string of little white settlements dotted the mountains westward — kibbutzim with the half-joking nicknames that their inhabitants had earned for them — Brisbane, Brooklyn, Odessa, Calcutta, Warsaw, Glasgow...

Beside him he heard a gasp of horror. One of the sentries was peering through his heavy Zeiss night-glasses — peering in the direction of the head springs where the mill stood, their outpost.

"My God," he said, "I can't believe it."

His hands were shaking so that he nearly dropped the glasses.

"What is it!" cried David sharply, snatching the instrument from him. He too turned the lenses on the northern corner where the Jordan, spinning out from the rock wall, fanned smoothly out into a wide green stream, pouring down the rich, lily-dappled meadows. Something was moving there on the river, something heavy which moved with a slow, halting rhythm — as if uncertain of its direction; something which turned slowly as it moved down towards them. He too caught his breath now as he focussed sharply on it...

The clumsy cross-beam of the water-mill must have been crudely sawn off to make a shape which was that of a Christian cross; there was a human figure crucified to it with bayonets. Naked, its side had been pierced so that blood dappled the white flesh and flowed down in a wave to its toes. It took some moments to realize that it was the body of Karam, and that the apparently beatific smile on the old man's face was really a rictus of intense pain. It was impossible to tell if he were dead or not. Slowly, hoveringly, the heavy cross moved down towards Ras Shamir, grazing the banks of the Jordan, turning and spinning swiftly in its own eddies.

"Run," said David in a voice choking with anger. "It must not reach the camp. Run I say!"

Hardly comprehending what or why, the two sentries followed the one who had himself seen the thing first. They dropped their guns and raced like hares across the fields towards the river, to head off this grim trophy of hate.

David gave a harsh sob. "They must have surprised them," he said. "How *could* Towers allow..." (Of course Towers knew nothing of it — it was Daud who lightened the boredom and loneliness of his illness with that original notion.)

David's glasses swept the nearer reaches of the river where the three men, up to their waists in water, grappled with the cross and its body, steering it to land; then there was no time for any thought other than the kibbutz and its danger.

It was only when the first ripple of machine-gun fire fell like hail on the corrugated roofs that he gave a sigh of exultation, almost of relief. At long last the final decisive engagement was to take place. Though the kibbutz was now a hive of unfamiliar activity, nevertheless there was no suggestion of haste or panic as the kibbutzniks moved each to his appointed place in the shallow emplacements which the tractors had ploughed for them, and which they had surrounded with a shallow defensive field of barbed wire.

On the calm evening air, David could hear the voices of the section leaders as they ordered their files into position along the perimeter: women and men took their places in the front line, training their weapons. Down by the sawmill there came the clatter of machinery, and it was with a splendid roar that the farm tractors now crawled out to take their place in the defensive scheme. Upon each was mounted one of the cherished light machine guns bequeathed to them by the kindly Macdonald.

In all this activity, Grete played no part. She had been forced to accept, much against her will, the role of children's warden. Indeed, she had come near to an acrimonious exchange with Anna over the business, so anxious had she been to share the front-line dangers of David and the men. But there were not enough guns to go around as it was, and Peterson herself had settled the argument abruptly by saying:

"There are so many more important things to do. Stop being child-ish and do as you're told. Your place is with the children."

So she now found herself locked into the great barn-like cellars with the smallest of the children — those who were ten years old and upwards had been given tasks to do which had a direct military bear-ing, acting as powder-monkeys, carrying ammunition, messages from those in the outer perimeter to the central command, and medical supplies.

27

The Ultimatum

Trouble began to spread now like burning oil on water, and every day brought its quota of ugly news and rumour, tidings of riot and burnings within, of menaces and provocations without. Yet still the valley lay in the winter sunlight, deceptively at peace, while the whole country was going through a convulsion around it — death-struggle or birth-pangs — who could say? By now the ugliness of Arab threats, and the fact that their armies were poised on the borders, waiting to pounce, left the kibbutzniks in little doubt that they would not escape the onslaught in this one small and remote sector.

But when Towers did get the order to move down into the plain and invest Ras Shamir, Daud was lying ill with fever and a new haemorrhage; it was plain that he would not be able to play an active part. He lay among the coloured cushions, exhausted, with flushed cheeks, and told Towers: "You will advance anyway, Towers." Towers grunted and nodded. "I am bitterly sorry not to ride with you," said Daud, but the old man said: "You will miss nothing. I am sure they will surrender. No shot will be fired. You will see. If I move we shall have the place in our hands in a couple of hours." He really believed this himself; indeed, to such a degree that he repeated it almost word for word to his staff as they sat by swinging lantern-light, making their final preparations for the morning start. It was to be a thoroughly orthodox operation — a "bus-ride" in Towers' expressive phrase. They would move down onto the plain and advance with the armoured cars in dart formation, infantry in open order.

So it fell out, exactly as planned, but of course no such operation could be conducted invisibly, and with the very first move of the scouts in the pass, with the first trails of dust rising from the lorry convoys with their infantry, the look-out at Ras Shamir picked them up and reported the fact. Pete watched them keenly for a second and then blew her whistle for general assembly. "I think we have a little time before they get here," she said soberly. "Send out the markers to mark the minefield." A dozen children raced out to mark the low pickets and tracery of wire with death-head signs and the forbidding words "DANGER — MINES". The men and women went slowly, purposefully, down to the magazine to draw their weapons, and then each went to his or her allotted place. Judith was in the second section with a group of yellow-haired Poles and four other girls, among them Anna who was the section leader. A deathly hush had fallen upon the settlement now, broken only by the low talk and murmurs of the defenders as they took up sighting positions.

Slowly, like a brown stain on the greensward of the plain, Towers' infantry debussed and formed up in battle line. Then the whole mass began its cumbersome movement forward, walking behind the armoured cars. Towers, who scorned armour, walked at the head of his section, grim of face; the existence of a hitherto unnoticed minefield infuriated him as an example of faulty intelligence. Nevertheless, it might be a fake minefield for all one knew. The intention was to advance up to the wire and call for a surrender, but they were already within a few hundred yards when a long rippling glissando of machine-gun fire broke from the perimeter of the settlement and swished among them like a scythe gone mad. There was a moment's hesitation and Towers called to his section-leaders to reform and continue the advance. "Bless my soul," he said to himself, almost with an academic pleasure, "at least four heavy machine guns. Who would have thought it?" Another long slither of fire, and he saw some of his middle section fall. He gave the order to halt and lie down, while he himself walked forward to the wire with the bullets flickering about him, cutting the heads off flowers and sending up puffs of soil. He walked slowly and thoughtfully, like a professor approaching a blackboard to make a demonstration of an academic fact. At the sight of this solitary figure advancing, the fire tailed away and ceased. Towers advanced to the wire, producing a white handkerchief from his sleeve, and made a vague and somewhat indefinite gesture towards the Jewish lines. It was the sort of half-modest movement that a public entertainer makes when imploring an audience to desist from further applause in order that he may complete an encore. "He wants to parley," said Anna grimly. A moment of indecision, and then they saw the minatory figure of Miss Peterson, Sten gun across her shoulder, advancing to meet the officer; it was a well-calculated choice of sector, too, for she was able to advance along the broad path between the fake minefields, thus offering an apparent indication of a safe road through them. But she was in fact walking over the grass and bramble-covered pits they had so laboriously cleared and covered. Towers, waiting for her, grunted and made the deduction he was supposed to make — the wrong one. He was extremely put out to be faced by a woman. He saluted and put on a quacking Camberley accent in order to disguise his confusion. "My orders are to call on you to surrender," he said. "Nobody will be harmed — you have my word for it."

"We are not surrendering," said Pete.

"I shall be compelled to use force," said Towers in his new blustering tone. "Much against my will."

"Is that all you have to say?"

"Yes."

"Then our answer is NO."

Pete turned on her heel and started her slow histrionic walk back to the perimeter. Towers called after her: "I will give you — " he glanced at his watch and named the time — "until then — to discuss the matter. Unless you surrender, I will attack."

She did not turn. Towers watched her broodingly. An idea had begun to stir in his mind, to germinate. He looked at his watch. "Donner," he called, "I have an idea. They seem better armed than I thought.

If they are going to resist we may have a bit of a dust-up — but it certainly means they expect to be reinforced. Detach three cars and command the eastern cross-roads." He watched the order conveyed and the great cars start to rumble off through the silence. Where the devil could hypothetical reinforcements come from? A faint biblical tag, something about "lift up thine eyes to the hills", crossed his mind. The camp lay quiet, ominously quiet — the hands of his watch circled to the appointed hour. No messenger appeared with the hoped-for white flag. "All right," said Towers, and addressed himself systematically to the task of reducing the settlement.

∼

Meanwhile, Aaron drove at full speed along the dusty roads towards the east, his mind buzzing with anticipation and anxieties. He had chosen a point some two miles away as a hypothetical point of concentration for his army of reinforcements. He knew they would need to form and concentrate if they were to be brought to bear on the enemy in any force. By now they must already be pouring down the dusty tracks among the hills, a motley crowd of farmers, blacksmiths, women... Some would be lorry-borne, some on tractors; some armed with nothing better than pitchforks or blacksmiths' hammers. But the call had gone out and been answered.

Civilians all, whose most distinctive feature of dress was the gentian blue pants of the field workers, and whose habits and culture spanned half the globe. The hills disgorged them slowly but certainly. Some swung in to marching tunes culled from many armies and many lands — Russian and Hebrew and Polish tunes hammered out in the distant past by armies of the line which had learned that to sing while you marched enlivened monotony. "John Brown's Body" and "Waltzing Matilda" carried their haunting overtones of Tobruk, Rimini and Caen; even "Lili Marlene" brought her sagging melancholy to swell the chorus.

Behind him in the distance, faint plumes of smoke rose from Ras Shamir — vague inchoate movements altered the lines and contours of the plain. Within an hour or so he should have his force concentrated and on the white road. He sat among the olives, savagely chewing grass and watching them roll in. He tried to keep his mind off Judith playing her part in the defence of the settlement. In his imagination he could hear the long dry chuckle of the automatic weapons, chattering like magpies.

But now the plumes of dust along the hills swayed and swelled as they approached him; he was at last a general with an army.

28

The Kibbutz Embattled

In the annals of that winter and spring of bitter fighting — the birth-pangs of the new state — the siege and defence of Ras Shamir does not bulk very large: many a kibbutz suffered the same hardships and endured the fierce onslaught of regular Arab troops with the same bitter obstinacy of purpose. Today, the only visible reminders of that pitiless struggle are an odd statue or a memorial plaque, or the withered garlands hanging from the turrets of the "home-made tanks" which line the long winding road which leads to Jerusalem. As for Ras Shamir, the single armoured car which managed to breach the perimeter stands today a rusty burned-out wreck on the green grass by the schoolroom. As the action opened, the two leading cars lumbered like elephants into the pits which had been cleared for such an eventuality; but the third, by a swerve, managed to find solid ground and burst through the perimeter with a roar. But here a swarm of youngsters clung to it like limpets and petrol-bombed it. It swung on like a crazy animal in pain, burst through a thicket of saplings and ground to a halt below the tower. Here it was systematically finished off like an iron bull; it gushed yellow smoke and flame and hissed like a great kettle. But it had unluckily revealed by its mad charge across the wire that the minefield was a fake.

The subsequent fighting was fierce, and in many places hand-to-hand. Time existed for them not like a continuous thing, but in a series of vivid impressionistic actions — of alerts and alarms — of deafening gunfire and slaughter. They saw it, the survivors, like so many highly coloured pieces of glass from a smashed kaleidoscope; the shrill powder-monkeys feeding the gunners, the stretcher-bearers moving about purposefully, the water rushing from the pierced towers. The noise and the confusion also had their own shape, their formal proportions. Lines broken were reformed. Little incidents stuck out and were swallowed again in the general pattern. The charge of the six Herculean Poles armed with scythes and hay-forks? Would the relief never arrive...?

So the long hours wore on; drenched in their own sweat, the defenders held on. Relief, when it did come, seemed to come from nowhere. The Arab infantry suddenly sagged at one corner like a curtain bellying out in the wind, faltered and then reformed with a new orientation. Afar off, now, the kibbutzniks caught sight of the little blue dots moving across their field of vision like a sea: the relief from their mountain comrades had arrived.

Aaron had been delayed by an encounter with the three diverted armoured cars at the eastern cross-roads; but his new army was not disposed to be trifled with by mere steel and rubber. It included veterans from many campaigns who knew all that is to be known about the blind side of tanks; they stalked the cars and captured them, turning them back upon their tracks. They formed a welcome and effective addition to the rescuing force, as it swept down the dusty roads. But Aaron was anxious now, for there had been a long delay: already evening was casting its first shadows under the rosy cliffs and escarpments. Nor was there time for any fine tactical manoeuvring. He could do little more than order a general engagement. It was, indeed, hardly an army but a ragged mob of angry and unshaven men which rushed down on Towers' flank with a shock that echoed like thunder. But Towers himself was dead, as was Donner; in fact, few of the British officers remained to rally and reform Daud's forces. Under the impact of the Jews, the lines sagged, wavered and began to give ground slowly but surely.

The defenders watched them as if in a dream — a strange incoherent dream of a retreat and a victory; in the hubbub their hoarse cheers, coming from throats so parched, could hardly be heard.

As the shadows of darkness began to fall, they saw the clouds of battle move inexorably towards the pass, towards the border which Aaron had made it his intention to seal fast. Ras Shamir was safe now, but its defenders could hardly form a coherent thought, so dazed were they with fatigue. An enormous emptiness beset them and hunger was all they were capable of registering.

~

The defence of Ras Shamir was only one of the defensive actions to take place during those tragic and heroic days when the existence of the new Israel hung in the balance. Nor in the official history will it ever figure among so many other glorious stories of the time. But if Ras Shamir was held, it was symbolic of the way in which the whole country, with its scattered and defenceless network of kibbutzim, turned each and all of them into strong points to stem the Arab advance. From Tiberius to Gaza the same story was enacted, though in each case the original nationality of the defenders might vary from British to Indian, from American to Greek. Beside such epoch-making names as Jerusalem, Haifa, Gaza, Beersheba, Ras Shamir will certainly find its small and modest place. The laconic official communiqué issued after the battle read as follows:

> At dusk a massive assault was mounted from the perimeter of the kibbutz by Arab forces using cavalry and infantry in the first instance. These assaults were beaten off and very heavy losses were inflicted. The enemy must have got wind of the reinforcements converging upon Ras Shamir from the hills, for a very determined assault involving three I-tanks was thrown against a weak point in the perimeter. Fortunately, it was the only point where a shallow minefield had been laid which accounted for two of the tanks. The remaining one managed to break into the centre of the kibbutz where it set fire to

some of the buildings with their tractors and inflicted serious damage and many casualties before it was put out of action, by some of the children. At 10 P.M. help arrived and the Arab forces were successfully engaged on the water-meadows by the river. They proved to be less well equipped than had been feared and they were completely routed and driven back through the ravine into their own territory by 1.30 A.M.

~

If Grete did not follow the fighting of that desperate night with her own eyes, entombed as she was below ground in the cellars of the ancient fortress, she nevertheless heard enough of it to deduce the ebb and flow of its fortunes even down there, in the dark ground. They heard, but as if muted, the infernal racket of the mortars and the dull concussion of the shells that landed; they heard the hoarse cheers and shouts of their own fighting men and women in the occasional pauses between actions. It was like the faint sound-track of a disaster — complete with shouts and groans and the bark of weapons, but with nothing visual to illustrate it. Their fragile oil lamps and candles flickered in the gloom. A thin dust was shaken down by the mortar bombs hitting the fort; cockroaches were shaken from their hideouts among the packing cases.

The small children were at first disposed to show fright and whimper at this strange new departure from their daily lives — by now it was long past their usual bedtime; but Grete read to them in her firm melodious voice; read to them until they dropped asleep around her like drowsy insects. And when the last pair of eyes had closed softly, she sat staring unwinkingly into the light of a candle, feeling the dull weight of her premonitions lying heavy within her — the foreknowledge of David's certain death somewhere out there among the tangled lines of wire and the shallow trenches.

That the battle ebbed and flowed she knew from the changes in the sound of it — but in whose favour she could not guess. She looked at her watch. Then once more she stared at the yellow flame, feeling herself completely engulfed by it, swallowed up in the dumb fear of a new day through which she might have to live without a living David.

At long last the door opened — though she hardly noticed it — and Anna stood in the dark panel, gazing at her with a yellow weary face. Her cheeks were stained with mud and powder markings. She walked very slowly, like a drunkard. Grete cried out her name and Anna walked slowly into the cellar, blinking with fatigue.

"They've been driven off," she said and, giving a great sob, threw her arms around Grete; they clutched each other. "I'm taking over for an hour," added Anna. "You must go and have something to eat. Orders."

As she entered the half darkness of the camp and picked her way slowly towards the canteen, Grete became aware that she was ravenously hungry. The darkness concealed most of the damage done by the attack, but here and there were some heaps of rubble, and outside the schoolroom, like a relic from some Pleistocene age, stood a large tank, still burning. Yellow flames lapped the interior, and the metal monster hummed like a giant kettle on the hob.

The long refectory was like a scene from a medieval master's canvas: pale candlelight marked the tables and threw the faces of their occupants into relief — exhausted men and women with eyes enlarged by fear and fatigue, wolfing bread and draining great draughts of warm tea and cocoa. All around them lay items of equipment, bandoliers, gun tripods, machine-gun belts, and swathes of blood-stained bandages.

They hardly noticed as she took her place among them. They talked in low murmuring tones. Someone had a small radio on the table, at which he was working, scratching his way along the dial until at last he found a familiar call-signal and an anonymous voice which told them that, like Ras Shamir, Jerusalem was holding, Gaza was holding, Haifa was holding. A babble of voices broke out at this piece of news. Then, into the midst of the dappled darkness, walked the gaunt martinet they all recognized as Peterson.

"I want a fatigue," she said.

Nobody spoke.

"Anybody who is not dead beat," she added harshly, looking at them under drawn brows. "We must collect our wounded. The Arabs have been driven off; but there are many wounded of both sides out there on the battlefield. You can hear their cries from the wire. Who will volunteer?"

Weary as they were, there was something about her that was irresistible, and they rose groaning and yawning, picking up lamps and torches as they did so. Grete followed them, but at the door Peterson stopped her. The doctor stood in the darkness outside the tall doors of the refectory. Her gesture was rough, almost brutal, throwing out her strong arm across Grete's body. Her voice was harsh and grim.

"Grete," she said, "I have bad news for you. David..."

But Grete, unable to bear the sound of the message which she knew must follow, put her hand over Peterson's mouth.

"Please," she cried. "Don't say it."

Then she turned and leaned against the door, sick and faint; she felt as if her body had shrunk to half its size. Peterson stood, breathing heavily and staring at her with a kind of grim compassion. Then she put a hand on her shoulder; Grete turned her dry eyes upon her and said in a whisper:

"Where is he?"

Peterson cleared her throat and, turning to the darkness, shouted, "Tonio, are you there?"

A huge shambling figure moved slowly into the radius of the light. The two women stared at this great sloth of a man, one of the Baltic contingent.

"You know where David is?"

The man nodded with an air of shyness, of confusion.

"Take me," said Grete suddenly, sharply, and the huge man nodded and bobbed, touching his forelock. Peterson laid a restraining hand upon her wrist but she put it aside, saying:

"I must go to him, don't you see?"

Neither of them saw the small figure of David's son materialize from the darkness and come towards them, his face deathly white. He had overheard their conversation. They stood staring at each other, their white faces registering a strange doll-like surprise.

"I will come with you," said the boy.

"No," said Peterson.

"Yes, I must," he said gravely, looking from one to the other.

"No," said Grete. "Wait here."

But the child shook his head gravely and, advancing, held out his hand to the shy blonde giant, Tonio. There was no gainsaying authority. Tonio took the small hand in his and turned; and Grete now followed them, drawing her shawl across her face, like a peasant woman in mourning.

They crossed the smashed and tangled workings with their shattered wire and found themselves out on the dark floor of the battlefield among the trampled and bloodstained water lilies where the river flew silently, swift as a dart. Everywhere there were huddles of bodies, from every side the darkness rang with voices — the low moans and whispers of the wounded and the clear voices of those who had come to succour them. Back and forth, across the dark floor of meadowland, the lamps moved like glow-worms, making little puddles of light, pausing here or there, moving, criss-crossing.

In these small pools of light they saw scenes enacted, as if from the panels of some Byzantine fresco: miniatures of a horse being cut from its traces and shot, a naked man receiving an injection, a moaning camel being pegged down on the grass. And everywhere the wounded were being selected from among the dead. Stretcher-bearers made what haste they could with their burdens across the meadows. The sky was full of stars, glimmering like precious stones. It was cold. Grete found herself shivering as much from chill as from fear. Dawn was already coming up, to judge by the swift lightening of the mountain ranges to the east.

At last they came to a fold in the banks of the river — a green strip covered with wild orchids and meadow flowers. Here Tonio quested about for a moment like a greyhound. Then he gave a grunt and pointed.

David's sturdy form lay coiled up and very still at the bottom of a hollow of deep grass; one arm was doubled under him in an attitude which suggested some severe dislocation of shoulder and spine. The other, fully extended, was buried in the earth. The flickering light wavered and jumped upon the tremendous stillness of him as he lay there.

Tonio halted, uncertain what to do. He still held the child's hand. But now Grete was kneeling beside her lover, turning the dark head and cradling it in her arms as she bent over him. Suddenly she looked up and, almost beside herself with astonishment, called out, but in tones so unbelieving that they carried no conviction:

"He's breathing. He's alive."

They stood like figures turned to salt, Grete staring blindly up into the light of the torch, repeating "He's alive. He's alive."

Then, as if the sum total of the knowledge had suddenly gone home like a bayonet thrust, the huge shaggy Balt turned and shouted across the darkness to where the stretcher-bearers moved among the dead, seeking the living. A party moved towards them and Grete saw the lights advance and brim the hollow with whiteness. Strange voices crowded about them.

An orderly knelt for a minute and listened to the feeble heartbeat in the chest wall of the fallen man — as one might listen in a cave for the voice of an oracle.

"Yes," he said at last. "Yes."

Grete thought she had never heard a sweeter word. "Yes," she repeated with a sob. "Yes. Yes."

The small boy was looking at her. They had moved David onto a rough stretcher made of blankets. The party set off in the gathering light of the dawn along the river. And now it seemed as if some new power stirred within her as she walked beside them. David's muddy hand hung over the side of the stretcher, jogging with the movement. His son seized hold of it, softly, proudly. And as they walked they heard — with the delectation of people hearing the opening bars of some great piece of music — the groans of David. Grete put her arm about the small boy's shoulders.

"I was wrong," she said to herself, "and he was right."

29

After the Battle

Now that the pressure of the attack had been relieved, it was once more possible to organize, to improvise. And aid materialized from various quarters. Unsolicited lorries rolled in to help with the wounded who had overflowed the medical bays. The most serious cases were sent off by three-tonner or ambulance (whenever possible) to hospitals offering greater facilities than were available in the little dispensary of the settlement. Judith watched the hefty arms of the young Poles lift the victims softly into the lorries, and turned back in bitter resolution to the settlement. By now someone had restored the electric light unit, and the work was easier; but there was much to do. She was glad of it, and worked all night until she was practically asleep on her feet. She had not seen Aaron all evening, but knew he was alive and unhurt. Nothing could have given her more strength and determination. Relief she could not call it.

But the attack on Ras Shamir was only the most personal part of something which loomed much larger on the horizon, and which engaged their anxieties for months to come; it was strange that, all of a sudden, the concerns and pressures of war should make her feel the reality of Israel as an idea. But it was so. In April the stranglehold on

Jerusalem was broken. Haifa was liberated, then Jaffa. All through that spring and summer the war flared up and subsided, changing aspect and design, changing sector. Stubbornly, bitterly, Israel was contending for her very existence, forging her national spirit in the brutal fire of war.

All this news, the source of so much pride and relief to the kibbutz, was sheer exhilaration for Aaron. He was truly part of it, a fighting part. He wanted to be on all fronts at once, and almost succeeded. He scanned the papers and listened to the radio; and some of his impatient excitement seeped into the letters he wrote to Judith from every part of the country. They were a curious mixture of ardour and reserve — almost as if he was unsure as yet how far he could commit himself or how much depend on the durability of her own feelings and emotions. Then one day she got the opportunity of a lift to visit him in Jerusalem. It was a surprise; to their astonishment and chagrin they found themselves almost tongue-tied, like adolescents. Judith's heart beat so fast that she felt almost suffocated. "By God," he said, "you are a good-looking girl!" She took his hand and held it to her breast. "Aaron," she said, "how lucky I am. Darling I've been..." She was almost overcome by the nearness of it. She held up crossed fingers. Aaron had grown large martial whiskers. "And you look like an Albanian bandit," she said. "I hardly recognized you."

Aaron grinned. "I've missed you terribly," he said, trying to make the remark sound light-hearted and conversational, in order to hide his emotions.

"Do you think you could kiss through the foliage?" he asked. "I suppose one could get used to it?"

She had brought a small parcel of sweets and cigarettes, and there was also a little bunch of somewhat faded flowers. "They are from your country house," she said. "I picked them yesterday." For a moment tears came into his dark eyes, but he quickly embraced her to hide them. "I'm coming back to the valley at the end of the month," he said. "Will you still be there, Judith?"

She was surprised almost to the point of anger. "Why not?" she exclaimed. He shook his head, still smiling and said, "I don't know. I had a dream in which you went off in great pomp to America. More than one actually. It seemed quite logical."

"And since when have you started having prophetic dreams?" she cried. "Oh, Aaron — please!" But he only held her closer, still smiling, and somewhere inside him unconvinced. "Of course I'll be there when you get back," she said, and then suddenly felt a shadow cross her mind, a shadow of doubt. Aaron said: "We must see what the new Israel... ha, how does that sound to you?... the new Israel has in store for us both. You the unbeliever, and me the sabra."

"Ras Shamir will always be there," she said. "Why shouldn't I?"

"You must," he said. "You really must."

And yet the obstinate doubt persisted in their minds. Could the new Israel somehow separate them? She kissed him tenderly as she said goodbye, and promised to take any opportunity to visit him in the interval before his return. At the door she turned and stared at him for a long moment. He stared gravely back at her from under his dark brows, tenderly, yet unsmilingly. Then she turned and he heard her light step echoing on the staircase.

30

The Decision

But the day before Aaron's return she received a call from Professor Liebling in Jerusalem — so perhaps there was something to be said for prophetic dreams after all? She must hurry south to see him on matters of great urgency, said the message. So, with obedient reluctance, she entered the car which he had sent for her and set off through the green hazes of Galilee towards the capital city. She supposed that it had something to do with her father's invention and she was not wrong. The Professor was waiting for her with an impatient enthusiasm which made him more than ever expansive. He embraced her warmly and fluttered around his desk like a sparrow from twig to twig. "America," he said, "Judith — America!"

"What about America?"

With an incoherent gesture he indicated the papers on his desk. "Now where shall I begin?" he said. "Let us be logical. First of all the patents are out on your father's 'toy'. We can consider going into prototype now — offers are coming in from every side for production. Just what it's going to mean to Israel's oil future one can't say yet — but it is going to be important — very important!"

"So much the better." She smiled, sitting down.

"*Aber* — but that is not all. Here are invitations from almost every learned society, every foundation, every university... You will have to go and address them, travel about, perhaps stay a couple of years and work."

"Go to *America*?" The idea came as something of a surprise; she had not formulated a future plan for herself, though of course some such vague thoughts might have floated around in her mind. Princeton, for example, had always wanted her back.

"America..." she repeated like someone half asleep. The Professor grew impatient. "Of course, wretched girl!" he cried. "You owe it to your father, to yourself, and lastly, but perhaps most important, you owe it to Israel. You must see this invention through prototype and trial stages and into production; meanwhile you will also travel and lecture and work. How pleased your father would have been! Really, you owe it to his memory."

"Yes," she said doubtfully, hesitantly. And then fell silent. She looked at her hands in her lap. "I hadn't thought of any such thing, at least — for a while yet. Ras Shamir..."

"Ach! that damn kibbutz!" said Liebling with high scorn. "Have they bewitched you? That damned old Peter! Are you going to spend the rest of your life letting a committee decide what you have for lunch? Come — wake up, Judith. Everyone is calling you, everything is calling you — Gott in Himmel! Israel not least. After all — you are a Jew and here is something you can do for us all. It was we who dragged you out of Germany — remember?"

"I know," she said quietly, "I know." She lit a cigarette and smoked thoughtfully. Liebling looked at her with hardly concealed impatience; he stood on one leg and then on the other. He held the side of his face and swayed from side to side as if with toothache. "Ach, Judith," he said, bursting out at last. "You are half asleep, girl. Doesn't this make you happy?"

"Yes," she said sadly. "But I must have time to think — time to decide. It's a decision that needs thought."

"You what?"

"I need a little time — that is all..."

"I don't understand," said Liebling. "After all, you have nobody here, nothing to keep you here. And your work — your career — it isn't even as if you were a sabra!"

The word struck her like a smack in the face. She stood up and said: "Very well. I will think about it and let you know soon, quite soon."

She embraced the old man and left him staring after her in reproachful amazement.

That afternoon she set off for Ras Shamir again in a state of doubt and confusion. How familiar the landscape seemed now, how intimate! It was as if her trials and tribulations in it had, as well as seasoning her, made her part of it. Who was it, she wondered, who once wrote that places where we are unhappy are always dearer to us than those where we were happiest? She had been both at Ras Shamir. Finally, too, she must see Aaron again before any decision could be taken. That was perhaps the crux of the matter. The Professor himself was driving her; he planned to drop her at the settlement and go on to Safad, where he had some business to attend to. "On my return journey tomorrow," he said, "I'll come back and see if you have decided anything. Perhaps you will see everything clearly and be ready for me. I feel sure you will."

It was strange to walk the paths of the settlement again; to pass the schoolroom where the children were buzzing with laughter and reciting tables. In the main office Peterson sat in a characteristic mannish attitude, dictating a letter about apples. Judith climbed the staircase and poked her head in. "Ah!" said Pete. "Come in — come in! Why are you looking so sad?"

"Because they want me to go away," said Judith, and explained all that had taken place at the Professor's office in Jerusalem. Peterson struck her knee and cried: "Marvellous! Judith — of course you must go. Anyway, it was foreseen long ago, wasn't it? A girl with your gifts can't stay on and moulder away in Ras Shamir. Good Lord — what has got into you?"

"Something," she said. "Where is Aaron?"

"He came back. Probably in the mountains again." She paused expectantly.

"I wish to goodness I knew why I feel so confused," Judith burst out. "Anyway, why should I trouble you with all these personal problems? It seems to be the eternal fate of us Jews in this generation to be chased from pillar to post. I envy you your life here!"

"Well," said Pete with a laugh, "in my case — and by the way, it is a secret — you know that I am not a Jew at all, at least by race. I'm a Jew by choice, which perhaps makes me more Jewish than the Jews. I really think that you should go for your father's sake, as well as Israel's. Old Liebling is right."

"Very well," said Judith with a sigh, "but first I must see Aaron and ask him what he thinks."

"Beware!" said Pete with a grin. Strangely enough that day Aaron was not to be found anywhere in the kibbutz. Nobody had seen him. That night Judith slept restlessly, turning and tossing. She had actually packed her exiguous belongings in a little suitcase — just in case (she told herself) the morning brought her a decision. In which case she could simply climb aboard the Professor's car when it appeared and leave for Jerusalem. If there was to be a break with Ras Shamir, it must be a sudden and definitive one; Judith loathed protracted fare-wells, long-drawn-out partings. Yet somehow she could not decide definitively without seeing Aaron. The next morning she met the Professor; she had had an idea. "Will you drive me along the high road to the ninth milestone?" she said. "There may be someone there I need to see." Liebling looked quizzical but said nothing. They drove in silence to the final curve of the high road into the hills and here she descended and took a footpath among the olives. She was going to see if Aaron was by any chance at his so-called "country house". He was — he was in fact working in the garden, digging away. He gave a shout when he saw her and ran towards her, towards the breathless embrace which she had been imagining for so long. Somehow every-thing came back with it — her confidence, her self-possession. "I've been tidying up the garden." He grinned at last. "I had a sudden sort of wave of energy; it's as if for the first time the blasted place did seem to belong to me. Look…" Already some semblance of order was begin-ning to re-emerge from the tangle. "Oh Aaron," she cried, "I so much needed to see you. I hunted for you yesterday, everywhere."

"I was here."

"They want me to go to the States." She suddenly blurted out the whole story, wringing her hands as she spoke, or softly banging her fists together in fearful indecision. He gazed at her keenly with sparkling eyes. "Of course you shall go," he said. "Of course you must."

She looked at him uncomprehendingly; suddenly she realized why she had been feeling such indecision, such a momentous upset. It had nothing to do with either Israel or her father or the invention or the USA. It was quite plainly and unequivocally a decision which depended, as she herself did now, very much on Aaron. He did not understand the expression on her face and tried now, despite his own feelings, to seem excited, warm-hearted, congratulatory about the whole matter. Inside he felt quite hollow and sick, but he was determined that nothing should stand in the way of Judith's future.

"Of course," he repeated excitedly. "You simply must. But surely it was all to be expected? Why should a girl with your gifts waste them here? No. But there, over there, Judith, you can play a part which will not only fulfill your own capacities but be a direct help to us here, to Israel. We are still desperately short of trained brains." She was staring at him now with a slowly growing resentment in her eyes. "Besides," he went on, hastily, lying now in order to help her as he thought, "they want me to join the regular army now and I shall probably be leaving the valley myself for a command in the Negev. It's not certain but it's on the cards."

"So you don't want me to stay," she said in a harsh, small voice, as if talking to herself. "It's all this sabra business again; you don't feel I have any sort of stake in your blasted Israel. Very well — thank you for making up my mind for me."

"Judith," he protested, "I meant nothing of the kind. I certainly don't want you to go in this state of mind. Listen..."

But she was already walking back through the olive glade to the high road where the car waited for her. Thank God, she thought to herself, I am already packed up. I have my suitcase and can leave today. Aaron walked beside her saying: "Judith, please don't be unreasonable. We must not separate on these false terms. I know you will come back sometime; and I'll wait for you — I promise you..."

But she climbed into the car and slammed the door shut. "Goodbye, Aaron," she said, and motioned to the driver with her hand. Aaron stood in exasperated silence, biting his lip and watching the car slide slowly away down the long avenue of trees whose green foliage waved in the wind like sentient creatures waving farewell. He sighed and folded his strong arms across his chest as he watched it dwindle to a dot. Then he started and felt the blood suddenly beating in his temples. The car had stopped. The small figure, infinitely diminished by the long green perspective, got down into the road. It waved the car on and, as the vehicle slowly disappeared around the bend, the familiar figure began to plod slowly and determinedly back. "Judith!" he said under his breath — but he did not move, did not breathe, for fear that it was his imagination playing tricks with him. But no. Gradually the figure was growing larger as it approached him.

Aaron now knew that a final and irrevocable decision had been taken, and that he was glad. Yet he still stood and waited patiently, separated from the distant figure by an eternity of time and space. Or so it seemed.

A Biography of Lawrence Durrell

Lawrence Durrell (1912–1990) was a novelist, poet, and travel writer best known for the Alexandria Quartet, his acclaimed series of four novels set before and during World War II in Alexandria, Egypt. Durrell's work was widely praised, with his Quartet winning the greatest accolades for its rich style and bold use of multiple perspectives. Upon the Quartet's completion, *Life* called it "the most discussed and widely admired serious fiction of our time."

Born in Jalandhar, British India, in 1912 to Indian-born British colonials, Durrell was an avid and dedicated writer from an early age. He studied in Darjeeling before his parents sent him to England at the age of eleven for his formal education. When he failed to pass his entrance examinations at Cambridge University, Durrell committed himself to becoming an established writer. He published his first book of poetry in 1931 when he was just nineteen years old, and later worked as a jazz pianist to help fund his passion for writing.

Determined to escape England, which he found dreary, Durrell convinced his widowed mother, siblings, and first wife, Nancy Isobel Myers, to move to the Greek island of Corfu in 1935. The island lifestyle reminded him of the India of his childhood. That same year,

Durrell published his first novel, *Pied Piper of Lovers*. He also read Henry Miller's *Tropic of Cancer* and, impressed by the notorious novel, he wrote an admiring letter to Miller. Miller responded in kind, and their correspondence and friendship would continue for forty-five years. Miller's advice and work heavily influenced Durrell's provocative third novel, *The Black Book* (1938), which was published in Paris. Though it was Durrell's first book of note, *The Black Book* was considered mildly pornographic and thus didn't appear in print in Britain until 1973.

In 1940, Durrell and his wife had a daughter, Penelope Berengaria. The following year, as World War II escalated and Greece fell to the Nazis, Durrell and his family left Corfu for work in Athens, Kalamata (also in Greece), then Alexandria, Egypt. His relationship with Nancy was strained by the time they reached Egypt, and they separated in 1942. During the war, Durrell served as a press attaché to the British Embassy. He also wrote *Prospero's Cell*, a guide to Corfu, while living in Egypt in 1945.

Durrell met Yvette Cohen in Alexandria, and the couple married in 1947. They had a daughter, Sappho Jane, in 1951, and separated in 1955. Durrell published *White Eagles Over Serbia* in 1957, alongside the celebrated memoir *Bitter Lemons of Cyprus* (1957), which won the Duff Cooper Prize, and *Justine* (1957), the first novel of the Alexandria Quartet. Capitalizing on the overwhelming success of *Justine*, Durrell went on to publish the next three novels in the series—*Balthazar* (1958), *Mountolive* (1958), and *Clea* (1960)—in quick succession. Upon the series' completion, poet Kenneth Rexroth hailed it as "a tour de force of multiple-aspect narrative."

Durrell married again in 1961 to Claude-Marie Vincendon, who died of cancer in 1967. His fourth and final marriage was in 1973 to Ghislaine de Boysson, which ended in divorce in 1979.

After a life spent in varied locales, Durrell settled in Sommières, France, where he wrote the Revolt of Aphrodite series as well as the Avignon Quintet. The first book in the Quintet, *Monsieur* (1974), won the James Tait Black Memorial Prize while *Constance* (1982), the third novel, was nominated for the Booker Prize.

Durrell died in 1990 at his home in Sommières.

This photograph of Lawrence Durrell aboard his boat, the *Van Norden*, is taken from a negative discovered among his papers. The vessel is named after a character in Henry Miller's *Tropic of Cancer*. (Photograph held in the British Library's modern manuscripts collection.)

One of Nancy Durrell's photographs from the 1930s. Pictured here is the *Caique*, which they used to travel around the waters of Corfu. (Photo courtesy of Joanna Hodgkin, property of the Gerald Durrell Estate.)

This photograph of Nancy and Lawrence Durrell was likely taken in Delphi, Greece, in late 1939. (Photo courtesy of Joanna Hodgkin and the Gerald Durrell Estate.)

A 1942 photograph of Lawrence Durrell with his wife Nancy and their daughter, Penelope, taken in Cairo. (Photo courtesy of Joanna Hodgkin.)

This manuscript notebook contains one of two drafts of *Justine* acquired by the British Library as part of Lawrence Durrell's large archive in 1995. (Notebook held in the British Library's modern manuscripts collection.)

A page from Durrell's notebooks, or, as he called them, the "quarry." This page introduced his notes on the "colour and narrative" of scenes in *Justine*. (Photo courtesy of the Lawrence Durrell Papers, Special Collections Research Center, Southern Illinois University Carbondale.)

"As well as serving delicious food in an idyllic setting, the Taverna Nikolas at Agni has strong links with the Durrell story in Corfu," says Joanna Hodgkin of this 2012 photo. Durrell lived in the neighboring town of Kalami, where his famous White House sits right above the shoreline. (Photo courtesy of Joanna Hodgkin.)

Copyright © 2012 by the Beneficiaries of the Estate of Lawrence Durrell

Introduction copyright © 2012 by Richard Pine

Cover design by Jason Gabbert

Published by permission of Françoise Kestsman, literary executor for the Estate of Lawrence Durrell

ISBN 978-1-4532-7080-6

Published in 2012 by Open Road Integrated Media
180 Varick Street
New York, NY 10014
www.openroadmedia.com

EBOOKS BY LAWRENCE DURRELL

FROM OPEN ROAD MEDIA

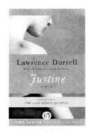

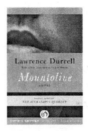

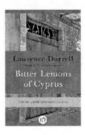

Available wherever ebooks are sold

OPEN ROAD
INTEGRATED MEDIA

Open Road Integrated Media is a digital publisher and multimedia content company. Open Road creates connections between authors and their audiences by marketing its ebooks through a new proprietary online platform, which uses premium video content and social media.

CPSIA information can be obtained at www.ICGtesting.com
Printed in the USA
BVOW041419190313

315851BV00004B/4/P